continued . . .

ALSO BY CHERYL ROBINSON

In Love with a Younger Man
Sweet Georgia Brown
It's Like That
If It Ain't One Thing

When I Get
Where I'm Going

cheryl robinson

NEW AMERICAN LIBRARY

New American Library
Published by New American Library,
a division of Penguin Group (USA) Inc.,
375 Hudson Street, New York, New York 10014, USA
Penguin Group (Canada), 90 Eglinton Avenue East, Suite 700, Toronto, Ontario M4P 2Y3, Canada
(a division of Pearson Penguin Canada Inc.) • Penguin Books Ltd., 80 Strand, London WC2R 0RL,
England • Penguin Ireland, 25 St. Stephen's Green, Dublin 2, Ireland (a division of Penguin Books
Ltd.) • Penguin Group (Australia), 250 Camberwell Road, Camberwell, Victoria 3124, Australia (a
division of Pearson Australia Group Pty. Ltd.) • Penguin Books India Pvt. Ltd., 11 Community Cen-
tre, Panchsheel Park, New Delhi - 110 017, India • Penguin Group (NZ), 67 Apollo Drive, Rosedale,
North Shore 0632, New Zealand (a division of Pearson New Zealand Ltd.) • Penguin Books (South
Africa) (Pty.) Ltd., 24 Sturdee Avenue, Rosebank, Johannesburg 2196, South Africa

Penguin Books Ltd., Registered Offices:
80 Strand, London WC2R 0RL, England

First published by New American Library,
a division of Penguin Group (USA) Inc.

First Printing, September 2010
1   3   5   7   9   10   8   6   4   2

LIBRARY OF CONGRESS CATALOGING-IN-PUBLICATION DATA:

Robinson, Cheryl.
When I get where I'm going/Cheryl Robinson.
p. cm.
ISBN 978-0-451-22947-2
1. African Americans—Fiction.   2. Sisters—Fiction.   3. Dysfunctional families—Fiction.
4. Domestic fiction.   I. Title.
PS3618.O323W47 2010
813'.6—dc22   2010019145

Set in Garamond • Designed by Elke Sigal

Printed in the United States of America

For my sister, Janice

ACKNOWLEDGMENTS

I know how I feel when I read a good book. How I'm transported into another world that feels so real that I don't want to put the book down, and how much I appreciate that great escape. God gives each one of us gifts, and I want to thank Him for providing me with the immense sense of joy that I receive each and every time I sit down to create a story that I pray readers will enjoy.

I am so grateful that I've been able to publish five novels with New American Library in the past five years. And I do have my agent Marc Gerald to thank because, as the saying goes, it's harder to get a literary agent than it is to get a publishing deal. Of course, I am also very thankful to Kara Welsh and all of the good people at New American Library/Penguin Group. I give special thanks to my new editor, Jhanteigh Kupihea. I feel that I've grown as a writer as a result of working with you. I would be remiss if I didn't also thank my former editors, Kara Cesare and Lindsay Nouis, who edited my previous four books and believed in me. And to Kathryn Tumen for all the hard work you do to get the much-needed publicity for your authors. I really appreciate all of your effort. It truly means so much!

One of the major themes of this book is sisterhood—along with family, dysfunction, and betrayal. But ultimately it is about unity and unconditional love. And in that regard, I don't want to forget those people who have always been there for me in my own family. I am especially grateful to my parents. My dad, who in some ways—*some* ways—I am very much like, I love very much. My mother is the sweetest, most wonderful woman I know and fiercely loyal to her family. Thank you for all your support through the years and for believing in me. To my late brother, Benny, who I miss very much. You are my angel always looking over me. You are my muse, and I carry your picture with me every day. To my nephew Brandon, I know distance prevents us from seeing each other and over the years we have lost contact, but I just want you to know that I love you very much and so did your father. To my sister, Janice, to whom I dedicated this book, I appreciate how with each passing year we become even closer. I love you very much. To my nephew Sterling, who's out in LA trying to make it. I'm proud of you and your stick-to-itiveness. And, of course, you know that I love you. Stay true to yourself and always follow your dreams.

A special thank-you to my hometown, Detroit. I read reports that call Detroit one of the dying cities, but I still have faith that one day something is going to turn around. I realize the more I write stories set in Detroit and I have a chance to discover places I never even knew existed, that despite the negative press, Detroit has a lot to offer—more than most people outside the city and the state even know. When I think of Detroit, I think of a city that is not only referred to as "the D" but also a city where Motown started. I remember Motor City when it was at its height. Hopefully, one day, Detroit will rise again and become one of the greatest cities in the United States. Detroit has a lot to offer and great people who live there, so I'm confident that whether it's with the help of the film industry that's moving in or some other industry, Detroit will pull through.

To Emma Rodgers. Your encouragement helped me to press on . . . and I owe you many thanks.

To my friends who have encouraged me along the way, I hope I don't miss anyone, but if I do, I'm sorry. An especially big thank-you to Green Moss III for all of his tireless help in promoting my last two novels and for being a family friend for more than thirty years. Also to Chris Elliott, Leah Evans, Shawn Beasley, Darren Sanders, Shannon Scott, Sherry Murray, Dewhana Jones, Agatha Clark, Corey Jones, Nekosher Dillard, Valissa Armstrong, Cynthia Taylor, Regina Smith, Charmette Brown, Derek and Nina Burke, Brian Christian, Laverne "Missy" Brown, Pia Wilson-Body and Anthony Body, Kyra Brown, Jacquelyn Theriot, and Karen White Calloway.

To the late E. Lynn Harris, who was a great inspiration to me and to so many others. To Electa Rome Parks, always a friend and a great person who keeps me laughing and encouraged along the way. To Cydney Rax for the friendship. To Kimberla Lawson Roby for the encouragement and advice.

To Carol Mackey, Tanisha Webb and the KC Girlfriends Book Club, the Ocala Readers Book Club, Stacy Luecker, Chandra Sparks Taylor, Trese Kennard and the entire family of the late Darrent Williams, Toka Waters, Lawana Durisseau Johnson, Yasmin Coleman, APOOO, Rawsistaz, Vee Jefferson, Dr. Nedra Dodds, Ella Curry, Idrissa Uqdah, Heather Covington, Joy Farrington and Nubian Sistas Book Club, Pamela Walker-Williams of Pageturner.net, Divas Read 2 Book Club, Marlive Harris, Assel Hannah, Debra Owsley of Simply Said Reading Accessories, Troy Johnson of AALBC, Ron Kavanaugh of Mosaic Books, SistahFriend Book Club, aNN Brown, Radiah Hubbert, and Peace in Pages Book Club. And to all the many book clubs, bookstores, retailers, libraries, media, and avid readers who have helped me spread the word along the way.

Thank you all and God bless.

CONTENTS

"I don't believe an accident of birth makes people sisters or brothers. It makes them siblings, gives them mutuality of parentage. Sisterhood and brotherhood is a condition people have to work at."

—MAYA ANGELOU

When I Get Where I'm Going

It is Wednesday, the day after the Mega Millions drawing. Two sisters—Alicia Day and Heaven Jetter—are at the bank where their other sister works. The purpose of their visit is to reclaim a missing link—Hope Teasdale, their sister who feels she doesn't belong, but only because she doesn't want to. Since they know she won't pick up her phone, they are going to let Hope know in person that they played Mega Millions the day before and matched five of the numbers (but not the Mega Ball number), for a total of $250,000 before taxes.

When the two sisters leave the bank, they're going to drive ninety miles on the interstate heading west to the lottery headquarters in Lansing, Michigan, so they can claim their prize. Heaven, the youngest of the sisters, picked the numbers. She used all three of their ages—twenty-one, twenty-seven, and thirty-two—along with Hope's birth month and day. For the Mega Ball number, she selected the number twenty-nine. Alicia, the eldest of the sisters, contributed twenty dollars toward the purchase of the tickets Heaven bought.

This is the truth—the whole truth—so help them God. And they do need help—all three of them.

Two of the sisters, Heaven and Hope, have the same mother and father, but neither parent is present in their lives now, and neither has been for quite a while. Alicia is their half sister. The three share in common a father, a man Alicia has seen only once and doesn't remember at all. What she knows of her birth and her biological father is what her mother has told her—that she was born when both her parents were still in high school and that it was a big mistake, though her mother reassures Alicia that she is not part of the mistake. But Alicia doesn't believe in mistakes. If she did, she would assume moving to LA when she was nineteen to become a star was a mistake, because after thirteen years of trying, after thirteen years of not giving up on a dream she's had since she was six years old, she still hasn't made it.

Life is full of experiences.

Consequences.

Not mistakes.

Eventually her mother moved on to a wonderful man, and they married and had a son, so Alicia now has a stepfather who treats her like his own daughter, as well as a younger brother. Growing up, however, she never had a relationship with her sisters. Up until recently, Alicia's life revolved mostly around her dreams of making it in Hollywood. Occasionally she fantasized about marriage—her plan B—in particular, marrying someone who could help her career. But time has a way of changing things, and now her life has changed. Having temporarily left LA, she is now back in Detroit living with her parents in their suburban condo while she makes plans for her personal reinvention. Her dream hasn't changed—just the way she plans to realize it.

Alicia and Heaven enter the suburban Detroit bank as a unified pair. They are so excited to share with Hope the good news that all three of them are winners; even if their past life hasn't always told them so, now their lotto ticket does.

They stand near the entrance, not far from Hope's desk, and wait patiently for her to finish with her customer—a badly burned man—who makes himself very comfortable at her desk. He has the front section of the *Free Press* sprawled over the seat of the chair beside him, and he occasionally sips from a bottle of water that he holds in his good hand. Hope pretends not to see her sisters standing to her right. But who can ignore two women, one with bushy hair and the other nearly bald, lingering inside the bank for no discernible reason? It appears that no one can, including Hope. *What happened to Heaven's hair?* Hope wonders. She knows Heaven didn't cut it. Not someone like her sister, who always wanted long hair. Maybe all the quick weaves, hair colors, and box relaxers finally took their toll.

Only after Hope walks her customer to the door does she cast her eyes in her sisters' direction, flashing a bothered look. No sooner has Hope walked over to join the two of them than four men, their faces covered by black ski masks, barge into the bank carrying high-powered automatic rifles and handguns. They instruct everyone inside to hit the floor—everyone but Heaven. One of the bank robbers has her in a chokehold as he presses a 9mm handgun against her temple, bartering with her life so two of the robbers can gain access to the inside of the teller station and the vault while the fourth robber removes jewelry and other valuables from the customers lying on the floor. Frozen with fear, Heaven closes her eyes and prays. Beads of sweat slide down her forehead. It's ninety-two degrees outside, yet she is cold and shivering. She has never had a gun pressed against her temple; she has never imagined how extremely painful the pressure of the metal barrel shoving against her skull could be. She imagines the damage a single round could do, shattering bones and giving her absolutely no chance of survival at such close range. Lying on the ground next to her feet is Alicia, who, so accustomed to Hollywood, is still waiting for the director to yell, "Cut!"

But this is no movie set. This is real life. And it is the fear of losing her life, or losing either of her sisters, that causes Alicia to cry. She's been back in Detroit for only a couple of months, and just like that her life may be over. This is what Alicia's acting coach had asked her to master—finding her overall objective. She not only wanted Alicia to be able to pull from a real-life experience in order to stir up enough feeling to evoke tears when a script called for it. She wanted her to understand the emotion itself in order to replicate it. But Alicia could never cry when it mattered most. She was never able to produce tears at an audition, when securing a role could change her life; she could cry only when she thought her heart was hurting—when a man had left her or she'd been wronged by a supposed friend.

The bank robbers enter and leave quickly, dragging Heaven outside to a waiting van before shoving her to the ground, but not before snatching from her tight grip her large red canvas bag printed with white hearts. They leave behind only the bamboo handles for her to cling to. Heaven remains on the ground, beating the hot concrete with the palms of her hands.

Heaven was going to use her portion of the winnings to move to an apartment downtown, buy a new car and a puppy. She was going to start a new life and never look back. And now, her bag and the lottery ticket are gone, and so is all of that money she'll never have.

Alicia wanted the things money can't buy, to become a star—what comes to some because of luck. The day before, after learning they'd hit Mega Millions, was the luckiest she'd ever been. Now today feels like so many other days she's had before.

Hope, oblivious to the reason they even came to her job in the first place, stands inside the bank, near the entrance, and peers out at Heaven, who has always played the victim well, but Hope can ponder so many reasons why she doesn't believe this is a simple robbery. However, this isn't a story about the lottery or the winning ticket that was stolen from the sisters. This is a story about all of the other things that have been stolen from their lives, some of which they are fighting to reclaim.

PART ONE

Another Part of Me

Five Months Earlier

May

My Dearest Heaven,

I pray this letter finds you in good health and spirits. Your nana finally gave me your new address. I've been writing to the one on Franklin Road. She just got around to telling me that you moved about a year ago. I guess she thought somehow I already knew. I hope all my other letters got forwarded to your new address. And for the ones that came when you were still living on Franklin, I can't say why I never heard back from you. All I know is I always pray during mail call that I'll receive letters from you and Hope. But I never do. I just want you to love me and forgive me for what I did. I don't know if that's even possible, though. And that's been the hardest part for me while I do time—not hearing from my girls in thirteen years. I'm doing a little better, though. I just got accepted into a program where I train dogs. I got my first one three weeks ago—a bullmastiff puppy named Temple. I also got a new cell—a bigger cell—and Temple is my only cellee. He goes everywhere with me.

Nana told me you lost your job at that school. Sorry to hear that. She told me you really liked being a secretary too. She tries to keep me abreast of things. She said money's tight right now for everybody and as bad as she wants to see you, neither one of you has the money to travel. I wish I could help you somehow. That's the hardest part of being in here, not being able to help my girls. Times are real bad now for everybody, but one day they will get better for you and Hope. I promise.

I really need to talk to you and Hope. Your nana said she hasn't spoken to Hope and that you don't speak to her either. That's really a shame; you girls need to be tighter than tight to get through the hard times in life.

With you and Hope not speaking, I think now is the time to tell you some important news, something I've been hiding for a long time. You have an older sister. Her full name is Alicia Nova Day. She was born in 1977 at Henry Ford Hospital when I was still in high school. Her mother's name is Krystal Day, if she's not married by now. They used to live in Detroit on Greenlawn. I want you to try to find her. I know it's easy to find people nowadays with the Internet. I've been meaning to tell you for years, but it never seemed like the right time. But now that I have, I'm leaving the rest up to you. I pray you and your sisters can all come together as a family.

Love,
Your father

Heaven Jetter enters the probation office on James Couzens in Detroit for her 10:10 a.m. appointment with her probation officer, Mrs. Debra Thomas. As she pulls back the door to enter, she says a quick prayer that Mrs. Thomas won't drug test her. Her best friend, Trina, and Heaven's boyfriend, Donovan, are both bad influences— both love weed entirely too much. *Damn*, she thinks. *How could I have been so stupid and gotten high the day before I had to report to the probation office?*

The police officer who stopped Heaven last year found controlled substances in her car; a little marijuana and a few ecstasy pills. As for the marijuana, just about everyone she knew smoked weed. But the ecstasy pills were a fluke. She had gotten the pills from a friend that night to give to Trina, but there was no hope of explaining that when she was pulled over for failure to follow right-of-way requirements at a stop sign at the intersection of Wright Street and Jos Campau as she was leaving her friend's downtown apartment at River Place. On top of that, she had a blood alcohol level twice the legal limit.

One month later she was in court. The sentence she received after everything was said and her misdeed had already been done was one year probation, a five-hundred-dollar fine, thirty days suspended license, six points on her driving record, and three hundred twenty hours of community service. She has finished only one hundred sixty of those hours, most by preaching to high school students about the dangers of drunk driving, and the rest from her forty-hour substance abuse class.

She didn't agree with most of what she'd told those students. One of her friends helped her put together two paragraphs that started with, "On that fateful evening, I made a grave error in judgment." And she felt funny while she was reading it—reading something that was supposed to come from her heart but didn't even sound like something she'd say. It wasn't in her own words, but the students didn't know that, her friend told her. The truth, in her own words, would be that she had three drinks that night—three, and that was it. Other times she'd had more and still made it home just fine.

She would have told those students in her own words, "Can somebody please explain to me what's so wrong with drinking? I'm not an alcoholic. Alcoholics drink every day. I'm sure some of you drink too. I know I started when I was in high school. My freshman year I got drunk in my friend's car in the parking lot at Pershing and fell asleep in my English class, and I still graduated. Personally, I couldn't have made it through high school without drinking every now and then. All I can say is, if you drink, just don't drive." It's not that she loves the taste (except for Dark 'n Stormys). She loves the way it makes her feel. When she has a buzz, nothing else matters, and if life could naturally feel that way, then she wouldn't need to drink. Maybe, for some, that's how life is, but it's never been that way for Heaven.

She drinks only when life bothers her. Is it her fault that happens a lot? Yes, she likes to indulge now and then to destress. A lot of people do. But she doesn't use any hard drugs. A little marijuana from time to time—so what? In her opinion, it should be legal in every state . . . and not just for medical reasons. Hope, her sister, swears she has a problem and believes she's an alcoholic. But Hope also believes her husband is still alive even though he died in an accident two years ago. So that should tell people a lot about Hope and her opinions. Sometimes she just doesn't make sense.

Drinking helps Heaven forget that her father went to prison for life for killing their mother. If people knew how lonely her childhood had been, maybe they wouldn't be so quick to judge.

She doesn't even have a chance to flip through a magazine at the probation office or cross her legs before she hears Mrs. Thomas' raspy smoker's voice say, "Heaven, come on back."

Heaven trails behind the fashionable probation officer in her early fifties who reminds her of Miss Swann, one of the teachers at the middle school where she used to work. Just like Miss Swann, Mrs. Thomas always has her shoulder-length hair done really nicely. Heaven isn't sure if it's a wig or not. She knows it's not a weave. She can spot a weave a mile away, even the ones that are done correctly. Mrs. Thomas always wears the nicest high heels too, and the most expensive outfits.

Heaven's going to get through this appointment the same way she gets through them all: by avoiding most of Mrs. Thomas' questions and answering many of them with a question of her own. Mrs. Thomas takes a seat behind her desk and leans back in her leather chair to relax.

"So, Heaven, how you doing?"

Heaven takes a seat in one of the chairs in front of Mrs. Thomas' desk. "How should I be doing under the circumstances?"

"Have you found a job yet?"

"Has any unemployed person in Detroit found a job yet, Mrs. Thomas?"

"You're not lying about that. I know my husband hasn't. But have you even been looking?"

"Mrs. Thomas, why wouldn't I be looking for a job when money makes the world go round? Wasn't your April DTE Energy bill as high as mine?"

Mrs. Thomas slaps her left hand, bejeweled with a large diamond wedding ring, on a stack of files on her desk. "Girl, don't make me start cussing up in here. It was way too high, but that's beside the point. Now, how many more community service hours have you completed?"

"Did you know it's not easy to complete community service hours?"

"Why isn't it, Heaven?"

"You don't know the kind of runaround they put you through just for one of them to sign and date a piece of paper," Heaven says as she takes out her chart that tracks her completed community service hours.

"Heaven, while you're not working, you should knock out as many of these hours as you possibly can. I want to see at least thirty hours completed by next week."

"Thirty hours, Mrs. Thomas? Are you for real?"

"Okay, forty? Does that sound better?"

Heaven's eyes roll. "Why not fifty, then?" Heaven asks sarcastically.

"Now, see, I was trying to work with you with the thirty, but you're trying to get all smart. If you had gotten one of the other POs in here, especially that asshole in the office next door," Mrs. Thomas mumbles, "he would really tack on the hours. Is that how you want me to be with you? I'm trying to work with you. So how many do you honestly think you can do, and don't say ten. Work with me, please."

"Does twelve sound reasonable?"

"Girl, if you don't remind me of my oldest child, always trying to be so nickel slick. Why would you want to be on probation any longer than you have to be? You have only two more months and a whole lot of hours to complete before then. I want to see fifteen hours next week. Now, get on out of here before I change my mind. I don't have to drug test you, do I?"

"Now, Mrs. Thomas, why would you think you would need to drug test me?" asks Heaven as she stands and removes her favorite purse—a red canvas bag with white hearts—from the chair.

"You're a mess and you know it. Girl, get on out of here before I change my mind about that too. And keep looking for a job."

Heaven heads out of her office with a sigh of relief. She made it through another appointment. She can't wait until she finally has her last one. But in the meantime, she is going to stop at the Sunoco Mart across the street to play the lotto and pray she hits it big.

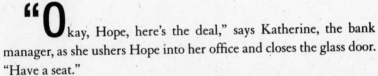

"**O**kay, Hope, here's the deal," says Katherine, the bank manager, as she ushers Hope into her office and closes the glass door. "Have a seat."

"This sounds serious," says Hope as she remains standing, "so I'd rather stand."

When Katherine sits behind her desk, Hope notices Mr. Hansen, her favorite customer, enter the bank. "Can you hold that thought for just one minute?" says Hope. "He always waits for me and I just want to tell him I'm in a meeting. You know . . . customer service."

"That's fine," says Katherine as she picks up her phone. "I need to make a quick call anyway."

She leaves her manager's office and walks over to Mr. Hansen. "Good to see you again, Mr. Hansen," says Hope with a big smile as she extends her right hand to shake his. She tries to ignore the stares in their direction.

"Ezra," he corrects her politely. "No need to be so formal."

Hope smiles and lowers her hand. "I'm in a meeting with my manager, and it could be a while. You're welcome to wait at my desk if you'd like, or see one of the tellers."

"Oh, that's okay. I'll come back another day. I prefer you to handle my business."

"That's fine—whatever you like."

Hope walks with Mr. Hansen. Just as they approach the door, a young boy around eight, the same age as Hope's daughter, walks in with his mother. He starts to point in Mr. Hansen's direction and says, "What's wrong with that man's face? Why does he look all nasty like that?" The boy tries to hide behind his mother, away from Mr. Hansen.

Hope is stunned—then outraged. She can't attack a child, even if she wants to at that moment. Instead, she lashes out at his mother. "Ma'am, please—your son. That was so unnecessary. You need to explain to him—"

"Hope," says Mr. Hansen, lightly tugging her suit jacket while he shakes his head. "That's okay."

Hope lets out a deep sigh. "It's not okay," she says as she walks away from the woman.

"I don't know what it is, but I seem to get that reaction a lot," he says jokingly.

But Hope isn't smiling. It's not funny to her that Mr. Hansen is severely burned over thirty percent of his body and suffered third-degree burns over his face, neck, upper chest, right hand, and right arm. People—not just children, adults too—feel they have the right to point and stare at him. They feel they have the right to make cruel comments like the boy did. Yes, Mr. Hansen's right hand is charred, stiff, and inflexible. His left arm and hand, however, aren't burned at all, and he still wears his wedding ring, just as Hope does, even though they are both widowed. And yes, he does have severe burns to his scalp that have made him permanently bald and terribly scarred, but he's still a human being.

He walks out of the bank with his head down.

Hope casts her eyes in the direction of the boy's mother, who is standing in line waiting for a teller, as she walks back toward her manager's office. She wants to tell that woman she needs to do a better job of teaching her son how to treat others who aren't like him. But then she wonders what Havana would do if she were to see him. Just because Havana is a straight-A student and mature beyond her years, it doesn't make her equipped for these kinds of situations.

"I'm sorry about that," says Hope as she reenters Katherine's office, still shaking her head at the behavior of the child. She takes a seat this time.

"That's so sad," says Katherine as she watches Mr. Hansen pull out of the bank's parking lot. "I can't imagine how that poor man must feel. Can you? Imagine being burned like that. I wouldn't even want to leave my house."

Hope's shoulders drop. It's not a rare disease, she muses; it can happen to anyone. "As my nana would always say, there but for the grace of God go I," she tells Katherine.

"So true." Katherine sighs, then shakes her head, getting her mind back to the reason she'd called Hope into her office in the first place. "I just want to give you a heads-up," she says, lowering her tone. "I know you had an offer at Bank of America at one time. Well, you may want to contact them to see if you can still get in."

Hope stiffens. "Why? Am I getting fired or something?"

"We may all be getting fired or something," Katherine says, dropping her head. "Word from corporate is the Feds will be visiting here any day."

"The Feds?"

"The FDIC may be coming in to shut us down. My contact at corporate said they sent a cease and desist order three months ago warning them to start turning down risk borrowers and raise cash by pushing the deposit accounts, but we didn't comply. Can you believe that?" asks Katherine. "We didn't comply."

"Yes, for some reason, I can," Hope answers. "My luck hasn't been that great lately."

Mercury is a bank with a reputation for aggressive real estate and development lending policies. The rumors had spread for several months about the bank's troubles. Hope had an opportunity to leave for Bank of America, but she turned it down. Mercury had been good to her. After her husband's boating accident, she took four months off, the bulk of the time at Katherine's discretion. And now, just over a year and a half later, all eight of their branches, which had been operating for forty years, could be seized by the FDIC.

"You've been a good employee and you're part of our management team, so I wanted to give you a heads-up. It might not happen . . . so please, whatever you do, do not mention it to the staff."

"I don't even talk to the staff . . . not that water cooler–type stuff, just strictly business. . . . You know that."

"I know, I know. And that's exactly why I confided in you."

Hours later, on Hope's short drive from the bank to her home on Church Street, she listens to Michael Bublé's "That's Life" once in its entirety. And she wishes she could truly believe in the song's message. Each day it gets a little better and one day, she tells herself, she'll accept that all the things that have happened—all the good things and just as many bad—are all just part of life. And perhaps one day she will be back on top.

A call comes in from Heaven on her cell phone as she is pulling into her driveway. She hasn't heard from Heaven in a while—almost long enough to miss her, but not quite. So she lets the call go to voice mail. She wants to forgive her sister for Havana's sake. Havana always asks where her aunt is and why she has stopped coming around. And even though Hope's told her how Heaven isn't living her life right, Havana still asks. But Hope's not ready to forgive her just yet.

The butterfly sensation that flutters inside Alicia Day's stomach is her nerves. She hesitates before extending her slender leg outward, nearly stubbing her big toe on the bottom edge of the open limousine door. The last thing she needs is to ruin a fresh pedicure on this of all nights—the night of the Primetime Emmys. Although she is certain Helena at Paradise Nails on Sunset would gladly repair her big toe *gratis* the next morning, it would be too late. Everything about her appearance has been calculated for tonight. It's all about tonight. How awful she would look draped in a black Christian Dior gown, clasping a clutch by the same designer and wearing Fred Leighton jewels around her slim neck and wrists, if her Manolo Blahnik's revealed chipped polish on her toes.

Alicia sighs in relief as she safely exits the limo while a crowd of paparazzi swarm around her. But one photographer, in his haste to snap a photo of her date, Barr Edmunds, steps on her sandal with his size-twelve shoe. Not only does he chip the white tips from three of her toenails, but he also splits one in the process. She grits her teeth to fight back tears. Talk about being in pain.

But she's at the Primetime Emmys. At that moment, she is acting.

She is smiling and pretending everything is wonderful—simulating a Hollywood star.

Cameras continuously click as more A-listers prance by. "Miss, can you please step to the side for a moment so we can take a few shots of Barr by himself?" a photographer asks Alicia. Her smile freezes as she politely takes a few steps back.

"Barr, look this way. Barr, please, just one more shot." Barr is tall, dark, handsome, and in his late twenties—younger than Alicia, but only by a few years. But the best part about him, aside from his British accent, is the sincere look in his brown eyes when he says her name.

Before she and Barr enter the Nokia, a man approaches them, and Barr briefly introduces him to Alicia as his agent, Ari Gold.

"Who is this beautiful creature?" Ari Gold asks Barr as he kisses Alicia's hand.

"This is your agent?" Alicia asks Barr.

"Yes. This is Ari."

"But this is Jeremy Piven. He only *plays* an agent on *Entourage*," she says in bewilderment.

"I know. This isn't making any sense right now," Ari says, wildly gesticulating with his hands. "But don't you worry your pretty little head over any of this. Let me handle the minor details. Don't sweat the small stuff, and it's all small stuff, right? What I want you to concentrate on right now is the fact that one of the biggest directors in town wants to do a movie with you. Might you know whom I'm referring to?" He winks suggestively at Alicia.

"Steven Spielberg?" Alicia asks.

"I'll give you another try. . . . Does the name 'Coen' mean anything to you?"

"The Coen brothers?!" Alicia exclaims.

"Well, I've only convinced Joel so far. I've arranged for him to be at our table tonight," Ari says with a self-satisfied smirk.

"Just like that?" Alicia asks skeptically.

He swats his hand dismissively. "You're guaranteed to be in his next movie. And, I haven't even told you the best part yet—you're an A-list star now, baby."

"Just like that, I'm an A-list star?" Alicia arches her right eyebrow.

"Of course you are. Don't you know who I am?"

"Ari Gold from *Entourage*?"

"'Call me Helen Keller, because I'm a fucking miracle worker!'" He looks upward. "I hope you brought an umbrella," he says as he points to the sky that has just turned green. "It's getting ready to pour."

"Oh my God, my hair," Alicia says frantically.

"Don't worry about your hair. Just have your hands ready. It's raining money, baby."

Alicia twirls around, grabbing bills as they rain from the sky. "What's going on? This doesn't seem real." She examines the money closely. "I didn't even know they made thousand-dollar bills."

Ari laughs uproariously. "This may be Hollywood, but if you think I'm getting you in a Coen brothers' film and thousand-dollar bills are falling from the sky, you really are dreaming."

Alicia's eyelids quickly flash open, and she finds herself sprawled across her bed. Disappointment weighs her heart down. *Why do I keep having this same kind of dream?* she wonders after she picks up her remote control from the bed and turns off her TV. This is the first dream she's had with Ari Gold in it, but since she'd fallen asleep watching *Entourage,* she isn't surprised. Her dreams are often filled with celebrities. As for Barr, although she'd fantasized about him often before, he'd never made an appearance in her dreams either. She's disappointed she isn't actually attending red-carpet events on the arm of an A-list actor, but she takes comfort in the fact that one of her best friend's Aubrey agreed to introduce her to the black Brit soon.

But what would he want with her? Although she has been called beautiful in the past, LA has made her self-conscious. Her high cheekbones, large dark eyes, and naturally tanned and enviously even skin tone have gotten her nowhere in the business. Ten years earlier, she was dating among the rich and famous. But she discovered quickly that she was merely one of many attractive women in a town where image is everything and beauty is mandatory.

Now Alicia can only find fault with herself. Fewer free drinks arrive at her table when she's out clubbing. It's a good thing she doesn't actually drink, or else she'd be broke on top of it all. She wonders whether it could be her thick curly hair. It's not easy being natural. Casting agents can make a perfect ten kind of woman question herself. One casting agent in particular pointed out things about her appearance she'd never noticed—uneven cheekbones; her left eye is smaller than her right; interesting hair, but with the potential to cause problems if she was unwilling to relax it since there was too much to stuff underneath a wig. One agent had the nerve to hand her a plastic surgeon's business card just in case she ever considered getting a chin implant and a little Botox under her eyes.

She thinks about the dream some more. It seemed so real before quickly turning nonsensical, she muses, as she rolls from her side to her back to stare at the ceiling. It was a recurring dream that always opened with Alicia at the Primetime Emmys, but never the Oscars, though she wants to work in movies. *Lord, even in my dreams I have lowered my expectations.*

She reminisces about her childhood and the 1983 Oscars, which inspired her to be an actress. She was six years old. Her entire family was in the den, their eyes glued to the television. While *Gandhi* swept most of the categories, what Alicia recalls most of all, aside from Richard Pryor cohosting the Oscars and Louis Gossett Jr. being the first black actor to win best supporting actor for his role in *An Officer and a Gentleman*, was that Sophie won for best actress. In her mind, she always closely identified Meryl Streep with her character in *Sophie's Choice*; she was never Meryl.

Her aunt Olena made a big deal about taking Alicia to see the R-rated *Sophie's Choice*. Alicia had been only five at the time. Her aunt made her swear she wouldn't tell anyone she'd seen the movie.

After the show they had a full discussion about the movie. The characters seemed as real to Alicia as her family members, so when Meryl Streep took the stage to accept the award for best actress, she was amazed to see that she wasn't acting like Sophie at all. When she asked Olena about this later, she said, "Meryl Streep is an actress. She gets paid to pretend she's other people."

"Like an allowance?" Alicia asked her aunt.

"Yes, like an allowance, but a really big one. So big it can't fit in your little piggy bank."

Alicia's eyes enlarged. People got big allowances just to pretend? She had always loved pretending, mostly when she was playing with her Barbie dolls. She would go off to her bedroom and enter another world. So to her, being an actress was just like being a Barbie. She never knew a person could grow up and become one. Gilligan was Gilligan. And he and the Skipper and the Professor and Mary Ann and Ginger were all trapped on that island.

At least that's what Alicia believed until she figured out they were just pretending. She never knew it was an option. She'd never once heard any one of her classmates say, "When I grow up, I want to act." The boys always wanted to be firemen, police officers, or doctors. The girls wanted to be teachers or nurses. Later in the school year, when her teacher asked everyone what they wanted to be, she proudly said, "I want to be an actress like Meryl Streep, and I want to win an Oscar." Aubrey, one of her best friends, laughed, and Alicia refused to speak to her for a full day because of it. To make matters even worse, Mrs. Barnes patted her on the back, almost like a pity pat, and started speaking to her slowly, as if worried Alicia might not understand. "You're a very smart little girl and it's okay to have a dream, but always remember, school wasn't designed to teach you how to dream. School was designed to teach you how to learn."

From her bedroom window, Alicia has a clear view of the Holly-wood sign, which is the only reason she rents the pricey two-bedroom apartment. Thankfully, she had convinced her friend Benita to move with her two years earlier and split the rent. But now as Alicia peers at the Hollywood sign, all she sees is false promise, and the more she gazes in its direction, the more she wonders how long it will take for her lifelong dream of stardom to ever come true. Who would ever leave such a perfect apartment? she used to ponder. Only someone who had either made it or got sick and tired of staring at a sign, a symbol, perhaps even a myth.

The former tenant was an aspiring actress from Wichita, Kansas, who overdosed on sleeping pills. Alicia doesn't know her name, but she privately calls her Dorothy. And now Alicia realizes what might've pushed Dorothy over the edge. Alicia can only hope she won't someday be driven to those same feelings of desperation.

Alicia remembers so vividly the conversation she had with her aunt Olena just last year and how she'd considered moving to Atlanta to live with her, since neither movies nor men were working out. She'd had it all planned. She would work at one of the M-A-C stores and audition for Tyler Perry. She even considered whether she could at least marry a star if she couldn't be one herself. Her aunt had told her, "It's not a man that should make you feel more alive. Life should, in and of itself."

For now, Alicia's mind is back on track with her goal. She'd read *A New Earth* at her aunt's insistence. The book helped, but that wasn't what changed her mind. She honestly believes acting is her God-given talent. But she never wants to get so caught up in Hollywood's hype that she loses all sense of self and forgets to take time, as one of her best friends Sir always says, to smell the roses. But what, other than Hollywood, could be as sweet as a rose?

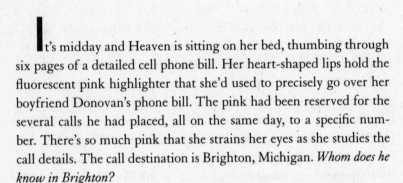

It's midday and Heaven is sitting on her bed, thumbing through six pages of a detailed cell phone bill. Her heart-shaped lips hold the fluorescent pink highlighter that she'd used to precisely go over her boyfriend Donovan's phone bill. The pink had been reserved for the several calls he had placed, all on the same day, to a specific number. There's so much pink that she strains her eyes as she studies the call details. The call destination is Brighton, Michigan. *Whom does he know in Brighton?*

Her eyes flit around the room restlessly. There's nothing fancy about the three-bedroom frame bungalow she lives in. Even the steel security door at the front needs replacing. The welding is coming loose. The only furniture inside is a double bed, a single dresser and a nightstand, and a soon-to-be-obsolete analog TV, all on the upper level where Heaven is now. The only things she owns of any value are a Nikon camera, photo lenses, and a Macbook Pro. But those aren't really hers. She bought her camera and computer using her sister Hope's credit without permission. This is the main reason they no longer speak.

Up until recently, she didn't own a cell phone with a decent airtime package, relying instead on an inexpensive prepaid Tracfone, which for the most part did the trick. But she'd be lying if she didn't admit to being ecstatic after Trina, her best friend, got her a refurbished iPhone on a hookup. Her stove and refrigerator are on loan from Rent-A-Center. There's nothing fancy about her life.

She is, however, proud to be an aunt, even though she never gets to see her eight-year-old niece. She is also proud that she graduated from high school, especially since so many of her friends dropped out. And she's particularly proud of the job she held for nearly two years as a secretary at a middle school on Detroit's east side. But now she depends on MARVIN for most of her income. She's not as proud about this, but at least MARVIN is not a man. MARVIN is Michigan's automated response voice interactive network that she calls every two weeks for her unemployment.

Heaven has an endless list of things she wants to change, and after studying Donovan's phone bill, his name is at the top of that list. With her cell phone resting on her bed beside her open laptop and her best friend, Trina, on the line doling out advice through the speakerphone, she ponders her tumultuous nearly-one-year relationship she's been in with Donovan that isn't worth salvaging; she knows it isn't. But for some reason it's hard for her to break free. And she's tired of her friends and her family—especially of her nana—telling her how to live her life when none of them have even figured out how to live theirs. It's not as if she knew what he was about when she met him. He'd told her all the right things. But maybe she should have just known—gone off what he did and not just what he said.

"Do any black people live in Brighton?" Heaven asks Trina. Heaven's index finger taps her computer touchpad to awaken her sleeping screen. "Probably not a one. I should Google the town and find out."

"Does it matter?" asks Trina.

"Yes, because I know he was more into white girls before we met, so maybe she's white."

"No, what I'm saying is, who really cares who or what he's into or whether she's black or white? The point is she isn't you."

"Trina, you don't even like men, so that's real easy for you to say."

"I like 'em—I just like women better," Trina says with a laugh. "I prefer men for money and women for everything else."

Heaven positions both hands in front of the computer screen and studies her scant nails. She bought the clear OPI polish with purple, red, and blue glitter strictly for the name—Too Good for Him. And she is too good for him. Too bad the polish is chipping. But what remains of it will be removed soon—and so will he. She continues studying the bill. "I can't believe him. There's a record of one of our calls and him taking this Brighton chick's call on call waiting. He got off the line with me for her? I really don't believe this."

"This song right here should be your anthem, girl. . . . Just listen to the words. . . . Just wait a minute," says Trina. And within seconds, "It Kills Me" begins to play. "Please listen to the words," Trina stresses.

Heaven listens intently to the first few verses. "Who is that?"

"Melanie Fiona. Her CD just came out, and you're listening to your birthday present right now."

"Girl, you already got me this phone. I don't expect anything else."

"The CD was on sale for seven ninety-nine, so it's not a big deal."

"Oh, okay, cool. Start it over from the beginning."

Trina starts the song over, and while Heaven is listening to the lyrics, she stops going through Donovan's cell phone bill and scrapes the polish from her nails. "Yes, I do know he's messing around," says Heaven, talking to the song. "And a part of me does want to leave." Heaven's head shakes. "I can't believe I'm going through this mess once again." Her voice quavered. "Why am I even wasting my time with this man?"

"That's what I want to know. Why are you crying over him? Girl, don't waste your tears."

"I'm so tired of being cheated on."

"Please stop. This conversation is so last year. We already figured this dude out. We already know Donovan's a fraud. What do you expect from somebody you met at the probation office? He isn't the first no-good man, and I'm sorry to break this to you, but he won't be the last man to cheat on you. But who cares? We have much bigger fish to fry and they're on the hook right now . . . at Nordstrom. I can't have your mind on anything other than that. Does he work? Does he even have a job?"

"No, but I don't have one either."

"I'm not talking about you right now. I'm talking about him. You had a job, but when has he ever worked?"

"He makes money too." Heaven goes through the pile of mail on her bed that she'd pulled the cell phone bill from and tosses her father's unopened letter to the side.

"You don't need him. Don't even worry about it, okay, girl? Just move on."

Later that night, Heaven pretends to be asleep and normally would be at four in the morning, except that Donovan is just now getting home and deep down she's fuming. He's drunk and doesn't know her snores aren't real. He drops his jeans on the floor beside the bed. She can smell the alcohol on his breath as he cozies up to her, and she tries her best not to say anything, not to ask where he's been. She has to literally grit her teeth when she feels like speaking. He falls fast asleep. Within minutes she hears heavy snores. She lies still for several more minutes, and then she slides out of bed.

She slips his cell phone from his front jeans pocket, then tiptoes down the stairs and into the bathroom. The last outgoing call from his cell phone is the Brighton number, but there isn't a name attached. He also has a picture mail from the same number, so she clicks on the link to launch the photo and waits several minutes for it to load. She has to try twice, due to poor reception, but finally a small photo that she can barely make out pops up. She hits view media for the photo to enlarge. Enormous breasts with pink nipples fill the screen. She screams and accidently drops the phone on the checkerboard tile floor. He told her he wasn't even a breast man. Obviously that was another lie, strictly for Heaven's benefit since she is barely an A cup.

She picks up his smartphone and calls his voice mail. She tells herself the only reason she's doing this is to make sure his phone is still working, not to try to retrieve any messages. *No service is currently available* appears on the screen. Her heart begins beating rapidly. He will kill her over his phone! She tries dialing his voice mail again, and a woman's voice says, "Please enter your password; then press pound." She doesn't know his password and can't even begin to guess. She goes back to the envelope icon and thumbs through pages and pages of sexting. "No . . . oh, hell no. I'm so much better than this," she says as each new nude picture is revealed . . . mostly of breasts. "I'm way better than this here." She tosses his phone in the toilet. "If he wants his phone, he can get it."

It is five o'clock in the morning, and Alicia Day is wide-awake, restless in thought. Sometimes she suffers from insomnia, but she refuses to take sleeping pills, because there are just too many people in Hollywood who are addicted to something, and she doesn't want to be the next one to fall victim. She deals with her discomfort by nestling in her sleigh bed on top of her beautiful floral-print queen-sized comforter between mounds of decorative pillows. Usually she has a leather-bound journal filled with several empty lined pages pressed against her chest. She is running out of things to say. She is tired of writing *I tried* at the top of another page. She wants to do more than try. She wants to make it. She wants to hear her Lupe Fiasco "Superstar" ringtone trill and know that her agent is on the other end with good news—a big role that Alicia will sink all of her acting skills into. She imagines Oprah screening her film and then calling her and asking, "Have you picked out your dress for the Oscars yet?" Instead, she is usually the one phoning her agency, only to have her calls screened by her agent's assistant. And she seriously doubts Oprah has seen any of the *Gigi Mama* movies, and if she had Alicia wouldn't want to know because her performance in all but the last one were far from being Oscar-worthy.

"Maybe something big is about to happen," she says to herself as she eases out of bed, always trying to remain positive. She notices a large dried spot on her sheet. "Again," she screams. *Oh my God*. Her period is the one thing that can disturb an otherwise positive mood. "When I said big, I didn't mean my period." She clasps her legs together tightly and leans forward to grab the bath towel resting on the edge of her dresser.

Her roommate, Benita, bangs on her bedroom wall, cursing Alicia in Spanish, then in English, and says, "Thanks a lot. I had three more hours to sleep—*tres horas*—but once I wake up, I'm up," she shouts through the wall. "Let me see if I can catch some reruns of *Gigi Mama*," she says sarcastically. She knows how much Alicia hates being associated with that DVD movie series of which Alicia is the star.

"I'll make it up to you after I win an Oscar, I promise." Then Alicia mumbles, "If I ever win an Oscar. If I can ever get cast in a movie . . . something besides *Gigi Mama*."

Security gates and large garbage Dumpsters line the ritzy street. The exclusive area is quiet and well maintained, but Alicia is feeling skeptical as she follows the winding road. It is hard for her to imagine Aubrey living in one of these colossal mansions. This is quite an upgrade from her nice little three-bedroom duplex on Craig Drive in LA that carried a million-dollar price tag. How does one go from that duplex to this estate in just two short years with only one major movie during that time? But, then again, it would be just like Aubrey to do something like that—to forego owning in order to rent a massive estate that was most likely way out of her price range. Not that Alicia signed Aubrey's paychecks and knew exactly what she was making, but a million or two a picture seems right. At least, that's what Benita said Aubrey was getting per picture ever since her Oscar nod four years earlier. And Benita usually knows how to track those things, but now that Aubrey is reading scripts for leading roles, she may earn even more soon.

"Fly to Detroit for what? I haven't been home in thirteen years," asks Alicia as she talks through her speakerphone to one of her best friends Sir while she is driving behind a black Nissan Sentra with an IF YOU RIDE MY ASS YOU BETTER BE PULLING MY HAIR bumper sticker. Sir is someone she has known for what feels like her entire life, ever since they were four years old. She talked to Sir nearly every day when she first moved to Los Angeles. But as the years passed, it fell to a couple times a week.

Now it had dwindled down to a few times a month to every now and then. This is more her fault than his, she acknowledges. Even though having his own business keeps him busy, he always manages to make time for the woman he refers to as his little sister on some days and the love of his life on others. "I need a man!" she'd told her aunt almost two years earlier. "There's always Sir," her aunt reminded her. But Sir is one of her best friends. Sir is not her husband. Hollywood is. Hollywood is who she is married to but doesn't fully trust, because Hollywood cheats and she knows Hollywood can never be faithful. Hollywood will always be looking for the next best thing.

"But this is for a role," says Sir. The last time she spoke to Sir was in January. He had just moved into a new loft—a historic 1920s art deco–styled high-rise and former toothpaste factory in downtown Detroit on Park Avenue in the theater district. Above his favorite bar, Centaur, it's also just down the street from his favorite sports bar, Hockeytown Café.

"As in movie role? That would be more believable if you said Atlanta instead of Detroit. ATL, not the D, is the black Hollywood."

"Next time you're on the Internet, look up the site Michigan-MakesMovies.com. I have a friend whose wife is a screenwriter."

"Oh," huffs Alicia. "I smell another hookup that's bound to go wrong. So, is this Michigan Makes Movies Web site your friend's or something?"

"No, it's not his site, but since you want to pretend like you're not from the D and you want to put down your hometown, I just wanted you to check out that site and see for yourself that a lot of films are being made here."

"So, tell me about this friend of yours."

"I wouldn't call him a friend."

"You just did a minute ago."

"Well, I shouldn't have. I don't know the guy that well."

"Great . . . So it's not even a hookup, then."

"Not really."

"How do you know him?"

"My lease was up, so I bought a Three Hundred from the guy's dealership. And we got kind of cool."

"Wait a minute? A Three Hundred as in Chrysler 300? What happened to your Benz?"

"As I just said, my lease was up, and as you may or may not know, we're in a recession—"

"I'm so tired of hearing the word 'recession.'"

"That's because you're off in Hollywood, the land of the flighty, but if you were back here in the D where the recession is hitting the hardest, you wouldn't be so tired of it. You'd want something done."

"Trust me, it's hitting LA hard too. So he sells you a car by claiming he can give me a hookup with a movie."

"I love you and all, but the only way anyone is going to sell me a car is by giving *me* a hookup on a car, and right now the American carmakers are doing so badly, they're giving away cars, but you wouldn't know anything about that because you don't keep up with anything going down in the Motor City anymore. Not even me."

Alicia tries to ignore the last part. "So how did I come up in this car transaction?"

"We got to talking, and he told me about his wife being a screenwriter and that she couldn't get anyone to buy her script, so she decided to produce it independently. I guess she got some funding through Detroit Economic Growth. I don't know. All I know is that I told him about you and he told his wife, and if you want, I can get a script to you."

"That's fine. You can send it to me and I'll take a look. But I doubt if I can be there next month for auditions."

"That was just an approximate date anyway. He said sometime over the next few months."

"Well, I doubt if I can get there in the next month or even two. There's really nothing in Detroit that I want to come back for."

"How would you feel if I said that about LA?"

"Stop acting so sensitive. You know I don't mean you. So she has the financing or at least some of it, but does she have distribution?"

"I don't know about all that. I don't even know how any of that stuff works."

"She probably doesn't. That's the hardest part for these independent filmmakers . . . and she's a woman too. Good luck. What's her name so I can Google her?"

"His last name is Townsend. Can't remember either of their first names off the top of my head."

"First name, Robert, I hope."

"Yeah, right, I'm sure you do. I think her first name might be Corliss."

"I'm going to Google her tonight."

"Listen," Sir says, "I'll talk to you later. I have a meeting that I'm late for and it's pretty important."

"How is your business doing anyway, Mr. CEO?"

"It's not—hence the Chrysler instead of another Benz. And that's why this meeting is so important. Hopefully I'll be driving a Bentley next year. I'll call you tonight, sweetie."

Alicia's other line beeps. "Hold on for a minute."

"No, you can go ahead and take that. . . . I have to go, okay?"

"All right. Don't forget to call me later," Alicia says.

She clicks over to her other line. It's a call from her doctor's office to confirm her nine o'clock appointment for the next day. If not for the friendly reminder by telephone, Alicia would have forgotten all about the appointment she'd made more than a month earlier with an ob-gyn she'd found on the Internet.

She is finally going to do something about her fibroid tumors that have recently started to enlarge—aside from trying to flatten her bulging stomach with Spanx and camouflage it with a cleverly coordinated outfit. She has restricted her diet by eliminating all soy, avoiding red meat and ham, and anything else with estrogenic properties. Every day she tries to take two tablespoons of blackstrap molasses; a natural source of iron, it's supposed to slow menstrual bleeding and boost energy. The problem with the molasses is that it tastes so bad, she usually skips the recommended dosage. She is tired of being asked by strangers if she's expecting, tired of her tumor being mistaken for a baby bump, tired of missing yoga due to her heavy menstrual cycles.

"Tomorrow?" Alicia asks, suddenly remembering an audition she just landed. "Oh, I can't make it. How about the next day?"

"Dr. Patel's next opening is Wednesday, June 18 at three."

Alicia sighs. "Well, I don't want to wait that long, but if that's all you have, put me down for that."

Once Alicia drives through the gates of Aubrey's estate, she parks on the open motor court. *The Power of the Actor* rests in her passenger seat. She has an acting class at seven. But it's still early, so she has plenty of time for a visit. Aubrey will probably give a quick tour around her new mansion. That will in and of itself take a solid hour, as big as the place is. And then Alicia figures they'll order a pizza from Two Boots with Sicilian crust and nearly every topping, heavy on the sopressata and tasso. Maybe they'll watch a DVD while they eat and critique the acting, just like old times. She brought along *The Curious Case of Benjamin Button*, just in case.

Aubrey greets her at the front door with a face full of makeup, including an extremely smoky eye and bold, colorful lips.

"Wow, you're dressed up," says Alicia.

Aubrey flutters her cat eyes. "This is loungewear." Skimming her size-four frame is a cheetah-print mini coat dress belted at the waist, exclusively designed for her by a previous *Project Runway* contestant

Aubrey loves to brag she retained as her personal designer before another A-list actress could. Each of her nails has a Minx film coating that matches her outfit exactly. She is standing in a pair of red leather four-inch open-toed sandals with a zipper strap across the ankle. Her hair is lighter and shorter for the moment—heightened into a Mohawk. And even though Aubrey can wear just about anything and look stunning, Alicia is praying this particular look is for a new role and not for real life.

Alicia assumed this was just going to be a casual get-together to catch up on missed time since Aubrey had been filming on location in Montreal for the past several months. So Alicia dressed accordingly, in jeans and a scoop-neck T-shirt with flat-heel gladiator sandals. She'd adjusted the double elastic straps to her crocheted headband with wooden beads from her Andrea's Beau headband collection through her hair to create a curly Afro puff. The one accessory she is the most proud of—a small black Italian and cowhide leather clutch with gold-tone hardware—is looped around her tiny wrist. It retails for $395. She lucked out in the Fashion District and paid a mere $125, thanks to Benita's talents as a budget-conscious personal shopper. And during this time of the month, she keeps her eco-friendly, multicolored tote made of nylon rice bags and juice packs by her side to carry the many sanitary napkins and tampons she'll need to change into throughout the day.

Alicia follows Aubrey into the Moroccan room, admiring her floor-to-ceiling opalescent tiles and gem-tone finishes as a butler pours white wine into their wineglasses. *She has a butler*, muses Alicia. *But she doesn't just have a butler. She has a chef, two bodyguards, a personal assistant, and this big-ass house.* Clearly, Aubrey wasn't suffering from the recession. *One to two million a picture can't be right. She wouldn't be able to afford all this.*

"You know I don't drink," says Alicia.

"Maybe that's your problem. Maybe you need to start doing things you don't always feel comfortable with," Aubrey coos. And Aubrey would know. If Page Six and *The Hollywood Gossip* were right,

Aubrey was addicted to all manner of prescription drugs, including Vicodin.

"Okay, one glass, but can you put crushed ice in it?" Alicia asks the butler. This way, if she can't stand the taste she can always suck on the ice—one of her recent favorite pastimes.

The butler retreats to the kitchen and returns quickly with a glass of crushed ice that he pours the wine into. Alicia takes the wineglass and rests it on the coaster on the table in front of her.

Sitting beside Aubrey is a young man with a grungy look. He is wearing a two-zipper dark gray hoodie with faded straight-leg jeans. His hair is mussed, as if he merely ruffles his fingers through it. He seems to be in an intense state of thought, or under the influence of some very powerful drugs.

Aubrey introduces him as John Ruckus, but he quickly says everyone calls him J.R.

"Essentially, this is an Indie film," J.R. continues, after explaining he's a writer, director, producer, and the next Tarantino. His spiel sounds so familiar to Alicia because she's heard it hundreds of times before and fell for it at least a dozen times, only to end up earning a few thousand dollars with the promise of more if the movie ever found a home—a distributor, and financing. What he is saying reminds her of what the director of *Gigi Mama* told her almost verbatim. She should have known from the name that that movie was going straight to DVD, but at least she was able to star in five of them.

She's never been thrilled about playing a stereotype. Her favorite actress is Meryl Streep and she wants to play the same kinds of characters she does. She does not want to get boxed into urban films as someone's best friend or love interest or a Gigi-type, described as being a sexy, ride-or-die "redbone" whose husband controls a notorious drug cartel. She found the first two movies to be disgraceful, and even used the alias Hunter Jones, but at least it was work and miles above porn, which she never considered doing. Thankfully, the story line improved as the series became an underground hit.

J.R. continues. "And I'm confident I'll secure backing during

Sundance, because I can easily see this film winning the Grand Jury award."

"So you must also be confident you'll get into Sundance?" asks Alicia. *Gigi Mama* was never accepted into the film festival, though the director had essentially made the same promise.

"I know I'll get in," he says through laughter. "I've always gotten in."

"Oh, so you've made other movies?" asks Alicia. "Which ones?"

"Foreign films, mostly in limited release. More art films than anything, and not necessarily something a major studio would be interested in. But this film is different."

"Oh yeah, how so?" asks Alicia, ignoring her drink. There's no need for her to take a sip; no need to try anything different, because so far all she's listening to is more of the same old nonsense.

"Because the screenplay I've written fits into the Hollywood blockbuster formula. I've done enough movies for the love of it. I'm ready now to make some real money."

"Well, good," says Alicia, taking a sip of her wine. His last statement was worth drinking to. "Because so am I." She spits up her words, nearly choking on the wine. "Sorry, this went down the wrong pipe."

"Continue," says Aubrey with a mischievous grin. "Tell her why she's here."

"I want you to play the lead in my next movie—my future Oscar-winning movie."

"You think it's a future Oscar winner, and you want me to play the lead?" Alicia asks as she continues to cough. "Seriously?"

"Aren't you secure with your talent?" asks J.R.

"I mean," Alicia says with a shrug, "you don't know me. Have you even seen my work?"

"He saw a few of your *Gigi Mama* movies," interjects Aubrey. "He thinks you're perfect for the part."

"Yeah, I do, and I noticed that they really love you in the direct-to-DVD world."

Alicia says, "I have nothing against you and what you're trying to do. I definitely respect anyone on their grind, but I've paid my dues. I've done stage plays and straight-to-DVD films. The only thing I haven't done is a reality show, but I've thought about it. After thirteen years, I need something bigger."

"I understand your reluctance toward me, since I'm an independent filmmaker. And I realize my name may not be as recognizable as Quentin Tarantino's, but just like him, I have heart and determination."

So did the director of Gigi Mama. The unfortunate part, muses Alicia, is that he isn't anyone she's heard of—anyone she respects and would die to work for. She hadn't heard of him the same way most studio heads and casting directors hadn't heard of her. And she wonders how he assumes he can go to a major studio asking for blockbuster-type money if he's already cast the lead. She's so tired of helping out these would-be directors who always talk such a good game and never deliver. When the deal is said and done, the results are still the same—straight to DVD, if they get that far. On the other hand, he is offering something she doesn't have now—money.

"I can give you a twenty-five-thousand-dollar advance. If, for some bizarre reason, the movie doesn't get made, you don't have to give me the money back."

"Seriously?" asks Alicia. She could use a quick cash infusion.

"Yeah. Let me give you the script and the contract. Think about it, but not too long, because I need to get started."

"I have an agent I need to run all this by."

"Heidi will be cool with it," says Aubrey. "You know how hard it is for you to get her on the phone."

"Will you try for me?" asks Alicia. "She'll pick up for you."

Aubrey nods. "No problem."

After J.R. leaves, Alicia excuses herself and goes to Aubrey's bathroom with her tote bag so she can freshen up before hitting the road. She is in awe when she enters the guest bathroom. She's never seen a bathroom so large, or one with a chandelier and solid gold fixtures.

Thirteen years ago Alicia and Aubrey moved to LA together and they each brought along one suitcase. Alicia still has hers, but now Aubrey has all this.

After Aubrey walks Alicia to the front door, she says, "We have to go to Guys and Dolls tomorrow night to celebrate. And don't worry, you can drink, because I'm having my driver pick you up."

"Wow, we're going to go out to celebrate my getting this role?" asks Alicia with a smile.

"Of course, you're my girl . . . and Barr will be there," she says with a wink. "You finally get to meet your crush."

"I wonder what I should do about the auditions tomorrow."

Aubrey shrugs. "You already know you have this part, but if you want to, go and see."

"No, I'm not going. You know how much I hate going to open auditions anyway."

Her friend is finally coming through for her. And Benita thought she'd never help her, but Alicia knew she would. They go back too far for her not to.

Later that evening Alicia receives another call from Sir.

"I want to make sure I have the right address," says Sir. "I'm going to FedEx the script to you. I picked it up today. She said to let you know it's not the final draft and she probably won't start casting for several months."

Alicia shakes her glass filled with crushed ice. "Don't send it. I think I already have a role—I got offered one today." She bites down on the ice. "Aubrey hooked me up with an up-and-coming writer and director. She is finally coming through for me. And she's throwing me a party to celebrate my first real role, *and* she's introducing me to Barr Edmunds. You know who that is, right?"

"Oh yeah, you mean that real nonmasculine-looking guy that you ladies seem to like."

"Nonmasculine? You're saying that just because he's clean shaven."

"I'm clean shaven, but he doesn't even have a mustache."

"I love his look. And besides, he's big-time out here . . . and there's nothing nonmasculine about him."

"He's big-time out there?" repeats Sir. "I'm big-time out here."

"Don't hate."

"I'm not hating. . . . I just don't get all into the hype. He might be a celebrity, but he's not God. He's human with a recognizable face. Don't blow him up to be more than that."

"True, but I don't want you to steal my joy right now, so I'm going to let you go. But I'll call you after my party and tell you how it went."

"I'm happy for you," says Sir. "I just don't want you to put all your eggs in one basket or, in this case, one very nonmasculine man."

"Don't say anything else. I'm trying not to come down from my natural high."

They say their good-byes and she hangs up, wondering whether Sir was a little bit jealous, but quickly shakes that thought from her head and continues eating more ice. Finally, Alicia feels as if her dream of becoming a working actress might actually materialize.

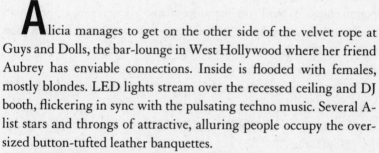

Alicia manages to get on the other side of the velvet rope at Guys and Dolls, the bar-lounge in West Hollywood where her friend Aubrey has enviable connections. Inside is flooded with females, mostly blondes. LED lights stream over the recessed ceiling and DJ booth, flickering in sync with the pulsating techno music. Several A-list stars and throngs of attractive, alluring people occupy the over-sized button-tufted leather banquettes.

Tonight is supposed to be a celebration for her new role. But it sure doesn't feel like one. Alicia is perched on one of the sofas arranged on the main floor. Hanging above her head is a grand display of small chandeliers in a voluminous cluster. Directly beside her is the actor Barr Edmunds, whom, before today, she knew only through his weekly television series and interviews—and her dreams.

She wants to speak to him, but she doesn't know what to say. She keeps thinking about what Sir said about Barr—about how he's just human, but if that's true, why can't she look at him without her vision blurring? Her eyes nervously scan the lounge and spot Evan Ross, an up-and-coming celebrity popular with the tween crowd. He's so cute but so young. She's not like her aunt Olena. She refuses to fall in love with a younger man right now. She'll wait for her forties. She also notices Aubrey in a nearby banquette dancing in her bare feet with a drink in her hand, not a worry in the world. Some celebration, muses Alicia. Aubrey has barely said anything all night to her aside from hello. And she still doesn't understand why they didn't ride there together. If she'd known before she stepped foot into the black SUV that Aubrey wasn't inside, she never would have agreed to get in. Call it her paranoia or whatever, but aside from not feeling comfortable with riding alone in an SUV with tinted windows and a strange-looking man behind the wheel, it also would've been nice to arrive with Aubrey like old times.

"You seem bothered," says Barr in a British accent that has the power to make Alicia swoon. He gently places his hand on her thigh and rubs her leg with sedulous care. He then picks up a small bowl of potato chips. "Would you like some crisps?"

"Did you say crisps or chips?" asks Alicia for clarification. She smiles at the richness of his accent. She loves to hear him speak, infatuated as she is with his presence.

"These are crisps," Barr clarifies as he holds one up for display. He has been in the States only a couple of years and is still getting used to the shift in vocabulary. "What you call fries over here, we call chips."

"How funny."

"The differences can be quite hilarious," he says with a smile that make his dimples more pronounced. "I'm going to pop outside and light a fag. Care to join me?" he asks as he takes out a cigarette from his pack.

"That really doesn't translate well over here. You might want to stick to calling them cigarettes. . . . So you smoke?" Alicia asks peevishly, wrinkling her nose.

"Yes," Barr says as he draws his face away from her. "I'm sorry. Let's not have a row over a fag—I mean a cigarette. Please pop out with me. The air may do you some good."

They step out onto a crowded covered patio situated in the front of the bar-lounge. He takes the cigarette and acts as if he is going to light it in the outdoor fireplace, but Alicia grabs his arm, and he strikes a match instead. "I wasn't actually going to stick my hand in. I was teasing you," he says.

All of the seating is occupied. And she wants to go back inside, but she knows the sofa they had is now taken. And she hates standing. It would be one thing if she still had a flawless body that she wanted to flaunt like many of the women there, but unfortunately that isn't the case. She still has her period and even with her Spanx and an outfit that conceals her belly, she feels like she looks pregnant, particularly from a side angle.

"Has anyone ever told you that you look"—she braces herself and says a silent prayer: *Lord, please don't let him say* pregnant—"like Halle Berry?"

Thank you, Jesus. "Occasionally," she admits.

"Halle Berry is sexy as hell." He bends down to whisper in her ear. "Would you like to leave?" She tilts her head back and peers up at him. She finds tall men incredibly sexy, and he towers over her, despite her four-inch heels.

"I'm not sure Aubrey's ready to go yet, and I plan on riding back with her."

"Oh, I thought this was our night to celebrate," he whispers. "I had the concierge book us a room."

"A room? For what?"

"Why simply dream about me?" he asks with a smile while checking out a slim blonde who breezes by.

She flinches. "Who says I dream about you?"

"Does it matter who said it? You have your dreams, and I have my own fantasies." He takes a swig of his drink.

"And what is your fantasy?"

"Halle Berry, of course," he says smoothly.

Alicia is completely turned off. "I'm sorry, but I'm not interested in fulfilling anyone's fantasies tonight," she says, forming a barrier between them with her hands. "There're enough women in here; I'm sure that hotel room won't go to waste." She turns to walk away.

"Can I at least get your mobile number?" Barr asks, whipping out his phone. "Oh, and your name again, or should I just put it under Halle?" Completely disgusted, she walks back inside the lounge, leaving him outside with his cigarette.

She finds Aubrey near the bar not too far from Matthew Perry.

"Hey," trills Aubrey. "Are you having fun? Where's Barr? Not this bar. Your Barr," she says, laughing at her own stale joke.

"He's not my Barr," says Alicia. "I need to talk to you."

"Okay, hold up for one second. I want another drink, and this is my party, so I shouldn't have to get my own drink, but it is what it is, I guess."

"You're right, it is what it is, and I thought this was *my* party?"

"Well, it's our party. I have a new movie to celebrate too."

"You always have something to celebrate. I need to talk to you right now," Alicia says as she puts her hand on her hip and huffs.

"What's wrong?" Aubrey follows Alicia into the ladies' room.

Once behind the door, Alicia blasts, "Why would you tell him that I dream about him?"

"Tell who, Barr?"

"Why would you do that? Now he assumes I'm just some groupie he can sleep with. He had the concierge rent a room for us. He's trying to fulfill some Halle Berry fantasy."

"That's a compliment."

"No, it isn't. I'm Alicia Nova Day, not Halle Maria Berry and I don't want to be with a man who's fantasizing about being with somebody else."

"Look, when are you going to learn that you have to give a little in this town to get a lot? He knows people." Aubrey leans into the mirror to reapply her lipstick.

"Groupies do stuff like that, and I'm not a groupie."

"No, but you are an aspiring actress and there's not that much difference." She chuckles as she twists down the tube of her lipstick, covers it with the cap, and tosses it inside her expensive clutch. "And come on, who better to give some to but an up-and-coming young actor like Barr. Some consider him to be the next Brad Pitt, which would mean you might be the next Angelina."

"Angelina was a star before Brad. You know what? Forget it. I'm going home with Benita."

"Ugh." Aubrey's eyes roll. "When did she get here?" Aubrey and Benita have never gotten along ever since all three of them were roommates six years earlier, before Aubrey hit the big time. It started with a dispute over a cable bill and escalated to small claims court. Benita won her case, but Aubrey still hasn't paid her the $463 she owes.

"She's not here yet, but I'm calling her to come get me because I don't want your *driver* taking me home. I'll never forget what happened the last time you had someone you supposedly knew take us home."

"Don't be silly. He really is my driver."

"I'm not being silly. I'm being safe."

"Be whatever," says Aubrey dismissively as she leaves the ladies' room, while Alicia stays behind to call Benita. "Come get me," Alicia says into her cell phone. She is standing inside one of the stalls with her head leaning against the wall.

"What time is it?" asks Benita.

Alicia checks the time on her cell phone. "Almost one."

"I'm working tomorrow . . . early," Benita says, sounding slightly annoyed.

"I know, but I could really use your help. Can you please come get me?"

"What happened to your ride? Let me guess: She left you stranded."

"Come get me, please."

"Where are you?" Benita's voice drags.

"West Hollywood."

"Where in WeHo?"

"Guys and Dolls. Next to Jerry's Famous Deli."

"I barely have gas, and I don't feel like going to a gas station tonight."

"Just drive my car. The keys are on my desk in that brown leather pen holder. And bring me some crushed ice."

Benita sighs. "Why are you so into crushed ice?"

"I don't know, but just bring it."

"It'll probably melt by the time I get there."

"Not if you put it in my travel mug."

"Just give me the address, please."

Alicia spots Benita as soon as she drives up to the building and parks on the opposite side of the street. "I don't even want to know what happened," says Benita as she gets out of the car and walks around to the passenger side so Alicia can drive. She's wearing holey sweats and an oversized Kobe Bryant jersey. Her hair is swept off her face and held in place by a large banana clip. "I bet they'd still let me in even dressed like this," she says jokingly while Alicia's eyes roll. Alicia knows Benita really believes this. While many women grapple with self-esteem issues, Benita is just the opposite. She loves to compare herself to Jennifer López as if they're twins, but, while Benita is an attractive woman, the only thing she has in common with Jennifer Lopez is her nationality.

"Thank you for coming to get me," she says, changing the subject as she puts the car in drive and pulls off. "And you brought my ice." She picks up her stainless steel insulated mug, removes the lid, and pours the crushed ice into her mouth.

"I don't want to know what happened. I mean it. I don't want to hear it, because as long as you keep dealing with that *person*, things like this will always happen."

"I've known her practically all my life."

"My condolences. But seriously . . . go ahead and tell me what happened."

"No, you don't want to hear it."

"I at least want to hear what happened with Barr. Is he as fine in person?"

Alicia huffs. "I don't have good luck with men." She stops for a red light and keeps her eyes focused straight ahead. "Do I look like a slut? Why would a man assume I'm going to sleep with him when I don't even know him? He didn't even buy my drink."

"You don't drink."

"But he didn't know that. And he rented a hotel room. Didn't even ask me. Who does that? And then he said he wanted to fulfill his Halle Berry fantasy."

"That sounds like a bit much."

"Then he steps outside with a fag."

"Oh my God, the blogs are right? He's gay?"

Alicia huffs and shakes her head. "The blogs." She hated some of the blogs and wished they'd just let actors continue to be shrouded in mystery the way they used to back when she was little, before the Internet took on a life all its own—back when she first fell in love with Hollywood. "If you listen to some of the blogs, every male actor is gay—singers too—and all the actresses are pregnant. If I were famous, they'd have a field day circling my stomach. 'Is Alicia Day pregnant? Check out her baby bump.' News flash: Some women have bulges without babies inside." She shakes her head as she reflects further on the night's events. "So, in answer to your question, no, I don't think he's gay.

"And by the way, I thought you knew not to use that word for a gay person. Your career will be ruined before it even gets started."

"What word?" Alicia asks, and then realizes the word Benita is referring to. "Oh, no, I was mocking Barr. That's what cigarettes are called in the UK. . . . Yes, he smokes too, and you should know how much I hate that habit. I'm so pissed. But the worst part is Aubrey had the nerve to tell him that I dream about him. He actually said, 'Let's go to the hotel so you can stop dreaming about me.'"

Benita's eyes widen. "That's messed up. I'm going to stop watching *True Blue*. His character is too cocky anyway."

"We have nothing in common."

"Nor do you and Aubrey."

"Aubrey doesn't know any better."

"Oh yes, she does. And don't give me that same old story about how you've known her since you were four."

Alicia chomps on a mouthful of ice. "Five . . . It's Sir I've known since I was four."

"She knows better."

Alicia shakes her head. "No, I honestly don't think she does. This is really going to make me sound like a hater, but I'm still going to say it because it's true. Aubrey got where she is today by going to hotel rooms. And she's been to a lot with a lot of different people, from actors to agents to directors. And if this business means that much to her and that's what she chooses to do, then I guess that's her business. And I'm not saying I don't want to make it, but I'm not going to whore myself out to do so. I'm not."

Alicia shakes her head. Even though it's true, she regrets saying it. She wonders how Benita will interpret that information. Will she think a top black actress can only become a major star by sleeping around? Is that really what she wanted to say about her friend, even one who'd pissed her off tonight?

"I shouldn't have said that," Alicia says, trying to recant her words. "I don't know who Aubrey has slept with."

She looks over to find Benita who, by then, has closed her eyes. She won't be calling Sir to tell him about her night. She didn't want to admit that he was right . . . again. He'd warned her about Barr. He'd warned her about Hollywood. When was she going to listen to him?

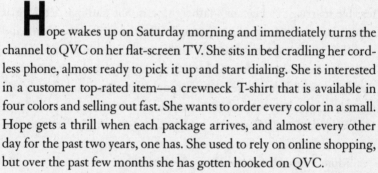

Hope wakes up on Saturday morning and immediately turns the channel to QVC on her flat-screen TV. She sits in bed cradling her cordless phone, almost ready to pick it up and start dialing. She is interested in a customer top-rated item—a crewneck T-shirt that is available in four colors and selling out fast. She wants to order every color in a small. Hope gets a thrill when each package arrives, and almost every other day for the past two years, one has. She used to rely on online shopping, but over the past few months she has gotten hooked on QVC.

TV has become her refuge—a great escape, just like shopping. Putting the two together is like magic for her. For Havana, there's no magic in TV; Hope can't help but be grateful for this. Havana finds magic in things like the Harry Potter books. She loves to tote around books as big as Bibles. But Hope doesn't want to waste the mental effort on imagining whole worlds. She has enough going on up there—enough to make a grown woman crazy, if she wasn't already. She'd much rather get lost in the foolish antics of reality TV. She finds comfort in a manufactured reality that tells her she's not the only one in the world with problems, though other people's problems aren't nearly as real as hers.

Dealing with a deceased husband when she was only twenty-seven—a man she considered to be her soul mate—would be enough to make any woman have a nervous breakdown, especially when years earlier her mother had been murdered by her father. But there was more to the story with her husband. She never really bought into what happened to him that day. Out of the three people on the tiny boat who'd been with him during his fishing trip, only one man, Michael Beck, survived. And his story just didn't add up. Hope's husband was a Navy SEAL. He'd had four weeks of cold-water-survival training in Alaska. He, of all of them, should have survived out there. But he didn't.

She didn't need to tune in to *CSI*. She was dealing with real-life drama.

She had been so happy when she met Roger, especially after her terrible marriage to Havana's father, Morris. She had married Morris when she was just out of high school. Their marriage was brief and their love even more short-lived. And though he's still alive, unfortunately he's a dead-beat dad to Havana, opting to provide adequate care for the stepchildren his new wife brought into the marriage but not contributing a dime toward his own child. And that's his cross to bear.

She dials the QVC number and gets a customer service representative.

"Mom," says Havana, picking up the line.

"Hang up the phone. I'm on it."

"Are you ordering more QVC?"

"Havana, hang up the phone," says Hope as her patience runs thin.

"Mom, you promised."

"Okay, Havana. Hang up," says Hope, tightening her lip.

Havana lets out a discouraged sigh. "I can't let you order more QVC. You told me you didn't want to put any more stuff on your bill, remember? You're trying to get out of debt. Suze Orman says—"

"Suze Orman has money because of people like me. I'm your mother, and I say hang up the phone."

"Your breakfast is getting cold," says Havana before slamming down the phone. Hope senses disappointment in her daughter's bruised tone, but what about Hope's disappointment in losing a husband she loved? Who says her grieving has to end when the memorial service is over? Who says it ever has to? She needs to cope somehow.

"She's right, you know," Hope says to the customer service rep. Why should she continue shopping like this when she may not even have a job soon?

"Would you like to cancel your order?" asks the customer service rep.

"No," she says as she takes a look at the woman on television raving about a set of Westinghouse solar lights for the introductory price of only $22.93. "I want to add item M-19765 to it." In just under thirty minutes, Hope has spent $438.23 on numerous products. As soon as she ends the call, she feels worse than she did before she dialed.

At the breakfast table, before Hope even takes the first bite, she can already imagine how the meal will play out. Her daughter will offer to decorate her pancakes with strawberries and whipped cream. Then her daughter's friend and next-door neighbor, Grace, will enter wearing stretch-fit designer jeans on a body built for sweats. Grace will want more pancakes, but will be too embarrassed to ask—at least while Hope is present. Havana will slyly reserve another stack inside the microwave just for Grace. This will be in addition to the four pancakes Grace will have already eaten. She will also want more whipped-cream topping, but instead she will complain that Havana is spraying on too much, and then she will lie and say she is on a diet. Her daughter will garnish her friend's plate with too many strawberries, and Grace's next complaint will be that she's allergic to fruit. She's also allergic to vegetables and water and anything that's considered healthy, muses Hope. Havana will give her friend a tall glass of chocolate milk and a shorter glass of orange juice. She will tell Grace to help herself to anything else she likes, but halfway through eating, she will pretend to be full, until Hope retreats back to her bedroom, at which point Grace will devour as much as she wants.

Grace is obese, and Hope's daughter is not only her best friend; she is also her enabler.

At the breakfast table, Hope remains quiet while Havana serves up pancakes and bacon. Havana loves to cook breakfast. Hope can cook. She just doesn't. For tonight, she has already decided that she will place a carryout order for Buddy's Pizza, because they both love pizza and especially Buddy's. Hope will make a salad to go along with their pizza. That much she can do. The night before, they ate corned beef from Bread Basket Deli. The night before that was Chinese from Stanley's Other Place. They eat out every night.

"You know you're not helping Grace. I know she's your best friend, but she eats at her house and then she comes over here and eats."

"No, she doesn't," says Havana, repeatedly shaking her head. She doesn't want her mother to get started on her friend.

"Havana, she does. Why do you think her grandmother moved down here?"

"To take care of her while her mom's in the hospital."

"And why is her mom in the hospital?"

"To lose weight."

"That's an understatement. You saw the fire department pull up to her house and spend all day trying to get that woman out of it. If you keep feeding Grace, she's going to die."

"Stop being so mean," Havana shouts as she slams the can of whipped cream on the table and takes a seat across from her mother.

"Mean? You think I'm being mean? If I was mean, I'd send you to go live with your great-grandmother. Now, that is one mean woman. She's like one of those evil people from your book—the ones that suck all the happiness out of a person."

"A Dementor?"

"Yeah, that's exactly what she is. Do you want to go live with a Dementor?

"Granny Nana isn't that bad."

"Oh yes, Granny Nana is. I lived with her for four long years."

Havana huffs. "Mom, Grace is my friend and I don't want you saying she's going to die. She wants to lose weight. She's trying her best to. And so many people laugh at her and tease her, and she has a hard enough time." Hope's heart tears for a moment as she thinks of how hard it must be for Mr. Hansen, her favorite customer, who she knows gets his share of negative words. "She's only twelve, and people talk about her like she's not a kid and she doesn't have feelings."

"That's another thing, why is a twelve-year-old hanging out with an eight-year-old? When I was twelve, I never would have done that if it wasn't my sister. Can't she find a friend her own age?"

"No, Mom, she can't. And you want to know why? Because most people in this world are a lot like you—worried only about their own problems and they don't have time for anyone else's." Havana scoots her chair back so hard it leaves black streaks on the kitchen floor. She runs into her room in tears. Hope sits at the table shaking her head and asking God to forgive her daughter for being so disrespectful.

"Lord, she's going through a hard time right now, just like I am. I'm glad she can see Grace for who she is on the inside and not how she looks." Hope sees a lot of herself in Havana, or at least the way she used to be. She can tell that Havana will be the kind of woman always trying to please and protect anyone she befriends. That behavior will eventually follow her into adulthood and bleed into her relationships. Then she will marry a man when she is too young to make the right decision, only to be disappointed.

There may be a call today for Havana from her father. He calls on occasion in what Hope assumes is an effort to appease her so she won't pay a visit to Friend of the Court. But there's nothing from him she needs; nothing from him she wants. If she accepts his money, he has the right to see his child; she doesn't want to give him that right. But today turns out differently from what she expected because Grace calls Havana and tells her she isn't coming over for breakfast and Havana's father doesn't call at all.

It is just before sunrise and Heaven is sitting inside her car, which is parked at the south end of the Cass Corridor. She wants to take advantage of the best light. She always takes her time to compose her shot. Her lens focuses on Patty, a prostitute she's been photographing for several months, bending over a garbage can in a frayed skirt so short that the thin red string from her thong is caught in the image. She loves taking pictures. She finds the entire process so mentally freeing by allowing her to focus on something other than Donovan.

She zooms in on her subject.

This time she steps out of her '95 Eclipse and slowly moves forward. She ignores the fact that she is shooting with an expensive digital SLR camera and has a wide assortment of interchangeable lenses packed inside the camera bag slung over her shoulder, all of which would fetch a pretty penny at any pawnshop. She also ignores the fact that there are enough addicts in need of scoring a fix to make her their next target. She is not afraid. She is a street photographer, and she wouldn't be as good as she is if she didn't live by the principle that without risk there is little reward.

She chooses different angles to shoot from. Patty is a great model.

Heaven is certain she must have been an actual model in her former life and somehow landed on the streets selling her body for money, and now maybe even for drugs, judging from the track marks. Even though Heaven doesn't like her models to establish direct eye contact with the camera, Patty looks directly at the lens. She even strikes a pose to go along with the smile she flashes. The gap in her mouth that's created by her two missing front teeth show Heaven that Patty's life has obviously been a hard one.

Heaven heads back to her car. Over several months, she has taken thousands of pictures, all in the Cass Corridor, and with every snap, she adds a new scene to her portfolio. Put together, they reveal a touching story of struggle and heartbreak, loss and survival. Sometimes she looks for Jamal, someone she went to high school with, and someone she has seen down there a couple times. But he isn't around today. She hopes nothing bad has happened to him. Her subjects have disappeared before. The summer before, she photographed Leslie, a prostitute, for a few months. Leslie enjoyed getting her picture taken more than Patty. She'd never miss a free photo op. So when she vanished, Heaven figured something must've gone wrong. She started asking around and discovered no one had seen her since she'd gotten into a john's car one night. And to this day, no one has seen her. In Leslie's case, Heaven is afraid that no news is bad news.

Out of nowhere Jamal appears, dashing across the dead grass of one of the abandoned Victorian-styled homes, too quick for Heaven to snap a frame.

Heaven's phone trills. She digs through her favorite purse, pulling out the unopened letter from her father in the process. She answers on the third ring and puts the call on speaker.

"Girl, what are you doing?" Trina asks. "Oh, wait. Let me guess. Taking pictures," Trina says before Heaven has the chance. "I'm just calling to let you know I'm not going in to work today. There's no point. The more I think about it, the more I know we can build up a little enterprise with the right number of people and a good enough plan."

"Don't get ahead of yourself," Heaven says. "Nobody's trying to make a living from stealing. Trust me, you can only do that mess for so long. Like my nana always says, everything done in the dark eventually comes to light."

"Yeah, yeah, whatever, but when that light comes on, I won't be nowhere to be found."

Heaven lets out a sigh. "Sometimes, I think I'm going about my life all wrong. Do you?"

"All I can think about right now is getting high. Girl, I got us some Gosling's Black Seal rum and some Vernor's Ginger Ale. So you already know what that's gonna be about. When you come over later, I'm going to make us some Dark 'n Stormys. Then we're gonna smoke some weed and just chill and not worry about a thing, especially not some man trying to get his little freak on."

"You took off from work just to get high?" Heaven asks, dragging her voice. As much as she loves Trina, she knows she needs to get a new best friend; someone who won't be such a negative influence on her; someone who has her own life together and would encourage Heaven to start making some changes, and even show her how to get started. But why would that kind of person want to be her friend?

"Who takes off to get high?" asks Trina. "I'd never be at work if that were the case. I took off because I wanted to. Because I didn't feel like dancing tonight. Pretty soon, I won't have a club to dance at anyway if the city council gets its way."

Heaven shakes her head. She's mad for feeling tempted, but Dark 'n Stormy is her all-time favorite drink. The marijuana, however, she can pass on. She swore off that stuff after her last visit with her probation officer. "Girl, why are you being such a bad influence on me when you know I can't be doing that stuff anymore? I have a DUI— remember?"

"So? It's not like you're going to be driving. Just spend the night."

"How am I going to spend the night? You know how Donovan is."

"Since when do you care? You live in Detroit, not Brighton, remember? I'm sure he'll be gone tonight like most nights anyway."

"I don't know." Heaven's voice drags. "We'll see."

"Excuse me for wanting to have a little fun so I can get my mind off a few things. We're young—we're supposed to be having fun right now. If not now, when? But if you're stepping into a convent soon, Mother Teresa, hey, just tell me. . . . Let a sister know right now."

Heaven starts up her car. "Nah, girl, not me. I'm just—"

"You're just what?"

As Heaven slowly drives by Patty, she watches her flash her middle finger. "Nothing, girl, forget it. I'll be over there later." Heaven rolls down her window. "Patty, why are you giving me the finger? What did I do?"

"Where's my picture at?" Patty shouts.

Trina says, "Girl, you better stop talkin' to them crack hos."

Patty walks up to the car and places her hand on Heaven's window frame. Her acrylic nails are raised and dirty. "You said you were going to print me off a picture and put it in a frame. Where is it at?"

"How do you know I didn't?"

"Where is it, then?"

Heaven pulls out a manila envelope from her purse. Inside the envelope is a five-by-ten color image of Patty. "I was waiting until I got a frame for it." She slides the picture out of the envelope to show Patty.

Patty smiles. "Well, when is that gonna be? I want it in a frame so I can give it to my little girl."

"You have a little girl, Patty?" Heaven's smile lights up her face. "You never told me you had a little girl."

"What I got to tell you anything for? You're not my momma or the First Lady or Oprah Winfrey either," Patty rants. "I don't owe you no explanation for what I push out of my body. My real name might not even be Patty. What you think about that? Just because I'm standing here doesn't mean my mind is in the same place as my body. I'm an astronaut and I'm on the moon right now. This is the Apollo landing right here. See, you have no idea, so don't come judging me," she screams. "You're judging me. You need to stop judging me!"

"I'm not judging you, Patty. I'm not in any position to judge you or anyone else."

"Yes, you are judging me."

"Roll up your window," says Trina. "That woman sounds crazy."

"Next time I see you, you'll have your picture in a frame," says Heaven as she slides the photo back inside the manila envelope and places it on the passenger seat.

Trina says, "Let the crack ho go . . . and hey, don't forget to get those jeans and that top. You remember which top, right?"

Heaven sighs heavily and pulls away. "Not really. Which one?"

"You don't remember the top, Heaven? You must be slipping—the blue Robert Rodriguez one with the metallic studs and the tie front. I need one in a medium and another in a large."

"It has a keyhole opening, right?"

"Exactly, now you coming back around. And the jeans, don't forget the True Religions."

"I know . . . I know. That's the main thing you wanted."

"I need to return these, please," says Heaven as she approaches the sales clerk standing behind one of the sales counters of the high-end department store. She tries not to look around. She tries not to look suspicious, but she's so tempted to. It's early afternoon, past lunch hour on a workday, and it's relatively quiet inside the store without many customers or sales people inside.

"Do you have a receipt?" asks the saleswoman.

"Yes, I do," says Heaven as she plops her large red and white canvas purse on the counter and begins rumbling through for her wallet. "I know I have it." She opens her shopping bag and searches through. "There's nothing wrong with the jeans—I just need a larger size. Do I need a receipt for an even exchange?"

"Not for an even exchange. But I will need to get some information from you if you don't have your receipt. Did you use your credit card for the purchase? We can track it that way."

"I paid cash."

"Did you want to make an exchange?"

"Excuse me, but I'd like to purchase these," says a well-dressed white woman with blond hair as she cuts across Heaven and places two pairs of jeans on the counter. "And I have one pair I need to return, please." The woman glances down at her luxury watch. "And I don't have all day."

"I found my receipt," says Heaven as she pulls the receipt from her wallet.

"Good, do you want to make an exchange?" the saleswoman asks Heaven.

"I do," Heaven, says, "but I don't really have time to try them on and I'm not sure what size I am. Maybe I can just try 'em on real quick," says Heaven, grabbing a pair of jeans off the rack. "I'm going to try to do this real quick. Can I leave my shopping bag with you?"

"Sure," says the saleswoman as she reaches for the handles of Heaven's shopping bag as Heaven passes it over to her.

The blond woman huffs. "I'm also short on time." The customer eyes Heaven suspiciously and rolls her eyes. "Unbelievable."

"Excuse me?" asks Heaven, snatching her shopping bag back. "You know what? Just go ahead and help Nancy Grace."

The white woman shakes her head. "No, just forget it. Hand me back my things and just forget it. This is what happens when the bus system starts running a line from the ghetto to the suburbs."

"Hold up—what did you just say?" asks Heaven with bulging eyes.

"Do you understand English or are you fluent only in Ebonics?"

"Do you understand sign language, because my hand's about to be all up in your face."

The saleswoman takes two steps back from the counter.

The blonde jumps back with her hands held up. "I don't need

this." She tells Heaven, "You can't use your food stamps to purchase clothes. Did you know that?"

Heaven takes a deep breath, but refuses to raise her voice. "Are you bipolar or something? You do know people in Detroit get killed for saying less."

"Oh, so now you're threatening to kill me? Did you hear her threaten me?"

"I did not threaten her. I just stated a fact. Did it sound like I threatened her?" Heaven asks the young saleswoman.

"I'm not really sure what's going on," the saleswoman says.

The customer grabs the two pairs of jeans, throws them in the bag, and huffs out of the store.

The young saleswoman bats her large eyes and says, "I am so sorry for that. She was so rude. Did you still want to make your return?"

Heaven takes a deep sigh while she presses her hand against her chest. "That really shook me up. Hold on, I'm trying to compose my-self," she says as tears stream down her face. "You know what . . . No, I'll look around first and come back. That didn't make no kind of sense," says Heaven as she places a pair of jeans inside her shopping bag that already has a pair inside.

"I'm truly sorry about that."

"No problem," says Heaven as she strolls confidently toward the exit. Her heart races as it always does before she is safely in her car and out of the large parking lot.

"Wait!" screeches the saleswoman as soon as Heaven steps one foot out the door. The woman's voice is so loud it sounds like an alarm. She rushes behind Heaven who is frozen with fear and afraid to turn around. It's over. The light has finally come on. The woman walks around to face Heaven. "You forgot your cell phone," she says as she holds it out for her. Heaven gives a sigh of relief. "And again, I'm truly sorry. Some people in this world are just plain ignorant."

"You are so right. Some people are just plain stupid, really." Heaven takes the phone from the saleswoman's hands. "Thank you."

"And she gives me my cell phone back, and your text message is right on the screen clear as day saying, 'Stacy's in the store with the jeans. She's going to make a scene at the counter. Play along.' I drove home the entire way thinking what if she had read my text?" Heaven says later at Trina's apartment.

"I don't live in a world of what-ifs," says Trina. "She didn't, so let's just move on. Five pairs of three-hundred-dollar jeans, that's what I'm talking about. Did they even have any left?"

"One pair," says Stacy as she snuggles up to Trina.

"And you," says Heaven, downing her drink and pointing at Stacy, "have the nerve to say, 'And this is what happens when the bus system runs a line to the suburbs from the ghetto. You can't pay with food stamps.' You were taking your role-playing a little too seriously, because I was ready to role-play an ass kickin'."

"You called me Nancy Grace. I should have kicked your ass for that alone. I don't look anything like her," says Stacy. "I'm like twenty years younger than she is, maybe thirty. How old is she anyway?"

Heaven waves off the question. "I just wanted to throw that girl's mind off so she wouldn't know if she was coming or going," says Heaven.

"Well, whatever y'all did, it worked," says Trina, folding up the jeans. "But where are my tops?"

Heaven's eyes roll. "I didn't have time to get the tops, but I got an extra pair of True Religions, so just sell that pair and buy the top."

"Girl, you're joking, right? I can't even remember the last time I bought clothes."

"Hey, where did you get the receipt you showed that salesperson?" asks Stacy. "Had you really bought some clothes?"

"That was from Family Dollar. I went there earlier to pick up a cheap picture frame. I just flashed the receipt like this." Heaven demonstrates. "I did it so fast she couldn't read what it said."

They all burst out in laughter. And then Stacy's cell phone vibrates across the cocktail table.

"Oh, well, I have to go, ladies," says Stacy after she reads a text. "It's been fun."

"Who was that . . . your husband?" asks Trina with attitude.

Heaven studies the pair. Trina's lifestyle is her business, she reminds herself, but Trina obviously isn't any better than Heaven when it comes to picking a mate.

"I'll call you later."

"Don't bother," says Trina as she flops on her sofa and reaches for the joint of marijuana that Heaven passes to her. "Go on home to your husband, but leave my jeans." Trina throws one of her four-inch heels at the front door to her apartment as soon as Stacy closes the door behind her.

The next afternoon, Heaven is sitting on Trina's living room floor. Her head isn't pounding nearly as hard as she'd expected after her drinking binge the night before.

Her laptop is resting on the glass cocktail table as she stares at Alicia Day's Facebook page. She doesn't have many pictures—nothing of a personal nature; just a few headshots that, judging by all the cropping, were taken by an amateur who didn't know what he was doing. And Heaven knows for certain she can do a much better job. She wonders what would happen if she moved to LA to meet the sister who up until today she never knew existed, and if she tried to make it as a celebrity photographer. The plan sounds good, but her life is hard enough to handle as it is. Why add an unknown city to the mix?

Alicia's bio says she was born in 1977, which correlates with what Heaven's father, Glenn, wrote in his letter, but it doesn't give a city or state. She is an American actress best known for her role as Gigi in the popular direct-to-DVD movie *Gigi Mama*.

"An actress?" Heaven asks herself. "Have you ever heard of the movie *Gigi Mama*?" she asks Trina.

"Nope." Trina is stretched across the leather sectional, sticking her head out from underneath a mauve blanket.

"Me either," says Heaven without looking up from the screen. "So how is it popular? Maybe Donovan will download it for me."

"Don't say his name, because hearing it makes me sick." Trina covers her face with the blanket.

Heaven notices a video attached to Alicia's Facebook page. She double-clicks on the video and gets launched into YouTube and a video entitled *My Natural Hair Journey*. Seconds later Alicia's open-captioned video begins to play, revealing a series of photos set to the song "Freedom" from the 1995 *Black Panther* soundtrack. It shows her days as a small child to her first relaxer at age fifteen to her first big chop where she was practically bald at age twenty-one and a second big chop at age twenty-eight along with all of the photos of hairstyles in between, from braids and two-strand twists to Afro puffs and blowouts. "She looks just like Hope, only with bushy hair." She clicks on her Starlet username and goes to Alicia's personal YouTube page. Her last sign-in was eighteen months earlier. Her "About Me" says, "A star was born and now I'm just waiting to be discovered." Her hometown is listed as Detroit. *Bingo.* "This is my sister. It has to be."

Trina comes from underneath the blanket and says, "She didn't even call me back yesterday. Can you believe that?"

"That's because you told her not to." Heaven carries her laptop over to Trina and hands it to her.

"That's your sister? She's pretty. She looks just like Hope. "

Heaven nods and asks, "What's wrong with you?" She reaches for the plug attached to the blanket. "Girl, I know this isn't an electric blanket . . . in the summertime, Trina?" Heaven laughs so hard she falls to the floor while she is pulling the plug from the wall socket. "Girl, and I thought I had problems when it came to staying warm. But you really have some, sitting up as hot as it is with an electric blanket. Why do you think you're sweating?"

"It's not summertime. It's *May* and we live in Michigan, so it's never really hot here." She sighs deeply. "I hate love."

"You'll be back with her next week."

"Not this time. I'm not like you are with Donovan. I don't easily forgive and forget."

Heaven bursts out in more laughter as she picks herself up from the floor.

"What's wrong with you?" asks Trina. "Are you still high from last night, or do you find my problems to be just that hilarious?"

"I'm not laughing at you. I'm just laughing at the situation. I mean, you're always telling me how to be with Donovan, but if you have to deal with all the same mess as I do, why be gay?"

"Whatever. I won't even dignify your question with my response. As long as I've known you I've been gay. Anyway, just tell me about your sister," says Trina.

"I found her on Facebook."

"Good for you . . . So send her a message and call it a day," Trina says with a grumble. "I wish my life was that simple. I wish the only thing I had to worry about was finding a sister. I'm trying to lose the ones I got."

"Girl, what is your problem today? I thought you would be happy you had another day off."

"So what I got the day off? I'll be back shaking my ass down there tomorrow. Oh, God, why me?"

"If you don't like stripping, don't do it. Go back into real estate. I thought you liked that."

"I'm not sure what I want to do with my life. Real estate was okay, but working for GM was better. Besides, now the only people buying houses in the city are investors looking for cheap HUD houses. I may not like stripping, but at least it pays my bills."

"Nobody told you to buy a BMW. I paid cash for my car."

"It's a ninety-five Eclipse. How much did it cost—twenty dollars?"

"Ha . . . ha . . . ha. Well, whatever it cost, at least I don't have a car note."

Trina tosses her blanket over her face. "Just plug my blanket back in so I can sweat to death."

"You better be careful or you might speak that into existence." Heaven retreats back to her spot, taking along her computer. Trina's constant mood swings were the reason Heaven decided to move out of their two-bedroom apartment at Franklin Park Towers in Southfield the year before and rent a home in Detroit on the northwest side; it turned out to be a big mistake, what with Heaven's subsequent layoff just a few months later and the rising cost of her utility bills. She feels stupid now, as if she is doing what her nana said she was doing, "going about her life all wrong."

She composes her thoughts for the message she's ready to send to her sister. She knows it would be better received if she had already watched *Gigi Mama* and could compliment her performance. But she doesn't want to wait. She's too impatient to wait.

"In the letter, did Glenn say why he waited so long to tell you about his other child?"

"You know Glenn—he said something that didn't make no sense."

Heaven types up something quickly, then rereads her message before hitting SEND. This is what she wants more than anything; more than she wants to make her relationship with Donovan work—way more than that; more than she wants to take pictures of gritty scenes throughout the city. She wants a family—a sister who won't shut her out, since she has to accept that she will never have a mother or father. She wants someone whom she can relate to and who loves her unconditionally . . . without any strings attached. She wants someone she won't fear will leave her; someone who won't disregard her the way her sister Hope has.

Hope has already logged off her work computer. She can't be late. She has been telling herself all day that if she is going to make it on time to her friend Taite's engagement party, she has to leave as soon as the bank closes. She can't stick around and help the tellers who are out of balance, especially since that means helping Rico Johnson, who is always out of balance, probably because he, himself, is out of balance.

She is supposed to rush right out, but then Mr. Hansen strolls through the door. As usual, he is draped in lots of clothing, even though the temperature today is in the mid-eighties. And even though Rico Johnson isn't helping a customer at his teller window, Mr. Hansen walks over to Hope's desk and sits down.

"How are you, Mr. Hansen?" A rare smile surfaces on Hope's face. "Do you have a deposit you'd like to make today?"

"Ezra," he reminds her again, before nodding. He reaches for the white envelope sprouting from his blazer pocket. "You know me."

Mr. Hansen removes the envelope from his pocket and slides it over to Hope. She stands. "Would you like any cash back?" she asks. He shakes his head. Hope takes the check and walks over to the only free teller, the one she detests—Rico Johnson. He is the one who somehow manages to keep his job though he's terrible at it; the one who can't make it back from break on time and calls in too often; the one whose ex-girlfriend drove to the bank and made a scene in the parking lot while their baby was strapped in a car seat in the back. At least she had sense enough to strap her child in, Hope had thought. Rico Johnson is also the one who pulls his dress pants down to show his underwear and removes his shirt and tie before leaving work, then races out of the parking lot with hip-hop blaring from the bass of his speakers. More often than not, Hope listens to David Garrett, Josh Groban, and Andrea Bocelli, and every now and then she switches to Michael Bublé or Colbie Caillat. And it doesn't bother her that the black employees don't relate to her, and even some of the whites. She is her own person. Always has been and always will be. So gaining the validation of her coworkers is not something she cares about. The only person she needs to impress is her boss, Katherine, the woman who hired her and can also fire her.

Rico Johnson needs to be thankful Hope wasn't the one who conducted his job interview, because he would still be unemployed. She was convinced he would flunk either the drug test or the background check. But, instead, he passed both with flying colors. Rico Johnson, the guy who came to the company picnic two weeks earlier with a white girl perfectly suited for Fox's upcoming reality show *More to Love*. A few of the black women at the bank immediately started complaining the minute they saw her, though none of them was remotely interested in him. "White girls got all our men," they complained. The solution is simple, thought Hope. Do what she did—marry a white man, or a man of another race.

"I don't see how you do it," Rico says to her.

"Do what?" she snaps, avoiding eye contact with him. She stamps the back of the check FOR DEPOSIT ONLY and writes Mr. Hansen's account number underneath.

"I mean, I know he's a good customer. He's got all this money and stuff, and I get that, but how can you look at that man directly in the face like that? Ugh." Rico's face twitches and his shoulders shudder.

She pries her eyes away from the check to snarl up at him. "You know, it's easier for me to look him in the face than it is for me to look at yours. Now, if you don't mind, can you please deposit Mr. Hansen's check?"

He pauses, tempted, she is certain, to let the real Rico Johnson come out. And she welcomes him to do so because then she'll have a valid reason for why he should lose his job instead of the biased fact that she despises him for simply being who he is.

Rico processes the deposit quickly. When he is done, Hope snatches the deposit slip from his hand and walks it over to Mr. Hansen, tucks the folded slip into his pocket, and returns to her seat.

"How are you holding up?" asks Mr. Hansen.

"I'm okay. It gets a little better as time goes on." Hope pushes her stapler beside her monitor. "I'm late for my friend's engagement party. I don't want to go to begin with, but since I promised, I don't want to be late."

"Don't let me make you any later."

She grabs her purse from inside her desk drawer, then locks her desk.

He stands when she does.

"Maybe we can talk about what we're going through outside of the bank."

"Outside of the bank?" she asks.

"I go to grief counseling. Maybe one week you could go with me. Then maybe we could go to dinner afterward."

"Maybe, we'll see." She shrugs. "I mean, okay that sounds like something I might do." She doesn't want to make any promises. "Or rather, might can do . . . *will do* one day soon."

"Perhaps . . . maybe . . . possibly," he says.

She smiles wide this time. Her eyes catch a glimpse of Rico in the background in a cluster with two other coworkers. He is shaking his head as he stares in her direction with contempt.

"Are you making fun of me, Mr. Hansen?"

"No, Mrs. Teasdale. Never. I'm in no position to make fun of anyone. Think about that grief counseling and let me know."

After the last customer leaves the bank, Hope edges toward the door. Three minutes remain before closing. No one will miss three minutes. She notices a sizable crowd lingering outside. She wonders where all the people are coming from. Only two of them attempt to enter; a tall, stout man with salt-and-pepper hair who looks to be in his early fifties, and a heavy-set woman around the same age wearing a pair of stylish metal-framed glasses and an ensemble that screams Macy's mannequin. Both carry large black briefcases.

"I'm sorry, but we're closed," Hope says as she attempts to politely shut the door in their faces. She is anxious to get to Taite's engagement dinner.

The odd couple flash their badges and tell Hope they are from the FDIC. They ask if she is the manager. "I'm the customer service manager."

Katherine is in her office but steps out when she sees the worried look on Hope's face. It's Friday. It's closing time. Both she and Hope know what this means. "Katherine, they're from the *FDIC*," Hope emphasizes as Katherine approaches. Several employees stare as a Michigan State Trooper secures the doors. Two employees stand at their desks with their mouths dropping; one dangles the cord of her handset in her hand. The tellers stand by their windows, most of them with stunned expressions on their faces, except for one man, David Nelson, whom Hope secretly calls Mr. Smiley Face because he smiles all day for no good reason.

The people from the FDIC walk into Katherine's office, closing the door behind them, and remain inside for several minutes. They return and stand in the middle of the bank. The man announces, "Your pay stopped with Mercury Bank at six p.m. As of six oh one, you are employees of the FDIC. You will be paid for any unused vacation time, and the bank will reopen at its normal opening time tomorrow morning with its usual hours of operation."

"Make sure no one enters without an FDIC badge," the woman tells the sheriff deputy who has just walked in, along with three other people with badges attached to their suit jackets. They post a public notice on the front door before a team of roughly eighty people enter, many rolling large black cases.

Mr. Smiley Face raises his hand and clears his throat.

"Yes," the FDIC man says, acknowledging him.

"Stanley Hudson . . . Are there going to be layoffs?"

Several employees chuckle at Mr. Smiley Face, who is obsessed with *The Office* and has just asked a very serious question while using the name of one of the program's characters. Hope, however, doesn't find the situation humorous at all.

"How can people laugh at that?" Hope whispers to a coworker. "How unprofessional of him."

"Oh God, he's using Stanley Hudson's voice and everything," the employee says, wiping away tears of laughter.

"As of this moment you are employed by the FDIC until we can find an interested buyer. When and if that happens, you will learn more."

"Question," says Mr. Smiley Face in a different voice this time. "If that doesn't happen, can we then assume layoffs, and if there are layoffs will we be provided with a package—a monetary parting gift, if you will?"

"Now he's Dwight Schrute," the coworker whispers to Hope.

Hope rolls her eyes. Now she's convinced that David Nelson is as weird as she thought he was. "*The Office* again?"

"Yes." The woman nods. "That's my favorite show. Do you watch it?"

"I haven't seen one episode and thanks to David's sneak preview, I never will."

Hope surveys the bank for Katherine, who, at the time, is surrounded by several employees of the FDIC.

They assign each one of the bank employees to their FDIC counterparts and proceed to conduct an audit.

"If any of you had plans to go home, you may want to call and make alternate arrangements. No one can leave until we complete our audit," the female half of the odd couple says.

"Katherine, I have to go," Hope pleads. "I have a very important meeting to go to."

"Hope, you heard what the woman just said. If you had plans, call and make alternate arrangements. No one can leave. You can use the phone in my office if you like."

"I don't care what the woman said. This meeting is very important."

"Please, Hope, if you need to use the phone and call someone, then do, because I really don't think these people will care about your situation."

Hope huffs over to her desk and picks up her phone to dial Taite to tell her what happened.

"Hope, is everything okay?" asks Taite.

"Yes, they said we'll still have our jobs. This sort of thing is happening all over, what with the economy and all."

"No, I don't mean about your job. My engagement dinner isn't until tomorrow—Saturday. Remember, we just spoke yesterday because I hadn't received your RSVP, and you said Saturday was perfect. You're too young to be this forgetful."

"I've had a lot on my mind," Hope says with a sigh, "but don't worry. I'll be there."

Hope enters the lobby of the Westin Book Cadillac Hotel, peeved. She arrives to dinner solo by choice to drive home her point that even a *young* widow doesn't have the right to move on—does *not* have the right.

She is almost thirty minutes late, even though the invitation clearly states for guests to arrive *promptly at seven*. Taite better not be angry, she muses. She better not say one thing to her about her tardiness. It's better to be late than not come at all. And she didn't want to come at all. It's not easy finding a babysitter, especially since she's sworn off Heaven. But Havana is spending the night at Grace's house next door. Grace's grandmother is doing a really good job with Grace, making sure she eats much healthier now. She's already lost ten pounds in two weeks. But what actually caused Hope to run late was the article she'd taken time out to read in the *Detroit News* about Michael Beck shortly before she left her house for the engagement dinner. It mentioned his forthcoming memoir. The man she believed killed her husband and Taite's husband was writing a book. He was going to be profiting from their loss, and she wondered if Taite knew about that or if she would even care anymore now that she's getting remarried. Maybe now isn't the right time for Hope to mention the article, but if she somehow finds the opportunity to do so, she will, because she'd want Taite to tell her.

She takes one step down at the entrance of Michael Symon's Roast and approaches the blond hostess behind the podium.

Taite is so predictable. Leave it to her to pick the restaurant of her favorite Iron Chef to serve as the backdrop for her engagement dinner, or maybe it's because her brother and his wife live in one of the condos upstairs.

"Dinner for two?" asks the hostess, grabbing two menus.

How presumptuous. Can't a woman dine alone? Hope wonders. Maybe she's just there for happy hour, she muses as she flutters her naturally long lashes, noticing how full the bar area is. "I'm here for the engagement party."

"Oh." The hostess tilts her head underneath the podium to return the menus and exposes her dark roots. "Please follow me."

Hope treads behind the conservative navy blue or black suit the woman is wearing; it's hard to tell the color because of the dim interior lighting. This is a plus because she's hopeful no one will notice the button missing from the center of her blouse replaced with a safety pin or the loose fit of her pencil skirt on her slim frame. She has no shortage of clothes in her closet, but most were purchased before her drastic weight loss. Her body has dropped pounds her naturally thin frame can't afford to lose. She dawdles after the hostess, slowly making her way through the main dining area into the party room.

She scans the small room, skipping over Taite's father's stylish angled cut that's tapered at the sides with some length on top, and Taite's mother's short pixie hairstyle, to quickly spot Taite's fall of red spiral curls that play around her shoulders. She is seated alongside her fiancé, who has a beach boy look, at a table adorned with a white tablecloth and an elegant floral centerpiece.

Hope tosses her a counterfeit smile and takes the only available seat at a table beside a large window facing State Street where Taite's brother and wife are seated. She shoots a quick smile to the pair and nods hello to both of them.

Forty guests—Hope can only imagine what the bill will come to.

"Do you want to try one of these beef pierogi?" Taite's brother asks Hope. "They're very tasty." He slides the appetizer plate over to her.

"What is it?" she asks as she sinks her fork into the fluffiness. To Hope, it looks like a deformed pot pie with meat oozing out of one side.

"It's good, trust me," he says, nodding with a wicked grin.

Hope isn't sure if she should trust Taite's brother, Bob, a man who cheats on his wife. But with encouragement from Bob's wife, she gives it a try.

She glides the fork of beef into her mouth and chews.

"Well?" asks Taite's brother.

"Well, I'm not exactly a food critic, but—"

"You like it, don't you? Go on and smile and admit it."

"I need to take another taste."

"Can we get a Tequila Fizz for the young lady?" he asks the waiter floating by. "It's good, isn't it?" he asks Hope, who begins nodding with approval.

"I wouldn't go so far as to say it's good. It's okay."

"Okay? You're crazy."

And then, a rare occurrence that even Taite takes notice of from the center of the room—Hope smiles, but not for long. Not after she realizes Taite is watching her. Not after she observes how she affectionately wipes the sauce from the side of her fiancé's lip with her bare hand. *How soon some of us can forget.*

Taite may be her friend, but she has no right to move on. Taite lost her husband the same day Hope lost hers. They were both on that boat. And according to Michael Beck, they'd given up in the wee hours of the morning he was rescued, releasing themselves to the sea. If there is one thing Hope is certain of, it is that Michael Beck is lying. And she wants to know the truth. She refuses to move on completely. She needs closure. Nothing about Beck's story made sense. A Navy SEAL doesn't give up before an unemployed carpenter. But not only did Taite decide she is strong enough to move on without her, she's going to marry the first man she moved on to.

Even more appalling to Hope than the fact that she can say "I do" after a mere three months of knowing her beach boy, is how big her second wedding will be. She's getting married at the Detroit Institute of Arts, for God's sake. Hope won't be surprised if she learns her friend's wedding dress is white with a twelve-foot train. And considering this year is the first time in the DIA's one-hundred-twenty-four-year history that they have rented space for weddings, she knows it comes with a hefty price. And yes, true, Taite can certainly afford it since she didn't waste any time declaring her husband, a professional baseball player, dead, and gaining access to his estate and insurance policy.

So go ahead and do it, but spare me every little detail, she muses as she sips her tequila. She doesn't need to know that the ceremony is taking place in the Rivera Court. She'll figure that out when she gets there—if she goes. Dinner is being served in the majestic Great Hall. *Whoopee*. Why is it majestic anyway, just because some reviewer from the *Detroit Free Press* says so? And finally, the reception will be held outdoors in the courtyard. *Who cares?* Hope doesn't.

Was Hope supposed to be impressed at the description of the Diego Rivera murals on the north and south walls of Rivera Court? *Who was Diego Rivera anyway?* Hope didn't know. As hard as she tries, she isn't as cultured as Taite. She didn't grow up silver spooned. And neither did Roger, Hope's husband. In many ways they struggled. It was also a second marriage for him, and he had had two kids by his first wife. Hope was the first black woman he'd ever dated. They got married at the Little Wedding Chapel in Farmington Hills, Michigan. Hope's daughter, Taite, and Taite's husband, were the only ones present. Heaven wasn't invited. They'd fallen out yet again. She couldn't even remember over what that time—most likely Heaven's poor choice of men.

She notices Taite get up from her table and head for the bathroom. She was going to wait until after dinner to speak to her about the *Detroit News* article, but now is a better time. Hope walks into the bathroom shortly after Taite. She stands near one of the sinks, waiting to hear her friend's toilet flush and for Taite to exit the bathroom stall. And when she does, Hope steps into Taite's view.

"Hope," Taite says, placing her hand on her chest. "You scared me. Were you hiding back there?"

"No, I was just waiting for you."

"Oh, well, I was just getting ready to come to your table to speak to you to see how you've been doing," she says as she stands at one of the sinks and washes her hands.

"Taite, did you read the article in today's *Detroit News* about Michael Beck and his book?"

Taite sighs. "No, Hope, I didn't. I don't read those articles anymore. I stopped following that story more than a year ago. And you should too. None of those stories are going to bring our husbands back."

"But don't you want to know what really happened?"

"We already know as much as we'll ever know, because we weren't there," says Taite.

Hope shakes her head. "There are some inconsistencies in his story. And do you know in this article he didn't even mention our husbands? It was all about him and how he felt hanging onto the hull while he prayed to be rescued. I know he's not trying to turn his story into something inspirational, becau—"

"Hope, stop," says Taite, sharply interrupting. "I am celebrating my engagement. I don't want to revisit the past. I've already lived through that and now I've moved on. You're a young, beautiful woman. It's not too late for you to find true love either. You've got to move on."

"You don't need to tell me what I need to do. I know what I need to do. Congratulations on your engagement, but I have to leave and go home now. . . . I have a child to look after and I don't want to burden my neighbor with watching her for too long."

Hope storms out of the bathroom.

"Hope, don't leave like this," Taite says as Hope is walking out of the bathroom. "Hope," Taite says as she opens the door to the bathroom and watches Hope march down the hallway.

Hope ignores Taite and continues to walk toward the front door of the restaurant.

Once inside her car, Hope sits behind the wheel and tries to summon the strength to put the key into the ignition and drive home, but the thought of what her husband told her right before he left for the boating trip stalls her for a few seconds. *I'm done. No more of these remote tours. It's taking a toll on our family. We've been married for three years and we barely see each other. I'm done ... done with the Navy.* He didn't reenlist. Eight years had been enough for him. That was going to be their time, but their time never came because Michael Beck, someone who could have tried to save her husband, was more concerned with saving himself. Hope knows for a fact that's what happened, but Taite's too blinded by new love to even care what the truth is.

Pictures are the first thing Heaven notices inside the stately home and what she gravitates toward. Pictures gleam through sterling silver frames, displaying her boyfriend Donovan at various stages of his life. There are pictures of him as a newborn, flanked by his family—his parents and an older brother—at his baptism, high school graduation, standing in front of his college dorm. And then the shrine to him suddenly comes to an end.

Driving through the gate at the entrance to the Bloomfield Hills community made her feel as if she were entering another world. And now this house. This beautiful home with soaring ceilings and immaculate furniture makes her almost frightened; confused. Donovan and the way he was raised are a contradiction. Despite his upper-middle-class background and two-parent upbringing, despite being raised in the suburbs and attending private schools that required students to wear uniforms, despite going to Michigan State for three full years before dropping out, he's still trouble. He is a contradiction, just like the black and gray cross tattoo on his forearm with the words *born to kill* inked inside.

Donovan promised Heaven he was taking them all to dinner at

Heaven's favorite restaurant, Beans & Cornbread. Finally, she is meeting his mother after nearly a year; this was Heaven's ultimatum.

It took Heaven hours to get ready, doing her hair and nails herself. Nothing too fancy, Donovan warned—his mother is ultraconservative. To Heaven, that meant changing her quick weave, leaving out the burgundy pieces, and substituting mascara for her dramatic fake lashes. Straight black hair would be best for the occasion, she realized, and not the wavy texture she preferred.

She is wearing a floral Donna Ricco dress with a navy blue blazer. And even though Donovan complained she'd gone a little too far and now looks like a middle-aged schoolteacher, she decided to take it as a compliment. She admired some of the female teachers she used to work around—not just for the fancy cars that a few of them drove or the designer handbags and shoes most of them had, but because they had a college degree and many had a master's degree. They were going places Heaven had never desired to go before she started working there; places she had never thought possible.

She tries not to stare at his mother's traditional furnishings and the attention paid to every little detail, the candles that have never been burned that are perfectly placed on the glass coffee table, a cello resting between two distinctly different accent chairs, and two vases; one with lilies and the other with wild orchids resting on an end table. She doesn't want to seem in awe; like a girl not used to being around nice things, even though that's exactly who she is. Maybe she shouldn't be ashamed of it, but she is. She's ashamed more of her past and her parents and the fact that almost everything her parents ever brought into the family home was stolen.

Heaven hears Donovan's mother before she sees her. She is talking to two other women.

"Who else is here?" whispers Heaven.

"Sounds like my aunt and probably Mrs. Granger, my mom's best friend."

Heaven smiles at what this meeting could possibly mean and reconsiders the relationship. She is happy to finally meet Donovan's mother and wonders if she can be happy with him again . . . if she can trust him. At times, she can imagine spending the rest of her life with him, if not for the unresolved issue with that Brighton chick. He'd found his phone in the toilet, mentioned it to Heaven, but strangely didn't press the issue. He just took advantage of the insurance he had added to his account and got a free replacement—an upgraded model. She is sad that his father passed away when he was a child, just like her mother, and therefore she will never have the opportunity to meet him. But she is excited to meet his mother and of the possibility that one day the two of them could be as close as mother and daughter.

Now she is in the suburbs where the rich automobile executives live. It makes her wonder why her boyfriend would ever choose to act and talk the way some of the guys she grew up with in the hood did. Why he didn't turn out like his older brother and study law or become a doctor like his dad or do something with his life. But, then, she realizes if he had, she never would have met him.

His mother walks out with authority, leading the other two women, her shoulders straight. She has on golf shorts, a polo shirt, and two-toned leather loafers with a putter tossed over her shoulder. She smiles, but not at Heaven. His mother's eyes never reach hers. She isn't smiling at her son either. It's as if his mother finds the situation—Heaven—something to make light of. She focuses on her son. The introduction is brief at best and very dry. She can't imagine how dinner will be or the drive getting to the restaurant if they all ride in the same car. She prays the other two women aren't coming along, because neither bothers to speak to her. Instead, they both turn and head in the opposite direction when Donovan attempts an introduction.

"What are you doing?" his mother asks him.

"What do you mean what am I doing?"

His mother doesn't respond. She just stands, holding on to her putter and staring him down—communicating with her eyes. "Come here," she says as she turns to walk away.

He follows behind her and even though they are in the adjacent room, Heaven hears every word.

"You have one baby that you're not taking care of and now you have another on the way with that girl. Maybe if you learn how to control your temper, you can fix your relationship. What are you doing?"

"What are you talking about? Heaven's not even pregnant."

"Who is Heaven?"

"Heaven, Mom . . . the girl in the other room."

"I'm not talking about her," she says dismissively. "That other one. I don't even know who you are anymore. If your father were still alive, he wouldn't tolerate the way you're acting. I just don't know what to do, except let you learn the hard way. You already messed up your education. Look at you. And look at the type of women you choose to be with. I'm tired of meeting these tramps. Don't bring another one around my house."

Heaven's eyes widen. She turns to study herself in the hand-painted horizontal mirror hanging over the mantel. *What is so wrong with me that not even my Syms dress and this plain Jane hairstyle can't fix?*

For starters they order fried catfish fingers and a Harlem burrito. Heaven adds a cup of Louisiana-style gumbo, and Trina requests firecracker shrimp. Heaven's eyes can't stop roaming. Every plate on the serving trays coming out from the kitchen looks so tasty. She's already stopped one waiter to ask about an entrée he dropped off two tables over.

While they wait for their appetizers to arrive, they sip on grape Kool-Aid martinis and nibble on sweet-potato muffins. A savory aroma permeates the quaint restaurant, a reminder to Heaven of home-cooked Southern meals like Angelica's (her childhood best friend) mother made. Heaven wishes she could capture that same essence in a candle she'd name Unconditional Love. She would light the candle each evening and bask in the warm light as if it could be enough to solve all of her problems.

"I can't make up my mind," says Trina as her brown squinty eyes slowly peruse the menu, paying close attention to each entrée. Today, she is wearing a long, straight, layered wig with feathered bangs, but nearly every week, if not every day she wears a new wig—a habit she picked up after she'd changed her profession to an exotic dancer. "For some reason, I have a taste for meat loaf, but I really don't want to order meat loaf from a restaurant. You know what I mean?" She scours the small restaurant.

Heaven gives a half shrug. "If you want it, just get it."

"I thought they'd be here by now," Trina says impatiently.

Heaven looks down at her refurbished phone. "My sister sent me a message back." Her eyes start to water as she looks at the Facebook message. She needs family; she needs someone other than Trina to talk to. Ever since Trina lost her job, she wants to live her life recklessly, and Heaven needs a good influence in her life, someone who will understand her, or at least try to. If she had that, what happened the day before at Donovan's mother's house wouldn't have seemed as bad; an older sister would have been able to tell her if she overreacted. After she'd overheard their conversation, Heaven walked into the room and told his mother, "Ma'am, I don't think you should judge me when you don't even know me. I'm not a tramp."

"I don't need to know you because I know my son, and I know the type of women he deals with," Donovan's mother had said with a slight sneer.

But Trina made it all up to Heaven by inviting her to dinner at her favorite restaurant as an early birthday present and giving her the Melanie Fiona CD she'd promised.

"What did she say?" asks Trina, referring to the message she'd received from Alicia on her Facebook page.

"Here's my number. Call me if you can so we can discuss further."

"Why does she sound so formal?" asks Trina, turning up her nose and waving her hand. "You don't need to be bothered with that girl. I'm all the sister you need."

"I just want to know my family," Heaven says as she wipes away her tears with a white cloth napkin. "I have a sister and I want to know her."

Trina's fist pounds the table. "Please, no more of this. This is a celebration, so stop all that crying. You cry like you're getting paid for every tear."

"Everyone cries," says Heaven. "You don't understand. When Glenn wrote me that letter from prison and told me about his other daughter, I was so happy, happier over that news than over hearing from him. And to think that I almost threw his letter out before opening it like all the rest."

"Yeah, but you cry way too easily about everything. You weren't that way before you got with Donovan. I don't know how to explain what he's doing to you, but it's not good, Heaven."

Maybe Trina is right, she tells herself. Donovan could be smothering Heaven's potential. As mad as Heaven was at his mother, she was even more shocked after Donovan called his mother a bitch on their drive home. The word reverberated in Heaven's soul. Sheer disrespect is what her nana would say about that. "If a man thinks that little of his own mother, you ain't even a thought to him."

"What's wrong?" Trina asks as she fiddles with her iPhone. She sets her phone on the table as the appetizers arrive, looking as palatable as the pictures in the menu. "I mean, you can call her and talk to her. She might turn out to be cool."

"Right now I'm not thinking about her. I'm thinking about Donovan."

Trina's eyes roll. She sticks a catfish finger in her mouth. "What has he done now?"

Heaven sighs while she peruses the menu. "He hit me."

"What?" asks Trina. "Hit you? Hit you how?"

"Hit me how? He hit me hard . . . with his fist."

"Girl, you better take a PPO out against him. You can't let him hit you. If someone did that to me, they'd be saying hello to my little friend."

"I don't know what I'm going to do. I don't even want to think about all that right now."

"You better think about it. For one thing, people these days are crazy. He's hitting you now, but he might kill you next. You need to protect yourself. I want you to go downtown and file a PPO, and you need a gun for protection."

"A gun?"

"A LadySmith revolver like the one I have." She sticks another catfish finger in her mouth. "I'm gonna get you one. But please don't kill nobody, because then I'm an accessory."

"I don't want a gun. I want him to just go his way and I go mine."

Trina starts wiggling in her seat. "So why did he hit you, and was that the first time?"

"We got into an argument. Why doesn't even matter, and yes, it was the first time," she lies.

"I'm getting you some protection. And you best not turn it down. That's your problem—you're too nice." Trina looks around the restaurant. "What is taking them so long?"

"Who are you waiting on?"

The waiter approaches their table and sets their empty appetizer plates on his tray.

"Are you ladies ready to order?"

"We sure are," Trina says with a smile. "Because they should have been here by now. So I'll have the mama's meat loaf."

"And you, miss?"

Heaven looks down at the menu. "I'll take the baby sister's backyard-style ribs."

"Excellent choice."

"What, mine isn't?" asks Trina.

"You really can't go wrong with anything on our menu," the

waiter says to Trina, "but the ribs are my personal favorite." He looks in Heaven's direction. "Would you like a half or full slab?"

"Maybe I should get those too, huh?" Trina asks Heaven.

"Nah, you better stick with your first thought. I'll get a full slab and give you some of mine." The waiter finishes taking down the rest of their order and then walks away.

"Oh, there they are," Trina says, smiling at the two women who walk through the front door of the restaurant.

"Which one is your new girlfriend?"

"The beautiful one."

"The one who looks more like a girl?"

"I'm not into femmes anymore. That's the one I'm introducing to you."

"To me?" Heaven asks, and then laughs as the two ladies approach their booth. "Why would you introduce her to me? You know I'm not bisexual."

"Just be nice."

"That's my problem, remember? I'm too nice."

"Heaven, this is Nicolette."

"Hey," Nicolette says with a smile. She ogles Heaven as she takes a seat beside her.

"Hey," Heaven says, bobbling her head as she stares at the young woman's piercings, one amethyst stud in her right cheek, and a stainless steel ring with a dangling turquoise ball looped over her right eyebrow. Heaven doesn't want to make any assumptions about Nicolette's profession. Her supertight clothes with the midriff top that glitters; the belly button ring; the big hair; caked-on foundation and heavily made-up eyes; the boobs that look fake even hidden under her clothing; all of these things scream pole dancer to Heaven.

"And this is Kris," says Trina, introducing her other friend. "Nicolette's sister." She gives Heaven a suggestive look. Heaven sighs. Even with things at their worst with Donovan, she's not ready to experiment on the other side.

After dinner, in the parking lot of Beans & Cornbread, Heaven and the three ladies stand beside Trina's BMW.

"Is it okay if I call you?" asks Nicolette.

"Umm . . . yeah," Heaven says with a shrug.

"Okay, what's your number?" Nicolette asks, after taking out her cell phone.

"I'm not gay," Heaven says, glancing up at Nicolette who is standing tall in four-inch heels.

"Okay," she says with a half shrug. "I have straight friends too." She gazes into Heaven's eyes. "But I do think you're pretty."

"Aww, she thinks you're pretty," Nicolette's sister says.

"Get out of our conversation, please," Nicolette says firmly. She takes Heaven by the hand and leads her to the other side of Trina's car, away from her sister and Trina. "Okay, I'm ready for your number." Heaven rattles off her digits. "Do you live by yourself or—"

"I have a boyfriend. We live together sometimes—I mean, it's my house and he's there most of the time."

Nicolette nods and drops her cell phone inside her Gucci bag. "I'll call you soon, okay?"

"Yeah," Heaven says with a nod. "That'll be fine."

"Can I have a hug?"

"A hug?"

"Yeah, a hug won't turn you gay."

Heaven smiles and relaxes. "I know."

Nicolette gives Heaven a loose embrace. "You smell real nice. What is that . . . DKNY?"

"Nah, honey, this is Love's Baby Soft. I can't afford DKNY. I wish."

Nicolette smiles and says, "Get home safely, okay?" Then she walks off.

Heaven hops in the passenger seat of Trina's BMW and watches Nicolette and her sister walk over to a large black SUV. Nicolette's sister gets in the driver's seat.

"As long as I've known you, you have never done that to me. A girl, Trina? Really? A girl?" She shakes her head as Trina drives off, busy explaining that she made the introduction so Heaven could have another cool friend since Trina had been spending most of her free time with Kris. But Heaven is shocked even more that she finds Nicolette somewhat attractive. Either that, or she had way too much spiked Kool-Aid at the restaurant.

Alicia rouses to a ringing phone and a blaring television. A young woman is on the phone saying she's Alicia's sister.

"My who?" asks Alicia as she rubs her pounding forehead. It was her headache that had forced her into bed early, before she'd finished two-strand twisting her hair. After peeling off a pair of faded sweats, she had crawled underneath a dark patterned comforter in a figure-hugging chocolate Che T-shirt that outlined her modest B cups and a pair of black granny panties stretched over her hollow baby bump. Her slender body was temporarily bloated.

"My sister?" Alicia asks softly.

"Yeah, your sister . . . Heaven . . . from Facebook."

"From Facebook?" she says, vaguely recalling the reference. "Hold on for one minute." Alicia pushes herself up, resting her back against a body-sized pillow, and musses her springy ringlets. Two bath towels are lying lengthwise underneath her to prevent any unforeseen accidents on her favorite sheets. It's that time of the month again, just one week after her last one ended.

"Hello," shouts Heaven. "Are you still there?"

"I just woke up and I can barely hear you." Alicia mutes the volume to her TV, but now she hears music blaring. "Now, what are you saying? Who is this?"

"Heaven . . . your sister," she screams.

Heaven's voice drills into Alicia's throbbing head. "Okay, I *definitely* heard you that time."

"Oh, sorry, I was kinda loud, huh?" asks Heaven. "Don't you remember me? I'm the one who sent you a message on Facebook yesterday about Glenn."

"Yesterday?"

"Maybe it was last week. I've been real busy, and sometimes all my days run together. You gave me your number. How many sisters can you have? You said it would be okay if I called you. Honestly, I was planning on calling you way before now, but my boyfriend took my phone."

"He took your phone?"

"Yeah, he's a fool. But I don't want to talk about him. Don't you live in LA? It's a three-hour difference, right? So it's only a little after ten there. Is it too late?"

The girl is talking too fast, saying too much in a span of only a few seconds for Alicia to comprehend. And she sounds completely drunk. "Are you at a club or something, or is that the radio?"

"You can hear that for real? Wow, I'm not even inside the club, but yeah, I'm outside one. I work at one. I'm a photographer."

"Oh, okay," says Alicia. She needs a good photographer, but Alicia thinks a nightclub photographer seems sort of like a direct-to-DVD actor—not quite as good as the real thing, so maybe they have something in common. But Alicia doesn't want to think about photographers right now, because then she'll remember all of the money she wasted on the one Aubrey referred her to, the one who took terrible headshots. She thinks about what Benita said about Aubrey. "Don't you see a pattern developing? Bad agent . . . bad headshots . . . bad friend." And she remembers that her best friend referred her to her agent as well. No. Alicia shakes the thought from her mind. She won't go there . . . not today—not with a headache and a drunk on the phone. Aubrey is a friend because it's Aubrey who got her a movie role.

"It's my sister," Heaven shouts to someone in the background, causing Alicia's head to rattle once more.

Sister? thinks Alicia. *I don't even know this girl.* "Are you okay?" asks Alicia.

"I'm fine.... That's my man, always checking up on me about who I'm talking to. Don't let me start going through your phone ... again," she shouts. "Get away from me. Stop, I'm trying to talk. I didn't ask you to come down here. Get on. Go. Stop."

"Why don't you just call me back? You sound really preoccupied."

Her lips smack. "No, that's okay," says Heaven. "I'm fine."

"But I'm not." Alicia's not even famous yet and some crazy-sounding girl is already stalking her. Can she just get back to her recurring dream? Back to Ari Gold? Back to the Primetime Emmys? Who knows? Maybe the next time she closes her eyes she'll be at the Oscars or at least the Golden Globes. Her head is splitting. Her eye is twitching. She needs to get up and change her tampon and sanitary napkins and finish two-strand twisting the other half of her bushy hair; a project that could easily take an hour.

"Girl, I don't even feel like going back in the club. You know how when men buy you drinks, how some of them think you owe them something? I'm sure it's probably the same thing if you accept drinks from a woman. Right now, I just appreciate the attention and the free drinks. You know what I mean?" Heaven continues her rant as Alicia's eyes slowly close.

"Hello?" shouts Heaven. Alicia's eyes spring open.

"I'm here," says Alicia. She massages the skin just above her right brow, trying to relieve the tension from her throbbing head.

Heaven giggles. "You sure be drifting in and out. Were you asleep before I called?" Alicia's eyes roll. She had already told the girl once she was asleep—she clearly has listening issues. "But look," says Heaven, "I've been standing out here too long, and the crowd is turning kind of shady. Just 'cause the club's downtown, it's still in Detroit, you know what I mean? So, I'll just call you tomorrow so I can tell you more about me and Glenn."

"Who's Glenn again?"

"Our biological father, the one in prison . . . and your other sister, Hope."

"She's in prison too?"

"No, sorry, I should have finished that sentence. I was just trying to tell you that you have another sister named Hope—my full sister and your half sister."

"How old are you?" asks Alicia. She can tell the girl is young.

"You accepted my friendship on Facebook and didn't read my profile? You could've learned about me. I'm twenty, but just for a couple more weeks. I put up a bunch of photos on Facebook. You need to go check 'em out. I have only one picture of Hope. She's standing next to my niece, Havana. You and Hope look just alike. Her hair used to be long like yours . . . not curly. She wears it straight, but then she lost her mind and cut it all off."

"Lost her mind?"

"Yeah, seriously, like for real lost her mind. She didn't get put away or nothing. But she lost it after her husband died, but she was kinda off even before all that happened." Heaven has a slight buzz. Just enough to make her laugh at things that aren't really funny, deal with things she isn't in the mood for, and call up someone like Alicia, someone she doesn't even know, and tell her things that are none of her business.

"Okay," Alicia says, dragging out the word. She knew one thing for sure: Once she did make it, she wouldn't want Heaven to be a part of her entourage, because she gave out personal information too freely. She would be the tabloids' best friend.

Alicia sighs. Now she understands why her mother told her not to invite the other side into her life after she told her that a young woman contacted her online claiming to be her sister. So what if she is her half sister. She has scores of relatives she's known her entire life but hasn't spoken to in years and has no desire to. Why should she waste her time on someone she never even knew existed?

"Well, I know you have to go—"

"No, it's cool now," Heaven says, interrupting. "My boyfriend went in the club and I'm sitting in the car away from the ruckus, listening to my Melanie Fiona CD. So I can finally talk now." She lets out a sigh of relief. "I got my shoes off and my heat on, and it's nice and toasty in here. My nana would be like, 'Summertime and you blasting the heat. Girl, you better get yourself checked out. You must have low blood pressure.' She is so quick to tell somebody they have low blood pressure. I think most women like to be warm. Don't you like to be warm?"

"I do."

"My best friend was wrapped up in an electric blanket the other day."

"Well, I know you have to get back to work. You might be missing out on last-minute customers who want to get their pictures taken."

"The club doesn't close till three. And that's why people have cell phones with a built-in camera anyway. I work at Rumor Nightclub, not Sears. This ain't portrait studios. I don't take pictures like that. I take random pictures of people in the club, and when we have performers come in, I keep their Web site updated. It's a cool little part-time job. Not something I wanna do for the rest of my life, but it's cool for the little extra money. I do some of their marketing and promotions. I'm supposed to pass out their stupid flyers. They better go green . . . wasting all that paper. I got so many flyers in my trunk, if they only knew. I told them they need to focus on online marketing. Do you know they just now set up a MySpace page? I don't even check my MySpace account anymore. Tom probably shut me down. They're not even on Facebook or Twitter. But they're real old . . . in their forties and obviously don't have a clue," Heaven says without taking so much as a one second pause.

"I have to go . . . seriously. I'm not feeling that well."

"Okay, well, have a good night and I'll try and call you back, probably tomorrow."

But before Alicia can tell her not to bother, Heaven quickly hangs up.

"**N**ana, are you up?" asks Heaven. She is still sitting in the driver's seat of her car in one of the club's parking lots.

"What time is it?" asks her grandmother, sounding incoherent.

"Just after one."

"In the morning?" asks her grandmother, clearing her throat. "Why aren't you in bed?"

"I'm at work."

"You're at the club. That's not work. Nothing good happens after midnight. Child, this better be life-changing if you're calling me this late."

"It is . . . to me," she says with excitement in her voice. "Guess who I just hung up the phone with."

"It's about to be me."

"Guess who I was just talking to."

"President Obama."

"Nana," says Heaven, dragging the word.

"Who? Just tell me. I don't have time for this guessing game. It's one in the morning. . . . Who, child, who?"

"Glenn's daughter."

"Uh-uh. First of all, what I tell you about calling your father by his first name? You need to stop that nonsense. And now you're calling your sister *his daughter*. You two used to be so close. What happened? Why can't Hope come to her senses and accept that that man is dead? Probably in a shark's belly, and it's time to move on. I have never mourned one of my dead husbands that long. What is that child's problem?"

"I'm not talking about Hope. Did Glenn . . . I mean Dad," she says, rolling her eyes, "ever tell you he had another child . . . a daughter named Alicia that he had in high school?"

"A what? I don't know anything about another child."

"He has another child and she looks just like Hope . . . like her twin, only with curly hair."

"She can look just like my deceased momma for all I care. I don't know about her."

"Glenn wrote me a letter and told me about her himself."

"Who wrote you a letter?"

"Glenn . . . I mean Dad."

"So you are getting his letters?" she asks as if she's saying, "Gotcha." "I didn't want to tell him you were just ignoring him, but I figured. So have you written back yet?"

"No, Nana . . . not yet, but I will." She had been writing the letter she planned on sending Glenn for a few days now, but stopped once she realized what she had to say could take a while to compose. She had a lot to say . . . most of which wouldn't be nice. But mainly she wanted to know why he killed their mother.

"You better . . . and you better be nice. He is your father. And he's in prison for life . . . natural life, Heaven. Do you know what that means? That means your father is never getting out of prison. He's going to die in that place."

And for good reason, Heaven thought. Is she supposed to feel sorry for the man who killed her mother? Even if that man is her father? She thinks not. She thinks he should die in that place.

"He's got his dogs now," adds Heaven. "He seems happy."

"Dogs," her grandmother says, almost spitting out the word. "Having dogs is nothing like having your children—your flesh and blood. Only a fool would be happy in prison."

"And that's who Alicia is to him too, Nana . . . his flesh and blood."

"Don't you think I would have known about some baby my son had? I'm going to have to ask him about this myself. I can't believe he has another child. He tells me everything."

Heaven is sorry she even called. Almost as soon as her nana answered, she realized she'd made a mistake. "All right, well, forget I even said anything, then."

"No, I'm not going to do that either. I mean you called me all early in the morning for a reason. This must mean something to you. I'll talk to your father and get down to the bottom of it. If he does have another child, I want to meet her too, but if this is just a result of some woman claiming to have had a baby by him and he never knew for sure if it was his, well, we can't be so quick to bring her into our family fold."

Heaven laughs. "Nana, what could she gain from coming into our family fold? Our family doesn't have anything."

"Anyway," her grandmother says, dismissively, as she always does when she's done listening to whatever it is someone else has to say and she's ready to move on, "I want to know why you're not talking to your father. I stay up nights sometimes worried over it. Everybody needs somebody to love, but to have your own children turn their backs on you. I don't even know what that's like. Just wait until you have a child. Then you'll understand."

"Is it my fault that I can't accept collect calls on my cell?"

"That doesn't stop you from writing."

"I don't even feel like I know him. And I don't feel like that's something I have to do."

"You don't know your own father? Is that what you're telling me?"

"Look, I'm sorry for waking you, because this call wasn't supposed to be about—hello? Hello?" Heaven's grandmother had abruptly hung up. Heaven sighs. She was starting to get excited. For a brief moment, she assumed that having Alicia come into her life at that particular time was a blessing, but after speaking to her grandmother, she has her doubts again.

A few minutes later, Heaven heads into Rumor Nightclub. Passing through the metal detector, she nearly trips over her four-and-a-half-inch peep-toe wrapped platform pumps into the broad back of one of the male patrons. She mistakes the enormous man for Detroit Lions defensive tackle Grady Jackson until she remembers that professional athletes are not that club's clientele. Rumor is not in the same league with the popular V nightclub—located in the MGM Grand Detroit. Stars are flown in to host events that are attended by more than a thousand partygoers at that nightclub. But here, there is no resident DJ close to the level of V's DJ Captn20 and absolutely no visits from nationally known DJs either. They hire amateurs to spin their turntable or let a poorly produced mixtape play all through the night. There isn't a VIP room at Rumor. There's just a leather sectional in the back office that friends of the owners can use when they feel the urge for a quick one-night stand.

Rumor Nightclub is known for inexpensive drinks, a massive dance floor, and no cover charge before eleven. But the club is also a breeding ground for fancy fedoras, alligator shoes, and loud-colored baggy suits. Many of the women who frequent the club seem to take pride in wearing skintight outfits that aren't in the least bit flattering for their body type. Fights break out so regularly that a Detroit Police mini station had to open less than a mile away.

She and Nicolette, the young woman Trina had introduced her to, have been drinking Grey Goose all night, which could explain why Heaven has taken only five pictures. She dipped out long enough to call Alicia and her nana. And she isn't quite sure of the impression she made with Alicia. It seems to her that Alicia was rushing off the phone, almost as if she wasn't as happy as Heaven to learn she has a sister.

She'd been outside for nearly thirty minutes, and she wasn't even missed by the owners.

This isn't a real job. They don't actually need her photography services and she knows it. And she also knows that one day soon the two owners might decide to let her go. The only reason she got the job was because one of the owners wanted to sleep with her. Malcolm—the other owner, who is married with six kids—does too. Or maybe he just likes talking about how much he wants to. Both are too old and too gray to be Heaven's type.

"There she is," Nicolette says as Heaven approaches. "Just in time for another drink."

"Nah, I don't need to be drinking."

"Just one more," she says as she motions the bartender to bring another vodka. "You look so sexy tonight," Nicolette whispers into her ear while she holds Heaven's hand. "You gonna let me take you home?"

Heaven smiles, flattered by the attention. "You're gonna need to let a cab take you home."

"I'm all right," Nicolette whispers back. "I have a high tolerance level with some things."

"So, are you trying to get me drunk so you can take advantage of me?" Heaven whispers back.

"Do I really need to get you drunk?" Nicolette puts her arms around Heaven's waist and draws Heaven toward her.

"Is this the reason you put your little hooker dress on?" Donovan shouts as he wedges between them.

"Donovan, please, I don't have time for this. I'm at work."

"Work, is this what you call work?" Donovan snatches the drink from Nicolette's hand. "Thanks for the drink, bitch."

"Your woman's with me, not you, so who's the bitch?" Nicolette asks.

He tosses the drink in Nicolette's face and pulls Heaven away from her.

"So, you're gay? I wish I would have known, because I could've put another bitch up in the bed with us a long time ago." Heaven is speechless. He grabs her by her arms and begins furiously shaking her. "Say something!" He shakes her the way her grandmother used to when she was a child, and Heaven starts to laugh just like she did as a child.

"Leave her alone," Nicolette says, trying to pull Heaven away from him.

Security rushes over and pulls him away from the two women and allows him to leave without calling the police.

Malcolm plods over to Heaven and says, "Is everything okay? Do you need me to take you home?"

"I need to leave," she says, taking laborious breaths. "Can Big Mike and Reno walk me to my car?"

Two large bouncers wait for Heaven as she goes into the back office to retrieve her purse. She wants to remember this night and how crazy Donovan is—this time in front of other people. She wants to remember this night so she won't let anything he says or anything he attempts to do convince her that he loves her. He's crazy, and she doesn't need him in her life.

All Alicia wants to do is play one frame. In the very back of her mind are thoughts of the girl named Heaven, who called her the night before from a nightclub, and how lost she sounded. Alicia has no idea why, but she just can't get her off her mind, and she wants to forget about her. She needs to distract herself. But she doesn't want to dance, even though there's a hip DJ spinning all the latest jams. She doesn't drink, so there's no need to even pause at the well-stocked bar. She simply wants to bowl one frame without choking, because she can still remember the time she bowled a perfect game—a three-hundred score. Even though it happened only once when she was a sophomore in high school, the point is that it happened, and if it happened once, it can happen again.

Benita came to Lucky Strike Lanes with her. And the only reason Alicia has come at all is to congratulate Aubrey, who is throwing herself another party to celebrate another new role. She's landed the lead this time, and supposedly it comes with an even bigger seven-figure contract and includes a percentage of the box office. Before coming, Alicia pondered the question of what to buy someone who already has everything—and what to buy someone who already has everything when you yourself have no money. *Nothing*. And that was exactly what Alicia did. She had to be honest with herself. The real reason she's even at Lucky Strike Lanes tonight is to hand off the signed contract to J.R. He'd said he was going to be so busy revising his script that he wouldn't be leaving his house in San Diego for at least a month. And since she didn't want to drive two hours on Interstate 5 to hand the contract to him directly and pick up her check, this is the best way.

Alicia is inside the private VIP lounge where the party is being held, refusing drinks, but nibbling on plenty of finger food. She feels out of place, an unfamiliar name in a sea of A-list stars. Not surprisingly, Aubrey doesn't greet her, not even with her usual fake air kisses—one to each cheek. She's too busy buzzing around the room acting like a VIP, and soaking up all the compliments about how wonderful she is, how great she looks, and how talented she is.

"Do you have my contract?" asks J.R., who appears from nowhere.

"I didn't bring it inside with me," Alicia says, twirling her tiny clutch. "But I'm getting ready to leave anyway right after I congratulate Aubrey and maybe bowl one frame. Do you mind walking me to my car so I can get it? I didn't park far."

He checks his watch. "I've been here for an hour too long already. I have work to do on my script, but I'm staying right next door at the Renaissance. I didn't feel like driving back home tonight. Why don't you just walk it over when you're done?"

He'd given her his room number and told her he'd be up late.

"Um," she says, waving her hand in Benita's direction, "I'll just get it now. I can come back after I give you the contract. Just walk me to my car. It's right outside." Alicia grabs Benita and they head back outside. She isn't about to go out with him to her car alone. Alicia didn't just blow through this town yesterday. There is no way she is going up to his hotel room either. She'd learned her lesson the hard way instead of heeding the warnings of Aunt Olena and Alicia's good friend, Sir. They must have watched the same episode of *48 Hours Mystery*, because they both seemed overly concerned that

Alicia would somehow fall prey to a bogus producer with malicious intentions promising her stardom.

When she first arrived in Los Angeles, she'd made the mistake of getting into a car with two men whom Aubrey claimed she knew, instead of waiting for another cab to come pick them up and take them back to their apartment. It was late and Alicia was just a little buzzed, but mainly tired. She simply wanted to go home and climb into her bed, say her prayers for stardom, and start the next day off trawling for auditions. The two men Aubrey claimed she knew were well-dressed and clean-cut—not the best looking, but certainly not the worst either. There was nothing to be suspicious of, but after a few wrong turns, suddenly they were hidden away in a dark alley. She was in the backseat and the man who was sitting beside her was struggling to get on top of her, but there was no way she was letting him go any farther.

So she went wild. She kicked and screamed, biting him on his earlobe until she tasted blood, and then the next thing she knew she was free. She ran through the dark alley with one shoe and the sole of her bare foot touching the foulest of things. She ran and she screamed. The men pushed Aubrey out of the car and sped off. Suddenly, lights turned on, and within minutes police arrived at the scene. They filed police reports. But Alicia never told her family. If she'd told them what happened, it would have been the end of her dream. Her mother and stepfather would have driven out to California and personally taken her back.

That was the night she'd given up drinking, for the most part. Had she been as intoxicated as Aubrey, she wouldn't have been able to fight as hard as she did. Had she not had that buzz, maybe she would have thought twice about getting into the car with those men.

"There's something I meant to ask you," says J.R, right after she hands over the signed contract. "Is that going to get in the way?" he asks pointing toward her stomach.

"What?"

"Your pregnancy. I mean, when I finally start to shoot this film

I don't want you in a hospital somewhere about to give birth. Will I need to shoot your scenes first? How far along are you?"

Heaven is so stunned she can't even speak. She and Benita had planned out her outfit, and they were certain her stomach didn't look like it was protruding before she stepped out. Apparently they were wrong. She sighs. "I'm just a little bloated right now, but I'm not pregnant."

"I was going to say, if you are, that's fine, because I can rewrite the character to make her pregnant. It might actually work better. I'll let you know what I decide."

When Alicia returns to the VIP lounge, she slogs through a sizable crowd of pretentious-looking people to offer Aubrey something genuine—a hug. She offers no air kisses, just a hug and an "I'm proud of you." Even if she does feel a slight twinge of jealousy from time to time, who wouldn't? Alicia is praying that this movie deal with J.R. is the beginning of a better life—a new beginning, just as it was for her aunt Olena when she went on her one-year sabbatical.

"I'm doing so good out here. Don't you think?" asks Aubrey as she nurses her drink. "And so will you one day. Just give J.R. that contract. He's amazing. Just wait and see. I'm sure it'll all work out."

"I hope so. I really do, because I already gave it to him."

Aubrey pats Alicia on the back. "Good for you," she says, and for the first time Alicia feels as if Aubrey has said so out of pity, and Alicia doesn't like the way that makes her feel. It reminds her of the teacher's patting her on her back and telling her school wasn't meant to teach you how to dream. No matter how many years she's been at the same dream to no avail, she doesn't need anyone to feel sorry for her. She's going to make it. And she has to believe in J.R. Even if she doesn't trust him enough to go up to his hotel room, she still has to believe that he could be the real deal.

"I really want to bowl," says Alicia as she notices one of the four private lanes open up.

"Go for it," says Aubrey, now sitting at the end of one of the long leather sofas and sipping a new drink.

Alicia wants to bowl a strike. Aubrey shows her where she can get a pair of bowling shoes and makes sure no one takes the lane. Within minutes, Alicia is standing at the far-right lane. If she bowls a strike, she will know that agreeing to do the movie with J.R. is the best thing she could have done. If not, well, she really doesn't want to contemplate anything negative.

She takes a few long strides and releases the ball with perfect form; it seems to be dead-on and heading for a strike. She's so excited to see what she is certain will happen—all of the pins falling down. But one pin wobbles. And she waits, but it never falls.

One pin is left standing, and she asks herself what that means.

"Why is the door locked?" Donovan asks as he turns the doorknob to the bathroom.

"Because I'm in here; why you think?" Heaven says. She has her cell phone in the palm of her hand; the last-dialed number is to Alicia, but her call goes straight to voice mail. This is the third day in a row that's happened. Maybe Heaven should read between the lines or between the many left voice mails, she muses.

"What you doing, changing into something sexy?" he asks as he stands beside the door, stroking his bare chest. "It's been a while since you gave me some."

"Can I please poop in peace?" asks Heaven, sitting fully dressed on the closed toilet. She isn't having a bowel movement, but as usual she is having doubts. A few days ago he was calling her out of her mind and accusing her of being gay. They'd agreed they both wanted to give their relationship a rest, but their breakup lasted all of one day. That was their cycle. Break up, then get right back together.

"Why are you so crude?" he asks.

Crude? Whatever. She wants to turn him off, because she surely isn't in the mood to turn him on. They have problems and while she'll be the first to admit she may not know much, she does know that having sex won't solve any of them. She wishes she had learned years ago how to simply say "No."

On the sink's counter are six one-hundred-dollar bills, which is all of the money she needs for her past-due electric bill. Her DTE Energy bill ballooned after she missed one of her monthly installment payments and she was removed from the plan. She didn't ask Donovan, who always cries broke, where the money came from. And she didn't care. He had his hustle and she, of course, had hers. But he did stress that he needed her to pay it all back—and soon. Yeah, right. Just as soon as he gives back all the electricity he used while staying there.

She picks herself up, flushes the toilet, and shoves the money in her front jeans pocket. When she opens the door, he is right there—nearly naked. And seeing him that way is turning her off. Her nana always told her that the way you know for sure you're over a man is when you look at him and feel the urge to throw up. Heaven can feel the bile rising.

"I don't feel so good," she says, clasping her neck.

"I got something for you," he says, rubbing his body against hers. "It's going to make you feel better. Trust me."

"I don't want to have sex," she tells him. "Ever."

He draws back. "Ever? What, you've gone all the way over to the other side now or something?"

"Donovan, what are you talking about?"

"You only like women now or something? You must. Because we were having sex before that little incident in the club when I saw you all hugged up with that bitch."

"Why is it every female, including your own momma, is a bitch?" She shakes her head. "I'm so tired of this existence."

"Tired of your existence?"

"Not my existence . . . *this* existence. The way I'm living my life . . . you . . . not having a real job . . . being behind on bills . . . Detroit . . . ev-er-y-thing," she says with emphasis.

"But baby," he says, easing his arms around her waist, "it's been like two weeks since we've done something. That's way too long."

"Some married couples don't do it that much."

"Married couples? I don't want to hear that as an excuse."

"Gas getting too high or something? You tired of driving out to Brighton to get you some?"

"Here we go again with that. How many times do I have to tell you that girl is like my cousin."

"Like your cousin?" asks Heaven, laughing. "Does your cousin text you naked pictures of herself?"

"You don't ever believe anything I say. I don't have to lie. She is my cousin."

"If she's your cousin, call her. Call her and introduce me to her right now. Let me see if she's as rude as your momma." As soon as she says that, he explodes. His fist immediately hits the wall, creating a major dent. He starts his rant and starts telling her what she isn't; what she'll never be; how much better he's had. The only thing Heaven can do as she speeds out of her driveway at eleven o'clock at night is thank God she got the money she needs for her electric bill before he started acting more of a fool.

She can hear her nana saying, "People are responsible for their own misery ninety percent of the time." She was always telling Heaven she could take a bad situation and find a way to turn it into something worse. That's what Heaven is trying to avoid this time—something worse. So she doesn't stick around to watch his fists eventually land on her. Instead, she leaves him in her house. She takes the things she has of value—her Nikon camera, lenses, and laptop—and rides up and down Livernois. She passes Pied Piper Market where she usually purchases her lotto tickets. She crosses over Puritan and stops at Citgo to put five dollars' worth of gas in her gas tank. She ignores Donovan's calls. She passes by Mo' Money Taxes and Frank's Three-Dollar Car Wash before stopping at the strip club where Trina and Nicolette both dance.

Heaven walks under the pink awning and behind the green door, easily avoiding the six-dollar cover, because they all know her as Trina's friend. And Trina's name gets her in for free. Heaven had almost taken a job at the strip club when things had gotten really tight about six months earlier, but then Trina came up with the brilliant idea to shoplift, and the rest was history. At the time, Trina's plan sounded pretty good. After all, stealing is in her blood. She was six years old when she discovered what her mother's hobby was. They were out shopping in the Greenfield Plaza on the third floor during the Christmas season, browsing diamond rings in one of the jewelry stores. A man behind the counter was helping her mother try on a few when suddenly he asked, "Where's the ring?"

Heaven's mother looked around, as if confused. "Excuse me, sir, are you talking to me? I don't know anything about a ring," she said with a phony Southern accent. She fluttered her false lashes and adjusted the large brim on her church hat, clutching the Bible she was carrying even closer to her chest. Heaven knew, even then, that her mother couldn't recite one verse from the Book to save her life. But she never questioned her as to why she carried it around.

"The one you took," the man said. "Where is it?"

"Sir, I tried on a few rings while you were standing right here, but I didn't take anything. You were the one helping me. I don't need to take a ring. I have plenty of rings," she said, flashing her two hands and revealing seven rings.

"Well, I know my ring tray by heart. And I know either you or your daughter put a penny in this slot right here, where a ring used to be. And I doubt your daughter did, so you must've done it while I went to take out another tray," the white-haired man said, tossing the penny from the ring tray. "It was here a few minutes ago, and you're the only customers who've been near my counter. So, I tell you what I'm going to do since it's the season to be jolly. I'm going to count to ten, and if that ring isn't back in the tray, I'm calling the cops."

"My momma didn't steal your ring, mister," Heaven said with defiance as she crossed her arms, tapped her small foot, and huffed with anger.

The man started counting. Heaven stood shaking her head, consumed with anger. She didn't understand why that man was treating her mother, an innocent woman, that way. There was only one explanation. It had to be just like their nana said: The white man was the devil. By the time the devil counted to seven, Heaven noticed something strange. Her mother had heaved her large leather purse onto the glass counter, unzipped the front pocket, retrieved a diamond solitaire ring, and put it back in the tray where the penny had been.

Heaven was shocked by what was going on. Her mother tried to take Heaven by the hand and lead her out of the store, but Heaven snatched her hand away. She didn't want to touch her mother, but she yanked Heaven by the arm and hurried out of the store. When they got back to the car, where Hope was sleeping in the backseat and her father was waiting, they sped off, her father burning rubber out of the parking lot after learning their plot was foiled.

Later, after they'd all made it back to their east side home, a distraught Heaven cried into her pillow with thoughts of her mother being a bad person. Bad people went to jail. Her mother was going to jail. That's when Hope, in an effort to cheer up her little sister, slid her pink Easy-Bake Oven from under her bed. "Let's make a cake. That'll make you feel better. I ran out of icing, but it will still taste good." She didn't run out of icing. At twelve, Hope had an extremely sweet tooth and used to rip open the party cake mixes at night just so she could eat the vanilla frosting mixes that were inside. Back then, Hope was pudgy with a lot of what their mother wrote off as baby fat. "There ain't nothin' 'baby' about all that fat she carrying around," their nana would tell their mother. "It was one thing to buy the girl that oven, but did you need to buy her a lifetime supply of the cake mix to go along with it?"

"You want to help me bake?" Hope had asked Heaven.

"Did they steal that too?" Heaven asked after she hopped off the twin bed, dried her eyes, and went over to her desk where Hope was setting up the Easy-Bake Oven.

"They only steal grown-up things. Not the stuff for kids. Kids' stuff is cheap. Adult stuff costs a lot and they don't have money. But Heaven, we won't ever have to steal when we grow up. We're going to make lots of money." After Hope read the instructions for the cake mix, she said, "We have to go downstairs and get some cooking spray and two teaspoons of water. And that's all we need."

"How long is it gonna take to bake?" asked Heaven.

"Twelve minutes."

"Dang, that long?"

"But I'm going to let you make it." Hope never let Heaven stir the mix before. She always said she was too little and would make a mess, but not that time. That time everything was okay. That time Heaven felt on equal footing with her sister, who at the time was twice her age. They went downstairs and retrieved the cooking spray and water. When they went back upstairs, Hope told Heaven she could start working with the mix. Heaven sloppily poured out the mix. A small pile of white powder landed on the desktop. As a joke, Heaven bent her head down near the powder and tried to sniff it up.

Hope grabbed Heaven by the arm and said, "Why would you do that? That's not funny."

Laughing, Heaven said, "That's what I saw Momma and Daddy doing."

"You're not supposed to do that. They're not sniffing cake mix. They're sniffing something else . . . something that's bad for you. Look at me, Heaven," she said, guiding Heaven's head up toward hers. "We have bad parents. . . . They do bad things. All we can do is pray they get better and always stick together. I won't ever let anything happen to you. Ever. Okay?"

Heaven nodded, then said, "Okay." Hope scooped the residue from the desk into the palm of her hand and dumped it in the small plastic trash can beside the desk, and Heaven started mixing up the cake batter.

Heaven has always known stealing is wrong. For some reason, though, she can still do it and not feel bad. It doesn't bother her. And then, there is the alcohol. She can't honestly deny she has a drinking problem, and if she's around alcohol four or five nights a week, like she is now, it will only get worse.

Heaven stands at the entrance to the hallway leading to the dressing area of the strip club.

Dynasty, one of the top dancers at the strip club, says, "Are you waiting for Trina?"

Heaven nods.

"Come on."

Heaven follows behind Dynasty, who is alluring in a black stretch matte minidress with silver clip accents that tie at the neck and the back and has an extremely low rear cut that is open at the back and the sides.

"Look who the stripper dragged in," says Trina as Heaven walks into the fitting room. Trina is standing topless in the dressing room, slipping out of a blue skintight belted miniskirt. "What happened now? Did he hit you again?"

"Again?" Nicolette asks. She is sitting on a wood bench with her legs crossed, covered with spaghetti-strapped garter belts. Her right foot dangles a five-inch open-toe platform stiletto. She has on a short pink belted flared skirt with a matching halter top.

"Yeah, again," emphasizes Trina. "Is that what happened?"

"No," says Heaven. "I just had to leave. And I don't want to go back there tonight. Can I stay at your place tonight?"

"Yeah, but I'm having company."

"Oh, forget it. Maybe he left by now," says Heaven.

"You can stay at my place," says Nicolette as she searches through her purse for her keys. She pulls out a set of keys and removes one from the key ring.

Heaven looks down at the key that Nicolette is stretching out toward her. She is debating whether she should take it and hopes Nicolette won't think that means she's interested in her. She'd taken a few of her calls after that night at Rumor when Donovan tossed a drink in Nicolette's face, but she'd also avoided many of them. Heaven feels strange every time she talks to Nicolette. She feels like she's in the beginning stages of cheating on Donovan, and with a girl, and that really makes no sense to her.

"You sure it's okay?" asks Heaven.

"Yeah, girl," says Nicolette as she places the key inside Heaven's palm and closes it. "More than sure—positive."

She just finished washing down her last White Castle and a few onion rings with several gulps of Coke when she pulls up the long drive leading to the entrance of the same apartment complex Trina lives in. The arm to the security gate is up. She'd given Heaven the security code just in case, and told her there might be a security guard in the booth. But the booth is empty as usual. She parks her car underneath a carport near Trina and Nicolette's building.

A man in a conservative suit speaks to Heaven as he holds the building door open for her and she strides in. He is probably coming from a bar or a club, muses Heaven, who also imagines how much better her life would be in the suburbs. She can't think as far as another state because she'd never been outside of Michigan, and the farthest city she'd visited was Ann Arbor, when Donovan had surprised her when they'd first started dating by taking her to the fancy French/Italian restaurant—the Earle on West Washington Street. But she always enjoys going over to Trina's Southfield apartment. It feels worlds away from her own home, even though it's only eleven miles.

What a difference nice furniture makes, Heaven thinks as she enters Nicolette's apartment. Trina's furniture is cute too, but Nicolette's leather seems to be a few steps above. Heaven can't wait until the day she can afford to buy an Art Van collection of her own.

She makes herself at home just like Nicolette insisted. She kicks off her mules, stretches her short legs across the leather recliner, and flips on the forty-inch HD television hanging on the wall. *Can photography get me all of this?* She has some doubt. Not even shoplifting can buy her this kind of lifestyle.

Before long her eyes close.

A few hours later, she wakes up after hearing a knock at the door.

She tiptoes over to the door and peers through the peephole at a young woman. She wonders if she should tell the woman that Nicolette isn't home, that she's just her friend, but instead she remains silent, tiptoeing away from the door as the woman begins to beat on it.

"Heaven, open the door."

Heaven removes the chain from the door and opens it. "Nicolette? Why do you look so different? So . . . normal?"

Nicolette walks into her apartment with two plastic grocery bags weighing down each of her arms. "I guess because I don't have on my stripper costume." Her hair is pulled back into a side ponytail with a twist. And she isn't wearing makeup. She doesn't have on five-inch heels, so she and Heaven are close to the same height of five foot four. "Are you hungry? I went to Meijer and picked up a few things."

"Girl, I'm way ahead of you. I stopped at White Castle on the way here and ate four White Castles and some onion rings," says Heaven. "I'm full."

Nicolette walks into the kitchen to put away her groceries. "You sure you don't want a little something to munch on?"

Heaven's nose crinkles. She doesn't like the way she said that and wonders what exactly she was referring to. "No, for real, I'm fine."

"Oh, I already know you're fine."

Heaven shakes her head. "That was so corny. Be original, please."

"The truth is always original," says Nicolette.

"Hey, where did you get your furniture from? It's really nice," Heaven says, trying to change the subject.

"Gardella."

"I never heard of that."

"It's on Gratiot," says Nicolette as she poses at the arched entranceway leading into the kitchen.

"You live out here and you went all the way down there?"

"All the way down there?" she asks in confusion. "You know it's not that far from here."

"I know it's not far, but I'm just saying you could have just as easily gone someplace closer."

"But if I like something and I want it, it doesn't really matter how far out of reach it may seem—I'll go after it."

"That's a cute little analogy, but I'm talking about furniture right now."

"Do you want me to take you? Are you looking for some new furniture? I'll take you down there."

Heaven's head shakes. "Not right now."

"You have pretty eyes."

"Thank you," mumbles Heaven, and Nicolette returns to the kitchen. Heaven is still trying to get past the fact that Nicolette likes her in the same way a man likes a woman. And to her knowledge, Nicolette is the first woman to ever like her in that way. Not that she has ever come straight out and said that she did. She mainly just compliments Heaven a lot and calls her all the time. She also sends her text messages and pictures—nothing X-rated. But Heaven can just tell—the same way she can tell when a man does, only Nicolette's advances seem a lot more sincere.

Within minutes, Heaven hears pots clanging.

"You can turn on the television if you want," Nicolette yells from the kitchen.

"It's on. I just don't have the volume up. What are you doing?"

"Making something. Don't come in here. It's a surprise."

Heaven toggles through a wide array of DIRECTV stations, and several minutes later Heaven crinkles her nose again. "What's that smell?"

"What does it smell like?"

Heaven takes a whiff of air. "I can't explain it. Like something I've never smelled before. It's kind of strong. What are you cooking?"

"Just hold on."

After ten minutes, Heaven hears water running. Then, Nicolette stands in the doorway to the kitchen. "Almost done." She comes into the living room and sits in a chair across from Heaven.

Nicolette is quieter than Heaven imagined. For the most part, she just sits in the chair with an oven mitt in her hand.

After another fifteen minutes, Heaven says, "I smell brownies. How did you know I loved brownies?"

"Trina told me," she says as the buzzer sounds. "Hold that thought."

Heaven watches Nicolette as she saunters off. "I am not gay," she says aloud to herself. "But she does have a cute butt."

"Are you sure?" Nicolette asks from the kitchen.

"Am I sure, what? 'Cause I know you didn't hear that."

"Are you sure I didn't hear that? Are you sure you're not gay? Oh, and thank you . . . I work out five days a week on this cute butt."

Heaven's eyes bulge. Complimenting a woman doesn't make you gay. Does it? Saying she has a nice body. Pretty hair. Smooth skin. Women talk like that about one another. Don't they? Women observe things they like on one another. That's normal, right? Heaven ponders. "You have some good ears to hear through walls."

"That's not all I got that's good."

Heaven smiles wide and laughs inside her hands. She's embarrassed. She'd swear if her skin weren't so brown, she'd be beet red right now. Minutes later, Nicolette enters with a plate of brownies. "These are still hot, but Trina said you like yours really hot."

Heaven reaches for one. "I do."

"I made a little substitution for the oil," she says as she watches Heaven bite into her first one. "I used cannaoil."

"You mean canola oil, don't you?"

"I mean cannabis oil."

"Girl, you put weed in these brownies?"

"Just five grams."

"Can we get high off of these?" asks Heaven. "They taste just like brownies. They won't get me high, will they? I don't really like weed."

"You'll get high—trust me. Don't eat too many. Maybe just two or three."

Ten brownies later and Heaven is beyond a simple buzz.

"Are you okay?" Nicolette asks.

"I'm fine. How about you?"

"I'm cool, but I only had two brownies, but you—you killed them," says Nicolette, looking at the crumbs on the empty plate.

"I told you I love brownies. And those things taste just like—" She stops before the end of her sentence and stares at the large painting hanging on the wall before bursting out in laughter. "That's a naked woman with a fried egg in front of her. Why does she have guitar strings coming out her nipples and why is her head shaped like a guitar? Is that supposed to mean something?"

"I don't know. It was a gift. And you're high. Real high."

"A gift from who, your girlfriend? Do you have one?"

"No, I don't. We broke up. I haven't had a girlfriend in more than a year."

"You don't have a girlfriend with your cute butt? Why not?"

Nicolette strokes the side of Heaven's face. "Because I don't like dealing with women who can't make up their mind between penis or pussy. Can you make up your mind?"

"Well, seeing as how his is only this big," says Heaven as she uses two fingers from the same hand to measure off two inches, "I wouldn't be missing much." Heaven bursts out in laughter.

"You're high," says Nicolette, "and it's not fun to talk about a serious matter with someone high."

Heaven stops laughing and sits quietly on the sofa from where she continues to stare at the painting. There are eggs hovering above the nude woman—fried egg clouds. Nicolette scoots in closer to Heaven. "You are high, aren't you?" she whispers into Heaven's ear, swirling her tongue inside her ear canal and telling her, "When I masturbate I think of you." Nicolette begins slowly unbuttoning Heaven's blouse.

"What are you doing?"

"What do you think I'm doing?" Nicolette asks right before she takes a nip of Heaven's lip. She slides off Heaven's blouse, unfastens her bra from the front, and pulls it off her shoulders. Nicolette stands and steps out of her blue jeans. She pulls off her top and removes her bra and panties to reveal a bald pubic area just like Heaven's. She then pulls Heaven off the sofa and helps her out of her jeans.

"I'm sleepy," Heaven says with a forced yawn.

"That's funny, because I'm wide-awake." She guides Heaven's hands to her chest and says, "Squeeze them."

Heaven can hear exactly what her nana would say. Imagine the kind of freak she would call her . . . the kind of misguided fool. Heaven allows her hands to feel what Donovan's hands feel time and time again on a woman and tries to understand his fascination with big breasts. "Are these bought?"

Nicolette shakes her head and says, "I got 'em from my momma."

"These are real?" Heaven asks in disbelief, even though they feel as natural as she can imagine a woman's breast would feel; she hasn't ever felt any, and hers are too flat to use as a comparison.

"You can do more than just rub on them," she says, taking Heaven by the hand and leading her down a short hall into her bedroom scented with a pluggable Wallflower—Caribbean Escape.

Nicolette glides her body across her western king bed and says, "Come here."

Heaven crawls on top of the down comforter.

Nicolette wriggles over to Heaven and takes Heaven's upper lip in her mouth and sensually sucks it as she uses her soft touch to caress Heaven's lower region. And, at that very moment, in Heaven's mind, no one—not Donovan, not even her nana—could tell her that what she is feeling isn't right, isn't just as good, if not better, than she has ever felt with a man. But it's not until Nicolette's lips travel below Heaven's navel that every nerve in her body erupts with a tingling sensation. It's not until Nicolette's long tongue gently pries open Heaven's other set of lips and zigzags her clitoris before thrusting under her clitoral hood, that Heaven knows for certain she has crossed a point of no return—her G-spot—something she has never felt before, and the mirror on Nicolette's ceiling allows Heaven to see it all for herself.

Nicolette lets her hair loose and Heaven can't help herself. So she closes her eyes as she glides her fingers through Nicolette's hair. She is amazed when she doesn't feel any tracks. Her mind is telling her to pretend it's a man she is with, a man performing the best oral sex she has ever had. But the long hair tells her the truth, so she moves her hands away from Nicolette's hair and places them by her side instead. This way she can keep on pretending—pretending that Nicolette is a real man the same way she pretends Donovan is one. He may have balls, but he doesn't have character.

In the morning, Heaven awakes to the smell of fried bacon. She stretches her hands across soft king-sized sheets and then sits on the edge of the bed, reaching her arms toward the ceiling. She doesn't want to think about what happened the night before.

Heaven wishes she could blame her actions on the brownies. Her high only provided her with the excuse of acting out something she'd recently become curious about.

A text comes in from Donovan.

Where r u? hope not with that bitch. i'm sorry i was wrong last night & i miss u

She reads the message and sends back a response.

"Good morning," Nicolette says once Heaven enters the kitchen. "Breakfast is almost ready." Heaven brushes past her as Nicolette tries to kiss her on the cheek. "I'm making you hash brown egg bake with bacon on the side and sliced cantaloupe."

"You got up all early and did this?" asks Heaven.

"I love to cook. I'm in culinary school." Nicolette smiles at Heaven as she drags herself to the table and sits down.

Heaven notices a small wrapped box. "That's for you," Nicolette says.

"For me? When did you have time to do this?"

"Never underestimate the power of a stripper."

"I hope you're not giving me a gift some man gave you."

"When you open it you'll see I'm not."

"I put on your robe—I hope that's okay?"

Nicolette places a plate in front of Heaven and sits at the table across from her. "That's why I laid it on the bed for you."

"Aren't you going to eat?"asks Heaven.

"I forgot the orange juice." Nicolette jumps up and rushes to the refrigerator for the juice. "I nibble while I'm cooking. I like to nibble. I'm sure you could tell."

"Oh God, I don't feel good this morning," says Heaven, grabbing her forehead. "I don't even feel like eating."

"You felt like eating last night."

"Ugh, stop. . . . I was high, so don't get it twisted. I'm not a lesbian."

Nicolette sets a glass of orange juice in front of Heaven. "It's not as if you didn't know what you were doing. You've gotten high before. Lots of times, I'm sure."

"Yeah, but I don't mess with weed that much anymore."

"Oh, okay," Nicolette says, shaking her head and rolling her eyes.

"What's wrong with you?"

"I figured you would play the victim today. So typical. This is the very reason I don't mess around with straight chicks. Well, I know one thing—I didn't rape you."

"I didn't say you did. Chill. I was talking about the weed, not you. Are you okay? Are you on your period or something?"

"No, I'm not on my period. Why? Did you taste blood or something?" Nicolette asks with attitude.

Heaven's eyes roll. "Please stop talking like that," Heaven says. "I was just checking to make sure you're feeling okay."

"I'm okay. I guess."

"It's cool. We're friends."

"Friends?" Nicolette says with attitude. "I thought we were a little more than that."

"Are you serious? You know I have a man."

"You mean little d?"

Heaven smiles. "Please don't take this the wrong way, but I can't imagine giving up dick, even if it's little. Some is better than none at all."

Nicolette tosses her a look filled with rage. "It's my own fault. Trina told me you were straight, but—" She sighs and shakes her head.

"But what? Say it."

"She said you were curious."

"She said *I* was curious?" Heaven spits out laughter. "She's crazy if she said that."

"Yeah, I guess you told her one time that you were or something— I don't know."

"I don't ever remember saying that."

"All I've ever been with is a woman," Nicolette says quietly. "I don't even know what it's like to be with a man. Never even used a dildo."

Heaven had been with a handful of guys sexually, and each time she convinced herself after she'd started having sex with them that she was in love . . . only, once the relationship was over, she regretted everything . . . regretted knowing them, let alone becoming intimate.

"So how do you dance for men if you're not attracted to them?" Heaven asks.

"Dancing and having sex are two different things. Dancing is a job that I have to do two nights a week so I can go to school and pay my bills. The pay is good, and nobody else is hiring, at least not where I can make an easy two grand a week. If it wasn't for all the money I would lose, I wouldn't care if the city council ordinance did pass, because I hate giving lap dances and I don't mind keeping my distance from those men."

"I'ma tell you something," says Heaven, sticking a forkful of hash brown egg bake into her mouth. "But don't let it go to your head."

"I already know what you're going to say—you like my cooking."

"Yeah, I do, but that's not all I like. . . . I never liked kissing, but"—Heaven's eyes drop to her plate—"I really liked kissing you for some reason." She stares at Nicolette.

"That's just because I took your virginity."

Heaven laughs. "Nah, sorry, but that's been gone."

"I'm your first woman, though, right?" she says with a wink. "And hopefully your last. Now, open your gift."

Heaven slowly opens the package. "I knew it was perfume."

"You didn't know it was perfume."

"I knew it was perfume, and I knew it was DKNY." Heaven puts her nose to the bottle. "A man has never given me a bottle of perfume before."

"And whose fault is that?"

Heaven shrugs. "I guess mine. . . . I guess mine." And it was also Heaven's fault for replying to Donovan's text in the morning with a lie that she was staying at Hope's. Her confidence that he would believe that lie only proved he didn't really know much about her or her family matters, because if he did, he'd know there was no way that could even be remotely possible.

She feels guilty for being with a woman. . . . She feels guilty like the first time she smoked a joint, because now she has to question her sexuality. She has to wonder, just seconds ago when Nicolette said after breakfast she was going to take her into her bedroom with a can of whipped cream for a special dessert, why she was already game to continue what they'd started early that morning. Now, she has to question what the Bible says about homosexuality, since she already knows what her nana says. And then, suddenly her entire misguided life flashes before her—not just that she kissed a girl and enjoyed it, and did a lot more than just kiss a girl and still enjoyed it, but everything else she has done as well. She looks into Nicolette's eyes and envies her for knowing who she is and what she wants. She wonders when she'll be in that same place.

Chung's mini egg rolls are warming in the oven. Alicia stands at the bar that separates her kitchen from the living room as she oversees Benita making each of her friends a drink. Benita mixes together one and a half ounces of Absolut Los Angeles vodka in a highball glass with ice, adding an ounce of cranberry and pomegranate juice, along with a little lemon-lime soda and a dash of lime juice to create an Absolut La La Land. But Alicia doesn't want a drink, not even a nonalcoholic one. All she wants is some crushed ice. She takes a highball glass from the counter and fills it with crushed ice from the ice dispenser on the refrigerator door.

"If we were playing Family Feud, we'd all get the top answer right," one of Alicia's friends says as she relaxes on the sofa. "Except maybe not you," she tells Benita.

"What do you mean not me?" asks Benita. "What is the question?"

She slides two fossil stone drink coasters in front of the ladies on either side of her and deepens her voice in an impersonation of a game show host. "Ladies, we surveyed the top one hundred Hollywood agents, and the top three answers are on the board. Name *something* a black actress can't get in Hollywood to save her life."

Both ladies slam their hands down on the drink coaster at the same time, and the friend pretending to be the host makes a sound to simulate a buzzer.

"A leading role," both women shout.

"Show me leading role," the game show host says as she stands and looks at the bare wall behind them.

"Bing," says the host. "Number one answer: leading role. The next answer is supporting role and the final answer is any damn role."

"You could have said black and Latina," says Benita.

"Look, you have to admit Latina actresses don't have it as hard as black actresses. I'm sorry," one of the ladies says. "You all can even play our roles."

"How can we play your roles? You just said you don't get any damn roles," Benita replies jokingly.

"You're not lying."

Alicia's actress friends, a group of nine women not including Benita, are gabbing away about the industry while the mellifluous music of Maxwell's plays in the background. This is a monthly get-together, and the women always take turns hosting, usually on a Tuesday. The gathering started with Alicia's idea of a book-to-movie book club, but after half the members came to the first two meetings without reading the books, it transformed into a bitch-fest about Hollywood that everyone seemed to enjoy more than discussing books. But now, at least for Alicia, all their trash-talking is getting old.

Alicia holds up a copy of *Dewey: The Small Town Library Cat who Touched the World*. "We need to get back to being a book-to-movie club. I, for one, thought it was a good idea and something that could help us with our craft, especially if during our book discussion we act out the various roles. But our book club has turned into a bitching club."

"Your girl Meryl is supposed to be in that movie," says one of the women, referring to the book Alicia is holding. "And I, for one, am tired of reading the books of movies I auditioned for and didn't get a part in. So it's a lot more fun just to bitch about everything."

"Constantly complaining will get us nowhere." Alicia slams the paperback down on the granite countertop. "I'm trying to keep this positive."

"More vodka," says a young woman standing in the hallway near the entrance to the bathroom. "That should keep things positive."

"Look, we all know the Hollywood formula—it's simple," Alicia says. "Once you prove you can make money, you can make movies, regardless of who you are. Now that we have a black president, do you think I'm going to stand here and make excuses over a movie role?"

"Honestly," one of the women says, "I'm ready to give up. Look at the type of roles that are offered to black women. We can't win for losing. If we take a role that's perceived as being negative by our community, then we have to hear about how we let black folks down for playing a stereotype when all we're trying to do is work in this town and pay our bills like everybody else. Is it my fault that society is so narrow-minded that if some people simply see me playing a prostitute they'll think that means all black women are prostitutes? That's so stupid. I'm playing a character. It's a role, people! It would be one thing if there weren't any black prostitutes, but there are, so why can't I bring her story to life? Some of our people have so many hang-ups." She is venting about the last role she played, which she'd been so happy to secure. It was in a big film with a big budget, and she played a supporting role and got a pretty decent check to do so, but when the film was released, many of the bloggers and critics found her portrayal to be a setback for the black community and to black women in particular. "To say that it's time for black actresses to start turning down these roles isn't fair to us. If I'd turned down that role, I would've starved and so would my daughter. We are still eating from the money I earned off that role. I'm still paying my rent with that money and the movie was released last year. I'd rather play a prostitute than be so broke I really have to become one."

A young woman says, "And you better believe, if you hadn't taken that role, some other black woman would have. Hell, I probably would've. So it's a Catch-22. A white woman can play any kind of role, from a prostitute to the queen. It's just that we need more roles offered to us where we're playing a queen and fewer as prostitutes and drug addicts—a healthy balance. Personally, I'm still waiting for a movie on Madam C. J. Walker. That's one woman I want to play." She stands and says, 'I am a woman who came from the cotton fields of the South. From there I was promoted to the washtub. From there I was promoted to the cook kitchen. And from there I promoted myself into the business of manufacturing hair goods and preparations. . . . I have built my own factory on my own ground.' I have that taped on my mirror at my home. It's inspirational; she was the first black female millionaire and I want a casting director to try to tell me I can't play her."

"I think most studios would pass on a movie like that," says the woman who played the prostitute, "because they'll feel like they can't make money."

"Well, the studios aren't always right."

"True, but if you don't have an opportunity to make the movie to prove you can make the studio some money, then what? Why do I have to suffer because some black movie may have bombed and cost the studio money? It's a ten-year waiting period between roles for all but a handful of us because of that."

God, they sound so much like Alicia did last year. *Excuses, excuses*, muses Alicia. "Aubrey," Alicia says. "She's a perfect example of a black actress doing her thing." Aubrey may not have the best reputation, but she was making her mark just the same.

"Aubrey?" asks one of the women in laughter. "Is Aubrey black? Because if she is, this is the first I've heard."

"You've got to be kiddin' me," says Alicia. "Of course she's black. What did you think she was?"

The young woman shrugs. "I'm just telling you she doesn't acknowledge any race."

"It's not that she doesn't acknowledge her race," says Alicia, coming to the quick defense of her friend as usual. "It's just that she doesn't want to be typecast." And sometimes Alicia didn't blame her. Sometimes, Alicia wonders if it's time for her to lighten the color of her hair from chestnut brown to light strawberry blond; to transform herself into a society-friendly black female—one of the kind that have viewers assuming they're not black at all, or if they are, not all black; the kind that land on soap operas and get paired up with white men, but also the kind that are often hard-pressed to find their place in Hollywood because they aren't "black enough" or "white enough."

"Well, some of us don't have the luxury. I don't think people will ever wonder what race I am. And I wouldn't want to make it by pretending to be something I'm not. It's one thing to change your name, but your race is part of your identity."

Alicia had thought Aubrey was taking the "hater" term too far when she'd accuse actresses of hating her because she landed roles that many black actresses couldn't. But now she understands what Aubrey was saying. When Aubrey's name is mentioned, usually a black actress would clear her throat or change the subject. No one had to like her, Aubrey would always say, as long as the box office did.

Alicia wondered on many occasions how Aubrey managed to fool the audience. Perhaps she did so because she claimed to be a little bit of everything: Native American, Italian, Irish, French, and only if someone pressed the issue would she say her mother is part Jamaican. It gave her the right to avoid the issue of race and let her "exotic" looks speak volumes. No one could say for sure what she was, not even her Wikipedia page. She was that ambiguous.

But Alicia isn't fooled. She knows Aubrey's black and so are both of her parents. Now, what's in Aubrey's family line, she has no idea, because Alicia doesn't even know what's in her own.

"I think it's pretty hard for any woman in Hollywood, regardless of race. Older women, especially after thirty-five, forget it, unless you're Meryl Streep," says one of the women. Several eyes aim toward her like missiles ready to go on the attack. "But I'm not saying it's not harder for some . . . for us . . . more than others. I mean, I agree it is. Black women definitely can't catch a break."

"Latinas either," Benita adds.

Alicia says, "Right now the two of you sound like you're playing a game of 'who has it the hardest.'"

"Sounds like it might be fun if some men were here to play along with us," adds Benita.

"Name one black leading lady making the kind of money Meryl Streep does with a career like hers," says another woman.

"Is that racism?" asks Alicia. "Or is that talent on the part of Meryl Streep?"

"What's so great about Meryl Streep?"

Alicia's nostrils begin to flare. Meryl Streep is the reason she's acting. "Are you ignorant?" she says sharply. "She is the greatest living actress today."

"I'm ignorant just because I don't like your girl Meryl Streep? Maybe you're ignorant for envying someone you'll never be able to play opposite."

"Okay, so now you're God and you can tell me what's in my future?" says Alicia.

"Yeah, I can. You're with a small agent at a small agency that's crushing your big dreams," the woman says. "You need to take your big dreams to a big agency that can sell you to a big studio and put you in a big film. You've been here for thirteen years. It's time. Like you said, you need to make your own opportunities. All it takes is one break. That's it. If Aubrey can make it, you better make it."

A couple hours after all of her friends have left, Alicia, nursing a fresh glass of crushed ice, receives a text message from Heaven.

It's my birthday and this fool has the nerve to take me to Lou's....I love Lou's like the next person from the D, but not on my birthday!

Alicia smiles as she shakes her head and sends back a text that starts a chain of back and forth texts:

isn't it the thought that counts?

when it was his birthday he wanted a gift not a thought!

enjoy your counterman's treat!

:-) …Ha Ha …I see U remember Lou's

of course …my fav!

i don't get a specialty sandwich I like to make it my way … since it's the only thing I can make my way … unlike my life.

on onion roll i hope

always!!!!!

Two thousand miles away, at three o'clock in the morning Heaven listens to "Pretty Wings" on the car radio. She adjusts the volume so the song isn't blaring through the speakers while she sits in Donovan's Jaguar, peering out the window. She is waiting in the parking lot of a strip mall on Greenfield where Lou's Deli is located.

A text message from Nicolette comes through minutes after she finishes sending her last text to Alicia.

Heaven forages through the glove compartment in order to satisfy her curiosity about the car. Going from a 2004 Ford Taurus to a brand-new Jaguar is quite an upgrade. *Whose car is this?* she wonders as she sniffs the new-car smell. There's no registration; not even an owner's manual. Now what Heaven smells isn't quite as pleasant. Something's definitely fishy.

She watches Donovan as he negotiates his way around a few passing cars and steps from the walkway into the strip mall's parking lot. He's at the driver's door before she has a chance to turn off Maxwell.

"It's my birthday," says Heaven, her voice rising with frustration, "so please don't turn the station."

With a wave of his hand he responds, "Go ahead, girl. I don't care what you listen to." He puts the greasy bag on Heaven's lap.

"Stop, you're going to stain my dress."

"If it stains your dress, I'll buy you another one. But I definitely don't want the carpet or these leather seats to get stained."

"You haven't bought me anything yet."

"Stop lying. I just bought you a corned beef sandwich."

Her lips purse as she rolls her eyes. "I hope you remembered to tell them to put it on an onion roll."

"I told them whatever you told me to tell them," he says as he pulls off.

She rummages through the bag. "Well, then how come I don't see an onion roll in here?"

"It's not in there?" asks Donovan as he pulls both sandwiches from the bag after he stops at the first light he approaches.

"No, it's not, so go back."

"I'm not going back for a damn onion roll. Why do you want stinky breath anyway?"

"It's my birthday," Heaven says, darting her eyes in his direction. "I want my sandwich the way I want it on my birthday. Can't I get anything the way I want even on my own birthday? What kind of birthday is this anyway? It's three in the morning and we're just getting out. And don't tell me you had business to take care of either. What kind of business? What do you really do? Where did this car come from? Do you know there are women in this world who get cars like this for their birthday? I can't even get a bottle of perfume. Not even get a sandwich made the way I want. A six-dollar sandwich."

"Eight dollars."

"Eight dollars, and that's my birthday present?"

"Trust me, I'm going to give you something the way you want it when we get home."

"Don't bother," she says, rolling her eyes. "'Cause I don't get that the way I want it either."

"Oh, I'm going to put it on you real good tonight. Trust me," he says, rubbing her thigh.

She knocks his hand away from her thigh. "Put it on the onion roll I was supposed to have. I hate you. I really do, because this relationship ain't shit and neither are you."

"There you go. . . . There you go with that smart-ass mouth I'm sick of."

"I don't have a smart mouth. All I'm doing is telling the truth. I hate you," she screams. "I don't know what my problem is. I don't know why I can't just leave your ass."

Another text message comes through, the third in a matter of seconds. Donovan snatches Heaven's cell phone out of her hand. "What's up with all these texts?"

"Give me back my phone," Heaven says, trying to snatch the phone away.

Donovan slaps Heaven's hand away and toggles through her text messages. "'Enjoyed last night, baby . . . even better than the first time. Can't wait to see you again'?" he says, reading the first text. "'You taste so good. Luv, Nicolette,'" he says, reading the second text. "'Glad to be your first. If you ever miss getting dick, I can always break down and buy a dildo. . . . Trust me, I'll put it on you better than your man D with the little d does.'"

"That shouldn't be too hard to do," mumbles Heaven.

Donovan swerves to avoid hitting a car.

"So, what, are you really some kind of lesbian?"

"At least she bought me a bottle of expensive perfume."

"So what? I paid your electric bill."

"So, you needed to. . . . You might as well say you live there, just like me. Besides, you want your money back. Her perfume was just because."

He pulls his car over, stops, and unlocks the passenger door. "Get your ghetto ass out of my car. You let a bitch lick your pussy for some perfume? You two hos deserve each other."

Heaven takes in her surroundings. "I'm not getting out. Take me home."

"Call your bitch and tell her to come get you. Just get out," he says calmly. "And don't forget your birthday present." He tosses the bag out of the car on the curb as soon as Heaven steps out. She stands at the overpass of the Lodge Freeway. Several cars blow their horns as they pass by and view their exchange.

She picks the paper bag off the ground and throws it at his back window as he drives off.

Several minutes later, she is sitting inside a nearby White Castle with her cell phone up to her ear. She could have called Nicolette, but she didn't want to use her for a ride when she knows Nicolette is hoping for more. She prayed before dialing her sister's digits that she'd pick up.

"Hope, I need you to do me a favor. I need you to please come pick me up from White Castle. I'm at the one on Greenfield—the one by the Lodge. I'm stranded. I called Trina, but she has her cell turned off. I called your home phone and left you a message there too. I don't have anybody else to call."

Forty minutes later, Hope pulls her sunflower yellow Beetle into White Castle's parking lot and Heaven walks out.

"Thank you, thank you, thank you," Heaven says as soon as she opens the front passenger door and slides inside.

"Shh, Havana's asleep." Heaven turns and sees Havana balled up on the backseat with her head sticking out from a light blue blanket. "She's not feeling well."

"You could have left her at home."

"At four in the morning? Is that the kind of mother you'd be, the kind to run off and leave your child home alone with all the stuff happening in the world today?" Heaven sits quietly, leans her head against the headrest, and closes her eyes. "Doesn't it feel good to be able to close your eyes and rest while someone else does the driving?

Unfortunately, your little mishap cut into my sleep time, but I still have to get up bright and early to go to work. Have you found a job yet?" Heaven shakes her head while her eyes are still shut. "Don't you think you need to be looking for one? Or are you planning to live off unemployment? You do realize that the extension to those benefits will eventually run out?"

Heaven nods. She wanted to tell Hope about their sister Alicia, but the more she listens to her go on and on about the sleep she is being deprived of and Heaven's soon-to-be-dwindling unemployment benefits, she figures now is not the time.

Heaven circles the Coleman A. Young Municipal Center two and a half times. She passes the twenty-five-foot bronze *Spirit of Detroit* statue twice before lucking out on a metered space on Jefferson Avenue close to the entrance.

She parallel parks between an Action News 7 truck and a Jeep Wrangler. So Donovan thinks he can toss her out his car in the wee hours of the morning in the city of Detroit? She'll show him what a move like that will cost.

"Hey, girl," says Heaven to Alicia. "Is it a good time to talk?" Her cell phone is resting on the passenger seat and she has Alicia on speakerphone. "It's been a bad week for me."

Alicia yawns. "It's kinda early here. I had some friends over last night, and then you started texting me." Heaven picks up her cell phone and looks at the time. A three-hour difference means it's ten in the morning there. "Why don't you give me your number and I'll call you sometime today after I wake up?"

"Don't you still have my text messages?" asks Heaven.

"Oh, that's right, I do, so I'll call you later. Is everything okay?"

"Yeah, I'm okay. Don't forget to call me," urges Heaven. She thought about telling Alicia that she was downtown filing a PPO and asking her if she'd ever had to do something like that, especially since she's an actress. Maybe she has a stalker. She wanted to talk to someone about this because she's nervous. This could get Donovan in some serious trouble, she imagines.

She looks at the meter and realizes she doesn't have any money— not one quarter to her name. She curses because she knows for sure that even if she doesn't have to stand in a long line once she gets inside the twenty-story building, just getting where she needs to go will take longer than the ten minutes remaining on the meter. She can only pray the meter maid goes to lunch while she's inside, or that he or she isn't dedicated to his or her job, even though she's never known a meter maid to be lax. She knows she will probably get a ticket, but what other choice does she have?

She wants to do this today. She can't put this off. If she does, she may never do it. She has to file a personal protection order against Donovan. This morning was the last straw.

As soon as she steps from her car, her nose is seduced by the aroma of sautéed onions coming from the corner hot dog stand. Her mouth begins to water as if she's a dog in a Pavlovian experiment, as she recalls from a Psych 101 class during her one and only semester at Wayne County Community College. And now she has a sudden urge for a hot dog, especially one with sauerkraut, and of course, onions. She loves onions so much that she could eat one whole; take a bite out of a Vidalia as if it were a candy apple. When she was a kid, she'd always get teased for eating raw onions—mostly by Hope, who'd hold her nose while she told Heaven her breath stank. But Heaven would blow her hot breath into her own cupped hands and in her mind smell nothing but freshness . . . onion-scented breath that didn't stink at all. Besides, she brushed her teeth after every meal and every onion. An apple a day might keep the doctor away, but an onion a day would keep everyone else away, Hope would tease. Heaven tried to convince her sister that onions were healthy. And that she'd found a beauty secret. When all the girls were suffering through adolescence with pimpled skin, she was quite the opposite. Heaven never worried about acne.

She studies the menu board at the hot dog stand. A juicy New York–style hot dog is only one dollar and a Polish sausage is only two dollars and fifty cents. The meal is cheap. But again, she doesn't even have a quarter to her name. Such a shame, Heaven thinks as she heads toward the Jefferson Avenue entrance of the Coleman A. Young Municipal Center, only to discover everyone must enter through Larned Street—just one more thing to take away needed time from her meter.

There are a few officers standing near the entrance. Several visitors are filing in line. A metal detector and a conveyor belt put Heaven in a different frame of mind. She realizes the people working there mean business, and so should she.

Eyes immediately attack her large red canvas purse—her favorite carryall that has the white hearts all over it. She even has a wallet inside to match. Heaven has loved purses ever since she turned eight and Angelica, her childhood best friend, bought her a pink one for her birthday. She still has that little purse with her first Bible inside. Heaven attaches herself to certain things that motivate her. Much of her casual clothing is inspirational. The red tank top she has on says STAY STRONG. She feels most comfortable wearing bright colors; red and pink are two of her favorites. Sometimes, she wishes she could be more stylish, like her sister Hope who always coordinates and always has the perfect accessory for every item in her wardrobe. For Heaven, jewelry is an unnecessary distraction and for as long as she can remember, her skin has never liked the feel. However, her earlobes tolerate earrings; she prefers a pair that dangle without being too busy. She's never owned a watch, opting instead to tell time mostly through the aid of her cell phone. And if her skin could tolerate a necklace without itching, she'd wear a cross so she could feel closer to God. Regretfully, she has a few tattoos, but she's been using fade cream on the one on her neck of Donovan's name—a gradual process, but she's looking forward to the day when she wakes up and the tattoo, as well as the man who inspired it, is gone from her life.

"You can't come in here with that," the officer says sternly. She wishes Hope could be there to see what she is seeing; a man towering over her, at least six feet tall, fine and black, wearing a uniform. They really do exist, just like she'd been trying to tell her sister. Fine, black men with decent jobs are real. Even through his unsmiling expression, he's beautiful. She would attempt to flirt, but he seems like the type who takes his job way too seriously and would end up arresting Heaven on some bogus charge like disorderly conduct.

She firmly clutches the bamboo handles. "This?" asks Heaven for clarification. She is slightly confused as to why a purse wouldn't be allowed inside.

"Yes, that. Do you have a camera cell phone?" he asks. She nods. "Can't come in here with that either. We'd have to confiscate them both."

"When will I get 'em back?"

"You won't."

She tucks her heart bag closer to her side. "So what am I supposed to do?"

"You can come back," he says as he hands her a sheet of paper that lists all of the prohibited items.

She quickly scans the sheet, slowing down at items she knows she has such as a mirror and comb. She doesn't have any alcoholic beverages, at least not today. And she has no ammunition, of course. As for the aerosol or spray devices, she does have a fairly new ten-ounce bottle of Pantene Relaxed & Natural intensive oil spray that she just treated herself to the day before her birthday so that she can try to bring the life back into her dull micro braids. She doesn't have any cigarettes—she doesn't smoke. Nor does she have any brass knuckles, but in that case, Donovan's hands should be prohibited from entering. Yes, there it is; she sees it for herself—no large bags of any kind including duffel bags, backpacks, and oversized purses.

She pats her purse and tells the officer, "I'll come back." She folds the full sheet of paper into tiny squares small enough to fit inside her organizer wallet that matches her purse. She tries to stick the folded paper into one of the many slots—the one behind her freshly reinstated driver's license, but there's something already stuck down in her hidden compartment preventing her from doing so. She pulls the paper square out and then pulls out another paper. Her eyes pop. Folded down to an inch square is a five-dollar bill she remembers hiding for a rainy day so long ago she forgot it was there.

She rushes out of the building, heading to the hot dog stand on the corner of Woodward Avenue and Jefferson, in front of the *Spirit of Detroit* statue. She tries to decide whether to buy two hot dogs, a soda and a bag of chips for three dollars and fifty cents or one Polish sausage with a soda and chips for fifty cents extra. She'll take the change in quarters and feed the meter, hide her purse under the seat out of view, and start the afternoon over—heading back inside the Coleman A. Young Municipal Center without her oversized purse or any of the prohibited items. And hopefully, she'll follow through. But first things first—she needs to eat. Food is fuel for the body and hers is on empty.

"Give me plenty of onions," says Heaven while her eyes scan the condiments.

He nods. "What else do you want on it?"

"Everything . . . and more onions . . . Just smother both hot dogs in onions. And let the onions be the last topping."

"Any chili?"

She nods. "Just a little." She watches him spread on the chopped grilled onions. "More than that please, and I want raw onions too."

"More than this?" asks the man, his plastic spoon frozen over her hot dog. She nods as she sheepishly lowers her eyes, realizing her request is slightly unreasonable. "Okay, but I'll have to charge you an extra fifty cents."

"That's fine. May I have my change back in quarters, please?"

He nods. He prepares the hot dogs the way she wants them, bags everything up, and hands the bag to her along with her change.

She devours the first hot dog near the stand in just three bites. The flavor still lingers as her mouth breeds an odor unknown to man.

She strolls back to her car, cupping the second hot dog wrapped in aluminum foil in her right hand. A brown paper lunch bag with an unopened can of Faygo grape soda and an empty bag of Better Made sour cream and onion potato chips is inside her purse. The hot dog is so good she wishes she had enough money for a third one and a tip. But she doesn't. She only has enough for the two-hour limit on the meter. She spots the meter maid a mere one parked car away from hers. She wants to sprint to her car, but her hot dog is just too good to waste, and even if she attempted to run, the toppings piled mountainously high with one flimsy napkin tucked underneath the foil would make a mess all over her. So she downs the dog like she's in a hot-dog-eating contest—one bite and a few chews is all it takes—and she hightails her wide hips to the meter. She starts shoving in four quarters at the same time the meter maid pulls up beside her, steps from her three-wheeled vehicle, and just as Heaven feeds the last quarter into the slot, slaps a ticket on Heaven's windshield.

"But I just put money in," says Heaven.

"I was already writing out the ticket. Sorry."

"You're still going to give me a ticket even though I put money in?" Heaven asks with irritation.

"I was already writing the ticket. Sorry."

"This is unbelievable. Just because the city's broke I have to help pay for it? Whatever—"

"I'm just—"

"Doing your job, I know. But just because you're just doing your job doesn't mean you're doing a good job of it." Heaven huffs off. "That b—" Heaven almost uses the b-word, but as many times as she's heard Donovan call a female that, she just can't. She gets into her car and drives away. "I don't need this in my life today." There are too many signs that she shouldn't even be there . . . that a PPO isn't the answer. Monday is Memorial Day. Maybe that's what she should be concentrating on. Visiting her mother at the cemetery. She'll need to bring flowers. And she'll need to call Hope to see if she wants to come along. She calls her while she heads home. And surprisingly, she answers her phone.

"Yes, what do you need now?" snaps Hope.

"I wanted to know if you wanted to go to the cemetery with me to see Momma on Monday."

"I see Momma all the time. I don't just wait till the holiday rolls around. So no. You can go alone." Before Heaven can say another word, Hope hangs up.

June

Hope drives to historic Indian Village—a neighborhood comprising just three streets with more than three hundred fifty homes. A few of the former residents are prominent Detroiters—Edsel Ford, Arthur Buhl, and Bernard Stroh. The homes, many of which have been restored, were remarkably designed by some of Detroit's most renowned architects. Mostly all are very well maintained, escaping the rumors of blight that plague so many Detroit neighborhoods.

At six fifteen in the evening, she parks in front of a 1912 Albert Kahn–designed Georgian Revival complete with carriage house. She arrives early—fifteen minutes before most. She knows she is at the right place. An antique wooden sign is planted in the front yard—KAREN'S HOUSE.

Upon entering, she notices catered food being placed on a long buffet table in the spacious dining room. She is surprised, as Ezra had mentioned going out for dinner afterward. He'd asked her nicely one day after he phoned her at the bank if she wanted to attend grief counseling with him. Hope was hesitant at first, but then the more she thought about it, the more she wondered if sitting around with

141

a group of people experiencing the same emotions as she was really would help. That's why she's there . . . to find out.

On an accent table near the entrance is a stack of self-adhesive HELLO MY NAME IS stickers and several black felt-tip pens. She takes one of each and writes down her name. She sits quietly in the spacious foyer in a black cherry–stained wood bench with spindle backing. Her elbow is resting against the bent arm of the bench as she admires the elaborately carved wood moldings and the Pewabic-tiled flooring.

Ezra enters a few minutes later in a casual long-sleeved button-down shirt, black denim jeans, and a newsboy cap. She smiles, because she has never seen him dressed so casually. He is always in a suit and tie when he comes by the bank.

They take the small elevator up two flights. She and Ezra are the only ones inside. Her emotions are mixed. She is nervous because she feels like she is on a first date, which also makes her feel awkward, because as most first dates go, she doesn't know Ezra, not on a personal level. She knows him as a customer at the bank and as someone who is experiencing a significant loss just as she is, but that is the extent of her knowledge about him. The elevator seems to travel more slowly than it should. She doesn't want to peer at him; she is sure he gets tired of having people constantly stare him down to sum up his burns. But in her case she isn't looking at his burns. She wants to watch his stance, marvel at his confidence, connect to his strength. She glances up at him and he smiles at her. "Are you okay?" he asks. She nods. Eventually the elevator doors open directly into the enormous ballroom that is larger than her entire house.

The thirty-person group, which includes children, forms a prayer circle in the center of the room. A woman inside the prayer circle starts off the prayer. "Lord our God, we grieve. Today and every day we mourn. But in the midst of our sadness, we know that you are there. And so we give thanks to you, dear Lord, for bringing us together so that we may talk through our grief. We are no longer alone with our pain. Together we will and must press on, for it is the will of the Lord, the will of he who is with us when we laugh, and also with us when we cry. Lord our God, hear our prayers."

Collectively, the group reads from the Book of Ecclesiastes. And although Ezra previously asked Hope to bring her Bible, she accidentally left hers in her car, so she reads along with him.

> To everything there is a season,
> A time for every purpose under heaven;
> A time to be born, a time to die;
> A time to plant, and a time to pluck up what is planted;
> A time to weep and a time to laugh;
> A time to mourn and a time to dance.

The group is ushered downstairs for an informal dinner catered by a well-established seafood restaurant less than two miles away. Guests can select from broiled pork chops, boneless breast of chicken, and New Zealand orange roughy. As Hope mills through the buffet line, she scantily prepares her plate. Ezra asks, "Is that all you're eating?" He picks out a bottle of water from an ice bucket and hands it to her.

"Where's your plate?" she rebuts.

"I promised you dinner after, remember?"

She nods. "And I didn't want to get too full, so I'm not going to eat much here."

"But you're thin enough that you can stand to eat twice," Ezra teases.

She smiles. She's used to the comments about her wispy frame, and it's never really bothered her. She knows she eats. She eats three times a day and usually has dessert. But she can't seem to keep any weight on.

They break off into groups—adults in one, children in the other. The children meet in the library on the opposite side of the house, away from the adults. The adults convene in the spacious sitting room in the front of the house. Hope chooses the center cushion on the sofa facing the onyx fireplace. Ezra sits to the right of her, and an older woman sits to her left. It quickly becomes Hope's responsibility as the new person to stand and introduce herself—to share her story, but only if she is "ready," they say, to which she responds, "I'm not at this time."

Ezra is the first to start. As he will later tell her, he is always the first. Some of the mourners share their story every time they come, and he is one of those.

"For me, I think, the hardest part is that I didn't go with them," Ezra says from his seat. "The burns don't bother me that much. Some people think if I weren't burned, I wouldn't have to look at myself and see the accident every day. But being normal wouldn't make it easier for me to go on. There are days and weeks that I don't look at myself, but there's not one day that I don't see the accident. The moments leading up to the accident, I can't remember. I don't remember the impact. I don't remember being ejected from the car. But I do remember seeing the car burning with my family still inside, and my being pulled back away from the flames. I remember running toward the car and the heat, and then the next thing I know I'm in the hospital. People tell me all the time, 'Oh, you're so lucky to have survived. . . . You could have walked away with no burns, nothing, if you hadn't tried to save your family.'" He shakes his head as tears surface. "Well, I don't feel so lucky." Hope places her hand on top of his and interlocks their fingers.

Hope's intense stare tells the woman leading the group that she has something to say.

"Hope, are you ready to share your story?"

She nods, starting by first clearing her throat. Then, she says, "I found out about my husband's accident through my friend Taite. I'll never forget her voice . . . her screams . . . words I could barely make out at first. She was crying, but it wasn't like a cry that you've heard before. It was a sound that someone would make if they were in intense pain . . . maybe if they were dying themselves. . . . Two state troopers had just left her house, and they had told her that her husband was dead. Then I heard my doorbell ring and I answered it while she was still on the line. But when they told me the same thing, I dropped the phone. My knees buckled—here I was again, feeling just as alone as I did when my mother was killed.

"I was so afraid . . . with that same fear I had of my father. The fear that he'd turn the gun he'd used on my mother on me and my little sister was the same fear I had right then. It felt like murder. They had recovered the boat, but only one person survived. They didn't have my husband's body or Taite's husband's body . . . just life jackets and personal items. . . . How could I believe my husband was dead when I didn't have his body to bury? And if he is dead, Michael Beck killed him. One day my husband was there with me laughing, and the next day he was gone.

"I try to tell myself that if he died, at least he died doing something he loved. He went fishing near Ludington Harbor on Lake Michigan for king salmon and steelhead. But then I get angry and ask myself why they would take a twenty-one-foot Everglades fishing boat out so far. Didn't they know better?" she asks, as tears begin to form. "No, I don't have closure. I don't even have a body to bury, so I can't have closure, and knowing there's a man out there somewhere, a man who knows exactly what happened but isn't talking, tears at my soul.

"I tried contacting him. . . . In the beginning I called his house a bunch of times, but then one day his phone number was disconnected. The news talked about it for about a week, but before long it faded from the headlines. The media may not care anymore. Even my friend Taite has moved on. But I haven't. I need to know what happened. I'm angry, because I didn't have a chance to have a life with my husband. I'm a widow at the age of twenty-seven, so why wouldn't I be angry?"

Later that evening, she trails behind Mr. Hansen's car in hers to the downtown Detroit Fish Market. He orders two meals and insists she try to eat more than she did at Karen's House. They are both quiet—unusually so, and drastically different—changed—from the way they are at the bank. The group therapy, at least for her, had been draining. She didn't know what possessed her to speak, let alone bring up things from her childhood. What must he think of her, she wonders. Would he really have believed she could have a mother murdered at the hands of her father? He must think she's a nutcase. Then her husband disappears.... What kind of evilness does she breed? Why would he want to be her friend now? He has his own problems. He has no time for hers.

He studies her mannerisms; he observes how her fork rolls over her food, prodding and jabbing but never moving in the direction of her mouth. "Here," he says, taking an extra fork, stabbing a fried scallop, and placing the scallop to her lips. "Please eat." She reluctantly opens her mouth and pulls the scallop off the fork. "Now, that wasn't so bad, was it?"

"I eat. Sometimes, I eat a lot. I'm just picky about my food." He nods. She can sense that he's down, and she knows it all started before they left Karen's House.

"Are you okay, Mr. Hansen?"

"Last time I'm saying this—please call me Ezra."

"Ezra? Are you sure?"

He nods. "Calling me Mr. Hansen makes me feel old. I'm only thirty-one." Hope would have never guessed his age, she muses. He is only four years older than she.

He uses his good hand, the left hand, which he is trying to learn to write with, to remove his bifold wallet. Then he slides the wallet over to her.

"Open it. There's a picture of my family inside."

She opens his wallet and gasps at the sight of him. "That was you," she says, sounding nearly as shallow as Rico.

"I'm the same person on the inside," he says. "At least that sounds good, because honestly, I don't think I am the same person." He looks away from her.

"I'm sorry. I didn't mean it like that. This isn't my day. You had a very beautiful family," she says, looking down at his red-haired wife and their infant twins. She studies his image in the photo; the curly locks of golden brown hair are now just a memory. "And you are a very handsome man."

"I *was* a very handsome man, and I had a beautiful family."

She closes the wallet and slides it back over to him. Suddenly, she can't stop staring. He could have made a living modeling before the accident. He was a very handsome man. He still has the same piercingly beautiful brown eyes; not quite the same lips, but close. But that was basically all that remained recognizable. His right ear is just a knot; his nose is bandaged. She touches her nose as she looks at his.

"I'm undergoing some more reconstructive surgery on my nose, and I'll also have more skin grafts on my face, arm, and chest. Those seem never ending. I've had more than thirty so far."

"Oh," Hope says, not knowing what to say.

He shrugs. "It's just a nose."

"You have a nice nose," she says. "Nice hair . . . those big shiny curls."

"Had." The look in his eyes changes as he gazes into her eyes. It is a familiar one that she hasn't seen from a man in two years. He smiles, showing off his straight teeth. "I just want to say thank you."

"What are you thanking me for?"

"For not treating me any differently. You look directly at me. Sometimes, I come to the bank just to be around someone who treats me like everybody else. To think, the first time I went into your bank I was driving by and I needed to get a certified check . . . and there was one of the branches so I went in. And you were so nice to me."

"Well, I don't treat you like I treat everybody else. You should see how I treat some people. Like Rico Johnson . . . and my sister. Those two people are on my hit list."

"Rico Johnson at the bank?"

She waves off the comment. "He's just an employee, but I definitely don't want to bring him or my sister into the conversation."

"Family is important. Whatever the problem is with your sister, you should really try to mend that. Especially with what the two of you have gone through in your childhood."

She shrugs. "I don't want to talk about family. Family should be important. Mine never was, with the exception of my beautiful daughter. I'm not perfect. I've probably stared at a person before that I shouldn't have. You really have to thank my daughter. I learned from her. She sees only inward beauty. She's blind to everything else. I buy her the cutest clothes and all the latest fashions—she'll wear them, but she could care less. In that way, she's like my sister. She's always saying, 'You know, Mom, I don't wear things because of how they make me look. I wear things because of how they make me feel. So I don't care how cute it is. If it's not comfortable, I don't want it.' All my daughter needs is a good children's fantasy novel and she's all set."

He smiles. "Your daughter sounds sweet. I want to meet her."

Hope nods before releasing a big smile. "Okay. We'll see."

He looks down at her plate. "More food?"

"I'm eating," she says as she sticks her fork in a fried scallop and brings it up to her mouth. "So for you it's been four years...."

"Almost five."

"And it hasn't gotten any better? Not even just a little?"

"It has. It's gotten much better, but I go up and down. I tell myself that I was left here because of God's will, and if it's God's will that I didn't die with my family, then there's a reason, and so I need to figure out that reason." He looks down at his plate, picking over his food the same way Hope does. "And once I figure out the reason, I'll be much more complete." He looks up at her. "How about you? Are you accepting it any better?"

"I just need to know what happened. I know Michael Beck will never admit to any foul play, but since he moved and I have no way of reaching him, there's no way for me to find out. I'm just stuck with going over all of this in my mind."

Not that Hope envies Ezra for being there when his family died, but he was able to lay them to rest. All Hope could do when she found out about Roger was wait and pray for the best while feeling completely helpless. But the waiting never ended. She's still stuck in the same mode—still waiting; still praying.

"Maybe we can help each other," says Ezra. "I'd like to be around you outside of the bank if you're okay with that."

She smiles without showing teeth. It's the same smile she had in her kindergarten picture, the first school picture she'd ever had taken, so she hadn't been quite sure what was going on or what to expect. She feels the same way now as his brown eyes pierce hers. She has to respond. "I can't promise anything. I'm just not in the best place right now."

"I'm patient. All I want is your friendship . . . at least for now."

Alicia is in her acting class when suddenly her mind goes blank. She can't remember her lines—just like that. After rehearsing for two hours a day for the past two weeks, she can't even remember the first word. It must be the anticipation of putting up her scene for the first time with cameras present and an unusually full class size. There must be quite a few people auditing the class because she is not used to seeing a packed room. Her scene partner, Rick, landed a part in a reality show and he has cameras following his every move—chronicling the life of struggling actors. He is one of four characters the network will profile. He even tried to stage a little drama the other day between him and Alicia by canceling their rehearsal at the last minute for the third time that week. Before class, he came to her with a consent form to allow the cameras to film her. She had half a mind not to sign the form, but she did. She needed every little bit of exposure she could get.

And now she can't remember her lines, and Rick's almost done with his.

Standing at the table, Alicia peers at Rick who is playing the role of the judge. After the guilty verdict is read, her body goes limp and she uses the table to balance her weight. "I . . . did not kill my husband. I don't care what any of you think you have on me . . . what you think you saw on some doctored-up video recording . . . I can explain all of those things." All her lines came flooding back to her.

"You waived your right to testify."

"I'm innocent. I don't have to take the stand and explain anything to anybody. Because, you see, I know the truth . . . the whole truth . . . so help me God. Not the police. I would never kill my husband. I loved him. I've never broken the law and now I'm hearing people say I may have to spend my entire life in prison. My entire life away from my kids. Who's going to raise them?"

"Remove her from the courtroom."

"Give me back my rights now," she says, struggling with two men acting as bailiffs who attempt to remove her. "I want my rights back. I want to take the stand right now, Your Honor," she says as she looks over at Rick. The two students acting as bailiffs lead her out of the courtroom while she struggles to remain. "Who's going to take care of my kids? The state . . . the same state that convicted their mother? I didn't kill my husband. I am an innocent woman . . . a mother. There's going to be blood on each one of your hands," she says to the audience as if they are members of the jury. "Each one of you is a murderer because you took away my life, and I'm innocent. . . . I'm innocent." Her delivery is perfect. But where are her tears? Why can't she cry? After the first time she'd put up her scene, the instructor noted her delivery as pretty good but had still asked, if she had everything to live for and someone was about to take it all away, how would that make her feel? What emotions? She can't cry, but fear is present. It's in her voice . . . in her eyes. The class can see it. Her scene partner can as well.

After their scene wraps up and Alicia is walking off stage, her instructor approaches her. "There was a director auditing the class tonight. He's very interested in casting you for a role and wanted to speak with you, but he had to leave. Here's his card."

Alicia takes the card and studies it. "Is this for real?"

"Well, you've heard of him, haven't you, so I'd say, yes, it's for real."

"Oh my God," she says, her eyes still on the director's business card. She glances up at her instructor. "Do you mind if I step out and call him right now?"

"Please do. He wanted to hear from you right away."

She rushes to the hallway and fumbles with her cell phone as she slides it from the case. She can't dial the number fast enough. She doesn't even take time to figure out what to say and is in utter shock when he answers.

"Marcus Toller . . . Speak."

"Mr. Toller, this is Alicia Day, the acting student . . . well, actress, actually, that you saw in class today."

"Yes, Alicia. Look, I'm getting ready to step into a meeting, so I'm going to make this brief. I've been looking for my lead for quite some time. For this role, I want an unknown, and your name had been tossed around for a few months now. I'd finally gotten around to seeing you in action."

"My name was? Really?"

"Yours among others, but I've already ruled out the others, so if you could have your agent contact me on Monday, we can work everything out."

"Do I need to read for the part or something?"

"You already have. That was part of my script you read from."

Alicia is blown away. "So are you saying I have the part?"

"I'm saying I'm behind schedule and I need to cast this role. I loved your reading—it was almost perfect. I would have loved to have seen tears, but they'll come, trust me. Anyone working for me always cries, so just have your agent call me." Alicia is overwhelmed with excitement. This is exactly what her aunt has always told her. Luck is when preparation meets opportunity.

"I will—I definitely will."

Alicia is hoping for good news. She had been sitting on a bar stool at her breakfast bar since noon, facing her small state-of-the-art kitchen, her nails drumming on the granite top. It is now close to five in the evening and still there has been no call from her agent. She stood only to go to the bathroom twice and step out on the balcony once, hoping a change of scenery might calm her jittery nerves and even cause her "Superstar" ringtone to trill.

Now she is standing in her foyer.

"This has been a dream of mine since I was six years old," she says as she stands in front of the mirror holding a wineglass filled to the brim with cranberry juice. She sips a little of the juice from the glass so it won't spill as the glass sways in her hand. "I have so many people I would like to thank." She knows her Oscar acceptance speech well. She knew it would start just that way and she also knew she would thank God first and then her aunt. "The one and only person who truly believed in me." If not for her aunt's support, both emotionally and financially, she would have been forced to leave Los Angeles years ago.

She takes a deep sigh. She finishes off the juice in her glass and returns to her bar stool. She makes certain her cell phone is plugged to the charger so the battery won't die. And then she checks the time on the microwave—5:10. By 6:43, still waiting for the call, she realizes how low she has sunk that she would stay rooted to the same spot that long, grasping at hope.

She was so sure today would be the turning point. She's been waiting to hear the words, "You secured the role." Finally! Instead, she is biting her nails.

Several minutes later the "Superstar" ringtone trills, which can mean only one thing—her agent is finally calling.

"Listen, Alicia, I don't have a lot of time," says Heidi. "I'm in my car rushing to get to a meeting. I just wanted to call you real quick to say sorry, you didn't get the part."

Alicia's voice cracks first and then trembles. "I didn't? Are you sure?"

"Yes, I'm very sure. Sorry," she says brusquely. "I just couldn't work it out."

"Couldn't work what out?"

"You signed on to do J.R.'s movie at the exact same time this movie is filming. They really wanted you, but you can't screw the other production company, even if they are practically nonexistent," she mutters. "So instead you screwed yourself."

"That role that J.R. offered me is nothing compared to this. Absolutely nothing."

"You're the one who signed on to do it."

"He gave me twenty-five thousand dollars up front and I needed the money."

"Well, you could have had one point five million," her agent counters. "Which was an especially good offer for your first major studio role."

"And I can still have one point five million, Heidi. All you have to do is your job and get me that role," insists Alicia.

Her agent lets out an exasperated sigh. "Listen, I'm not the one you need to be angry with. You're the one who made an unwise decision and signed a contract without my knowledge. So now, it's too late. They're going with their second choice. Sorry."

"Which is?"

"Does it even matter?"

"Yes, it matters. To me it does."

"Aubrey."

"Aubrey who?"

"Aubrey Daniels. Who else?"

"Aubrey?" Alicia asks with a crushed expression on her face.

"I guess they just decided to go with a bigger name after all, but you were their first choice."

"That can't be possible. It just can't be possible. Aubrey told me she spoke to you and you agreed that signing on with J.R. was the right thing to do. She said you said it was a good deal and I should sign. Was she just trying to get me out of the way for this role?"

"I'm not getting between you and Aubrey. But no, Aubrey did not talk to me. If she had, I would have told her you don't sign on to do roles without my first reviewing the contract. You don't sign roles without sufficient out clauses, which that contract doesn't have. You don't sign roles on spec, especially not with some wash up like J.R. He might as well be kryptonite, because no studio is going near him."

"But Aubrey talked me into taking that role, and now she has the one I want, which makes it really seem like she set me up for failure, and I've known her practically all my life. She's done some bad stuff to people before, but why would she do this to me? This is all I've ever wanted. Why would she do that to me?" Alicia asks with a quavering voice.

"You'd have to ask her that. I have no idea. All I can say right now is that signing on with that other project is the single biggest mistake of your life. No studio is ever going to green-light that movie, so twenty-five thousand will be all you ever see from that deal."

"Please, you have to help me. I need that other movie. Please call them back and tell them I still want it."

"I could've sworn I just said there was nothing I can do. What do you want me to say other than I can't? It's unethical. Our agency also represents Aubrey, and besides, you entered into that bogus-ass contract with the other company, and it's binding. J.R. may not be able to write a decent script, but he did a hell of a job with that contract."

"I want you to tell me the truth. Do you even care about my career?"

"This is business. You can't take it personally. Do you want to know what I care about? I care about making money, and the way I do that is by having clients who make movies that make money, because then we all win. Not clients who make poor decisions and then have the nerve to ask me a dumb-ass question like do I care about their career. If you didn't care, why should I?" Next came the dial tone. Her agent had hung up. Alicia is certain her agent will mail out a termination letter, if she hasn't already. She'd always heard that with her agency you only had a few missed opportunities before you were long forgotten by them.

There's only one thing she can do now.

"J.R.," says Alicia frantically. "What's going on?" Alicia decides her first course of action is to call J.R. and see if he's willing to release her from a contract and a movie that she is certain will go nowhere fast. He claimed he was going to spend the next thirty days in seclusion in his house working hard revising his script to hand off to his agent to give to a major studio for a first reading. Yet, when she calls him, she hears loud music and people laughing in the background. She hears water splashes. He's either at a party or throwing one.

"This is J.R. speaking. Who's this?"

"This is Alicia. Are you having a party over there?"

"Yes, why, do you want to come?" he asks, sounding obnoxious and annoying.

"Listen, I called to let you know that I can't do your movie. I have another offer that I can't pass up."

"Yeah, well, you listen," he says as his voice rockets. "I already talked to your agent about your other offer when I faxed a copy of the contract to her, and I told her you will do my movie or I'll sue your ass."

Alicia's mouth drops open. It's as if she is dealing with a completely different person from the laid-back guy she'd met at Aubrey's. "I don't want to work with you anymore . . . especially not after the way you just spoke to me."

He erupts into laughter. "Honey, Hollywood is a cutthroat industry. Unfortunately, you don't have a choice."

After the call ends, tears stream down her cheeks as her trembling fingers dial her aunt Olena.

"You turned off your phone," Alicia says after Olena's prerecorded message plays. "I know you said I can do anything I set my mind to. Well, now I have my mind set on leaving California because I hate it out here. Call me."

She hangs up and her eyes pierce the doorknob as it turns.

"I had the worst day at work," Benita says as she kicks off her Giuseppe Zanotti sandals. "I spent the entire day running around trying to find Jennifer Aniston an outfit. Finally, I had to say, 'Jen, I can't keep Emma Watson waiting. My time is just as valuable as yours,'" Benita toys.

Alicia wails.

"My God, what's wrong with you?" Benita asks as she stares at Alicia, who is crying her eyes out. "Please tell me you're just in character."

"I wish I had a part I could be in character for," Alicia cries.

"What happened?" Benita throws up her hand. "No, don't tell me. Let me guess. Aubrey."

"Yes, Aubrey. She set me up, and she stole my role."

"Hmm, let me think." She places her hand on her chin. "Why am I not surprised? Remember that Andy Tennant film?"

"*Hitch.* Please don't go back and remind me of things I really didn't feel she had anything to do with. I want to be known, but not because I killed someone."

"You could have played Sara and you would have kissed who?"

"Will Smith. Please don't remind me. Do you honestly think I had a chance at that role?"

"Why not, you're just as pretty as Eva Mendes. If Aubrey hadn't lied about dropping your name with the studio head over at Columbia and telling you not to worry about auditioning, you would've had that role. When I tell you that she's a psycho lunatic liar, next time you better believe me."

"I've known Aubrey all my life. This makes no sense."

"In Aubrey's demented mind, there can be only one star."

Alicia snatches her cell phone off the kitchen counter. "I'm calling her to cancel brunch. I don't want to ever see her again."

Benita raises her eyebrow as an idea pops into her consciousness. "No, not so fast." She snatches the phone out of Alicia's hands. "Meet her for brunch. In fact, let's both meet her. Have some bread and a little wine and make this a little like . . . well, the Last Supper."

"Don't compare me to Jesus."

"Oh, I'm not comparing you to Jesus. I'm comparing that snake to Judas. And it's time for you to call her out."

Her conversation with Benita is interrupted by a call from Sir. They talk briefly, mostly about nothing. She is definitely in a funk, but even Sir seems to be in one, which is why she decides not to bring up her problems. Aubrey was his friend also. Maybe she treated her male friends better than her female ones.

Next Alicia calls Heaven. Heaven is feisty, she muses. A round-the-way type girl who'll make Alicia feel better simply by cursing Aubrey out for Alicia, and Alicia needs to hear that, not just from Benita but from as many people as possible. But once she gets Heaven on the phone, Heaven sounds just as down as Sir did; just as down as Alicia does.

"Are you okay?" Alicia asks, trying to sound normal—not cheerful, but not as if she's on the verge of doing what Dorothy did.

"I think I'm pregnant."

"Judging by the way you sound, I guess that's not a good thing," Alicia says.

"No, not at all," Heaven says, and starts to cry. "I don't want to be with him. And I don't want to have his baby. But this is my fault, because I keep saying I don't want him, but I keep being with him."

"You're young. When I was your age, girl, I did some of the stupidest things. So is the father that guy you were arguing with the first night we spoke on the phone?"

"Yes. And, we always argue and fight and have a dysfunctional relationship. If I have a baby with him, that means eighteen years minimum he'll be in my life. I don't even love him. Not anymore."

Everyone has problems, Alicia thinks to herself. *Everyone*—not just her—has things going on in their lives . . . game changers . . . things that could happen that make them feel the world has ended. The world doesn't revolve around her, she realizes. Other people's lives don't revolve around making it in Hollywood. God is bigger than just one thing, she tells herself as the tears roll.

At her northwest Detroit bungalow, Heaven stomps from the kitchen into the nearly empty living room. Her shadowed outline moves quickly across the shiny wood floors. Broken glass is at her feet, and two Detroit Police Department officers are knocking on her door.

Her relationship with Donovan has many problems, not the least being that Donovan doesn't support the one thing she is most interested in—photography. And while his main objection is that he doesn't think it's safe for her to take pictures in the Cass Corridor, sometimes referred to as Detroit's skid row, he never offers to tag along to give her some added protection. He opts, instead, to put down the thing she loves most, telling her it makes no sense if it makes no money. Why would she want to have a baby with him? Oh, wait, she doesn't, but she may not have a choice. She doesn't want to have an abortion, and if she carries a baby for nine months, she's keeping it, so adoption isn't a choice either. She missed her period. She needs to stop procrastinating and buy a pregnancy kit and find out the truth—whether it turns out to be a total disaster or not.

He had come over high, angry that her cell phone had been turned off and convinced that he had seen Nicolette sneak out the back door. She had told him to stop being paranoid, and he had thrown a water glass at her head. The glass missed, smashing against the mirrored living room wall. She rushed to attack him, but he was too strong. He slapped her against a wall and yanked a fistful of braids so hard she thought he was going to pull the hair from her scalp. She wanted to tell him she might be carrying his child, but he didn't care about the one he already had or the other one on the way. If anything, knowing she might be pregnant would probably make him angrier.

Furious, she kneed him in the groin, and he had slumped against the wall as she ran to the kitchen to call the police.

Now she stands with her fists clenched tightly in front of Donovan in the living room and shoots her boyfriend a cold glare as she struggles to listen to his excuses, but she can't imagine his words will make a difference. She knows she has finally reached her limit.

"Donovan, I'm through with this," Heaven whispers fiercely. "I'm this close to throwing open that door and letting the police in."

"Shh," Donovan says as he presses his finger against her plump lips. "Remember, you and me are on probation. If you let them in here, it'll be bad for both of us."

"Correction. I got off last month," Heaven lies, "and besides, what's that have to do with this? I'm the one who called 911. I'm tired of you hitting on me." She turns away from him and makes for the front door.

He grabs her wrist and yanks her back toward him. "I got six more weeks . . . six more weeks and I'm off probation. Heaven, listen to me," he says, taking a firm hold of her arms. "Please don't do this to me," he pleads.

"You should have thought of that before you put your hands on me," she says, snatching away her arm.

"I have weed in here. You want a possessions charge?"

"It's your weed. You deal with it if they find it."

"Last I checked, it don't have nobody's name on it," he says, tilting his head, "and you rent the house, not me, so you're the one in possession. Didn't you have weed when they arrested you for your DUI?"

She narrows her eyes in his direction. "You can't be serious. Really?" Heaven asks as her voice rises. "Really, Donovan, that's how you're gonna do me?"

"You called the police on me, remember?"

The bangs on her door grow louder, and one of the officers announces, "We can hear you inside, and we need Miss Jetter to come to the door. We aren't leaving until she does."

Donovan places both of his hands on her shoulders, plants his black high-top sneakers on the hardwood floor, and peers down at her. "Baby, I'm so sorry. You gonna forgive me? Please, just answer the door and make them go away."

Heaven sighs. She knows she should open the door and tell the truth, but she can't risk his pinning the marijuana on her. Going to jail would be her worst nightmare come true.

"If you hit me again, I swear to God," Heaven threatens, shoving her finger in his face. Donovan smiles at her gratefully, grabbing her hand and kissing it.

"I promise I won't," he says. Heaven isn't so sure, but she straightens her peace-sign T-shirt, walks to the front door, and pulls it open, showcasing a broad smile.

"Are you Miss Jetter?" asks one of the officers.

"Yes, Officer."

"May we step inside?"

"Yes, Officer," she says as she steps to the side and allows them to enter.

"We had a 911 call. Possible domestic abuse. Did you make that call?"

She shakes her head. "No, Officer."

"No?" he asks, looking over at his partner. "So who made the call? Are you Heaven Jetter?"

She nods. "Yes, Officer."

"Do you have a driver's license that we can take a look at?"

"Yes, Officer, I do." Heaven picks up her canvas purse from the floor, retrieves her license from her wallet, and hands it to the officer.

He studies her license briefly. "Someone called from this residence and said her name was Heaven Jetter and that her boyfriend was threatening her and throwing things and saying he was going to kill her, but you're saying that wasn't you?"

"Yes, that's what I'm saying."

The officer peers around the house from the entryway. Donovan had quickly shoved the glass out of sight before she let them in.

"We take domestic calls very seriously," one of the officers tells Donovan, "so what I'm going to have to do is ask you to leave the premises for now."

"Leave for what?" asks Donovan. "She just told you she didn't make the call. So why do I have to leave?"

"We're not arresting you, but this potentially is a domestic issue and we need to talk to the young lady alone. So is one of those cars parked out there yours?"

"Yeah."

"Okay, so you have transportation and you can leave the premises."

"What if I don't have anywhere to go?"

"We can always take you down to the station and you can wait there until you find someplace to go. But I'm trying to avoid doing that."

Donovan cuts an evil eye at Heaven as he grabs his keys and leaves. Within seconds, he is pulling out of the driveway.

The officer turns his attention back to Heaven. "The reason we asked him to leave is because we need to talk to you alone in case you felt endangered while he was here. Does he live here with you?"

"No."

"Did you call 911?"

"No."

"Your right eyelid looks a little puffy."

She turns away from them momentarily to look at herself in the mirrored wall. "Oh, probably just because of my allergies."

"Okay, well, we are going to leave since you don't appear to have any physical signs of abuse and the house looks to be intact. Obviously, if he comes back, you have the option of not opening the door, and if you do and he threatens you, you can always call 911 again."

"Officer, I didn't call 911 the first time."

"Well, I just want you to know your options." The officer looks long and hard at Heaven before turning to leave.

Heaven retreats upstairs to her bedroom. She spots a bag of marijuana on top of the television and knows Donovan's coming back tonight. There's no way he'd spend a night away from his weed.

Morning arrives unwelcomed and sooner than expected. She can just barely open her right eye. Surprisingly, Donovan never returned. Heaven tossed and turned all night. She is too sleepy after last night's events to spend the day photographing the city's urban plight. She'll leave that for the next day. And besides, as she stares into a compact mirror at her swollen eye, she doesn't feel like going out all bruised and battered.

The next afternoon, Heaven sits inside her car on the opposite side of the street in the middle of the next block, positioning her camera at his face. He has just made an exchange—cash for a small plastic bag, and Heaven had caught it all through her lens, snapped the picture with her Nikon digital camera at just the right moment. She didn't need the men's faces in the photo; it was all in the hands.

Just as she is changing her camera lens for a closer look, her phone trills.

She answers without looking at the caller display. "Yeah . . . hello," says Heaven. Her voice sounds rushed.

"Hey, this is Alicia. Did I catch you at a bad time?"

"No, I'm good."

The young man she is photographing glances around to quickly survey the area. He takes a few steps back and enters an abandoned building—a former liquor store. Heaven takes another picture of him entering the building and then one of him leaving. Then, he simply disappears—vanishes after crossing the street and weaving between two buildings.

"Girl, I am so glad you called me back," says Heaven.

As she is switching from her zoom lens to a telephoto, she hears knuckles tapping on her glass. She jumps. Her heart thumps heavily. She is frightened. Should she pull off right now, she wonders, and risk being shot? A lot has changed since high school. And besides, he didn't know her then, so of course, he won't remember her now. "Let me call you back," she rambles off quickly, before ending her call with Alicia.

She takes a deep breath, shoves her sunglasses on, and lets down her window.

"What's up?" asks the young man as he places his hand on the door's window frame.

"Nothing," she answers sheepishly.

"Something's up. Why you down here all the time taking pictures of me? You were down here last week and the week before that too. Weren't you? You pulled off right before I could get to you both times. So what's up? You with the Feds or something?"

"Me?" Heaven sputters as a puzzled expression crosses her face. Her lips pucker. "Come on now," she says. "Do I really look like I'm with the Feds?" She wants to tell him that she'd seen him several times before, near Tomboy Supermarket and once, a few weeks ago, as he was walking down Woodward Avenue in Highland Park near Hollywood Video in the Model T Plaza as she was driving. She decided right then to go ahead and follow him, but she'd lost him after he walked through the McDonald's parking lot. Still, she'd recognized him as Jamal, that fine boy from her high school—the one who was a senior when she was a freshman; the one she had a crush on. It had been more than a crush—if she hadn't already lost it the summer before, she would have wanted to lose her virginity to him.

"I'm a photographer, and I'm just down here taking pictures."

"I don't know about all that. Photographers like taking pictures with nice scenery. Nothing's down here but a bunch of boarded-up buildings, and homeless people, and crack hos, and . . ." His voice trails off.

"And what?" asks Heaven, waiting for him to go on. *And drug dealers, perhaps?*

"And nothing's down here to take pictures of. Why don't you get out of your car so I can take a closer look? I might want to take your picture."

She steps out of her car for Jamal . . . Jamal. . . .Jamal is his first name, but she can't remember his last name. She can't wait to step out so he can see what he could have had seven years ago.

He grins as he takes a closer look. He likes what he sees.

"Do I look like a Fed to you?"

He shrugs. "I might need to pat you down to make sure you're not wired."

"Go right ahead, Jamal," she says as he proceeds to run his hands slowly along the length of her body—pinning her up against the car.

"You don't appear to be wired."

"I'm not, Jamal."

"Why do you keep calling me Jamal?"

"Because that's your name. You want to know how I know?"

"Yeah, how do you know? Because you with the Feds and I'm under surveillance?"

"Because we went to high school together, but you were a few years ahead of me. I was a freshman when you were a senior, but I don't expect you to remember all that. Do you?"

"You went to Glenville?" he asks as he stands directly in front of her, his hands placed firmly on her waist.

"Glenville? I went to Pershing," says Heaven. "I never even heard of Glenville. Where's that?"

"In Cleveland."

"Oh my God. I don't know you," says Heaven, wrinkling her nose and pushing the man away from her. "Who are you?"

"I'm Lucas, as in Frank Lucas. Only Lucas is my first name. Who are you?"

"Lucas?" she asks.

"You're Lucas too?"

"No, I'm Heaven. So you're not Jamal Bashi?" she asks, suddenly remembering his last name.

He shakes his head. "Never heard of him. But if I ever meet him, I'm going to shake his hand and say thank you."

"Oh well, so much for fulfilling my high school fantasy," she says. Her eyes take a slow crawl over her phony crush—his wheat nubuck Timberlands and baggy jeans; the crisp white T-shirt partially tucked inside his jeans exposing the front buckle and part of the white leather to his belt; the large diamond earrings in both ears. She pets his fresh haircut. "But you are just as fine."

"Okay, I'm Jamal, and yeah, I went to Pershing, so let's go ahead and fulfill your fantasy."

"What street is Pershing on?"

"You went there. Don't you know?" he asks.

"Oh, yeah, I sure do know. Because I went there, but I don't think you know, because I don't think you went there."

"It's on Dexter," Lucas says matter-of-factly.

"Dexter," she spits. "Wrong. I can't believe you were feeling all over me like that."

"And I can't believe you were letting me feel all over you like that."

She puts her hands over her sunglasses and shakes her head. "I can't believe I did that. I am so embarrassed." She tries to get back in her car, but she can't because he has his hand against the door. "What are you doing?" she asks.

"Are you hungry?" Lucas asks as he stares at her freshly glossed lips and leans his face toward hers. "I feel like having a big, fat, juicy . . . burger to sink my teeth into."

She places her hand on his chest to prevent him from coming any closer. "Move back."

"You game for that?"

"I don't know you, so I'm not letting you in my car."

"I know you don't know me. I'm not asking to ride in your car. I have my own transportation, so just meet me there?"

She smiles. "Meet you where?"

"Checker."

"I don't know. I mean, things are getting bad. I watch the news; I know about crime."

He shakes his head. "If you watch the news and know about crime, what made you come down here? If I really wanted to hurt you, I could do that right now, right here. I don't have to take you to lunch first," says Lucas as he walks away. "Just meet me at Checker, girl."

"Girl?" asks Heaven to his back.

"That's right, girl," he yells back without turning to face her.

His pants are sagging a little, but not nearly as much as they do on Donovan; not so much that his underwear is showing; not so much that it turns her off. He disappears behind a different abandoned building and Heaven waits for a few minutes before eventually pulling off, waiting to see his car drive down the street before she heads for Checker Bar and Grill. Within seconds, she notices a black motorcycle in her rearview mirror closing in on her as she approaches a red light. "Slow down," she says to the rearview mirror as she watches him race toward her. "I know it's you."

He switches lanes right before she presses down on the brakes to stop at the light, and he stops beside her and flips the shield protector on his helmet up. "Do you know where you're going, or do you need to follow me?"

"Do I need to follow you? Which one of us is from Cleveland? Maybe you should follow me. And by the way, I don't like the way you handle your bike."

He shrugs. "It's just a bike. Trust me, I handle my women much better," he says with a wink, then flips the shield down and speeds across the intersection as soon as the light turns green.

When she walks into the restaurant, he is already seated in the front near the door, beside the window and in clear view of his motorcycle parked in front on Cadillac Square. A waitress comes over to them and places two glasses of water on the checkerboard table.

"I'm going to go to the restroom," says Heaven as she sets her camera bag on the seat beside his. "Can you watch my stuff?" He nods. "And just order me whatever you get." She dashes to the restroom to make a quick inspection of her face in the mirror after she removes her sunglasses. She wants to see if the makeup she is wearing is completely covering her bruise, because she can't imagine eating with her glasses on. She applies more of the heavy powdered foundation to her face, washes her hands, and yanks paper towels from the dispenser. The first two are to dry her hands off and the next two are to hold the door handle as she exits. She steadies the door with her foot, balls up the paper towel, and tosses it in the wastebasket—a perfect free throw.

"You want a drink?" asks Lucas before she can take her seat across from him. Heaven's mouth waters at the very thought of alcohol. "It's taking you too long to answer. How old are you anyway?"

"I'm legal."

"Let me see your license." She digs her hand inside her large purse, pulls out her wallet, and retrieves her license. He snatches the license from her grip and examines it closely. "You just made it. Nice picture." She smiles while she watches him continue to study her license. "Do you want some wine? They have a good selection here." She shakes her head. "Do you want a Coke?" She shakes her head again. "What do you want to drink?"

"Bottled water," she replies, even though she wants something much stronger than water, stronger than wine, but she tells herself she has willpower and doesn't need to drink just in case she's pregnant.

"Water's free," he says, nodding his head in the direction of her red tumbler glass as he picks up his glass of water and takes a sip.

"I need my water to be filtered. Tap water is nasty."

"I don't buy free water," says Lucas. "It's the same water that's in this glass, but just because it's in a bottle I'm supposed to pay for it? Not hardly."

"So you're treating?"

"Yeah, I'm treating. I'm the one who asked you to come," he says.

The waitress returns. "Do you need anything to drink?"

"Just a refill on this free water," he says to the waitress. "Drink up," Lucas says to Heaven.

The waitress leaves the table long enough to fetch a pitcher of water. She comes back and sets it on their table. A few minutes later she returns with the food Lucas had ordered for them.

"Appreciate it," he says to the waitress. "You got a man?" Lucas asks Heaven right before he sinks his teeth into a half-pound beefy burger loaded with bacon, ham, grilled onions, cheese, and sautéed mushrooms. Half of his toppings drop onto his plate.

"I almost forgot how good these burgers are." He takes a napkin from the metal holder and wipes the grease and sauces from his mouth. "Well, does Heaven have a man?" She shrugs. "Either you do or you don't, and if you're shrugging, that must mean you do, but you're not happy with him."

"Wow." Her eyes widen. Her situation is a little more complicated than a simple yes or no. She's still with Donovan, but none of her mental or physical bruises have healed completely.

"I'm right?" He nods. "I'm right. I'm always right. Why are you with a man who doesn't make you happy?"

"Who says I'm not happy?"

"It's not what you say. It's what you don't say. A woman in love with her man, first off, wouldn't even be having lunch with a stranger. At least not in my opinion," he says with a shrug. "But, I guess you're thinking, what does he know?"

"You're not a stranger. You're Jamal."

He smiles. "I guess that's who you want me to be. Isn't it? So you can fulfill a fantasy. So let me ask you. If I were Jamal, what would you do to me?"

"I don't like questions like that. It doesn't matter what I'd do because you're not."

Lucas takes another large bite of his burger and washes it down with more water. "*If* you had a good thing at home, he wouldn't put his hands on you."

"Why are you trying to pretend that you're a mind reader? Who says he puts his hands on me?"

"Actually, I don't read minds. I pay close attention."

He takes a napkin from the holder, removes Heaven's large sunglasses, and starts wiping away foundation to reveal a bruise under her right eye. "I bet you're so much prettier without all this stuff caked on." He shakes his head. "I don't understand women like you."

"And I don't understand men like you."

"Then we just don't understand each other. You want anything else before we leave?" he asks. She shakes her head. "Well, I do. I want you to stop letting Donovan beat you. You're better than that."

Shocked, Heaven says, "How do you know his name? Do you know him or something?"

Jamal's head shakes. "You have it tattooed on your neck. That's got to be one of the dumbest moves—tattoo the name of someone you're dating on your body. What fool does that? And in your case, it's the name of a man who beats you. Didn't your mother teach you better than that?"

Heaven stares him down with contempt. "No, as a matter of fact, she didn't. And he doesn't beat me. We just got into it—that's all." He raises one brow and shakes his head. "Don't judge me. Just like I don't judge you for your lifestyle, don't judge me for mine."

"You don't even know what mine is. You just think you do."

"And you don't know mine either. You just think you do. And," she says with a shrug, "why do you even care? You don't even know me."

"I know you in a way."

"In a way how?"

"Look, I have a confession to make, but I need you to promise me right now that you won't get mad."

"Get mad about what?"

"Promise first and I'll tell you."

"Okay, whatever, I promise."

He laughs. "I am Jamal." Heaven smacks his arm. "You promised you wouldn't get mad," he says.

"I'm not mad. But I'm not sure I believe you now."

"I went to Pershing. I was a senior when you were a freshman. Pershing is on Ryan Road. I had Mrs. Glitch for English."

"Oh my God, I knew it was you. You haven't changed. I used to watch you walk into Mrs. Glitch's classroom. Do you remember me?"

He eyeballs her braids. "Yeah, you always wore your hair real long and wavy . . . real, real long. And your clothes never matched."

"Whatever. I have my style," she replies, shrugging off his words. The waitress comes back to the table to drop off the check.

"I always thought you were cute, though, just color-blind," Jamal says with a laugh.

Heaven flutters her eyes. "So why did you lie?"

He shrugs as he stands. He throws down twenty-five dollars with the check and walks away. "It was kind of fun pretending to be someone I'm not."

After he steers her out of the restaurant over to her car, he removes her cell phone from her hand and begins keying in his name and phone number. "If you're interested in getting to know me," he says as he hands over her phone, "call me."

She takes the phone, gets into her car, and starts the engine, a smile playing on her lips. At the stop sign on the corner, she grabs her camera off the seat, anxious to get another glimpse of him. She wants to see all of the old pictures she took of him over the weeks. She toggles through the images and can't find one of him. She thinks back to the restaurant. She'd left her camera in the booth beside him. He must have erased them while she was in the ladies' room.

She grabs her cell phone and looks in her address book. She smiles when she sees it and calls him immediately.

"You erased my pictures?" Heaven asks as soon as he answers the phone.

"No. I erased my pictures that I never gave you permission to take. Drive carefully. It's starting to rain."

"Those were my pictures."

"Call me when you want to see me again. Not when you just want to fuss. And who is Nicolette?"

"Huh?" Heaven asks, stunned. How could he know that name? She doesn't have it tattooed anywhere.

"I saw her name on your phone when I took it from your hand. Your phone was connected to her number."

"My phone was? For how long?"

"I don't know how long. You'd have to ask her that."

Heaven doesn't waste any time calling Nicolette. But she doesn't ask her if she received a call or if she'd heard anything. She just pretends she had been thinking about her.

"I know why you're calling me," Nicolette finally gets around to saying after a very dry ten-minute conversation. "Yes, I was on the phone when you and some man you went to high school with were having lunch, and I listened to your entire conversation for more than an hour. And do you know what I came up with? That you're not ready for me. You like girls . . . or you're bi. . . . That much I know, because nobody can fake it that good, but I don't mess with women who mess with men. I should have known after that first night, but I guess I was fooling myself."

"So what does that mean? You just want to be friends with benefits?" jokes Heaven.

"No, I don't want to be anything. You can chalk it up to experience while I, on the other hand, got hurt again. I don't need to be friends with someone who hurts me; someone who lets a man hurt her."

Heaven is stunned after Nicolette hangs up the phone after telling her never to call her again. How can she be so strong? As much abuse as Heaven has taken off Donovan, all Heaven did was have lunch with someone . . . lunch? And now Nicolette wants to throw away their friendship over a hamburger.

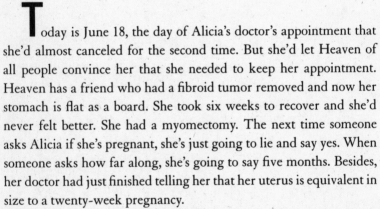

Today is June 18, the day of Alicia's doctor's appointment that she'd almost canceled for the second time. But she'd let Heaven of all people convince her that she needed to keep her appointment. Heaven has a friend who had a fibroid tumor removed and now her stomach is flat as a board. She took six weeks to recover and she'd never felt better. She had a myomectomy. The next time someone asks Alicia if she's pregnant, she's just going to lie and say yes. When someone asks how far along, she's going to say five months. Besides, her doctor had just finished telling her that her uterus is equivalent in size to a twenty-week pregnancy.

Less than an hour after arriving at her doctor's office, Alicia learns from the doctor that she is severely anemic from the large tumors inside her uterus. And the tumors account for her heavy periods. She is also at risk of a heart attack due to the anemia. "And yes," the doctor says to Alicia in response to one of her questions, "your anemia is causing your cravings for ice." He referred to the disorder as pica. The ultrasound reveals several tumors. Two are very large—eleven centimeters each. She asks the doctor to just remove them. Embolization? Not an option. Myomectomy? Not one either. He tells her that he can remove the tumors, but he'd also have to remove her uterus, and possibly her ovaries. Maybe even her cervix.

She'd be left with nothing.

She is thirty-two and basically that's how she feels—that she would be left with nothing at all. She would be at less risk of cancer—ovarian, cervical, and uterine—but none of the women in her family have fallen victim to any form of cancer, so she has never felt at risk to begin with. Nonetheless, with her hemoglobin at just a five, when twelve is considered normal and anything below a nine is a risk, her doctor is amazed that she has been functioning at all. He is surprised she hasn't been rushed in before now in need of a blood transfusion. Now he's really scaring her. A blood transfusion? She doesn't want that. Even if things have changed since Arthur Ashe and Kevin Peter Hall and contaminated blood is more of a rarity now than then, it's still possible, her doctor admitted. She needs to do something soon, because she is losing too much blood during her menstrual cycle each month, and being anemic can end her life if she doesn't take action. She sits numb. She was not expecting to hear such bad news. She doesn't have health insurance. Struggling to become an actress doesn't come with benefits. That's when she decides that if she is going to have a hysterectomy, she isn't going to do it before getting a second opinion, and she isn't going to do it without her mother by her side. She needs to go home. There's nothing in Hollywood—not anymore. She needs to go to Detroit, the city she hates and makes no apologies for. She explains all of her concerns to her doctor. He advises her that whatever she does, she needs to do soon. "I will gladly forward all of your records to the doctor. Do you have the doctor's name you're going to use?"

"I'm assuming I'll see my mother's ob-gyn."

"All ob-gyns aren't surgeons, so if you need a referral, I can give you a few I know of in Michigan."

It isn't until she reaches her car that the tears fall. She calls her aunt first and gets her voice mail at both her home number and cell. When she gets home she calls her mom. She has always been very close to her mom, but she usually calls her aunt Olena first because there are certain things she can discuss with her aunt that she can't with her mom. Her mother is her mother and would react the way mothers do—with too much concern . . . and possibly even panic.

"Mom, do you know why Auntie hasn't been picking up her phone?"

"Yes, but please don't say anything. I found out from your grandmother just today, and she told me not to say a word to anyone, including you. She was laid off. Your grandmother thinks they let her go because she didn't come back from her sabbatical. She extended her leave by three months. Something about taking care of some friend of hers. They said they were downsizing due to the current economic conditions, but you would think they would want to keep their best employee. But I guess anyone's dispensable. You know how these companies are. They don't care. It's all business." Alicia's eyes roll. The last statement her mother made sounded like something her agent would say, and that was the last thing she needed to hear again. "So she's avoiding everyone. She told your grandmother she was going to write full-time."

Her mother was late with her information. Her aunt had already told Alicia months ago that she received a buyout from her company. But Alicia didn't know she was going to write full-time.

"So she got a book deal?" asks Alicia.

"No, but she feels pretty confident."

Alicia laughs. "Yeah, I did too . . . about a lot of things."

"What's wrong?"

"Well, let's see." She lets out a sigh of lament. "Where do I start? I did what you said. I went to the ob-gyn. Do you think I'm too young to have a hysterectomy?"

"A hysterectomy? Why would you need a hysterectomy?"

"I have large fibroid tumors."

"What kind of doctor would suggest a hysterectomy to a thirty-two-year-old?"

"The doctor said if I don't remove my uterus, I may not live to regret it."

"Fibroids aren't a reason to have a hysterectomy."

"They aren't?"

"No. Do you know how many black women have fibroid tumors? If we all started ripping out our uteruses, none of us would have children. I have fibroids. So do your aunt and your grandmother, and none of us have had a hysterectomy."

"But what he said scared me."

"What did he say?"

"Let's see . . . that I could die."

"From fibroids?"

"No. From being anemic. And I really need to start getting either blood transfusions or iron infusions . . . but actually I think I'd have to have both."

The phone went silent.

"How do you feel?"

"Sick."

"You never told me you felt sick."

"I never thought feeling tired was feeling sick. I just thought it meant I was doing too much ripping and running as Grandma would say. And then there's my heart."

"What about your heart?"

"It flutters a lot."

"Alicia, why haven't you ever told me any of this?"

"I don't know," she says, even though she knows the reason she hasn't is because her mother would worry. "My heart just started doing that recently. . . . Oh, and my stomach—I look pregnant."

"You look pregnant?"

"People ask me all the time how far along I am."

"You're coming home. Alicia, you are coming home," her mother declares.

After she hangs up with her mother, she collapses on her bed, brooding over the day's events, eyes toward the ceiling. Going home—she gets to see her parents again. She gets to finally see Sir face-to-face for the first time in years. Maybe she'll even get to see her sisters—Heaven in person and meet Hope. And on another bright note, she'll finally be able to go to White Castle and order about a dozen sliders and gorge on the tiny square hamburgers and some onion chips. Now that she thinks about it, maybe going home is exactly what she needs.

Heaven slides the pregnancy test stick from the foil package and removes the purple cap to expose the absorbent tip just as instructed. She'd broken down and told her nana she thought she may be pregnant. And after Nana stopped fussing, she told her to do the same thing Alicia had suggested. "Take one of those home pregnancy tests just to be sure. Get one from Cunningham's—" *Cunningham's?* "I mean Perry's." *Perry's?* "Well, whatever the name of the store is now, just get one."

"Rite Aid?"

"Wherever you can go and buy you one of those tests that tell you if you're pregnant or not. And just pray. Pray that you're not, because a child is the last thing you need right now. You're still a child yourself. Still making decisions like one."

Heaven holds the pregnancy stick by the thumb grip and places the absorbent tip downward, inside her plastic cup of urine. After twenty seconds, she removes the absorbent tip and places it on Trina's sink with the window facing up. In two minutes she'll know if she's pregnant. A plus sign in the round window means she is. A minus sign means she isn't. She waits behind the closed bathroom door for the results. A baby is the last thing she needs right now. She doesn't have a job . . . and doesn't have a decent man to help.

Suddenly, she hears a loud knock on the bathroom door.

"Can't you wait for two minutes?" asks Heaven as she whips Trina's bathroom door open. "What's the problem?"

"Your sister is on the phone."

"Which sister?"

"You know it's not Hope."

Heaven rushes out of the bathroom into her living room, holding the pregnancy stick that still hasn't registered a result. She grabs her cell phone. "Hello?"

"Hey," says Alicia, her voice dragging.

"What's wrong? What did the doctor say?"

"Do you really want to know?"

"Yes, I really want to know," Heaven says.

"Well, let's just say I won't be having any kids of my own . . . not any time soon . . . not any time at all. I have to get a hysterectomy. I'm not a candidate for a myomectomy. My fibroids are too large. What about you? Did you find out whether or not you're actually pregnant?"

Heaven looks down at her pregnancy stick and the plus sign that is beginning to form.

"My test is coming back positive as we speak," says Heaven with tears in her eyes. Now what? Now what is she going to do? Is she supposed to try to make things work with Donovan so her baby won't grow up like her . . . without a father? She's so confused . . . angry . . . at herself more than anyone. "I don't mean to get off the phone, but I don't feel so well right now, so can I call you later? I made a big mistake, and I'm not ready for all of this."

"Sure, you can call me later . . . tonight or whenever . . . and hey, no mistakes. Life is full of experiences. Consequences. Not mistakes."

"My life is full of mistakes," Heaven says, and then ends the call. She didn't need a pep talk; she needed a time machine that she could step inside and go back to the day she was leaving the probation office when Donovan approached her in the parking lot. If only she could go back to that day. This time she wouldn't stop after he asked her name. She would just get in her car and drive off. She wonders where would she have been now if she had done that.

In Michigan, most people look forward to summertime, the change of season that ushers in sunshine and eighty-degree temperatures to bring them out of hibernation to the downtown festivals, parks, outdoor concerts, and the ability to mill around without depending upon layers and layers of heavy clothing, winter coats, and snow boots. Today is the first day of summer, and for Hope, summertime is the most dreaded season of the year—the time when her husband died.

Hope stands in front of the TV with her arms folded. She feels sick, watching Michael Beck on C-SPAN, always so willing to speak to the press lately. He'd written a book—a memoir about his life as if he were someone people cared about. What, besides the fact that he held on to a boat after forcing two others off it, is so important about his life? His publisher is taking him on a national book tour. Hope writes down a few of the dates and locations. His tour is starting off in Three Rivers, Michigan, at Lowry's Books. He may have moved out of state, but to Hope the fact that the signing starts back in Michigan proves he can run, but he will never be able to hide. It's time for her to confront Michael Beck in person. Come this time Saturday, when she's sitting in the front row at the bookstore for Michael Beck's signing, she'll find some justice.

Who is this man? Hope wonders. Or better yet, who does he think he is? Does he think he's important enough to have security and arrive in one of those black chauffeur-driven SUVs as if he were John Grisham?

Hope practically camped outside the bookstore as if it were Black Friday to ensure she'd be among the first to take her front row center seat. She got there early in the morning, a solid two hours before the bookstore opened, and she was the first patron to enter when it did open.

That was nearly three hours ago. The signing is set to begin soon.

A bookstore representative is attending to Michael Beck's every need, placing a bottle of water by his side along with several ballpoint pens.

He doesn't recognize Hope because he's never seen her, unless of course, her husband showed him one of the several pictures he had saved on his cell phone. But even if he had, she looked completely different now that she had chopped off nearly all of her hair.

She'd seen him before on the Internet in a photograph that looked like it was from his college days. But he looks much larger than she was expecting in both height and weight. He is tall and muscular, reminding her of a bodybuilder, a man who could definitely fight her husband and possibly even win.

A tall, extremely thin man in relaxed-fit jeans and a polo shirt pushes a cart with stacks of books over to the table where Michael Beck is sitting. Hope hears a woman say, "We're going to have you get started signing some books right now, and then we'll start the reading in about fifteen minutes. After that, we'll have the line form here and we'll have one person handing the books out as the people approach you."

"As long as they know I'm just signing my name—not personalizing."

"We'll have someone announce that as well."

As soon as there is a small gap in the conversation, Hope raises her hand. The skinny man who had been carting books marches over to her and stoops to her level.

"Will there be a Q and A?" Hope asks.

"I think just a reading," whispers the man, "but let me check for you. I'll be right back."

She keeps her eyes on the skinny man as he glides over to the lady who appears to be coordinating the signing. She peeps at Hope and flashes a smile while the man Hope asked the question of repeats her question to the woman.

The woman nods and says, "A brief one."

By now, Hope's heart is pounding so loud she is certain the man, who comes back over to her with the answer she's already heard, can hear it as well.

She tells herself that she has to be the first one on her feet with her question, the first one at the microphone. So she makes the decision to retrieve not one, not two, but three of his hardcover books, and an audio version, and to stand at the microphone directly in front of him in the middle of the aisle. She stands there and waits. Maybe she looks like an anxious fan or just plain weird, but whatever the case, she doesn't care, because finally he will have to say something, even if he still refuses to tell the truth.

The section reserved for the signing is beginning to fill up. She waits . . . and waits; she stands there with the three books, plus the audio version, and the besetting desire for the truth weighing her down. She waits for him to finish reading, to finish droning on about his childhood. Nothing he has said so far piques her interest.

Finally, it is Hope's turn to ask the questions that have been haunting her for two years. The bookstore representative, who remains standing beside Beck with a microphone in her hand, fields questions.

"Young lady in black, you've been waiting very patiently. You have a question?"

"I guess I want to know how you feel about being the lone survivor."

Michael Beck lowers his head. "I ask myself that every day. I ask myself, why me? Of the other two on the boat, why was I the only one to survive? I'm not sure why. I guess it was God's doing."

Hope's head is shaking. "You still haven't answered my question. I want to know why you think you were the only survivor," she says as her voice escalates slightly. "My husband was a Navy SEAL. Do you understand the training and dedication it takes to rise to that level?"

"I'm sorry, what did you say your name is?"

Hope ignores him. "I just want you to admit what you did. Admit that you fought with my husband and Taite's husband so you would be safe on that boat, because the hull was too small for all three of you—for anyone other than you."

Michael Beck turns beet red. He turns toward the woman sitting beside him and whispers in her ear.

The woman stands and says, "If you don't mind, please step aside. We can only allot a few minutes to each question."

"I'll gladly move," Hope says calmly, "as soon as Mr. Beck answers my question. Did you push my husband, Roger Teasdale, off the hull of the boat so you would survive?"

"Miss," the woman says firmly. Mr. Beck reaches his hand out and touches the woman, who lowers her head to his mouth so he can whisper. She stands up straight after he finishes. "Mr. Beck will gladly speak with you after the signing concludes." And even though there is a long line of people behind her who probably know exactly what they want to ask, Hope doesn't move. She remains planted in the same place. She can't move.

"Miss, please," the woman says.

Hope finally steps out of line and sits down at the only empty seat in that section. She is anxious to find closure. She still needs answers, but now she has to wait at least another hour to get them. The other attendees, a bit shocked by Hope's presence, ask Michael Beck only about his personal life and his family upbringing—things that Hope couldn't care less about.

A little more than two hours later the bookstore representative ushers her to a semiprivate area in the back of the bookstore so that she can speak to Michael Beck.

He can barely look at her, and Hope isn't surprised. He looks around nervously and decides to move their talk outside. They exit out the back door, an entrance used by bookstore employees.

"What are you running from?" Hope says in an accusatory tone. "I already know what happened. You don't have to take me out back to admit it. I already know what you did."

"It's not what I did."

"It's not? Well, who did it, then? You were the only survivor."

"No," he shakes his head. "No, see—"

"You were the only survivor. Weren't you?"

"Of the fishing accident . . . yes."

"Well, isn't that what we're talking about?"

"That's what you think we're talking about, but that's not what's going on here." He buries his hands in his pockets and sighs. "I don't know how much I can say. I don't know what I can tell you. This is not good."

"What are you talking about? Will you just go ahead and say whatever you're trying to say to me?"

One of the bookstore representatives sticks his head out the back door and asks Michael Beck if he needs anything.

"No, I'm fine. Do you need them to get you anything?"

"All I need right now is for you to tell me the truth," she says as the bookstore representative walks back into the store.

"The reason I avoided you all of this time is because I didn't know what to say. I didn't know what I could say without getting myself in trouble. I should have just been honest from the start. One lie always leads to another and another."

"So, you did it—you killed them? Didn't you? Just be honest now so I can move on. I want closure," she says in tears. "I want to be able to enjoy life and participate in things and have my daughter see her mother happy. Just give me closure," she says through gritted teeth.

Michael Beck's head shakes. "No. I didn't kill anyone. And your husband isn't even dead. I haven't told anyone this, not even my wife. The initial statement I gave to the police wasn't completely true. Your husband wasn't even on the boat."

Hope pauses, eyeing him suspiciously. "What? What do you mean he wasn't on the boat? He was *on* the boat."

"No, he wasn't. He just told you he was so he could do other things. Do you know what I mean?"

"Other things like what?"

Michael Beck shifts uncomfortably. "He was cheating on you, okay. We all took women out there, but he only stayed the first night. He never went out on the boat with us."

"You're lying. . . . If he wasn't on the boat, then he would be alive and he'd be with me."

"But he's not. And he wasn't on the boat either. I didn't know your husband as well as Tim did. I knew him, but he wasn't a close friend of mine."

Hope rolls her eyes and shakes her head. "I don't believe that story for one minute. Why wouldn't he come home to me on his own if he was alive?"

Michael Beck shrugs. "I have no idea, but I am telling you the complete truth. What would I get from saying he wasn't on the boat if he was?"

"Lots of men cheat and don't fake their death, if that's what you're suggesting."

"I'm not suggesting anything, because I don't know why he didn't come home. Only your husband knows that. All I know is he wasn't on the boat."

"Don't you see how ridiculous this all sounds? He wouldn't fake his death to cover up an affair."

"Listen, you wanted the truth, and now I've given it to you. I guess you can go with that information. Call his naval office—maybe they have some information."

"He didn't reenlist."

Michael Beck begins to pace. "I don't know what to tell you."

"So who else was on the boat, then?"

"Look, does that even matter? I've already said too much. I swear to you, Roger wasn't on there. And Tim's wife knew. They got into a big argument about it. She told him she wasn't going to cover for him if you asked her anything."

"Wait a minute. Taite knew? Is that what you're telling me?"

"She knew Roger left Ludington after the first night. Look, what I'm telling you could get me in trouble. I'm just telling you because I think you deserve to know the truth."

She looks into his eyes and can tell he isn't lying. He has no reason to twist and turn his story. No one, except her, was accusing him of anything. He could've stuck with his original story until the day he died.

"I don't plan on telling anybody else what I just told you. So, if you go to the police and tell them, I'm not going to admit to it. I can't. I have a family. I'm restarting my life. I'm not going to lose what I have on account of your husband. I should have just told the truth to begin with, but—"

"But?"

Michael Beck just hangs his head, ashamed. Hope turns on her heel and walks away.

As she takes exit 34A and from US Route 131 north merges onto Interstate 94, heading east toward Detroit, she asks herself if it's possible that she has spent two years mourning a man who isn't even dead. And she realizes that, in life, anything is possible.

Alicia, Aubrey, and Benita are eating brunch at a ritzy seaside restaurant in Santa Monica. Their table for four is situated beside a twenty-foot-high window with a direct view of the sand and ocean. The crashing waves should have given Alicia a sense of calm, but instead her nerves seem to be even more on edge.

Aubrey greeted her with her phony set of air kisses to each cheek. And Alicia wanted so badly to slap her, then curse her out and leave. But she wasn't going to rush what she had to say. She was going to take her time—the same way Aubrey had with her deceitfulness over the years.

The empty chair holds three purses. Aubrey's Zagliani crocodile puffy satchel overpowers the two smaller and less expensive handbags, serving as just another obvious reminder to Alicia of how much more Aubrey has than she does. Not to mention the ten-bedroom French-inspired château she is renting in Bel Air, California, in contrast with the modest two-bedroom apartment Alicia and Benita share.

Aubrey proceeds to run down a list of upcoming movies she'll be appearing in. "I told Stuart I need to be busy for the next three years. Two movies a year is what I've committed to. Actually, three this year, and then two the next if none fall through, and then I'll take two years off . . . a year off . . . maybe. I'm getting all my money now. I'm not stupid. This train won't run forever."

First look with Aubrey Daniels, Alicia thinks as her eyes roll.

"We get the point," Benita says. "You're working. I'm *working* too. I'm a stylist."

"If you call working at a Ross Dress for Less being a stylist, then, okay, you're a stylist," Aubrey says, making air quotes with her fingers.

"I work at Ross part-time and Saks full-time, and yeah, that's exactly what I call it. The niche I've carved as being a personal shopper for those who want to look like a million bucks without spending a million bucks is catching on with a lot of people now that we're in a recession. So you don't have to put me down, because I let you talk about all your movies, even though some of us don't need to feel like we're logged on to your IMDb page. It's good to have your face out there, but too much exposure is just as bad as not enough. Because I'm sure people are going to get sick of looking at you. I've only been looking at you for thirty minutes and I'm already sick of your face. And, I'm curious. Why aren't you mentioning all of the roles you auditioned for but lost out on?"

"So you're a personal shopper and an agent now too? Glad to know you think you know something about my industry."

Alicia places her orange juice on the table. "You said Stuart. I thought we had the same agent."

"We do. We have the same *agency*."

Alicia shakes her head. "I don't have Stuart. I have Heidi . . . Heidi, who hates me. You have Stuart, the one who owns the agency. How did that happen?"

"We have the same agency. Not the same agent. I never said we had the same agent. Stuart isn't going to take you on—you haven't done enough."

"And why is that?" asks Benita. "Is there a reason she hasn't done enough?"

Alicia throws her hand up in front of Benita's face. "I can handle this."

"Is there something to handle?" asks Aubrey.

Benita nods. "Don't play dumb, even if in your case it's not an act."

"Benita, I can handle this."

"What's wrong, honey?" asks Aubrey in a condescending tone.

"I'm not your honey. And I don't need you to patronize me. Do you care about me? Because I have always loved you like a sister, and if I had made it before you, I would have helped you. I never would have taken from you."

"What did I take from you? What exactly are you trying to say?" asks Aubrey as she stops typing on her BlackBerry, sets it by her side, and takes a sip of her blueberry mojito before pointing in Benita's direction. "And why is she here?"

"Who, me?" asks Benita, pointing to herself.

"No, your twin . . . yeah, you. Why are you here?"

Benita closes her eyes as she shakes her head. "Lord, give me the strength. I know this is supposed to be Alicia's moment, but I want one of my own with this tramp."

"Tramp?"

Benita's eyes open. "You remind me so much of Phyllis, because you're definitely the type to push someone off a cliff."

"Phyllis?" asks Aubrey.

"*The Young and the Restless*, skank," says Benita.

"Oh my God," Aubrey says. "Benita, can you just join us in the real world for a minute? You really are a sad state of affairs and such a waste of my time. The only reason I know you is because of Alicia. And I curse the day I let her convince me to move in with you and her."

"You curse the day? You're the one who can't pay your cable bill."

"So sue me. Oh, that's right, you already have," she says, letting out a wicked laugh.

"Here you are, sitting here bragging about all of your films, and you can't even pay off a four-hundred-dollar judgment."

"The only reason I know you is because of Alicia. She is the only reason I tolerate your ass."

"You won't know me after today," says Benita. "In fact, you won't see me after today."

"And I won't miss you after today either."

"Do you think I'm invisible?" interrupts Alicia.

"What?" Aubrey asks, turning and looking at her with confusion.

"Why did you refer me to that photographer?"

"What photographer?"

"The one who had to be the worst photographer in the business; the one you claimed was also yours, but when I got to his studio, I didn't see any photos of you hanging up."

"I guess he just didn't hang any of them up."

"He had hundreds up, but not one of any celebrities. That man was mean and rude and extremely unprofessional . . . and to prove he had bad karma, I lost one of my favorite earrings there. The only reason I even agreed to use him to shoot my headshots is because you referred me to him, and guess what? They look horrible. That is just one example of the many ways you have steered me wrong."

"I'm sorry. He was good when he shot mine. What, do you think it was intentional?"

Benita nods her head in disgust. "Yes, she does."

"I didn't think so then, but now, yes, I do," Alicia says before clearing her throat. "I will never forgive you for what you did."

"I can refer you to another photographer."

"I'm not talking about the photographer. You set me up to sign on for a movie that will never be made so you could take my other role—a role that probably would have been a breakthrough one for me. How could you do that?" asks Alicia, tears forming in her eyes. "You knew, didn't you? You knew they wanted an unknown. . . ."

You knew Marcus Toller had my name for months. . . . You knew all of that because you make it your business to know."

"They didn't want you. They wanted me."

"That's not what Heidi said."

"Heidi, what does she know?"

"A lot more than I've given her credit for."

"She's a subpar agent. They wanted me. I have a name; you don't."

Alicia stands with the bowl of soup she'd ordered but never ate and allowed to cool—Manhattan clam chowder—and calmly pours it all over Aubrey's head and her off-white outfit.

"Oh my God, why did you do that, you bitch?" Aubrey shouts in surprise. "Tommy!" she screams, frantically summoning her bodyguard as she pushes back her chair and stands, dripping red soup from her hair and face to her blouse. She grabs a cloth napkin from the table and starts to wipe herself off. "You ruined one of my favorite outfits," Aubrey cries. "And my hair!" She starts stomping her feet.

"And I still didn't get even because you ruined my life. Besides, you did say my meal was on you, right? Well, now it really is."

"Tommy," shouts Aubrey.

"Call your bodyguard on me, and I'll make a living selling everything I know about your ass to the tabloids. You know I'd make a fortune on the sex tape you made with Mr. Sands in eleventh grade—you know, the one you had me hide for you. I still have it."

"Wait, Tommy." Aubrey throws up her hand to stop her bodyguard. "I want that tape."

"I bet you do. Just like I wanted that role."

"And on that note," says Benita, linking her arm with Alicia's, "we're leaving."

"It's not my fault you couldn't make it on your own," Aubrey says as Alicia and Benita walk away.

"I don't need your help. I can and I will make it on my own."

"Not in this town you won't."

Benita throws up the peace sign to the bodyguard as they pass him.

"Do you really have a sex tape?" mutters Benita as they walk out of the restaurant.

"I had one. But that was fifteen years ago. Who knows which box it's lying in now. But Aubrey doesn't know that, so let her sweat."

"So she slept with a married schoolteacher? Hmm . . . Why am I not surprised? I'm sure it was a class she was failing."

"You'd be right about that." Alicia says as she releases a sigh filled with discontentment. She believes there are some things in life that must happen; things that would be so much easier to deal with if a crystal ball came along for her to sneak a peek into her future. But that's where her faith needs to step in, she reminds herself. So many things in life are easier said than done, Alicia realizes. "First, you must understand," her aunt would always stress, "that God is bigger than just one thing. He's bigger than just one thing." But what if that one thing is the only thing you want? Is God also big enough to give it to you? If you know for a fact that that one thing is all you want, will he do that one thing for you too?

PART TWO

Between a Rock and Detroit

July

"**C**an you take your sunglasses off for me, please?" Daisy asks Heaven. This is Heaven's first appointment with Daisy, who came highly recommended by a woman Heaven stood behind in the checkout line at an ALDI Food Market on West Eight Mile Road in Ferndale. Heaven was there for the twenty-four pack of ten-ounce purified water that was on sale. She'd complimented the woman on her hair that she had initially mistaken for a weave, because the loose hair hid most of the braids underneath. Heaven asked the woman if she had a card for her braider. And as many times as Heaven had asked that very same question of women whose hair she'd liked, this was the first to pull a business card from her purse—and not just one business card, but a stack of business cards. She also had a five-by-seven flyer with a picture of the inside of the salon on the front, Daisy's picture in the upper-right-hand corner, and all the services listed on the back. Daisy was the woman's daughter. "I'm her walking billboard," the woman said. "She doesn't supply the hair, so you'll have to bring your own. These are tree braids," the woman said, revealing the cornrows underneath. "If you want your braids done like mine, take three eighteen-inch bags of wet and wavy human hair with you.

She'll probably only use two, but better to be safe. She doesn't take walk-ins, but she should be able to fit you in."

"I'm trying to go natural, but I'm having a real hard time because right now I hate the way my hair looks and I'm so tempted to put my weave back in," Heaven told the woman.

The woman took out her cell phone and called her daughter as they stood in the ALDI parking lot. After a minute, she snapped her phone shut.

"She just got a cancellation. You have an appointment tomorrow."

Now Heaven is in the salon chair. But she doesn't want to remove her glasses because she doesn't want to show her bruised face. After she and Donovan came home from Rumor Nightclub the past weekend, they got into a big fight, and instead of punching the wall in or throwing a chair across the room, which she definitely would've preferred, he hit her so hard she was rendered unconscious for a minute. She wasn't sure for exactly how long; all she knew was when she opened her eyes, Donovan was holding her up in front of the bathroom sink and splashing water on her face. Blood was gushing from her nose. She couldn't open her left eye, and her head was pounding.

"Sit here and don't move," Donovan told her after placing her on the closed toilet seat. He took a face towel, wet it with cold water, and placed it on her eye. "Tilt your head back," he said, referring to all the blood pouring from her nose.

"What happened to me?"

"You fell," he said, but she knew he was lying.

"Did I fall before or after you beat me?" she asked sarcastically.

"It wasn't like that. Don't you remember?" But of course she remembered. Donovan was already outside waiting when she pulled up to the house. She was tired of his coming to the club where she worked every weekend to keep an eye on her.

"As far as I'm concerned, I didn't do anything wrong. He offered me a drink and I took it. I was just being nice." But that word *nice* seemed to set him off, because he pushed her against the hood of her car and, then, cursing and calling her awful names, tramped into her house. Once they were inside, her fear turned to anger when he tossed his cell phone on the kitchen counter and she picked it up and started perusing his text messages, spotting a picture of a woman's breasts—but it didn't look like the same pair as before, which she assumed belonged to the woman in Brighton.

"Another chick sent you a picture of her titties?" she asked in outrage.

Donovan snatched his phone away from her and said, "That's my business if she did." Heaven started screaming, telling him she may have small titties, but he had a small dick, and that's the last thing she remembers.

Daisy moves the wig away from the side of Heaven's face and notices the bruises. "I'm going to make an exception and do you in my private room," she says as she tugs at the bottom of her black asymmetrical beauty tunic; the mandarin collar seems to strangle her sizable throat. "You and me gonna have a little talk." Daisy's bell-bottom uniform trousers flap as she marches off in her comfy leather mules.

Once they relocate, Daisy pulls off Heaven's wig after she takes a seat in her stylist chair. She starts combing through Heaven's real hair so she can assess the condition. "You just took braids out of your hair recently?" Heaven nods. "Your hair is very dry and damaged, but we can repair it. So what's the deal?" asks Daisy as she saturates Heaven's hair with a mixture of water and extra-virgin olive oil.

Heaven shrugs. "I don't have soft hair like my sister's. My hair is coarse like my mom's."

"I'm not talking about your hair. I'm talking about your face. What's up with your black eye?" Daisy uses a Magic Star wide-tooth comb with a light touch and sections Heaven's hair with butterfly clips.

Heaven sighs. "It's a long story."

"I got time," says Daisy as she pulls off Heaven's glasses to reveal a frightful sight. "I almost want to tell you to put them back on. How did that happen? Did a man do that to you?"

Heaven's face collapses into her hands. "It's complicated."

"It's not that complicated. Trust me. Do you see this?" asks Daisy as she points to the hearing aid behind her right ear. "Let's just say I didn't lose hearing in my right ear from natural causes. The man who did this told me he loved me every day, whether it was a day he beat me or not."

"Wow, how did you get out of the situation?" asks Heaven.

Daisy takes a swig of her bottled water. "Oh, I killed that fool," she says matter-of-factly.

"You did what?"asks Heaven, assuming she couldn't have heard the woman correctly. She couldn't have said she killed him.

Daisy swivels Heaven's chair around until Heaven is facing her. "Four years ago, my ex-boyfriend at the time came into my house and I shot him. He'd already threatened to kill me, and I had a protective order placed against him. He called me calmly one day and said he was just letting me know he was coming over to kill me. He told me what time he was going to be there, like he was one of my clients making an appointment or something. 'I'll be there in five minutes and I'm coming over to kill you.' But what he didn't know was that I had bought a gun for protection, and when he burst through that door, I shot him, because I knew he was crazy enough to do it and after all the abuse I'd taken, I wasn't going to wait to see if he was joking."

"That's kind of stupid to give somebody the heads-up," Heaven says, shocked.

"The man wasn't necessarily a genius. I thank God every day for that heads-up, though."

"Did you have to stand trial?"

"Stand trial for what? He broke into my house. The police questioned me as part of their procedure, but there was a long documented history of violence in our relationship and I had a PPO against him. I was protecting myself. And now I counsel high school girls on dating violence. Did you know that one in five high school girls has reported being either physically or sexually abused by her partner?"

Heaven shakes her head. "No, I didn't know that," she says as she follows Daisy over to the shampoo bowl.

"It's true. And, in all fairness, men can also be the victims. But I only counsel the girls." Heaven wonders if that's something she can do to fulfill the rest of her community service hours. She really wants to get that out of the way because it's just one more thing hanging over her head.

Heaven momentarily closes her eyes as the warm water runs over her head, but as Daisy's hands begin to vigorously shampoo her scalp, she opens them.

"Could you not shampoo my head so hard?" Heaven asks. "Any other time I'd appreciate it, but today my head is a little sore. The shampoo smells good, though. What is it?"

"Creme of Nature Kiwi and Citrus Ultra Moisturizing Shampoo," Daisy says as she starts gently massaging Heaven's scalp.

"Creme of Nature," Heaven says, laughing. "My mother used to shampoo our hair with that when I was real little. She hated doing my hair and I hated her doing it."

"So, I've told you all my business," Daisy says as she applies conditioner. "Now, what's going on with you?"

"Well, obviously, I'm in a bad relationship."

"Obviously."

"He does have some good qualities, though."

"Listen, any man who puts his hands on a woman does not have good qualities. He might have potential if he's young and gets counseling, or even if he's not young and really wants to change, but is his potential worth risking your life? I'd say not, and I hope you'd say so too."

"Our relationship isn't as violent as yours was. But we're both possessive and he's real jealous, just like I am. Put the two of us together when we're both in a bad mood, and some major fighting will go down."

"You can sit up," says Daisy. "I want the conditioner to sit for a few minutes." She walks over to her station to retrieve a portable mirror. "Have you taken a real good look at yourself?" She hands Heaven the mirror. "Judging by the look on your face, you're not winning the fights." Heaven holds the portable mirror up to her face and stares at her puffy eyelids and dark circles under her eyes. She can still hear a ringing in her ear. "If your head is sore from a shampoo, how do you think braids are going to feel?"

Heaven covers her eyes with her hand and shakes her head. "I never even thought of that."

"I can do them loose, but you'll probably have to come back in four weeks instead of six if I do. And I charge a hundred and ten dollars."

"Can you discount it some since I'll have to come back quicker?"

Daisy shakes her head. "I'm not trying to be funny or anything, but why should I have to discount my services due to your situation? That would be like me condoning it. And I don't. But you know what I think? God probably put you and me together so I can minister to you, because I know how hard it is to break free from an abusive relationship. And trust me, killing the person isn't the preferred method of doing so." She guides Heaven's shoulders back. "You can lie back. God has a way of bringing people together, especially when someone may need help. Did you know that?"

"Yes, ma'am. You're right," says Heaven as she lays her head back into the shampoo bowl while Daisy washes out the conditioner. "Braid it loose and I'll come back in four weeks."

"And let me tell you something. . . . It may get to the point where you need to go downtown to the courthouse and ask a judge to grant you a personal protection order just like I did, because that's your right."

Heaven says, "I tried that already."

"Tried. And what happened? The judge didn't grant it?"

Heaven shakes her head. "I never saw the judge. I just left."

"Why would you do that?"

"It's a long story."

"You're addicted to the wrong type of man. That's not a long story—that's the story of a lot of women—and you probably went down to file a protective order and then told yourself you shouldn't go through with it. You didn't want to get him in trouble. You could leave the relationship on your own, but if that was true, you would've by now." Everything she is saying is exactly right, except for one thing. Now Heaven is pregnant, and she doesn't want her child's father in prison like her father. Heaven can work this out herself without involving the law. It might take a little more time, but it won't take forever, because she wants a family, a healthy loving one. And that doesn't mean she needs to stay with Donovan.

A couple hours later, after Daisy finishes styling her hair, she hands Heaven a mirror. Heaven smiles at what she sees. She is very pleased with her new free-flowing locks, a welcome change from her usual wigs, braids, and quick weaves.

"To be honest with you, tree braids will usually last two to three months, but for you I'd say maybe six weeks since I tried not to cornrow you too tight." She uses her fingers and combs through Heaven's hair. "As for your upkeep, lightly oil your scalp between these parts twice a week and spray the rest of your hair with oil sheen. I prefer Organic Root Stimulator Olive Oil Sheen Spray. And you should use that daily. Also, you should use a braid spray or a liquid leave-in conditioner on the cornrowed base of your braids once or twice a week."

"Should I wash my hair?"

"Definitely . . . once a week. You can buy Creme of Nature."

"Do you sell it here?"

"No. My customers keep asking me to start selling products, but I don't have time for that. That's the salon size," she says, handing Heaven the bottle of shampoo as an example.

"But they have much smaller sizes at the beauty supply stores. And I don't have to tell you that you need to tie a satin scarf over your head, do I?"

"No, you don't have to tell me."

Heaven walks out of the salon extremely content with her hair, but she vows not to return—not only because she doesn't have that kind of extra money, but also because there is something about Daisy's story that just doesn't sit right with her, perhaps because of what she witnessed as a child between her parents. She'd much rather have a hairstylist who is either happily single or happily married and has pictures of her beautiful family taped to the mirror of her workstation to prove it, instead of an article from the *Detroit News*—"Detroit Woman Shatters Silence on Abuse to Teen Girls." Daisy seems like a nice woman, but her story is just too familiar to Heaven's life—past and present—for Heaven to be able to sit in her salon chair comfortably.

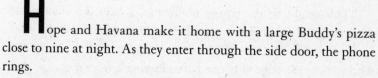

Hope and Havana make it home with a large Buddy's pizza close to nine at night. As they enter through the side door, the phone rings.

Havana runs inside the house ahead of Hope and answers the phone. "Hello."

Alicia hesitates for a moment after hearing a child's voice. "I'm trying to reach Hope Jetter."

"Hope Jetter?" asks Havana. "You mean Hope Teasdale, right?"

"Hope Jetter is right," corrects Hope. "Who is that on the phone?" she asks as she locks the door behind her and sets the pizza box down on the kitchen table.

"It's a woman for you." Havana hands her mother the phone.

"Hello."

"Is this Hope?"

"Yes, this is Hope. Who is this?"

Alicia clears her throat. "Hope, my name is Alicia Day. This call may come as a shock to you. I got your number from Heaven."

"Whatever she did this time, I can't help her anymore. I have my own problems."

"No, she didn't do anything. . . . I'm . . . I'm your father's daughter . . . which would make me your half sister."

Hope stands frozen. *Father's daughter . . . half sister . . .* "I'm sorry, you have the wrong number."

"Are you Hope Jetter . . . or, I mean, Hope Teasdale?"

"Jetter," she snaps a correction. "No."

"But you said you were Hope."

"I misunderstood your question. Hope isn't home. Try back tomorrow." Hope slams the phone down.

Havana stands in front of her. "Why did you lie, Mom?"

"I didn't lie. She said she was my sister. I don't have another sister."

A few minutes later, Hope's phone rings again.

The same number with the 818 area code appears on caller ID.

"This might be the wrong number . . . ," says the voice on the other end, and the answering machine records Alicia's words.

Alicia sits on the edge of her bed after leaving a voice message, shaking her head and mulling over the fact that the woman named Hope is avoiding her call. This must mean reaching out to her was as bad an idea as she had told Heaven it would be. But Heaven insisted. She said her sister would take it better coming from Alicia than she would from her, but evidently not.

Two red Samsonite bags are lying on Alicia's bed. Red is a powerful color and Samsonite is strong and durable; made to last—all of the things Alicia didn't seem to be at the moment. After thirteen years, she is heading back to Detroit with one more bag than she had when she'd first moved out here.

Benita looks around Alicia's room. They are both trying to figure out where to start.

Alicia surveys her bedroom. Thirteen years is a lot to pack up. Her walk-in closet alone is a territory that should be off-limits to everyone—including her. "Thank God I still have a few more days to get all of this stuff together."

"You are coming back, right? So you don't have to take everything."

"Hopefully I'm coming back."

"What does that mean? You paid your three months' rent in advance, and you told me you'll be back. I'm counting on you to come back. Your dream is here."

"And you need a roommate."

"No, I can always find a roommate. I have a big family. I just want you to promise me that you won't give up on your dream. And even if you decide not to come back, still promise me that I'll see you again, if not in person, then on the big screen."

Alicia nods. "You will definitely see me again . . . in person. I can't promise you about the big screen because apparently that's not up to me." It was a dumb thing to want—a vain thing, muses Alicia. But she still can't give up on it, which she realizes as she picks up the book *Acting Is Everything: An Actor's Guidebook for a Successful Career in Los Angeles* from her nightstand. She flips through the pages and considers throwing out the book—tossing it out the window. But then she notices a faded yellow picture marking the chapter entitled "Dealing with Rejection." The picture is of Alicia as a child when she was around five. She's sitting in the middle of a pink blanket sprawled over a grassy section of a park, sitting beside her father and his infant daughter Hope—her other half, who refuses to take her calls.

Her mouth falls open. She had wondered where the picture was; she knew she had one. She'd had the book for a few years—at least four. Even then, as she stares at the picture, she tries to tell herself what her mother had told her so often. They didn't matter; certainly not her father who wasn't even at the hospital when she was born, and not her sister either. She had Aubrey as a sister—and having Aubrey used to be good enough.

Alicia was seven when her mother married. And it didn't take her long to warm up to her new father. After all, he was around her every day and he moved them out of Alicia's grandparents' home and into one of their own that was bigger and still relatively close to Sir, who used to live on the same street as she did. She'd overheard her grandparents saying that her mother had married a good man—an older man, which was just what she needed. Back then, she thought he was so much older than her mother, but there was only a seven-year age difference. He was an engineer for General Motors, and his movie-star good looks made him an instant hit at her school. All the female teachers' eyes seemed to light up when he walked into their classroom for parent/teacher conferences, which was something her mother didn't like but got used to once she realized none of them was a threat. He cherished the ground Alicia's mother walked on. He had never been married before and never had children. Being a father was new to him, but he seemed to cherish that too. She could never replace her stepfather—he was the one who raised her, called her "honey," and fiercely protected her from the boys who meant her no good. And even though Alicia kept her mother's maiden name, he was her father.

A few days later, Alicia is at Los Angeles International Airport.

"Why does it sound like you're at an airport?" asks her aunt Olena.

"Because I am," says Alicia as she waits at her gate for the departing flight. "I'm going to Detroit, actually."

"You're going there? For what? I thought you said you never wanted to go back."

"I'm going for an operation, and I'll have to stay there for a while . . . at least two months while I recover . . . maybe longer, who knows. I just have to figure some things out right now."

"Back up . . . an operation?" asks Olena. "What kind of operation?"

"A hysterectomy," Alicia says nonchalantly. By this time she'd told her mother and grandmother, and now the disclosure felt like second nature, in a way.

"Isn't thirty-two too young to have a hysterectomy?" asks her aunt. "Is that really your only choice? Because there's no coming back from that. There's no putting your uterus back in once it's gone. So please be absolutely sure."

"My doctor in LA said I don't have a choice. It's either that or die. And I didn't want to have the operation here, so I'm going to Detroit to my mom's doctor. He already has my records. I just have one appointment to assess me and then he's going to schedule surgery."

"Did you ask him what he meant by it's either that or die?"

"No, I just said okay, no problem, I'll die. Of course I asked him."

"You have fibroids. Since when do women die because of that? I've had them since I was nineteen and I'm still living. So how did your doctor possibly justify his asinine statement that you could die because of some fibroids?"

"Because, Auntie, it's not asinine. I'm losing way too much blood every month while I have my period. I wear four pads and a tampon, and I have to change those five times a day, so I'm severely anemic and more susceptible to a heart attack. If you don't believe me, Google it. But I don't want to talk about this right now."

"Google what?"

"Anemia," shouts Alicia. "I'm not in the mood for this!" The woman sitting beside her turns slightly and looks in her direction. Then she stands up and slowly walks away.

"Did he even take your blood? After watching the *Sicko* documentary, I don't trust the entire medical profession, insurance companies, pharmaceutical companies, anybody remotely connected . . . not even the magazines that go inside the waiting rooms. Did he take your blood, Alicia?" she repeats.

"Of course he took my blood," says Alicia more calmly. "How else would he know I'm anemic?"

"What was your hemoglobin?"

Alicia's sigh was even heavier. She dreaded even saying the number. "A five," she mutters.

"A what? A five? I know you didn't say a five. That doesn't sound normal."

"It's not normal, Auntie. That's why I could die."

"Did you know it's the second most common surgery among women in the United States? Doesn't that seem odd to you? Almost like a racket?"

"I don't think my surgery is a scam," Alicia says calmly. "Don't forget, I don't even have insurance."

"Well, then that explains why your doctor said you're going to die. No health care insurance and you die. It's all in the documentary. Watch it for yourself. Sometimes, even with health insurance you still die. Did you know that insurance companies consider paying claims to be a loss? That operation will probably be close to ten grand."

"Actually, it'll cost me more like thirty-two thousand."

"That's because you don't have insurance. I bet those insurance companies don't pay out thirty-two thousand for a hysterectomy. Where are you going to get that kind of money?"

"I have some money, and between my parents and your parents and you, I'll be okay."

"Me, huh? I'm laid off, remember?"

"You still have money."

"Why aren't you listed on your parents' policy?"

"Auntie, thirty-two may be too young to have a hysterectomy. But it's definitely too old to be listed as a dependent on your parents' insurance policy." Maybe it won't be so bad, muses Alicia. That's what a lot of women online were saying. She'd found a support forum for women who had or were going to undergo a hysterectomy. But Alicia occasionally grew tired of reading all of the posts, especially by women who'd gone through the procedure and claimed it was the best thing they'd ever done. They talked about a major surgery as if it were some whirlwind vacation, as if they'd just returned from Cape Town or taken to the high seas for a cruise to Antarctica. They had their uterus removed. And Alicia could definitely conjure up better things to do than that. Her doctor can't even say for certain if he's leaving in her cervix; he might even have to take both ovaries. *Is that what surgically induced menopause means?* What will stay and what goes all depends on what he sees when he gets in there. It's as if her womb were some forbidden cave he's exploring. She's scared. And as for age thirty-two being too young for a hysterectomy? When she told her doctor that, his response was simply, "Would you rather they say thirty-two was too young to die?"

Even her grandmother started freaking out when she heard about her thirty-two-year-old granddaughter getting a hysterectomy. She's worried about something Alicia isn't even concerned about—Alicia's sex life. All her sixty-seven-year-old grandmother kept saying was, "Please don't let them take your cervix or you won't feel a thing. You'll be as dry down there as the Atacama Desert." Not the Atacama Desert, thought Alicia. Her grandmother obviously watched far too much Discovery Channel.

"Is it possible I was born without a cervix?" added Alicia sarcastically, because she never felt much of anything anyway—never had an orgasm. She always just pretended to. She didn't even blame a man if he cheated on her. Sure, she'd get mad for a moment. But when it was all said and done, if she were a man, she'd cheat on her too, because she wasn't even that great at faking orgasms. If she were that good an actress, she would have made it in Hollywood, she muses, instead of waiting at the airport to go home.

"Listen," says her aunt. "I'm sure everything will go fine with your surgery, and just think, when you go back, you'll be ready to take on Hollywood period free, because I know you're going to make it."

The main reason Alicia wanted to talk to her aunt so badly was because she needed someone to remind her that people were still expecting her to make good on her promise. People still wanted her to succeed, maybe now even more than she wanted to. She used to think giving up on her dream would be impossible. "I'll never stop trying," she'd say. Of course, she had her moments when she felt like a fool for not going to college, probably Howard, and getting that "good government job" once she finished like so many of her cousins had.

Alicia hears a beep. It's her other line.

"Auntie, I want to take this call real quick, and then I have to get ready to board. I'll call you when I get to Detroit."

It's Heaven, and Alicia's happy to hear from her.

"Hey, guess what?" says Alicia, trying to sound excited. "I'll be in Detroit later today."

"In this Detroit?" asks Heaven.

"Is there another one?"

Heaven giggles. "For how long?"

"Two months."

"That's a real long time. I'm so happy. God answered my prayer."

"What was your prayer?"

"That I could meet you face-to-face one day. I used to have a direct line to God. As you know, my name is Heaven."

"Okay, well, the next time you and God have a talk, ask Him to slide a little favor my way. I just need a role. Just give me one role and I'll make the rest history."

"I will," says Heaven. "So, are we gonna see each other?"

"If you want to, we can."

"If I want to? Of course I want to. I prayed to, remember? And I haven't prayed in a long time."

Alicia hears a boarding announcement for her section. "I'll call you sometime later in the week as soon as I get settled," she says, rushing off the phone.

"Okay, I can't wait to finally meet you."

Alicia lands in Detroit a little after four in the afternoon. From her window seat, she watches a baggage handler, bundled up in rain gear, on the tarmac carefully loading luggage onto the conveyer belt of another plane. She's really home.

The plane beside her is getting ready to depart. But unfortunately for Alicia, she has just arrived. She releases a woeful sigh, muses over what lies ahead, and then she removes the picture she has of her sister Hope. Everything happens for a reason. Maybe Heaven and Hope are the real reason she's home.

"I'm here," she tells her aunt by phone after picking up her luggage from baggage claim. "Metro Airport sure has changed. They have a train."

"You mean the tram. That's nothing new. Lots of other airports have one, including Atlanta. So, do you even remember what your parents look like?"

"Auntie, what a stupid question. Of course I do. It hasn't been that long."

"Alicia?" a woman's voice says.

She turns, still holding the phone, and her mouth drops. "Mom," she says. For a minute there, she wasn't sure that Olena's question had been such a stupid one. She barely recognized her mother, who had cut her hair and gone natural, which made her look much younger than forty-seven.

"Where's Dad?"

"He's waiting on us outside."

"You look so good," says Alicia as she gives her mother a heartfelt embrace. "Auntie—"

"Tell your aunt you'll call her later," says Alicia's mother. "It's a perfect time to write, Olena," Alicia's mother says loudly enough for Olena, her sister, to hear. "The English Gardens are calling you."

"Tell your mom thanks for her support. Better late than never," says Olena.

"You're coming, right?" asks Alicia. "You'll be here for my operation. I need you here—I'm so nervous."

"Why do I have to come? You'll be fine. You should want me to conserve my cash under my circumstances."

"You have enough cash. Well, if you can't make it here, just pray for me." She ends the call with her aunt and follows her mother to the parking lot. Being reunited with her parents is bittersweet. Her parents never wanted her to move to LA in the first place. And once she was out there, her mother spent endless hours trying to convince her it was time to come back home. She can still remember her mother's words when she left. "If you go to LA, you're going out there on your own. Your father and I don't approve of this. You don't know anyone out there, and young girls go out there every day trying to become a star, and very few of them ever make it."

Back then, she was young and full of ambition. She felt like her whole life was ahead of her and it was going to be one filled with nothing but glitz and glamour. So off she went with one duffel bag stuffed with tees and tanks, hoodies and sweats, and a few skirts along with one wrinkle-free dress just in case she needed to go somewhere fancy. But fewer and fewer callbacks and auditions led to her growing doubts and to her current state of hopelessness. Now she was back, just like her mother had predicted.

"Have you given yourself a time frame?" her mother had asked one evening after Alicia had been in LA for a couple of years and was crying about her dead-end retail job. Funny, she'd always given herself a time frame when it came to how long she would work a regular job—how long she'd waitress, how long she'd work retail. Six months tops, and she'd quit on or before her deadline. But when it came to making it in Hollywood, she left the door wide-open. That explained why it hurt so much when it slammed in her face.

Detroit has changed quite a bit in the last thirteen years. In many ways she is relieved. Even though she would have preferred to return under different circumstances, she's surprisingly happy to be far from her wannabe lifestyle in LA—the too-expensive apartment with the awesome view; the used CLK she bought for image but couldn't even afford the oil changes for; her designer clothes. Almost everything seems make-believe now. Now that she has put her dreams of acting aside, she is starting to wonder what will be next. If life isn't about her career or a man or babies, what is left? In a way it is nice not to want much—to approach the world devoid of expectations and excuses. Even if Hollywood is one big conspiracy theory, what does it matter now? She is free. *Finally*, she tells herself. No Oscar nods to dream of. No big break to obsess over. Her "Superstar" ringtone is irrelevant now. And the more she tells herself how good this move will be, and how horrible Hollywood is, she's hopeful that one day she'll actually believe it.

Heaven is inside a huge beauty supply store around the corner from her house. She's desperate to do one thing—to get her hair together before she meets Alicia. After one week, her tree braids are keeping up nicely, but she wants to wash her hair, and when the braids start to loosen and she needs to take them out, she'll need the products necessary to do her own hair. She's decided to officially transition from relaxed to natural hair, which means she'll need something to fight that stubborn new growth.

Two days have passed and she hasn't yet heard from Alicia, but when she calls she wants to be ready . . . hair and all.

The night before, she prayed again. Right before she went to bed. This time she actually got down on her hands and knees and talked to God. She felt like she had to apologize—first for losing faith, and also for hardly ever talking to Him, and never going to Him for help when she needed it. And then she thanked Him for bringing her sister home. And then she asked for His favor—not for her, but for Alicia. That her dreams would come true. And for Hope. That she might one day forgive Heaven for all her past failures. And she said a special prayer for Havana, and she didn't leave

213

out Trina or her nana either, or even Donovan. But she did skip saying a prayer for Glenn.

"So I was watching TV last night," says Heaven as she stands in front of the glass counter encasing wigs and various bags of hair. She is holding several African Pride and Creme of Nature beauty products. "And I saw this thing that's like a flat iron advertised. It's called the InStyler, and I was wondering if you all carry it?"

"Me not know," says the Korean woman in broken English. "Ask him. He tell you."

"Do you carry the InStyler? It's a—"

"I know what it is," says a Korean man speaking slightly better English than the woman.

"Do you carry it?"

"We have."

"You do?"

"Yes, we have. You want? I get for you."

"Is it the InStyler, though?"

"Yes, InStyler?" he says, removing a set of keys from the drawer, then walking down the long glass counter to the other end. Heaven follows along his path, stopping when he does.

"That doesn't say InStyler," says Heaven as she watches the man remove a flat iron box. "I already have a flat iron."

"This same thing. This better than InStyler."

"Is it the same thing or is it better?" asks Heaven, becoming irritated.

"Same thing . . . It's better."

"Don't you know me? I come in here all the time and buy a lot of products. This is really important to me. I'm trying to do something I've never done. And when you're trying to do something you've never done before, you need to use things you've never used before . . . or something like that . . . and I've used that," says Heaven, jabbing at the flat iron box. "So do you have the InStyler or not?"

"No, we not have that one. Check back next week. You need anything else?"

"Yes," she says, dragging her voice and piling the products that are in her hand onto the counter to purchase with cash.

She didn't have access to the Internet, so she couldn't order the InStyler online. She didn't have a credit card, so she couldn't call and order by phone. She had her Visa check card, but she'd had a bad experience with ordering something over the phone with that. They charged her in three easy payments. By the time the second payment rolled around, she didn't have the money in her account, causing several other checks to bounce and putting her in a serious hole.

Sometimes she understood why some women chose to date for money instead of love. Love didn't pay a single bill and she had so many. Love wouldn't buy her an InStyler and neither would Donovan. But maybe Jamal would. During the welcomed absence of Donovan over the past several days, Heaven and Jamal began talking on the phone, covering various topics from politics—a subject she quickly switched from—to food. He asked what she knew about Chaldeans, finally putting to rest her curiosity about Jamal's ethnicity. She'd just spoken to him earlier that day, and they had arranged to meet at a Chaldean restaurant in Oak Park at one in the afternoon.

The next day, Heaven arrives at New Sahara Restaurant on Coolidge Highway, just minutes from Hope's house. After taking their seats near the front of the restaurant, Jamal places a large order for a variety of Chaldean dishes so Heaven can truly experience Iraqi food. Her cell phone is vibrating in her large canvas purse. There is no need for her to check the caller ID; she knows it's Donovan. For the past few days, he has said he wants to work things out. But she's been careful not to mention she's pregnant. Even though she knows their relationship is as good as over, she still wants what his mother wants for him. She wants Donovan to get his life together and to take care of his kids—the one he already has and the one on the way that Heaven didn't know anything about until she overheard his mother. He won't have to worry at all about taking care of the one she's carrying. This one he'll never know exists.

"You never answered my question about what you think of Chaldeans," says Jamal.

"You mean Arabs?"

"No. We're not Arabs. I mean Chaldeans."

"Aren't the people who live across Seven Mile and Woodward called Arabs? That's what we always called them. I know all about your people. You're Muslim, right?"

He snorts laughter through his nose before shaking his head. "You don't know much," he says calmly. "Chaldeans are Christians from Iraq. Many of us practice the Roman Catholic faith. We are not Muslim." He went on to explain that his ethnic group came from a village in Iraq called Telkaif. His family on his father's side had migrated from Telkaif to Baghdad before finally arriving in Detroit in 1972 when his father was just a young teen; his mother was born in the States. His mother's family had arrived in Detroit in the late forties, well before his mother was even born. Both his father's and mother's families settled in Chaldean Town. When his paternal grandfather first came to Detroit, he had hopes of finding employment at Ford Motor Company, but when that didn't pan out, he took a job at a small Iraqi-owned grocery store, and eventually took over ownership.

Jamal tries to explain so she will understand. "I am not anti-Arab, because to be anti-Arab would be racist, but I am trying to explain to you that I am not an Arab and not a Muslim. I am a Chaldean, and I am also Roman Catholic."

"This is why I don't like talking about race, religion, or politics. I would never ask a person who isn't black what they think of blacks. Look at the nasty things some of them say about our First Lady." Heaven shakes her head. "If they can talk badly about Michelle Obama, I don't even want to know what they'd say about me."

"You are the one who brought up race, not I."

"When did I bring up race?"

"Last night on the phone . . . You thought I was Mexican, remember?"

She shrugs. "Okay, you're right."

Even though Jamal's family considers themselves Westernized, they are still very proud of their own culture. Jamal points out that he loves Iraqi food; loves rice and stew, grape leaves, spinach pie and hummus, but as Heaven can testify, he also loves hamburgers and fries, and many other non–Middle Eastern dishes.

"Now, tell me what you think you know about my people. And I'll tell you the same," he says as they share a plate of appetizers, a Sahara Maza tray.

She shrugs. "Just what my nana always told me."

"And what is that?" he asks as he spreads hummus over his pita bread.

Her cell phone is vibrating in her favorite purse.

"I don't take too much of what my nana says to heart. Basically, she said that your people own all the grocery stores and gas stations in Michigan. And your people do better than our people because you don't have to pay taxes for seven years."

As she is speaking, Jamal shakes his head. "Where did that one come from? Do you think Uncle Sam would allow us to not pay taxes?"

"You all don't have to pay taxes."

"You're telling me what my people don't have to do. Don't you think I would know?"

She shrugs. "This is why I don't like talking about that kind of stuff."

"Go on. . . . Continue."

"I don't want to continue. I want to eat and enjoy my food. I don't want to talk about race or religion."

"She probably said we're all uneducated, right?" he asks. Heaven shakes her head. Heaven's grandmother would be the last person to pass judgment against another based on their level of education; she herself never made it further than the ninth grade and had her first child, Heaven's father, when she was only fourteen. "I'm surprised. Most people think that. In fact, my mother is a schoolteacher and my father is an attorney. Many of us are educated."

"What do you do?"

"Me?" asks Jamal with hesitation. "I help my grandfather with his gas station."

"I thought he owned a grocery store."

"He did, but he gave the grocery store to my father and bought a gas station. And my father gave the grocery store to my other sister's husband as a wedding gift a few years ago."

"Nice gift." Heaven picks up some baba ganoush from the Sahara Maza tray they ordered as an appetizer. "Now, can you tell me what I'm eating?" He explains to her what is on the tray—hummus, tabouli, faitoush, falafel, and grape leaves. He also ordered fried kibbee, a Sahara salad, jajeek salad, and two chicken shawarmas. He points to the hummus. He is surprised to find she has never heard of it as it is one of the more Westernized dishes.

"What is tahini?" she asks when she doesn't recognize one of the common ingredients found in a few of the items they are eating.

"It's a paste made from the hull of sesame seeds," Jamal explains.

Heaven spreads a large amount of hummus and tahini on her pita bread. She loves the Chaldean food because it is spicy and they use a lot of garlic, which she loves.

"My sister is in town from LA," she says proudly. "She got in a couple days ago."

"She went there for a vacation?"

"She lives there. She's a sister I just found out about. Long story, but I want to take her out to dinner. I wonder if this would be a good place to take her." She looks at the prices on the menu. "The prices aren't bad, but I'm looking for something cheap. Like, unemployed cheap."

"Take her to Toast in Birmingham."

"If it's in Birmingham, I know I can't afford it."

"Take her on Tuesday. They have two-dollar taco night every Tuesday."

Heaven's smile widens. "Now, that's affordable."

As they sit chatting together, Heaven realizes just how much fun she is having. She could never just sit with Donovan and have an intelligent conversation. He is always distracted by his cell phone and never really seems to be listening to her. But she is pregnant, and eventually she will start to show. Sooner or later, she'll have to tell Jamal, and at that point she wonders if he'll categorize her. Single black mother is the statistic she'll belong to.

Their lunch ends with a handshake as he walks her to her car and watches her drive off before he hops on his motorcycle.

She watches him through her rearview before he breezes past her and out of sight. He is nice and handsome and wants nothing but her friendship. She hopes he won't disappoint her as so many others have. But she knows his line of work isn't legal. She knows he sells drugs, and she has the pictures to prove it.

She stops at a nearby Walgreens to buy a Hallmark miss-you card and then drives by Hope's house. Hope's car isn't in the driveway, and she knows she's not at home yet because Hope doesn't park in the garage, and it's not even four in the afternoon so she's still at work. She places the card in the mail slot of her front door. Inside, on the blank side of the card, she has written:

> *I miss you and Havana so much. And I love both of you. You two and Nana are all the family I got. I know what I did was wrong and I swear to you one day I will repay you, but please forgive me. You know how important family is to me.*
> *Love always and forever,*
> *Heaven*

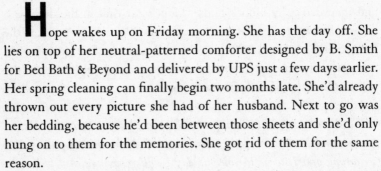

Hope wakes up on Friday morning. She has the day off. She lies on top of her neutral-patterned comforter designed by B. Smith for Bed Bath & Beyond and delivered by UPS just a few days earlier. Her spring cleaning can finally begin two months late. She'd already thrown out every picture she had of her husband. Next to go was her bedding, because he'd been between those sheets and she'd only hung on to them for the memories. She got rid of them for the same reason.

It was freeing for her to confide in Ezra, who was blown away by the revelation. The more they talked everything over, the more she realized it was true. And where Roger was suddenly didn't matter. Whether he was alive after two years or off somewhere dead, she just didn't care anymore.

A cool breeze from the floor fan planted at the foot of her bed circulates across her twelve-by-ten bedroom. An orange ginger votive candle that she'd forgotten to blow out before she closed her eyes six hours earlier still flickers from her nightstand. Sleeping long and sleeping well wasn't something she had been used to for the past two years, but now she has been sleeping a little more soundly . . . just a little. She is still not getting the recommended eight hours, but any more sleep than the three hours she used to get is an improvement.

This afternoon she is having lunch with Taite. She wants to know if Taite knew all along that her husband wasn't on the boat. And if she did . . . What kind of friend wouldn't tell her?

She sits in bed with her cordless phone to her ear, listening to the message from Heaven. No, she doesn't want to meet her and Glenn's other child at Toast on Tuesday. Two-dollar tacos? Who cares? She's an actress. So what? She can't be that good, because Hope's never heard of her. And the card Heaven had dropped off is already torn up and in her garbage can sitting on her curb, waiting to be picked up by the city of Oak Park. It's trash day. The fact that Heaven stole from her is only one straw. The way her sister lives, the poor choices she makes with men and friends, her overall lifestyle—these are all things she can't condone and doesn't want to be around. Period. Blood or not.

She is almost ready to start dialing.

She is interested in another customer-top-rated item being shown on QVC and selling out fast.

"Mom," says Havana, opening her mother's bedroom door. "Another package for you. Will you take me to the bookstore?"

"Havana, didn't I tell you about knocking first? Please put the package down."

She sets the small box on Hope's dresser. "You should lock your door so I can't just walk in."

Hope's eyes flutter. "Why don't you just do what I say to begin with so we won't even have to have this discussion? How about that? Please don't forget that I'm the mother and you're the child." She is more frustrated at herself than at Havana. Every time she snaps at Havana, she feels a pain in her chest. And she has to remind herself often not to take her anger out on her child. Havana didn't understand her loss then. And she won't understand now that what her mother truly lost was time, not a husband . . . and all faith in men.

"I'm sorry. But will you please take me to the bookstore?"

"Just let me think about it. It all depends on how I feel."

"Can I call Aunt Heaven back? She'll take me."

"No," snaps Hope. "I already told you about your aunt Heaven. She won't be coming back over here."

"Ever?"

"Never . . . You already know this, Havana."

"I didn't already know that she would *never* ever be coming over."

"Yes, you did, Havana. We've had this discussion. You have to start listening to me. There's more to life than a book filled with fantasy. Because, let me tell you something, life is fantasy enough. What you see isn't always what you get. Learn that lesson now so you won't be disappointed later."

Hope and Taite meet at the landmark Greektown restaurant, New Parthenon. They sit on the second level of the loft-style space and start off their meal with an order of saganaki, an appetizer of pan-seared cheese. The waiter brings it to their table and gives it a shot of oil that ignites into a large flame.

"Opa!" yells the waiter.

"I finally had an opportunity to speak with Michael Beck," says Hope after the waiter leaves. "I was beginning to think I never would."

"Oh, really," says Taite as she nibbles on the hot cheese. "And what did he say?"

"Did you know that Roger wasn't even on the boat? I don't even think he's dead. You had to know. You did know, didn't you?"

"Wait a minute. What do you mean he isn't dead?" Taite asks. "I had no idea. How could that even be possible? If he wasn't on the boat, where is he?"

"Exactly, where is he? Michael Beck said you knew he wasn't on the boat. Did you?" Hope asks even though she knows that's not exactly what Michael said, but she did want to know what she did and didn't know. She doesn't care about Roger, but if Taite knew all of this time and didn't tell Hope, she doesn't think she'll be able to forgive her.

"No, I didn't know that. I swear to you I didn't. How would I know that? Don't you think I'd tell you?"

"Michael Beck was your friend, not mine."

"He was not my friend. He was Tim's friend. I barely knew him."

"Well, he said you knew about Roger. Look, I know he wasn't on the boat. I believe that. I mean, if my husband could lie about being in the navy, he could lie about anything. He'd been dishonorably discharged more than a year before. So what did you know? Did you know that?"

"I knew what you knew." She shrugs. "I mean, I had suspicions that Tim was cheating on me at the time, but I had no idea Roger was cheating on you," she says, throwing both of her hands up. "And I definitely didn't know he wasn't even on the boat. I talked to Tim late that Friday. He told me Roger had left Ludington that night, and he asked me not to say anything to you. I went off. I told him that I was going to say something because that wasn't right. I think the only reason he even mentioned Roger and what he was doing was to throw me off him. I knew he was out there with some chick. I figured. Things weren't going well on the team, and he'd really been acting out. I asked him why Roger left, whom he left with. Then Tim quickly changed his whole tune and said Roger was coming right back and not to worry. I knew that part was a lie, but I didn't have proof, so I wasn't going to come to you with my suspicions. You don't break up a marriage over suspicions."

"Well, I believe him when he says Roger wasn't on there."

Hope knows things like that can happen. She knows a person can marry another person without knowing who they truly are. She's heard of that happening, but she never, in more than a million years, expected anything like that to happen to her. Maybe the marriage wasn't exactly what she thought it had been—obviously. And now, more obvious than that is that he wasn't—or isn't, if he's still alive—

who she thought he was. She realized then that her first husband, Morris, wasn't half as bad as she'd made him out to be. At least he had been honest enough to tell her he wasn't ready for their marriage. She may not have wanted to hear what he had to say since she was pregnant at the time, but he had been telling her the truth—that he was too young and too immature to be a husband and a father. He didn't know how to keep a family together because he himself wasn't together. He didn't have a steady job, and he was tired of constantly borrowing money from his family just to pay rent on a roach-infested apartment they both hated living in. She wasn't trying to paint Havana's father as perfect, but at least he was honest.

She now has to deal with the fact that she'd checked out of life for two years for a man who left because he didn't love her. It is the plain truth and no other. Who was the man whose last name she'd taken?

She realizes now that a wedding ceremony means nothing, whether it is as small as the one she had with just a few people present at an inexpensive chapel or huge like the one Taite is planning. What matters most is the person you choose to walk down the aisle with. Now, she feels the entire concept of marriage is completely ridiculous—saying, "I do" and intertwining your life with that of another person you really know nothing about other than what they've told you, in her case that having been just plain lies.

"Let me see, what makes me look less pregnant?" Alicia asks herself as she pulls outfits from her suitcase. "These jeans and this top. Maybe not this top . . . I think this one will look better." She pulls out a pair of black blue wash jeans and a printed ruched fabric top with short flutter sleeves. She is meeting Sir for dinner and strangely, she's nervous. Over the years, Sir has admitted to having feelings for her. In fact, as recently as last night, he'd joked about getting married. But she's never looked at her friend in that way.

Her phone trills. She assumes it will be Sir confirming dinner, but it is Heaven.

"So you made it to the D? I'm so jazzed about seeing you."

Jazzed? Alicia thinks to herself. "Me too."

"Well, I was just calling to ask you if I could take you to dinner tomorrow. I know you said you'd call me, but my friend was telling me about this place in Birmingham that has a two-dollar taco special on Tuesdays, and that is right in line with my budget. Will you go?"

"Count me in." They agree to meet at seven. Alicia ends the conversation after Sir calls on her other line.

The restaurant where Alicia is meeting Sir is situated in a renovated 1890s building, near the old Tiger Stadium. A black and red sign with fluorescent lights juts from the red brick building and displays the restaurant's name—SLOW'S BAR-B-Q—underneath the image of a locomotive blowing smoke from its engine.

A tall man stands near the entrance, wearing a tie with a red square print and matching hanky tucked neatly inside the breast pocket of his suit jacket. His face is cleanly shaven and his hair is in a close cut. He politely holds the door open for Alicia, who mutters a quick thank-you as she hastily walks past him.

She steps inside the restaurant and takes a look around, unsure of who it is she's looking for exactly and realizing, for the first time, she might not recognize him after thirteen years, the same way she didn't recognize her mother. But as she scans the restaurant, she's struck by a sudden realization, and a smile slowly crosses her face. She turns around. She walks back outside where the man is still standing.

"You knew it was me, didn't you?" asks Alicia as she walks up to him.

"Yes, I did. You still look exactly the same," he says, "but I had to mess with you."

"You don't look the same at all," she says. And he didn't. Was it possible for a man to get taller after the age of nineteen? Because he'd grown several inches, now reaching her ideal height of six feet.

"I only recognized you because you still have that baby face," she says, pinching his cheeks.

"Please don't." As Sir holds the door open, Alicia steps to the side to let a young couple pass her. The young woman smiles and says, "I love your hair."

"Thank you," says Alicia with a smile.

"Yes, I love your hair too. It looks very Jill Scott," says Sir. She doesn't respond. She knows he likes women to wear their hair straight . . . long and straight, the way she'd always worn hers in high school.

Inside the restaurant, Alicia and Sir make themselves comfortable in a wooden booth set against a brick wall. Even though Alicia doesn't drink, she decides to order a dry white wine to go along with her St. Louis spareribs and the pricey but tasty mac-n-cheese; Sir opts for pulled pork.

Today is a special day, a cause for celebration, the first time in thirteen years she's seen her friend and only one week before the big operation, so she's going to drink, but just a little.

As far as Alicia knows, Sir is still in the mortgage industry. He has been featured in several publications as one of the future business leaders to watch. Sadly, she's never read any of the articles he was featured in. Alicia doesn't sway much beyond *Variety*, *Daily Variety*, and the *Hollywood Reporter*. Oh, and she definitely couldn't live without her subscription to *Essence*. One day she was going to be honored at their annual Black Women in Hollywood award ceremony, because one day she was going to achieve the success she dreamed of.

"So how's the mortgage business?"

"I see you're still not reading anything besides entertainment news."

She shakes her head and says, "Not really."

"Well, there is no more mortgage business for people like me who specialized in subprime lending."

"Are you serious? So what happened to your business?"

"I had to close it."

"Oh my God," says Alicia, after letting out a loud gasp. "But what about all of the meetings you were having? I knew you weren't doing great, but I didn't know you'd have to close. I'm so sorry."

"Yeah, I am too."

"But on the bright side, you're a born entrepreneur. And I know you'll land on your feet," she says, remembering that he always sold the most candy for fundraising events for school and how he was the first among their friends to start working when he'd decided at twelve to take a job over the summer drying off cars at a car wash on Seven Mile. Alicia was fifteen before she finally agreed to babysit, and that was just to watch her little brother. Sir also worked while he went to Michigan State and paid for his own books, while his education was paid by a four-year academic scholarship. "You'll be fine."

"I know I will, but right now I'm having a moment, and I'm going to go ahead and take that because I lost a lot of money. A *Madoff* amount."

She gasps. "You mean you lost everything?" She shakes her head. That was the worst situation to be in—losing everything. Alicia knew that full well.

He shook his head. "I was so close to buying a loft at Willys Overlands. I'll have to take you there for a tour. You will be amazed. Detroit didn't have anything like that when you were here, and I am still going to buy one of those lofts one day."

"I'm sure you are."

"If I ever rebound. I'm talking about living in a loft, but I may end up living in a tent in Florida."

Alicia gasps. "Are you going to be homeless, Sir? My parents would let you stay with them. You're like family. But wait a minute—you have family. Your mom still lives in Michigan, doesn't she?"

Sir smiles. "It's actually not that bad. I was overexaggerating a little. I did close my business, but I have enough to tide me over for a while. When the mortgage business was good it was *real* good," he says, "so I put enough away for a rainy day to transition into something else—as soon as I figure what that something else will be."

"You had me worried for you for a second." She shoves the remainder of the mac-n-cheese down her throat without chewing, swallowing several large spoonfuls of the sharp and creamy dish before washing it down with a glass of water.

"How's Aubrey? You haven't mentioned her yet," Sir says as he notices Alicia's eyes roll. "Is something wrong?"

"Aside from the fact that she's a backstabber," she says firmly. "No . . . not really." She picks up her glass of wine and downs it.

"So you and Aubrey fell out? I didn't think I'd ever see that day come. I thought you two were like Oprah and Gayle."

"And she's Oprah, I guess," snarls Alicia.

"No, actually, I was going to say you were Oprah." Alicia smiles at him, and this time she looks into his eyes, realizing how much she's missed him.

"You're kinda cute," she says, already tipsy after just one glass of wine.

He smiles and says, "Thank you. Just kinda though, huh? So, are you going to tell me what happened between you and your girl?"

The waitress returns with the bottle of Muscadet and refills their wineglasses.

Alicia sighs. "It's going to take me this entire bottle to get through that story."

"I've got time, I don't have a business, so I have nothing else to do but listen."

"Seems like nobody has a job anymore . . . you . . . my parents . . . my aunt . . . Oh, Aubrey does—she has my job . . . *puta*!"

"Spanish? Who taught you that word . . . Benita?"

Alicia nods.

"What happened?" he asks her.

"I had a part in a movie and she convinced me to take another part and she ended up with the other part that I really wanted and could have had that would have paid really well. And now I'm locked into a film with this crazy guy she introduced me to who threatened to sue me if I don't fulfill my agreement. But he's just going to have to sue me."

"How much is 'really well'?"

"Well, Aubrey is getting seven figures," she says with a frown. "Oh well, I can't cry over spilled milk."

"Why not? You can cry over anything you want to, especially over something like that."

And that's when she lets loose. In the crowded restaurant, as Sir hands her napkins from the dispenser, she cries . . . and drinks . . . just one more glass. But with her low tolerance, that's too much alcohol in her system for her to drive back to her parents' condo.

Alicia prances through the eight-foot-tall entryway of Sir's home and enters the rented loft. She stands in the center of the large open space with nine-foot ceilings, not knowing where to go first or what to explore. Through a large window she notices a stunning city view. She's surprised Detroit can look this good.

He removes his suit jacket and tie and tosses them over a bar stool. She notices his little paunch, but she wouldn't dare tease. She's too self-conscious about her own belly.

"Wow, I really like this place," she says, making herself at home. She enters the kitchen first. Even though she doesn't cook, she's always told herself one day she is going to take gourmet cooking lessons. Her hand sweeps across the black granite breakfast bar and countertops. She thinks she is opening the dishwasher before realizing she needs to pull it out like a drawer. That is the first time she's ever seen a dishwasher like that, but she imagines that Aubrey's dishwasher is even fancier. All the appliances in his kitchen are stainless steel, including a side-by-side fridge with ice maker.

"Nice loft," she says.

"Nice rent also . . . or should I say high rent."

She settles in his living room on a large black leather chair with her feet kicked up on a matching ottoman. He sits across from her on the sofa. Eventually, with the assistance of Maxwell, Al B. Sure, and a little Whitney Houston—she starts talking to Sir about her impending surgery that she's so nervous about. She doesn't mention the big H word. She uses buzz words like tumor and cysts instead.

"So you're having a hysterectomy?" asks Sir, controlling the music with his remote.

"I didn't say that. And what do you know about a hysterectomy anyway?"

"My mother had one, and I dated a woman who had one . . . so I know a few things."

"With the woman you dated, was the sex any different?"

He shrugs. "I never had sex with her."

"Really? Now that's different. Did you tell me about this one?"

"No, I don't tell you everything . . . just almost everything."

"I just can't believe you didn't sleep with her."

"Why? Do you honestly think men sleep with every woman they date? Have you had sex with every man you've dated?"

"Hmm," Alicia says. "Just about," She pauses a second before saying, "I'm kidding."

"I can count on one hand how many women I've had sex with and still have one finger left."

"Four?" exclaims Alicia, turning up her nose. "Are you serious? I can't believe this is the first time we're talking about this. Four women? That's it?"

"Four women," he says. "The first time I had sex was in college. Sophomore year. And of course, I stayed with her all through college and a few years after."

"Madeline was your first. I knew that. I knew you got off to a late start, but I guess I thought you'd caught up by now. Okay, so let me think. After Madeline was Tiffany. And you stayed with Tiffany for two years, and after that relationship you took a break. And then last year you were dating two different women, but I can't remember their names."

"Neither can I."

"I think you're like that because of what happened to your uncle."

"I know I'm like that because of what happened to my uncle."

Uncle James was his father's brother who'd lived with them for a while. To say he was a ladies' man was an understatement. Sir's uncle was just as obsessed with getting women as Sir's dad was with getting rich. Sir's father used to always tell James, "You can't keep playing all these women or one day somebody's going to get hurt." And one day someone did—James and a young woman he'd fallen in love with were both found shot to death inside the woman's home. Police believed, but were unable to prove, that one of the women James had previously dated was responsible for the double murders.

"So you won't be able to have kids?" asks Sir.

"Nope. Isn't that sad?"

"Not for you, it isn't. You never wanted kids."

"Never wanted kids? Says who?" Alicia shakes her head. "I never said I never wanted kids."

"You've said that ever since the fourth grade. I remember, because at that time I was trying to figure out why you would even be thinking about having kids. At that age I probably still thought the stork delivered them."

"I might've said it in the fourth grade, but come on now, what does a nine-year-old know? Things have changed since then. I just knew you'd be married by now. You know, you men have more control over that sort of thing."

"I've never wanted children, and as for marriage, I won't rule it out, but most women want kids, or they'll lie and say they don't, figuring they can go ahead and have one anyway, but I had a vasectomy."

"I thought I knew everything about my best friend, and now I'm beginning to realize there's so much I don't know."

"I've always said everything happens for a reason and what happened to my uncle was a really bad thing, but it taught me not to lead women on. And as for kids, you know how many nieces and nephews I have. I get to play Dad enough."

"Well, I recently discovered I'm an aunt."

His eyes widen. "Maximilian had a kid?"

"No. I have two half sisters and one has a child. I haven't met any of them yet, and the older one won't take my calls, but maybe one day she will. The point is I'm an aunt."

"If you say so," Sir says. "It will really count once you can point your niece out on the street. So, how does having sisters make you feel?"

"Half sisters," Alicia corrects. "I don't know. I'm going out to dinner with the younger one tomorrow. I can tell she has issues—just don't know what they are aside from being in a bad relationship—but I think there's more to her story . . . a lot more. At times, it's depressing to talk to her. It takes me back to my twenties." Alicia contemplates her last words. "Well, for Hollywood, being in my twenties would be great. But not in real life . . . I don't want to go back there."

"Let me ask you a question," he says. He leans forward on the black leather sofa and is practically sitting on the edge of it. "What do you think about me?"

"What do you mean?" she asks, wrinkling her brow.

"Have you ever thought about me romantically?"

"Sir," she says blushingly. "No, never," she lies. "I've known you all my life like a brother. That would be like incest."

"No, it wouldn't, because I'm not your brother. What about that time we kissed?"

"You mean the time we got drunk and kissed when we were on our senior trip?" She had actually thought about that time only a few nights earlier. She remembered how awkward she'd felt afterward; how close they'd come to taking it farther than a kiss; how glad she was that Aubrey had forgotten her key inside the hotel room they shared and had to go back to get it. Her fist pounding against the door beat sobriety into both of them. And now she realizes if she had gone farther, they'd be each other's first.

"We almost took that kiss a lot farther. Remember?" asks Sir.

"We were both upset because the airline lost our luggage. We couldn't go out partying in Orlando. What else could we do but get drunk in the hotel room and kiss?"

"I guess you're right," says Sir as he takes a momentary glance down at his square-toed oxfords before peering into her eyes. "I love you."

"I love you too," she says.

"I really thought we'd be married by now."

"Married?" Alicia asks as she scrunches her face.

"We've known each other all of our lives you might as well say. And, let's not forget that we got married in nursery school."

"We won't have to worry about your getting senile, because you don't forget a thing. We got married on a dare during nap time," she says with a laugh.

"Still, we got married. So technically, you're my wife. We've just been separated for all of this time."

"I know we had a mock marriage and that was cute and all"—she shrugs—"but you never liked me like that, did you?"

"You think I never liked you like that? I loved you like that. If you don't believe me, ask my mother."

Alicia can't stop blushing. She feels so awkward. She wants him to change the subject so badly, but he won't move on to something else . . . anything else. "I'm not going to ask your mother."

"I don't see why not. She's your biggest fan. The reason I stayed a virgin in high school was because you were the only girl allowed to visit. The only time I was able to use her car was when I was going to see you. She used to always say we were going to get married one day. I love you," he says, looking deep into her eyes. "I'm being very serious right now."

"If you've loved me for all this time, why would you let so much time go by and not tell me? Let's get serious. I love you too, but I'm not in the mood to play. I'm getting ready to have a serious operation. I love you like a brother."

"Are you saying I've never told you this?"

"I'm not saying that. I guess you have, but not all the way. I'm not saying we haven't talked about this."

"Alicia, you know we talked about it."

She tries to allow her mind to process all that Sir has told her. One thing she loves about him is that he isn't afraid to open up and share his feelings. He is like a woman in that way. He enjoys talking on the phone to her as much as she enjoys talking. Their relationship has always been that way.

Alicia says, "I guess a man is the farthest thing from my mind right now."

"I understand. You're having your surgery soon, and I know your mind is focused on that. We can table this conversation for a later date after you've fully recovered."

"I feel like you're about to whip out your BlackBerry and schedule that conversation or something."

"No."

"Oh, good," she says, but laughs at him when he pulls out his Palm.

"What date is your surgery?"

"It's on Monday," she huffs.

"Next Monday," he says, going through the calendar on his smartphone, "and recovery is roughly six weeks."

"You know that because of your mom?"

"And the other girl . . . We're getting up into early September. What are you going to do with all that time?"

"Relax and get my mind right."

"Get your mind right?" he asks as he focuses on his phone. "It's going to take you longer than six weeks to get your mind right. I might not see you until sometime next year, and that's being generous, because we are talking about *your* mind."

"Shut up," she says playfully as she walks over to strangle him.

He puts his hands on her stomach and she draws back.

"It's okay—you don't have to be self-conscious with me. And just think, before you know it, this will all be gone," he says as he holds on to her waist. "But I won't ever be gone. Now, that should have your mind messed up for real."

Alicia pulls her mother's Prius into a metered space across the street from Toast. She's apprehensive—not about meeting Heaven, but about Taco Tuesday. Coming from Los Angeles, she can't imagine any place in Michigan that has tacos that could even slightly compare to her favorite LA taco spot, Hugo's.

In the window of the restaurant stands a life-sized Betty Boop statue. The interior sparkles with gorgeous wood floors and retro black and white wallpaper—a mixture of fifties retro with a stylish contemporary cozy feel that resembles a vintage home. The eclectic vibe boasts chandeliers and vibrantly colored cozy sofas with large bright accent pillows. In the lobby there is a wall display of floral art along with multicolored plates and cups.

An antique white stove with legs and drawers serves as the hostess station.

The environment is lively and casual . . . and somewhat loud. She surveys the room in search of Heaven, whom she's only seen on Facebook.

Heaven arrived an hour early at the insistence of Jamal to accommodate the usual wait that the popular spot demands. To her surprise, she was seated rather quickly in the cocktail lounge while she waited for a seat to open up either on the patio or in the main eating area.

Now, Heaven sits patiently, staring at the white deer's head above a fireplace filled with candles. For kicks, she looks at the drink menu—the Blueberry Pancake Martini sounds tempting as does the Bloody Mary, but she's pregnant. The baby growing inside her has cured her borderline alcoholism, replacing her urge to drink with what feels like an incurable sweet tooth that is further tempted by the fresh baked pastries on display in the restaurant's lobby. As she waits for Alicia to arrive, she indulges in a slice of rum butter cake with rum pecans and fresh berries. She's going to be a mother in seven or eight months. She's not even sure how far along she is. She hasn't gone to the doctor yet, but she has made an appointment because she's pretty sure she needs to start her prenatal care. There's probably a lot she'll need, so she plans to buy a few books on parenting so she'll do a better job than both of her parents did.

She starts to rethink her restaurant recommendation. It's not that the inside isn't adorable or that the plates coming from the kitchen don't look delicious, but it's a bit loud—both with music and conversation. The place is full of energy—seen as well as heard. People are having fun. White folks always seem to have fun, she muses. This isn't necessarily the best place to have the meaningful conversation with Alicia she is hoping for. The outside patio might have slightly less noise, but it's filled to capacity, much like the inside. *Two-dollar tacos*, she thinks, reminding herself why she chose the place.

Alicia contemplates her first hello, wondering if it will be as simple as a subtle smile followed by, "Hi, I'm Alicia . . . your sister." No, she doesn't want to say "sister." That sounds too personal. How can she be her sister when they have never met in person? Just "Hi, I'm Alicia" will suffice. She realizes how much easier it would be for her if she had made a name for herself in Hollywood, assuming most would love to have a famous sister. But who is she kidding? That isn't her life.

Alicia walks through a wide entrance into the bustling main section of the restaurant and is instantly reminded of LA. She searches the lipstick red banquettes for Heaven. She'd visited Heaven's Facebook page the day before and looked at enough of her photographs that she is certain she'd be able to pick her out in a crowd. But out of the few black females, she doesn't spot one sitting alone, so she does what anyone living in a technology age would. She takes out her cell phone and sends a text.

Where r u?

Lounge. Sitting on a sofa. got on red top w/ beads and got a big red purse w/ white hearts all over.

A few minutes later, Alicia approaches. "Heaven?" shouts Alicia so she can be heard.

"Alicia?" Heaven yells back. She stands, and Alicia gives her a hug. "You're so pretty. Those head shots don't do you no justice."

"What?" shouts Alicia. "Are you sure you want to eat here? It's real cute, but I can't hear you. . . . Can you hear me?"

"Did you ask if I can hear you?" shouts Heaven. "Yeah, a little bit. I heard you when you said 'Can you hear me,' but I didn't hear nothin' you said before that."

"This isn't going to work."

"I don't. I used to work at Hamilton Middle School as a secretary, but I got laid off," says Heaven.

Alicia shakes her head. "What? I can't hear you." Heaven sits back down on the sofa and Alicia sits beside her.

"I said I don't work. Isn't that what you asked me?"

"No."

Heaven shrugs. "I'm starving. You?"

"I'm hungry, but I'm not in the mood for tacos. Do you want to go somewhere else?" She looks over at Heaven and the strange expression that quickly surfaces. "Did you hear me?"

Heaven's eyes flutter. "Yeah, I heard you. But the tacos are two dollars. I'm not trying to come off cheap, but that's all I can afford right now."

"Don't worry. I'll pay. You don't have to get tacos."

"But I want tacos. Sorry, maybe I should've picked someplace else. Is that what you're saying? You should have told me you don't like tacos."

"No, I'm not saying that. I love tacos, but it's an LA thing, I guess."

"An *LA* thing? Tacos?"

"Yes, like Chicago is known for deep dish pizza and Philly for cheesesteak. LA is known for its tacos, but I'll probably still get some . . . some fish tacos."

"I don't think the fish tacos are two dollars. I think just the beef or chicken ones are."

"If it's more, I'll pay for it; don't worry."

Both sisters realize the meeting is off to a shaky start, but as they start talking, things start to smooth out. For nearly an hour they indulge in fish and chicken tacos and some light conversation. Alicia's impressed with the taste of the tacos, but she won't go as far as to say she prefers them to the tacos at Hugo's. Hugo's is an LA treasure. It was the first food she had on arriving in Los Angeles.

There's more staring than talking, mostly on the part of Heaven, whom Alicia catches gawking at her several times. Before long, a dispute over who should pay the bill ensues. They both want to treat the other.

"How about neither of us treats and we just go Dutch?" adds Alicia. "Because I'm going to add some dessert to mine."

"The rum cake is good. I had it while I was waiting for you."

"I don't like rum. I think I want a warm apple Betty. Should you be having rum in your condition?"

Heaven's eyes bulge. "I never even thought about that."

"It's not going to hurt the baby, I guess. There was only a little bit in it, I'm sure."

A table opens outside after they've eaten their taco dinner, so they move to the patio for dessert. After they take their seats, Heaven orders a flourless chocolate cake.

"You definitely have a sweet tooth, huh?" She looks at Heaven and suddenly feels distant, but she's not sure why. "So, how are you feeling about everything?"

Heaven shrugs. "You mean about being pregnant? I don't have any feeling about it yet. I don't feel pregnant. But in a way I'm thinking this will be a good thing. My baby will give me a sense of purpose. I could never think of a reason to live before, but now I have one. I'm going to make sure my baby has a good life. I have to think positive. Have to think of a good name for my baby . . . one with meaning. I was thinking about naming her Aailyah at first, out of respect for my idol, but maybe I shouldn't. My baby needs her own name . . . her own mark," says Heaven. "By the way, is it okay if I visit you in the hospital?"

"Yes, I don't mind. But don't feel that you have to."

"I want to. Maybe I can convince Hope to come with me. I invited her to come here. I left the invitation on her voice mail."

"She hides behind her voice mail, doesn't she?"

Heaven nods. "I can't get over how much you two favor. I wish she could see that for herself."

"We do favor a little. I saw her picture on your Facebook."

"You have to see her in person to see just how much you look like her. Y'all got the same exact nose. So, what hospital will you be at?"

"Providence Park in Novi. My doctor said I may be there for up to five days. Then six weeks for recovery at home. Just don't come visit me on the first or second day."

"What you gonna do for all that time while you're recovering? I got a bunch of bootleg DVDs you can borrow."

"Bootleg DVDs? Girl, you're talking to the wrong person. I

would never watch a bootleg DVD. I want to act, and piracy is the villain that won't help me accomplish that goal. So please don't bootleg. That's just as bad as theft. I don't get why people don't see that."

"Okay," Heaven says, though she doesn't really see the problem. Thankfully Heaven didn't let Alicia in on her hookup on True Religion jeans.

"I'll probably just reread my acting book and think about that role I lost to Aubrey. I wanted it so bad."

"You can't accept defeat that easy. I've been praying for you."

"What else am I going to do?" she asks after the waitress returns with their bill. "Demand that Marcus Toller give me the part? Tell him nobody can play that crazy woman like I can?"

"Yeah, that's a start."

"Well, Marcus Toller has moved on to someone else, so I need to move on as well."

Heaven takes out her iPhone. "I should've brought my real camera, but this will have to do. . . . Smile."

Alicia throws up the peace sign and grins. She hates that she ended the evening on a sour note and is certain she'll have another crazy dream involving Hollywood tonight.

Hope strides through the front door of the Borders bookstore in Beverly Hills, Michigan, resplendent in a paisley print maxi dress, gladiator-inspired flat sandals, and a pair of designer sunglasses resting on her head. A smile crosses her face once she spots Ezra sitting on a bench, reading a hardcover novel.

"Definitely don't like the title," says Hope, staring at *The Bourne Deception* cover of Ezra's book. Deception—she's had enough of that. "I promised Havana I'd buy the latest Harry Potter, so I want to get that out of the way."

"You should have brought her."

"I would have, but she's with her best friend today."

"Well, I beat you to it," he says, raising a shopping bag, "and I even added in an Artemis Fowl book that she may not know about. It's going to be my gift to her when I see her."

"That's sweet," she says, ducking down after she spots Heaven.

"What's wrong?"

"My sister is in here and I do not want her to see me."

"You're hiding from your sister?"

Hope whispers, "I know she's going to see me, because she's coming this way." Hope sits frozen on the wooden bench beside Ezra, arms tight against her sides. Seconds later, she hears Heaven say, "Hope . . . is that you?"

Hope takes a deep breath and turns her head slowly in the direction of her sister. "Hey, Heaven," says Hope, dragging her voice.

"Hey." Heaven beams as she comes swiftly down the aisle toward Hope. She stops beside the bench Heaven and Ezra are sitting on and smiles politely at Ezra.

Heaven is holding two books in her arms; *What to Expect While You're Expecting* and *The Baby Name Wizard: A Magical Method for Finding the Perfect Name for Your Baby*. "Are you pregnant?" asks Hope, after reading the title. Heaven beams again and then nods. "You're pregnant?" asks Hope again, her mouth agape as she prays Heaven's answer will change.

"I'm happy," Heaven says unconvincingly.

"Happy? Why? Do you even have a job yet?"

"I'll be fine."

Hope shakes her head. "Do you still have your house?"

"Yeah, I do. Why wouldn't I? Anyway, I met our sister for dinner on Tuesday. I invited you. I was hoping you would show. Did you get my card?"

"Yeah, I got it," Hope says, dragging the words.

"So our sister's name is Alicia. Do you want to meet her?"

"As far as I'm aware, you're my only sister, and, no, I don't want to meet her."

Heaven takes her iPhone from her purse and shows Hope one of the pictures she snapped of Alicia while they were having dinner at Toast. "How can you not claim her—you two look so much alike . . . like twins."

Hope studies the picture. Their faces are very similar, but so what. She shrugs.

"She's having surgery on Monday at Providence Park in Novi if you want to come with me to visit her."

"Visit her for what? I'm sure Glenn had a couple of children we've never met, knowing him, but that doesn't mean I have to meet them all."

"Hello, my name is Heaven," she says to Ezra. "Can't wait on Hope for an introduction because she'll never give one."

"Oh, I'll be glad to give one. Ezra, this is Heaven—my sister who stole my credit and charged close to ten grand to a Visa card that I never even signed up for. So if you shake her hand, make sure the other one is firmly clutching your wallet, because I'm sure she's one helluva pickpocket."

Heaven shakes her head. "Like I said, I'm going to pay you back every cent I owe you, plus interest. I never meant for you to have to pay that bill. I was making payments."

"Two payments hardly count as making payments."

"I got laid off and couldn't make any more."

Ezra stands. "Heaven, it's very nice to meet you." He turns toward Hope. "I'm going to let the two of you talk privately."

"You don't have to leave," says Heaven, "because we don't have anything else to say."

"You got that right—we don't," says Hope to Heaven's back. "I feel sorry for that baby."

Heaven's steps immediately halt, but she doesn't turn to face her sister. She shakes her head and continues toward the register.

"I've never seen you like that. You're always so pleasant at the bank," says Ezra after he rejoins Hope.

"You don't know her," she says, shaking her head. "You don't know that girl the way I do. Sure, she's looking innocent today and she's pregnant and all that, but there's not much that girl hasn't done and not much she wouldn't do either."

"I may not know her, but I do know that life is too short to hold a grudge, even over money," says Ezra. "My wife and her sister hadn't talked in nearly a year before the accident. They fell out over an inheritance. And my sister-in-law says there's not one day that goes by that she doesn't regret that. Love 'em. Love 'em while they're here. Love 'em while you're here."

Hope watches Heaven standing in line. That's her baby sister. And at one time not long ago, there wasn't anything she wouldn't do for her, but now the only thing she wants Heaven to do is stay far away.

By the weekend, Hope and Ezra are seated at a glass patio table on his terrace, which is larger than his dining room and kitchen combined, enjoying honey-soy broiled salmon. She had accepted Ezra's invitation to dinner for two at Willys Overland Lofts in Midtown. She'd thought it was a restaurant, but it is his house. Ezra cooked. He'd bragged he learned the fine art of gourmet cooking by obsessively watching the Food Network channel.

Havana is away for the weekend with her father and his family at Frankenmuth. Hope wonders why her daughter's first weekend outing ended up being with her father and his family instead of with her. Havana's father had brought all the past-due child support current. This meant a fifteen-thousand-dollar-check was presented to Hope when she went to court, and the very next day she took it to work and established an account for her daughter—something that she could set aside to help with college. He also told the court he could immediately start making the $275 bimonthly payments. He'd gotten a recent promotion at his city job. He is now a director at one of the city's recreation departments and after spending so much time with other people's children, he started feeling bad for not doing right by his own child.

Hope wanted to know where all of his cash came from and how he could all of a sudden afford to write her a five-figure check. He'd explained he'd taken out a loan in order to do something he should have done a long time ago. He also told the court a little more about his family, his wife, and her job, and how they could provide a stable and loving family as a second home for his child. He said he wasn't trying to take Havana away from her mother, but to Hope that's what it felt like.

The judge was impressed and therefore set visitation arrangements for Havana to spend every other weekend with her father, as well as Thanksgiving and, beginning next summer, the month of July. Hope objected to Thanksgiving and the entire month of July, even if that was a year off. "She's my daughter," she yelled to the judge, who demanded order. "I can't be without her for that long. Ask Havana what she wants. She's old enough to decide."

"I already have," the judge informed Hope. Knowing that the judge had discussed the arrangement with Havana when she was in his chambers without either parent present, just the judge and a children's advocate, made Hope angry. Hope was certain they had filled her daughter with lies to get her to agree to that arrangement. But on the drive home, Havana told her mother, "I love my father, and my father loves me. I love you too, Mommy. But please don't be mad at me if I have a big heart and I can love more than one person at a time."

"It's so pretty out here, so peaceful," says Hope. "Your entire loft is nice." And she loves his furniture. After looking at how he furnished his home, she realizes she needs to get on the ball. She did a decent job with her landscaping. She put a lot of knickknacks in the yard, but she could do better with the inside. She could make it brighter, give it a pulse, let it come alive. "This patio is huge."

"Which is exactly why I decided on this particular unit. I sold the house and bought this loft—should have moved to the city sooner."

"Why? Why move from the suburbs to here? The suburbs have so much more to offer—shopping, safety."

"Part of my healing process is to change my views."

"What are your views?"

"At the time my views of the city were that it was being run by a corrupt government and it wasn't going to turn around any time soon, if ever. I pretty much knew it wasn't safe. I didn't want my family in Detroit for any reason. We didn't come near the city. I was even offered a residency at the Detroit Medical Center, right down the street, and I turned it down. I thought I was doing the best thing by keeping them out of the city. But maybe I wasn't." He shrugs. "There's so much more to the city than I thought."

"You never told me you were a doctor. I should be calling you Dr. Hansen."

"Look how long it took me to get you to stop calling me Mr. Hansen. Let's not backtrack. Besides, I'm not a doctor anymore, and I really never got to practice outside of my residency." He looks at her plate. "You're not eating again."

"I'm thinking about my child. She's with her father. I don't like that. I know it sounds bad, but I just don't."

"Why?"

"Why?" she repeats, and then ponders her answer. "I don't trust him."

"What do you think he's going to do?"

"I don't know what he's going to do. I don't know him. I don't know his family. I met his wife and her kids, and they seem fine. His wife has a great job with Ford. She's an engineer. Her daughters are nice and well behaved, and they all get along with Havana, but—"

"But, is there really a but? It was sounding great so far."

"I have an issue with trust. I've figured out that in life things are rarely as they seem."

"But, also in life, you have to trust that while they're not always as they seem, they're not always bad either. Sometimes in life things are better than they seem. I never thought I'd smile again, but I've smiled a lot lately. I never thought I'd ever take my wedding ring off." She'd noticed he hadn't worn it the time before when they were at the bookstore.

"Why did you?"

"Because I'm ready to start living again. I have you to thank for that."

"Me?"

He moved his hand toward hers and held it. "I know I don't look like Prince Charming, but do you think you could ever allow me to show you how I can treat a lady I'm interested in?"

"What are you saying, Dr. Ezra Hansen?"

"I'm saying I want you to trust me. That's all I'm saying right now. Just trust me."

"Do you know what I want?" asks Hope.

"What's that?"

"I want to see you in a short-sleeved shirt and some shorts. Sometimes it's really hot, yet you always wear a long-sleeved shirt buttoned all the way up, and you always have on pants."

"I've never worn shorts. It's not because of the accident. I don't even have burns on my legs."

"You must have skinny legs."

"Not too skinny. I just never got into shorts. But yes, I do always wear long-sleeved shirts because of the burns and my bad arm. Next time, I might wear a short-sleeved one."

"I don't care about the burns."

He flashes a look of endearment. "You really don't, do you?"

She shakes her head. "No, I really don't."

After dinner they relax in front of the television on the contemporary sofa. He tells her to make herself comfortable. She kicks off her shoes and hugs her knees to her chest on his white leather sectional. "Can I make myself this comfortable?"

"It's just furniture."

She snuggles her head against his chest after he drapes his good arm around her. "How about this comfortable?" she asks as she slides her hand up his chest on the outside of his shirt.

He drops his head to kiss her hand when she slides her hand near his neck.

She smiles at him with her eyes. "I want us both to feel good again."

"I want that too," he says as he stands, turns off the television with the remote, and takes her by the hand to lead her into his bedroom. But before she can stand up straight, her cell phone buzzes. Anxious that it may be a call from her ex concerning Havana, she reads the incoming text.

Just want 2 remind u our sis has surgery tom@ Providence in Novi and she will be there 4 or 5 days. 47601 Grand River Ave ... 2484654100 Do u want 2 come with me?

"This girl doesn't get the hint," says Hope. "And I thought I made myself crystal clear at the bookstore that I didn't want anything to do with her." She looks up at Ezra. "I'm sorry, but now I'm really in a bad mood."

Ezra plops himself back down on the sofa. "To be continued."

She shoots her eyes toward the exposed brick walls and ductwork, toward the track lighting and the "Martini glass" fluted columns, admiring his loft. If only her life were as perfect.

Alicia feels naked—vulnerable. She dons a solid pink maternity dress she purchased the day before from Target. She's without a purse, cell phone, or makeup; not even lotion covers her pale skin. She studies her feet in a pair of Yellow Box jeweled thongs. She misses seeing her raspberry-colored toenails twinkle. Even though her feet are free of corns and bear no bunions, her toes aren't as appealing without polish. But nail polish is prohibited.

She studies the door.

She tries to will it to open. Mind games are playing tricks on her. Life or death games; *Will I live?* continues to pop into her head. *Why me? Is this just a dream?* More than a dream—a nightmare. It isn't too late to change her mind about the surgery; to get a third opinion as her aunt Olena suggested.

Alicia's mother is sitting beside her, nervously reading a magazine, or at least pretending to. She makes small talk with Alicia, who isn't in the mood for anything other than staring at the closed door across from her and occasionally watching Meredith Vieira host *Who Wants to Be a Millionaire* on the television fixed to the wall. She can't remember the last time she actually watched that show. It always makes her feel so stupid, because she can never get past the thousand-dollar mark. Maybe she'll go to college. If she survives her operation, maybe that's what she'll do—study something besides lines.

She sighs and drops her head. It's so hard for her to even imagine doing anything other than acting.

Her stepfather is sitting directly across from her, beside the door she is staking out. He is peeling an orange, the juice from which drips onto the front page of the *Detroit Free Press* resting in his lap. On any other day this would have bothered her. Today, she lets it go, trying to keep her mind calm.

A woman in scrubs opens the door and calls someone's name other than hers. Alicia studies the second hand ticking on the clock hanging over her father's head. The pre-op instructions said to be there at one. It is now ten after. Surgery is scheduled for three. After the door closes, she waits a few minutes before walking over to it. A sign posted says to knock before entering, which she does. She sticks her head inside. The same woman in scrubs—this time holding a clipboard—is standing nearby. She asks Alicia for her name, which Alicia politely supplies.

"It will be just a few more minutes."

Alicia nods and smiles. But inside she's more anxious than ever. No sooner has she sat down and begun engaging her mother in small talk than her name is called.

She closes her eyes and says a silent prayer. Then, head down, she walks to the door. She doesn't know what to expect. She has never had major surgery. Everyone is so nice on the other side of the door. All of them are wearing smiles that appear genuine.

The same woman in scrubs takes her to the staging area; she draws back the hospital curtain where a nurse is waiting. Alicia takes a seat. She is given a cup inside a clear bag with a BIOHAZARD stamp.

"Do you think you can urinate for us?"

She looks at the cup and feels weak. She shakes her head. "No."

"The anesthesiologist is requesting a more up-to-date pregnancy test." The nurse flips through the chart. "You had one during your pre-op, but that was last Thursday and she likes to be safe."

"I'll try." She takes the cup from the nurse and heads to the bathroom.

She sits on the toilet, waiting for the drip to begin so she can hold the cup in place. But nothing happens.

A heavy hand begins knocking on the door. "Are you all set in there? We're ready for you." A few minutes later Alicia walks out of the bathroom holding a cup of urine and hands it to the nurse. The nurse takes it and ushers her into the pre-op room.

Alicia Nova Day is thirty-two, and they are taking her uterus, cervix, and ovaries—and any dream she might have had of having children. Sure, she could adopt, her mother had suggested encouragingly, but those words were easily spoken by a woman who had birthed two of her own. The more she considers it, the sadder she becomes. She slips into a flimsy hospital gown and rubber-soled socks, then slides underneath the cool, thin white sheet covering the cot. She flinches before the needle even punctures her skin. The blood nurse searches for a vein. The mere thought of the thin needle piercing her skin sends Alicia into panic mode.

The nurse gives up on the veins in Alicia's arms. "These veins don't want to come up. We'll have to try to put it in your hand," the second nurse says, thumping Alicia's hand with her finger. "You have such dainty hands. You could be a hand model."

"Genes," she says, but considering what she is going through, she's not sure they're all that good.

The ob-gyn who is performing the surgery pays her a visit. He has a young face. The only thing that ages him is the gray in his hair. He asks if she is nervous and when she says yes, he says, "Me too," and makes his hands tremble. She laughs, even though she thinks it's a sick joke, but Sir would say anyone who would do that before surgery is confident nothing will go wrong. But many things can go wrong, according to Alicia's research. What if she doesn't wake up?

"The anesthesiologist is going to meet us in the hallway to give you a cocktail," one of the nurses says. "Just a little something she'll put in your IV to relax you, and then you'll get the stronger stuff in the OR."

The nurse pushes Alicia into the hallway and down a small hall. The anesthesiologist appears out of nowhere and injects the cocktail into Alicia's IV. But it doesn't seem to relax her—instead she feels even more alert. The nurse continues pushing the cart down another short hallway, then turns into a very large operating room, much larger than the one she saw on the set of *Grey's Anatomy* when she played a patient who dies during surgery. She prays that in this case art doesn't imitate life.

Heaven and Hope. She isn't sure why her half sisters suddenly pop into her mind. Maybe it's the effect of the cocktail the anesthesiologist slipped her. But she wishes they were there—even Hope, whom she has yet to meet. She has sisters . . . sisters . . . but she won't have children.

Alicia blinks her eyes into focus. She sees a woman's electric blue dress hanging in front of her hospital bed, which is adjusted to the upright position. Medium electric blue; it's more subtle than her favorite color red, but as her eyes ease open and she blinks a few more times, the image slowly comes into focus. It isn't simply a woman's dress. There's a woman wearing it—her aunt Olena.

"My God, did your fibroid tumors grow too?" asks Alicia, staring at Olena's swollen belly.

"I'm pregnant, silly." Olena flashes her three-stone emerald-cut engagement ring.

"Pregnant?" Maybe it's the drugs Alicia has been taking or the fact that she's been in the hospital for two whole days already. She can't have heard what she thinks she heard. No, her forty-five-year-old aunt is not pregnant. But if it's true, Alicia suddenly realizes how amazing the news is. At the same time, she remembers what was just taken from her.

"I'm having twins. That's why my stomach is this big this soon. I'm only five months."

"Why didn't you tell me before now? Does my mom even know?"

"Yes, she knows. She just saw me. Your parents just left to get something to eat, so they'll be back in a couple hours. And I was going to tell you, after I got over the shock, but I didn't want to tell you after I found out your situation."

"I'm happy for you. And you're having two, so you can just give me one."

"I might need to now that I don't have a job. I might need to give you both," Olena says with a chuckle.

Before Alicia can ask her next question, one of the nurses comes in to see if Alicia can urinate, which she hasn't done since the operation. The nurse unstraps her legs from the restraints used to help ensure proper circulation, and Alicia slowly walks into the small bathroom. It isn't difficult for her to get out of bed; in fact, it's definitely getting easier to move around. She still walks slightly bent over, protecting her fragile stomach. The doctor originally told her to expect a five-day stay, but as soon as she can urinate and pass gas he may let her go since the surgery was such a success. She didn't need a blood transfusion as her doctor had once cautioned might be necessary. They didn't have to perform a bilateral oophorectomy, which meant she still had both of her ovaries. And she was able to retain her cervix because the fibroids hadn't caused any other damage.

Alicia runs the water from the sink and waits to hear her own water come down. She sits on the cold commode with a plastic pan tucked underneath the lid positioned by the nurse. She hears voices—her aunt's and a man's. She wonders who he is.

She strains; she tries to concentrate on tinkling by listening to the water instead of their conversation. If she doesn't urinate, they will have to put the catheter back in, and she is sick of all the pricking and probing. If she doesn't urinate, she may have to spend another day in the hospital; she can barely afford the two days she's already been in.

"Forget it." She sighs, frustrated for the most part. "I can't go." She wipes to check for blood and is pleased to find none. Then she sighs again, takes a deep breath, and opens the door to find Sir and Olena waiting for her. He is holding a bushel of yellow roses with red tips in a clear glass vase.

She wants to scream at the sight of him, but if she does, she is certain her stitches below her bikini line will burst. She doesn't want Sir to see her like this, so she quickly shuts the door.

She looks at herself in the mirror. Her natural curls, which usually glow with a healthy sheen from Carol's Daughter Hair Milk, are thirsty for hair products, lifeless, flat on the top, and sticking out on the side. Her skin is pale and her nose red—she looks like Bozo the Clown.

"Come back tomorrow or the next day," she says at Sir through the door. Hopefully by then she'll be discharged from the hospital. But even then, he'll still have to wait six weeks for her to look like her fabulous self again.

Several minutes later, after her aunt tells her the coast is clear, she walks out and crawls back into bed. Alicia's skin feels itchy and prickly—much worse than the times before. It feels like hives. Her scalp is on fire, and her arms have several large clusters of small bumps. She digs her short, polish-free nails into her scalp and scratches furiously. Then her back begins to flare up. The feeling is discomforting. She yells for the nurse and suddenly feels as if her stomach is ripping open. She can only thank God for the heating pad that is resting on her stomach or the pain most certainly would have been unbearable. She looks over at her aunt's stomach again—and shakes her head. "The world sure is changing. Times are so different now. Women in their forties are having babies while women in their twenties and thirties are having their uteruses removed." She tries to smile, but the tears come. "I should have gotten a third opinion."

"You did the right thing," Olena says.

"I did the right thing? You were the one telling me I should get another opinion."

Sir reenters before a nurse does. "I forgot something."

Alicia's eyes widen. "Sir, why did you come back? What did you forget?"

"I forgot to leave this," he says, handing her an envelope with a get-well-soon card inside.

She puts the hospital sheet over her head. "Come back on day four . . . not day three anymore."

The nurse enters as Sir leaves the room, responding to her yells for help. She asks Alicia what the problem is.

"Right now I'm itching all over. And my shoulder is stiff. I can't seem to get comfortable. This leg brace thing makes me feel like I'm wearing a straitjacket."

"Those are for your circulation, and it's very important that you keep them on while you are lying in bed," she says as she straps Alicia's legs back into them.

"I'm itching and I can't take it," says Alicia as she furiously scratches her back.

"Could be from the Oxycodone," the nurse says. "We can try a different pain medicine."

"No. A cold shower would make me feel much better. It would make this itch go away."

"You have an incision that needs to heal first. The itchy feeling is common for women who have just had a hysterectomy. The way you are feeling is normal."

Alicia passes gas and the nurse smiles and says, "That's good— you need to pass a lot of gas. Have you been doing that regularly? It's very important that you do."

"I just started farting today," says Alicia, eyeing her aunt who is holding back laughter. "And they're very loud and painful. Is it supposed to hurt like that? It feels like my incisions are going to rip open."

"It's important to pass gas. You probably won't be able to have a bowel movement for a few more days, so if you can at least get that gas out, it's good for you." The nurse picks up the plastic AirLife respiratory aid from the table stand beside the bed. "Have you been breathing in this?"

Alicia's eyelids drop. Every nurse who comes into her room asks her that same question. Her answer is always, "Not really . . . no. I'm trying, but it's hard."

The nurse nods. "It's very important that you do." The nurse turns to Olena with the respiratory aid in her hand. "She needs to breathe into this at least ten times an hour so she won't get pneumonia. It's very important. I can't stress it enough. If she gets pneumonia, she's gone through all of this for nothing." The nurse hands the respiratory aid to Alicia. "Breathe in ten times while I'm here and try to get the indicator up between the arrows at the fifteen-hundred mark."

Alicia communicates with her aunt with her eyes. She's exhausted. She's ready to go home and have her mom take care of her. She wants to relax in a real bed. She's too afraid to take the pain meds because she doesn't want to wind up addicted. She wants all of the nurses to stop coming to her room every hour to rouse her out of bed so she can sit on the toilet and try to make something happen. And, more important, she wants to stop breathing into that plastic tube.

"If I do one, will you leave? I promise to do the rest under my aunt's supervision."

"Yes, for an hour, and when I come back I'll need you to do it again."

Alicia sighs heavily. She takes the breathing machine from the nurse's hand and struggles to release air through the tube, trying her best to push the blue indicator to the fifteen-hundred mark. After she takes one successful breath, the nurse leaves, and Alicia places the respiratory aid on the bedside table.

"What do I have to do to get you to breathe into this thing?" asks Olena, dangling the respiratory aid from her fingers.

"Who is the father of your babies? And if you say Matthew, I won't take one breath," Alicia says. Olena pauses for several seconds. "Tell me!"

"Jason."

Alicia gives a sigh of relief. "Thank God. Get him on the phone," she demands. "If you want me to breathe through that tube, get him on the phone right now."

"You will have plenty of time to talk to Jason. Right now, you have to get well."

"But you're not lying? The father is Jason? And that big ring on your wedding finger means what?"

"I'm engaged. Just waiting on you to get better so I can have the wedding. Can't have a wedding without my maid of honor."

Long after Olena has left, Alicia wakes up in the middle of the night after a different nurse rouses her from bed again to use the bathroom—still no urine, which means another day in the hospital.

This is day three at the hospital for Alicia. Her parents visited for several hours and had just left. Her aunt flew back to Atlanta that morning and didn't have a chance to visit again.

Alicia has a smile on her face as she thinks about Olena's story. She'd fallen asleep the night before, after her aunt told her that prior to Jason's prostatectomy he stored his sperm in a sperm bank, so Alicia had to conclude that her aunt was artificially inseminated.

Today, Sir decided to call first and ask Alicia if she was up for his visit. She kindly turned him away. She thanked him for the flowers and promised to see him as soon as she fully recovered. Seeing him now, while she's recovering, she tells him, may stress her out, and stress will slow down her recovery.

She hears a knock on her door and assumes it's another nurse coming to annoy her. But it's Heaven, who walks in with the baby book tucked under her arm and greets her with a very loud, "Hey!"

Heaven is wearing a red T-shirt with white letters that say LIVE YOUR DREAMS; the shirt she'd lifted from Macy's. She brought another one for Alicia to cheer her up.

"This is for you, Mama . . . I mean . . . *Gigi Mama*," says Heaven

as she sets the mint green Secret Sister gift bag on the bed beside
Alicia.

Alicia adjusts her bed to the upright position and reads the message printed on the gift bag. "'Your Secret Sister prays for you more
often than you'd guess that God will fill your day with peace, your
life with happiness.' That's really nice."

"I thought so too. I picked it up from a Christian bookstore."

Alicia reaches in the bag and pulls out the T-shirt. "Oh, you got
me a T-shirt just like yours. That's cute too. But we won't be wearing
it at the same time because that wouldn't be cute. . . . That would be
weird."

"Day three . . . only two more to go."

"Not if I can pee it won't be."

"Huh?"

"Once I pee, I can get out of here. Peeing and farting are very
important. Don't ask me why—ask her," Alicia says, pointing at the
nurse who enters.

"Are you doing your breathing exercises?" asks the nurse.

"Not yet, but I will. I promise," says Alicia, rolling her eyes.

The nurse turns to Heaven with the respiratory aid in her hand
and repeats the same words she muttered to Olena as Alicia mouths
the words behind the nurse's back. Alicia takes the respiratory aid. It
takes her almost twenty minutes to blow through it ten times.

"Please, make sure she blows through this every hour ten times,"
says the nurse, delegating to Heaven. She hands her the respirator.
"I'll be back in an hour."

Before long, Alicia, under the influence of pain medication, drifts
off to sleep. When she awakens a little more than an hour later, she's
surprised to see Heaven still in her hospital room, curled up with a
blanket in a chair that converts into a narrow bed.

"You're still here?" asks Alicia. "You mean the nurse didn't come
back in here?"

"She did, but I asked her not to wake you," says Heaven as she
continues reading *The Baby Name Wizard*. "I promised her I'd make

sure you breathed into that tube every hour." Heaven tosses the blanket off herself, sets down her book, and picks up the respiratory aid. "It's almost that time."

"If you bring that thing near me, I'll fart," Alicia says, partly playful but mostly annoyed.

"I promised the nurse," she says, handing her the respiratory aid. Alicia reluctantly takes the breathing instrument from Heaven. "Now breathe," says Heaven.

This time it takes Alicia nearly fifteen minutes just to take ten breaths.

"I figured out my baby's name . . . if I have a girl."

"Oh, really . . . what?"

"Harmony. It means a beautiful blending. It's going to be Heaven and Harmony."

"Which of your parents had an H-obsession?"

"Our mom. Her name is Hester." Heaven pauses. "Your mom and dad seem nice. Seems like they're really in love." Heaven smiles. "How long have they been married?"

"Twenty-four years. And they're best friends and so in love. When did you meet them?"

"Wow, that's nice. I met them in the hallway as they were coming out of your room. That's how it should be. Marry for love . . . and no other reason."

"I never asked you about your mother."

"Oh, my mother." She hesitates, wondering if she should tell the truth, but she doesn't want to. "She died of cancer when I was little."

"Oh, I'm sorry, Heaven."

"Yeah, I am too." She turns and heads back to her makeshift bed. "You have one hour, and then you need to give me ten more."

"Ten more what?" Alicia asks with attitude. "You're worse than these doggone nurses."

"I take my job very seriously, honey. It's been so long since I've had a real one."

"Who told you that you could spend the night?"

"The nurses did," Heaven says as she curls up under the blanket. "One hour."

"Good night."

"Good night for one hour," suggests Heaven. "Oh, but before I take a nap, I need to ask you something."

"Yes, Heaven?"

"When are you going to do a part six to *Gigi Mama*?"

"Don't make me throw up. A part six? Never! I didn't want to do the first five."

"Girl, I rented all of them, and I loved them . . . especially part five. Gigi is a trip."

"If I could move, I'd get out of this bed and go over there and smack you."

"I'm nervous," admits Heaven.

"I wouldn't really smack you."

"No, I mean I'm nervous about the baby . . . about everything really." She wants to go into detail—tell her about Donovan and the abuse; admit that there are a few nice department stores that would love to get their hands on her. She wants to admit what she'd done to turn Hope against her, but she's too afraid that too much information will only serve to turn Alicia away. Alicia seems so put together, and so do her parents.

"Having a baby is a blessing," says Alicia. "I always took that for granted until now . . . now that I know I'll never have a child of my own."

"But you can adopt," chirps Heaven. "There are so many kids out there who would love to have a home. Kids in foster care." Even though Heaven was raised by her nana, she can still remember the time both she and her sister spent in foster care after Glenn was arrested for killing their mother. Heaven was seven at the time. She and Hope became wards of the state for nearly a month, though it felt much longer, while the Department of Human Services searched for their living relatives. Their nana, who was away with one of the many men she'd dated and eventually married, finally surfaced, but red tape and a preliminary investigation caused their time in foster care to get prolonged.

"I suppose you're right. Adoption is always an option for later . . . much later."

"Kids need a family . . . not just kids . . . everyone." Heaven covers herself with the blanket.

Alicia looks over at the covered mound that's Heaven, smiles, and wonders what she can do to bring all three of the sisters together. A few minutes later, she decides to unstrap her leg braces and try to urinate.

She sits on the side of her bed for a second, trying to get the strength to take six steps into the bathroom.

"Do you need help?" asks Heaven.

"Just help me get down from the bed. I should be able to walk after that."

Heaven assists Alicia in getting down from the bed. Then Alicia walks into the bathroom on her own, turns on the sink water, and sits on the cold commode with the plastic pan tucked underneath the lid. Minutes later, Alicia shouts, "I peed." She holds her stomach out of pain, but she is so relieved that she can leave tomorrow.

It is a little after eight in the morning, and Hope is in the driver's seat. She is heading downtown with Havana to meet Ezra at Wheelhouse Detroit, a bicycle shop that offers rented bikes and bike tours. It was Ezra's idea for the three of them to take a four-hour bike tour.

Hope considered the offer. "Is that okay?" she'd asked him.

"Is what okay?"

"Can you be out in the sun? I'm not trying to offend you or get personal. I just thought burn victims couldn't be out."

"I'm already burned," he jokes as he often does about his condition. "What's a little sun going to do to me? What do you say?"

"There's something I want to tell you about my friend, Mr. Hansen," Hope says to Havana as she heads south on the Lodge Freeway. "Only because I don't want you to be shocked when you see him."

"What?" Havana asks as she peers over at her mom from the passenger seat.

"He's badly burned."

Havana shrugs. "Okay?"

"Mr. Hansen, my friend. His face and right arm are badly disfigured. One of his ears is just completely gone. It's not there. He doesn't have eyebrows. I don't want you to feel strange, like you can't look at him, because he is a very nice man who had a really bad thing happen to him."

"Why would I feel strange? He's been burned. Just like my friend Marcel in school whose house caught fire when we were in the first grade. Remember, I told you about that?"

Hope shakes her head. "No, I don't remember."

"Oh yeah . . . that's right, you probably don't," Havana says, suddenly remembering the time frame—two years ago when her mother didn't remember anything. "Anyway, I know about burn victims. I'm not one of the ignorant ones."

"Treat him just like anyone else. Just like you treat Grace."

"Treat him like I treat Grace? You mean like a human being? That's how I treat everybody, Mom. I got it. I'm not just a kid. I got it. He had an accident. He was burned. I'm not going to stare at him or say something rude like I don't have sense. I'm going to look at him and talk to him just like I look and talk to you. I've seen burns before. His burns aren't going to freak me out. You do realize that in addition to being an English professor, I am going to be a surgeon when I grow up. I think I've told you that, or did you forget that too?"

Hope says, "I may have," feeling chastised.

"Well, maybe now you can unplug your ears and listen to your daughter from time to time. I am pretty interesting."

Underneath his bike helmet, Ezra wears a thick nylon cap to cover his bald head. He is wearing goggle sunglasses, bike gloves, and more clothing than Hope feels is necessary considering it's summer and they are embarking on strenuous physical exercise. But they do still have a few more hours before it really starts to heat up.

They ride the trail, staying behind their tour guide by a bike's length, but they keep up with the few Creekside community residents who come along to assist with the tour. They ride through parts of the historic fifty-three-acre Maheras-Gentry Park. By a quarter to one, with close to eighty ounces of water consumed by Hope alone and several bathroom runs, they return to the downtown bike shop. And even though biking isn't one of Hope's favorite pastimes or something she would have ever suggested they do, she's pleased with herself for trying something different and not complaining once they set out.

"Did you have fun?" Ezra asks Havana. The three of them are in the parking lot of the bike shop standing between their two cars—Hope's Beetle and Ezra's Volvo.

"Yes, that was so fun. This was just so perfect."

"Good, I'm glad. We'll have to all do it again then."

Havana pops her eyes out at a woman, mid-thirties, who walks by them and then turns around to stare at Ezra. "That's okay," he snickers, "you don't have to take up for me."

"You saw me?" she says, covering her mouth in embarrassment. "I'm sorry. I just hate ignorance, and that woman was old enough to know better."

Ezra chuckles. "So, your mother tells me you like books." He reaches into his car and hands her a Harry Potter gift bag.

"I do," says Havana as her eyes light up. "And I love this bag. I'm never ever going to throw it away. It's just so perfect."

"Go ahead and look inside," says Ezra.

Her beautiful eyes sparkle while her two thick black braids swing back and forth as she drops her head to investigate the contents. She digs her hand through the green tissue paper. "And by the way, I'm not certain if my mother already told you this or if this just happens to be an amazing coincidence, but green is my favorite color."

"It's an amazing coincidence," Ezra says with a smile. "And she's how old?"

"Eight going on thirty," replies Hope.

She pulls out the first book, a hardcover, which is *Harry Potter and the Deathly Hollows*. "Book seven. Yes, this was on my wish list." She reaches in and pulls out the trade paperback, *Artemis Fowl*.

"Have you heard of that one?" asks Ezra. "That's the first book in the series."

"No, I'm not familiar with this one," she says checking the copyright date. "The year I was born. That's a great sign. I can't wait to read it," she says with a big grin. "I just can't believe that you got me a gift and you don't even know me. It was so thoughtful. I mean, I love to read. Thank you so much." She flips to the last page to check the number of pages. "And it's only three hundred and four pages, so I'll be done with this by tomorrow."

"Tomorrow?" Ezra questions.

"Easily. I'm used to Harry Potter books that are more than twice this size, and it takes me three days to finish those. Well, in all fairness, I really need to read the Harry Potter book first—I'm already committed to that series."

He smiles. "And you may not know, but we do share a common bond—we both love to read fantasy."

"You're a Harry Potter fan?"

"I am, I must admit."

"Perfect, because my mother's not, and my best friend isn't either. And I used to go on these forums to discuss Harry Potter, but my mother doesn't want me going on forums because she thinks they're full of crazy people."

"Well, you don't need a forum anymore. If you want to talk about Harry Potter, I'm your forum—if I'm not too boring for you."

Havana's smile lights up. "Wow, this has been the best day of my life," she says, then gives him a hug.

Ezra looks over at Hope with a smile as he hugs Havana. "I'm glad. I had a great time too."

After Havana settles in the passenger seat, Ezra and Hope linger between their two cars.

"You have a really sweet daughter. She's a testament to how good a mother you are."

"Well, I could be better. I have a lot of ground to make up."

Ezra notices Havana is puckering her lips and leaning forward, trying to give him a hint, and so he takes it. He leans in closer to Hope and kisses her on the cheek. Hope looks stunned. "I chose the cheek because your daughter's here," he whispers before opening her car door.

Hope climbs inside her car and pulls off, waving good-bye to Ezra as he stands near his car.

"He should have given you a real kiss," says Havana. "Maybe he's shy. He'll have to work on that."

"Shy . . . real kiss. You are growing up too quickly, young lady. We are just friends." As Hope drives home she thinks of Ezra and about how when she looks at him she doesn't see the burns. All she ever sees is a handsome man like the one in the picture but even more attractive; a man who has been through a lot just as she has, but who gets up every morning and goes on.

"You know what, Mom?" says Havana. "For once in my life, I can honestly say, I think you have found yourself a good one. Now, I just have to work on my aunt."

"First of all—"

"Yeah . . . yeah . . . yeah, I know, the two of you are just friends."

"That's what we are, but that's not what I was going to say. I was going to say that your aunt and I are finished, so you won't be able to work on her. She's bad news, I told you."

"I'm going to pray on that one, Mom. She's your sister, and one day you'll appreciate what that means."

August

Heaven is sitting on an examining table waiting for a doctor to enter the room. It is early August, two weeks after Alicia's operation. Heaven and Alicia have grown even closer together through daily phone conversations, while she and Donovan have grown even farther apart. Heaven is fairly confident their relationship is coming to an end. But what she isn't confident about is her pregnancy. The night before, while she was lying in bed, she felt her panties dampen. She'd assumed she may have urinated on herself by mistake. But then she saw blood . . . and not a few spots either, but enough to soak through her underwear, clothes, and sheets. She went to the bathroom, sat down, and blood clots came out. She was having persistent abdominal cramps. By the time she'd made it to the hospital, she was doubled over from the severe pain.

She hears a knock on the door and the doctor enters.

"Heaven, sorry for the wait, but I was waiting on the results of your hCG tests," he says as he opens her chart.

"What did you find out?" Heaven asks nervously.

"Basically, the reason you are bleeding is because you had a miscarriage."

271

"A miscarriage?" she asks, her heart sinking. "I lost my baby?"

He nods. "Yes, I'm afraid so."

Heaven's shoulders slump. No more Harmony. She had just gotten used to the idea of having a baby. She was becoming excited . . . and now this.

"But why?" asks Heaven. "Do you know what caused it?"

"Unfortunately, miscarriages are pretty common. They happen in about twenty-five percent of all pregnancies and there can be a number of factors. You're a young woman, so in your case, age isn't one of them."

Heaven hesitates. "What if I took a real bad fall?"

"Yeah, that could have done it. Physical injury is one of the causes. I'm very sorry, Heaven."

"Thank you." She shrugs. "I guess it just wasn't in God's plan for me."

"So you think you can keep me out just by changing the locks?" Donovan demands through the phone.

"It's over," Heaven says, dragging her words. She wants to tell him that he has no idea what she has been through lately. The day before, she learned the bad news. No more Harmony. No Hope. And if she's not careful, with the way she's been living her life, there'll be no Heaven either, in more ways than one.

"What's wrong with you, Heaven? You can't ever make up your mind. One minute you want to be with me, you say you love me, and then the next minute you don't."

Tears start to cloud her eyes. "Well, I've made up my mind this time. Don't you know that there's something wrong when the only thing two people can ever do is cuss each other out and fight? Can't you see that two people like that have no business being together? I called to tell you about a book you really need to buy." They are having a carryover argument from a few nights before that resulted in her kicking him out of the house and dumping his things in the alley along with all the other trash. Then the next day she miscarried.

The fight had started upstairs and she'd fallen down the stairs. Forget about all those other times she'd had enough—and there'd been plenty. Times that started off with his drinking a lot and ended with his kicking his foot through some door. This last time it was the bathroom door, and she'd managed to get to it before he did and she locked it, after which he proclaimed, "Next time it'll be your ass."

"No, it won't," said Heaven, steadying a knife in her right hand, which was the first thing he saw after he'd kicked his way in. It was a big butcher knife she'd hidden under the sink for a time just like that one. How sad to think she figured one of those times would eventually come. "Get out!" That time she meant it, because that time he had gone way too far. "Who's going to pay for this?" she shouted. Her eyes were engulfed with anger at the sight of the mangled hinges.

"Are you pregnant?" asks Donovan.

"No, I'm not pregnant," she snaps. "Why did you ask me that?"

"So why you reading a baby book if you're not pregnant and picking out names?"

"It's not my book—it's Trina's."

"Trina's gay."

"So what? Gay people can have babies too."

"If you're pregnant, Heaven, just tell me. At least that would explain why you are the way you are."

"And tell me, Donovan—how is that? How am I? Don't even answer that because it doesn't matter."

"Are you pregnant?"

"I said I'm not pregnant," she screams. "I don't have to lie to you. I only called to tell you that you need to read *The Black Male Handbook*."

"The what?"

"*The ... Black ... Male ... Handbook*," Heaven says slowly. "It's a book by Kevin Powell. He's a very intelligent black man and he was just on *Oprah* as a matter-of-fact."

"So? You read it, because I don't need that."

"Yes, you do. You need something," she shouts.

Heaven's doorbell rings. "Who's at your door?" he asks angrily.

"I have no idea," says Heaven. "Is it you? Because if it is, I replaced the knife I had the other night with a gun today." Donovan hangs up. Frustrated, she tosses her cell phone on her bed and heads downstairs for the front door to answer it. This is not the life she wants, but it is the one she expected to have—one so similar to her mother's that she wouldn't even be surprised if it ended the same way. She wonders if Donovan really is at the door. She wouldn't put it past him. She wonders if he was driving to her house while talking to her on the phone, even though it was pouring rain and the roads were dangerous. Twenty minutes earlier, the news interrupted *Oprah* right when it was getting good. Oprah was talking to men who'd beaten women. Kevin Powell was on the show via Skype, and Heaven had been hanging on to his every word. She'd written the title to his book down—*The Black Male Handbook*, then immediately called Donovan. Then *Channel 7 News* cut into the program with a severe weather report advising all metro Detroit residents to stay inside and avoid driving.

She peeps out the hole and sees her landlord, Mr. Williams, standing on her porch with a morbid facial expression. She assumes someone died, so she asks him about his wife. "She's fine," he replies. "In fact, she's waiting in the car." Heaven steps on the porch to wave.

"So what's wrong, then?" asks Heaven, wondering what can be so important that he'd come out when the weatherman told everyone to stay inside. The sky lights up and crackles. Rain is coming down hard and steady. "Did you know it's a tornado warning?"

"Actually, it's a watch."

Heaven shrugs. "Oh, I don't know the difference. Which is worse?"

"A watch."

She darts her eyes toward Mr. Williams and tries to nod sense into him. "So why are you out in it?"

"Well, we got caught in it on our way home, and we have to pass your house to get to ours—"

"And?" she asks in irritation. He isn't making any sense. She wants to know why he is mumbling in the midst of a storm. She wants to get inside so she won't get struck by lightning like the man three blocks down from her did the last time it stormed that bad.

"And because my wife told me I have to tell you now." He takes a deep breath. "I don't know how to say this."

A roaring burst of thunder crashes through the air, followed by forceful bolts of lightning. "Just say it, Mr. Williams, please," she says, feeling a bit frightened by the storm.

He takes another deep breath and sighs. "I'm being foreclosed on."

"They're taking your house?" asks Heaven, placing her hand against her chest.

His eyes shift nervously. "They're taking my rental property."

"Which one?" she asks. He couldn't possibly be referring to the property she is living in—not hers—but why else would he be standing there? she wonders.

"I only have one."

"One besides this one, right?" she asks, nodding and waiting for him to nod back in agreement. "It can't be this one. Right?" she asks, nodding some more. "They're not taking this one."

"I only have this one—had," he corrects.

"They can't be taking this one, Ralph," she says, dropping the formality. No more Mr. Williams; now he was just plain old Ralph. "I paid you every month. Paid you early. How can this be happening when I've paid you?"

He shoves his hands into the pockets of his work pants. "You're a good tenant. But . . ."

"I'm a good tenant, and there is no but. But what?"

"But I lost my job."

"What does that have to do with me? I lost my job too, but I still manage to pay my rent."

"The factory was shut down for only a couple of weeks at first, but then they decided to close the one I work at. Then my wife lost her job too. All we have right now is unemployment, and we had to use your rent to help pay our own mortgage. It was either that or be homeless."

Heaven stares straight ahead, looking past him. "So . . . now, instead of you being homeless, I'm going to be homeless. Is that what you're telling me?"

"Don't you have a sister?"

"And?" she asks irritably. Yes, she has a sister, she muses; she has two, but Hope isn't an option. And Alicia isn't one either. Heaven refuses to bring her messed-up real world into Alicia's make-believe Hollywood one. "This is how people end up on the six o'clock news, Ralph." It's times like these that people like Donovan come in handy, but she can't let that evil thought warp her otherwise caring mind.

"You know I'm a good person," says Ralph. "I didn't mean for any of this to happen."

She keeps staring straight ahead, her jaw clenched. She stares in the direction of Ralph's car and his wife, who is sitting inside, refusing to turn her head in Heaven's direction. "I paid you every single month. Rent was due on the fifth, and I paid you by the fifth and not a day after," says Heaven.

"I know you did." He shrugs. "I'm so sorry."

"Sometimes I even had to borrow money, but I still managed to pay you on time, and most of the time I paid you early," she says, pursing her lips.

"I know, Heaven. This has nothing to do with you. I entered this real estate game really not thinking it through."

"Game? This isn't a game, Ralph. This is my life."

"I was looking for an easy investment. I got suckered in. I should have bought a cheap HUD house or something and fixed it up and tried to flip it. That's all I needed to do. Not this. That's what I intended to do, but I couldn't sell it, so I rented, and you were a good tenant."

"I *am* a good tenant. And don't make excuses, Ralph. This isn't an expensive house. Trust me. I may be young, but I ain't stupid. Maybe it didn't cost you a dollar, but it sure didn't cost you a hundred thousand dollars either. Not even half that, so I doubt you were over your head. Banks are willing to make arrangements. Even I know that, so why don't you?"

"Who knew all this was going to happen with the economy? I'm sorry."

"So you still have your house?" asks Heaven as she stares him down with contempt. He nods. "And I'll be out on the street."

"I'm sorry."

She shakes her head and repeatedly asks the question, "What did I do to deserve this?" This is not only about the house. There are plenty of others she can rent throughout the city. But her bad luck is never ending.

"You didn't do anything. It's this recession keeping people down."

"No, Ralph, you can't blame this on the recession. This isn't right. I don't want to move. I paid you. I have proof I paid you. And you won't be getting away with this. I'm taking you to small claims court."

"I was trying to catch up. I made arrangements with the lender to make partial payments. I missed one, and that's when everything fell behind. I never wanted this to happen. But I understand you got to do what you got to do too."

"You seemed like such a good man. I trusted you," says Heaven, wiping away tears of anger. She is so upset that a man like Ralph, a husband and a father, an otherwise decent man, could be so irresponsible. She is upset that his actions would allow Hope the opportunity to tell her that she told her so if she ever found out about this. Hope didn't believe in conducting business with other blacks; a notion Heaven always thought made no sense. But for a minute, however slight, the thought crosses Heaven's mind, and she starts to doubt herself, which angers her so much she is forced to tears.

"I am a good man, but I have a family and I had to think about them. My wife is working now. I thought we were going to be able to catch up. I'm going to start working soon. It was just bad timing." Both he and his wife had more than twenty years invested in the same company, the kind of time that tricks a mind into feeling safe.

"Just tell me how long I have?" asks Heaven. "Ninety days?" she says before getting a response. Ralph's head drops. "Sixty?" He shakes his head. "How long?"

"Thirty days."

"Ralph," she says, shaking her head. Tears fill her eyes while anger takes a hold of her heart even deeper. Now she doesn't feel so bad about the bathroom door hanging off the hinges or the window Donovan busted in the back or the big holes he punched in a few of the walls. She doesn't even feel bad about the mouse she'd seen that had outsmarted the trap she set. In fact, she's hoping there are more where that mouse came from; it didn't matter if rodents lived there now that she wouldn't be. "I need more time than thirty days, and I know banks are giving extensions for hardship. I need at least a hundred and twenty days, and you better find a way for me to get it or I'll go straight to Steve Wilson and get Channel Seven on my side."

"Why are you gonna go to the news?"

"And I won't just stop at Channel Seven. I'll go to Fox and have Rob Wolchek put you in the Hall of Shame. I'll take it to CNN, too," she says, jabbing her finger in his face. "Don't mess with me. I need a hundred and twenty days," says Heaven, turning to walk back into her soon-to-be-foreclosed home. He stands on the porch, giving her the slightest satisfaction of slamming the door in his face. She peers through the living room window, standing witness just in case he miraculously gets struck by lightning.

"**H**ave you left yet?" Alicia asks Sir. It's been four weeks since Alicia's surgery, and she's finally ready to get out, especially now that she has a flat stomach and the doctor has given the okay to resume normal activity. Four weeks instead of six—not bad, she thinks.

"I'm on my way," he says, and within thirty minutes he's in the living room of her parents' condo talking politics with Alicia's stepfather. Sir's a Republican, but because he went against his party line in the last election and voted for Barack Obama, Alicia's stepfather doesn't hold that against him. Otherwise, he would've given him some flack.

Alicia is greeted with smiles from Sir as she strolls out in a pair of capris with a stretch waist even though she'd rather be wearing jeans. But wearing jeans four weeks after surgery or wearing anything that fits snugly at the waist isn't recommended because it could cause her belly to swell. She is so excited that she can finally wear a form-fitting top without worrying whether or not it makes her look pregnant.

The vase of exquisite lilies waiting for her on the table makes her eyes light up and she exclaims with delight, "Sir, these are so beautiful."

"And so are you," Sir says, causing Alicia's mother, who enters after her, to smile.

"Oh, I think you guys are going to end up getting married," her mother says.

"Let's go," Alicia says, ushering him out the front door.

Alicia and Sir's afternoon begins at the Main Art Theatre in Royal Oak for the one-thirty showing of *Adam*. The pair had been going to the art house ever since they were in the seventh grade. Aubrey used to come along, but she usually complained through the movie or fell asleep, interrupting their movie-going experience with her annoying snores.

Being back at the Main Art Theatre mostly brings back pleasant memories. His admission that he has recently joined the art house's film club to receive e-mails on upcoming movies and film screenings makes her remember how big a film buff Sir truly is. But she can't help cringing. Being at an art house also reminds her of J.R., who had recently sent a certified letter from a Beverly Hills attorney's office to her and Benita's apartment. Benita offered to forward the letter along with the rest of Alicia's mail, but Alicia told her not to bother. "I should be home pretty soon," she'd said.

Sir buys them each a Häagen-Dazs vanilla and almond chocolate bar from the concession stand. After the movie, he suggests they get something to eat, which sounds like a wonderful idea to Alicia because she feels her stomach rumble and she knows no matter how gently she presses against it, sooner or later loud, embarrassing sounds will erupt. They dine at Godaiko, a Japanese restaurant, at a small table for two, and eat sushi and chicken lettuce wraps and sip sake.

"For someone who doesn't like to drink, you sure love rice wine," he says as she swipes his cup and begins sipping.

"Well, you have to drive home, so I don't want you drinking and driving."

"Do you want to come home with me?" he asks with a wink.

"I'm still recovering."

"I'll give you some TLC."

"Thanks but no thanks. Although I did have my post-op appointment and the doctor did clear me for sex," she says with a wink back at him.

"Don't play—see, don't even play with me about that."

"I'm not playing. I'm just telling you. He said, 'I'm clearing you to return to normal activity.' So I said to him, 'So that means I can drive?' And he said, 'Most women your age ask about sex before they ask about driving.' And I said, 'Most women my age probably have a man. I don't have a man, or access to one, but I do have access to a car.'"

"You have access to a man—this man."

"I know, but right now I'm still dealing with a lot. My mind has been set on one thing for so long. And I remained positive for most of that time. I was so close, and to have it snatched away from me by a so-called friend whom I've known so long . . . That really hurts. And then there's the issue with Heaven and Hope. Take me out of the picture, and let's look at just the two of them. They're sisters . . . full blood, yet they don't speak. That bothers me so much. There's this tug inside me that tells me I have to do something to get those two back together." At that moment, a lightbulb goes off. "Let me use your phone."

"My phone?"

"Yes, your phone. You have a 313 area code. Maybe she'll answer if she sees a local number instead of my 818 area code."

Sir pulls his Palm phone from his pocket and slides it over to her. "Don't you think that's somewhat high school, though?"

"No, not at all. I think it's just me trying to reach Hope by any means necessary." She looks at her own phone to retrieve Hope's phone number while she dials on his. "Here, you ask for her so she won't hang up on me." Alicia shoves the phone over to Sir.

He stutters in hesitation after Hope picks up the phone. "Is this Hope?"

"Who is this?"

"I have someone who would like to speak with you," Sir says, handing Alicia the phone.

"Hi, Hope. This is Alicia. I just wanted to call—" She looks over at Sir and then hands the phone back to him.

"What happened?"

"She hung up."

"Of course she did. She probably thinks you're crazy. I know I would."

"You don't understand."

"Maybe I don't. Because I'm of the opinion if a person doesn't want to be bothered, just leave them alone."

"Which is why you're alone."

"But I don't feel like I'm alone," he says, reaching over to hold Alicia's available hand. "At least not anymore."

Later that night, after Sir drops Alicia back to her parents' condo, she phones her aunt Olena.

"What's wrong?" Olena asks right away.

"Why does something have to be wrong?"

"Because when you call me something usually is."

"I need your advice. I told you that I have two half sisters."

"No, you didn't—your mom did."

"Well, anyway, I knew someone in our family did. So, I'm getting close to one of them, but the other won't even take my calls . . . and she fell out with the one I'm close to."

"Over you?"

"No, not over me. I'm not sure what they fell out over. But I've never had a sister, and I need your advice. Since you and Mom have fallen out several times and aren't really that close—"

"Your mom and I are very close . . . now that I'm older. When we were growing up, she used to think she was so much older than I was and treat me like a child, but now that we're both in our forties, our relationship is much better."

"That's great for you, but I can't wait that long. What should I do, Auntie?"

"I'm curious, why didn't you ask your mom?"

"I don't know. I just didn't. Maybe because I know how she feels about my biological father. I just don't think she wants me getting involved with them at all, really."

"Well, Alicia, I think you should give it one more shot. You already know the phone doesn't work, so maybe you and the one you get along with should stop by her house. Maybe she'll talk to you in person. That's the best suggestion I have."

When she ends the call with her aunt, she realizes Olena was of little help. Alicia couldn't imagine going to Hope's house even if she did take Heaven with her. If Hope won't answer her phone, she definitely won't answer her door.

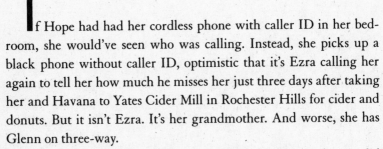

If Hope had had her cordless phone with caller ID in her bedroom, she would've seen who was calling. Instead, she picks up a black phone without caller ID, optimistic that it's Ezra calling her again to tell her how much he misses her just three days after taking her and Havana to Yates Cider Mill in Rochester Hills for cider and donuts. But it isn't Ezra. It's her grandmother. And worse, she has Glenn on three-way.

"Is this some kind of sick trick?" asks Hope. "Is that why you did it this way? Call her and then have her call me, because you knew I wouldn't pick up the phone?"

"Girl, your father doesn't have to trick you. He's your father. He did it this way because he didn't want you paying for the collect call. I'll pay for it. You probably don't know since you have never talked to your father, but collect calls are expensive coming from prison."

If she never accepts his collect calls it is because she never gave him her number to begin with—her grandmother did, and because she doesn't have anything to talk to him about. She understands, being a mother herself, how a parent can love their child like her grandmother loves Glenn, so much that even when they do something awful, such as commit murder, the parent remains by their side. But her grandmother refuses to believe Glenn did anything wrong; instead, she blames their mother's alleged infidelity as his reason for snapping.

"If you want to talk to me, you'll have to call me back direct. I'm not going to talk to you with her on the phone."

"Are you going to answer?" asks her grandmother angrily.

"He'll have to just call back and see."

"Do you hear how she's talking to me? Totally disrespectful after I raised her." *Raised me? If that's what she thinks she did. If that's what she wants to say she did, then I guess that's what she did. At least she didn't give us sleeping pills like Hester and Glenn did to make us go to sleep so they could run the streets.*

On that note, Hope slams the receiver down. Listening to her grandmother is fruitless. And even though her father didn't speak, just knowing he was on the other line angered her. If kids could choose their parents, Hope muses, there would be a lot of childless people in the world.

A few minutes later the phone rings and she answers it again.

"This is a collect call from the Chippewa Correctional Facility. Please press one to accept the charges or simply hang up if you do not wish to receive this call."

Hope presses one to accept the charges.

"If you have something to say, why don't you just say it, because I know these calls are timed and I don't have anything to say to you. Honestly, I'm not sure why I even answered."

"How are you doing?"

"I'm doing. Talk—don't ask questions."

"I'm worried about you and your sister, and I want the two of you to be closer."

"You want what?" spits Hope. "Do you really think I care about what you want? I wanted a normal childhood. Always afraid to go to bed at night because I never knew if this was going to be another one of those nights when the police knocked our door down or when you and Mom fought, so I could care less about what you want," she shouts. "You were never there for us."

"But you and Heaven have each other. You can't give up on your little sister. You just can't."

His comment gives Hope pause. "There was a woman who called me not too long ago saying she's my sister. Do you know anything about that? I don't even remember the woman's name."

"Alicia?"

"Yeah, I think that was her name."

"She called you . . . really? What a blessing. She found you and she called. Did you talk to her?"

"No, I didn't talk to her. Why would I? Is she crazy? She wants to be a part of this family only because she doesn't know what this family is all about."

"I'm praying for you . . . praying that God delivers you from your hatred."

"I don't want your prayers. Don't want them at all . . . because your prayers won't do me one bit of good." She slams the phone down on the receiver and collapses facedown into her pillow. It's not surprising that Alicia woman wasn't lying after all. It's not surprising, but it's not something she can deal with right now. Hope is trying to take one step at a time.

Everything is going downhill, Heaven tells Alicia over the phone, from losing Harmony to not being able to break free of Donovan to her hair. Heaven doesn't know who she is. She hates everything about her life. She hates living.

"I can help you, just don't give up," Alicia pleads with her. "You are so young. Things will get better."

"Help me how? The last person I remember trying to help me left town. Don't waste your energy on me."

"I wouldn't be wasting my energy. I'd be doing something other than focusing on something I can't have, and that's what I need to do right now. Let's go exercise. It's good for stress."

"Don't even talk about exercising," says Heaven. "I have a lifetime membership at Fitness USA, but ask me if I use it."

"I'm just saying if you want to lose weight."

"Hold up. I never said I wanted to lose weight. What, you trying to say I'm fat or something? I love my curves. Maybe Dove will hire me to do a commercial for their campaign for real beauty."

"You should do yoga with me. My roommate and I used to go to classes together. If I find a place for us to go, will you go with me?"

"Yoga?" asks Heaven, wrinkling her nose.

"Yes, yoga, I love yoga. It's so relaxing and energizing."

"I guess it couldn't hurt for me to lose five or ten pounds just to keep everything looking nice and toned. Sign me up—I'll go. Just don't get me stuck in a contract. I can't go through that again."

"Don't worry, no contracts. I don't plan on being here that long."

Heaven broods over Alicia's comment long after she ends the call. Eventually, Alicia is going to leave her just like her childhood best friend did and everyone else who Heaven loved that was in her life has.

A few days later on a Monday, Heaven arrives downtown within twenty minutes. She parks on Atwater Street and walks a short distance to the Rivard Plaza and Pavilion. While she waits for Alicia to arrive, she observes the standing glass map of the St. Lawrence Seaway. She notices Lake Michigan and thinks about Hope's husband and about how, after Hope lost him, Heaven had lost Hope, most likely for good. She is almost sure of it. And even though Alicia is really friendly and resembles Hope almost like a carbon copy, she's not her replacement. She loves Alicia, but it's not the same. She and Hope have history . . . memories. Within minutes, she retreats to one of the many benches lining the cobblestone path and stares out at the Detroit River.

This is the Detroit RiverWalk. She's never been here. She's never been on the beautiful carousel or strolled along the expansive walkway made for a perfect romantic date—probably because she's never been on a perfect romantic date. She can't believe she is down here so early. Yoga just isn't something Heaven ever considered. She'd always thought of it as something rich folks did; yet all she has to throw on is a pair of long johns under her pants in the wintertime and a V-neck shirt. She doesn't have a mat, but Alicia said she'd bring two.

Alicia arrives shortly after. She waves at Heaven and walks up to her. "Here're your mat and a bottle of water," she says.

"FIJI," Heaven says, twirling the bottle. "Isn't this stuff expensive? I have a friend who doesn't believe in buying water. He says Michigan has some of the best water . . . the same as what's in the bottle."

"I will not drink water from a faucet."

"I'm the same way." Heaven admires Alicia's curly locks. "You looking good . . . much better than you did in the hospital," jokes Heaven. "I wish my hair could get like yours. I'm trying to grow my relaxer out, but it's hard," says Heaven, touching the scarf she has tied around her head.

"I told you I can help you with your hair. But, if you're really serious, you have to be willing to do a big chop like my mom."

"Cut it off short like that? Don't get me wrong—your mom's hair looks cute on her, but she has a slim face. I have a round head. I'd look silly wearing my hair like that."

"If you're trying to grow out of your relaxer, you can either transition for a long time and get frustrated or cut off the relaxer and start fresh. It's a great way to work on your patience, because it will probably take a solid two years before your hair gets the way you want it."

Heaven stands when she sees a group of ladies forming on the lawn with mats. Alicia reaches out and gives her a hug.

"You sure like to hug."

"I'm sorry. I do like to hug. I guess you don't."

"I do. It's just that Hope and I never hug," Heaven says with a shrug.

"That's really too bad."

Heaven shakes her head. "No, that's just Hope—that's all that is. Once you meet her, you'll see what I mean. She has a serious attitude problem, and that started way before her husband died."

"Well, it's probably hard for her, being a widow so young."

"We're used to having it hard. We were orphans."

"Oh, yeah, with your mother and the cancer . . . and your father and . . . what is he in prison for?"

Heaven hesitates. "Murder."

"Oh wow. So he's never getting out?"

Heaven shakes her head. Alicia wants to ask who it was he killed, but she would feel awkward probing. Even though, technically, Glenn is her father too, but she doesn't feel even a slight connection to him.

After a few more minutes of talking, they join the group forming on the lawn near the river and start doing breathing exercises.

Heaven looks over at Alicia who is having no problem doing a downward-facing dog. Heaven has no problem getting on her hands and knees or tucking her wrists underneath her shoulders while her knees are underneath her hips. The difficulty arises after she curls her toes under and tries to push back and raise her hips to straighten her legs.

"I can't," says Heaven amid heavy breathing.

"Don't say you can't. You can do anything you put your mind to."

Heaven throws her an evil eye. She knows what she can do and what she can't. And if what Alicia is saying is so true, why didn't she become a big star in Hollywood? Hadn't she put her mind to that? Heaven wonders. "I haven't even done that much yet, and I'm already out of breath. This is getting on my nerves," huffs Heaven.

Alicia asks Heaven to start from the beginning pose. "When you're on the floor with your fingers spread out like this," says Alicia as she gets in the pose beside her, "curl your toes and just push back."

"It's easy for you. But I have all this right here"—Heaven pinches her thighs—"and all this right here"—she pats her behind—"so I can't just push back that fast, because that's a lot of weight I'm pushing."

"Just take your time," says Alicia.

Heaven nods in agreement. "That's exactly what I plan to do." She opens her bottle of water and begins drinking. "I think I should've consulted my doctor before I started doing this mess, because my back is killing me now." Heaven checks her watch. It is a quarter to eleven; the one-hour session is almost over. She decides to sit out the remaining fifteen minutes and watch the rest.

After the session, Alicia joins Heaven. "So, do you want to go somewhere and get something to eat?" she asks as she wipes sweat from her brow with a small towel.

"Looking like this? Downtown during the week when the business lunch crowd will be out in suits and I have a rag on my head?" asks Heaven, shaking her head. "No."

"You look fine. It's summertime and we've been exercising. There has to be a restaurant around here. Somewhere we can sit outdoors and talk. We have a lot of catching up to do."

Heaven shrugs. "I guess we should, huh? If we can eat outside, that'll be fine."

They end up at an Italian restaurant in the GM Building called Andiamo. They have lunch on the patio and both order from the "ten under ten dollars" menu. Alicia selects the portobello mushroom salad; Heaven picks linguine with littleneck clams.

"So tell me about this Donovan character. You must really love him."

"Why do you say that?"

"Because you seem to have a hard time leaving him, and I guess for me, I'm the complete opposite. I mean, when I'm done with a man, I'm done."

Heaven gives a deep sigh. "I'm almost done," she says, then laughs, because even she knows how ridiculous that sounds. "Physically I've established a distance, but mentally it's hard for me not to think about him. I just don't want to be alone and go through the whole dating thing again because I could be out there and meet someone worse. Meet someone with a disease that'll stay with me long after they're gone."

"Or, you could meet someone better . . . or, why worry about meeting anyone at all right now? Why not focus on Heaven for a change and making yourself happy? Work on your relationship with Hope. And the rest will come."

Heaven sighs. "Everyone gets, like, one strike with her, so I used that and now it's over. If it wasn't for Havana, I'd be cool with that, but I love my niece."

"Would you really be cool with that? You miss them both, don't you?" asks Alicia, noticing the sadness in Heaven's expression.

Heaven nods. "I'm not claiming to be perfect," she says, deciding to finally let Alicia know a little more about her. "I've done a lot of things wrong, but I'm going to make it up to her. I took money from her and I'm going to make sure I pay her back, and then some. I shouldn't have used her credit, but I had every intention of paying the bill, but then I lost my job."

Heaven didn't want to think about Hope, who, at times, could be as cold toward her as their father used to be toward their mother. She knows she let Hope down at a time when Hope needed her most. All she wants now is forgiveness.

"So, what do you like to do? Since it's obvious you don't like yoga."

Heaven shrugs. "Shoplift I guess," says Heaven, and watches Alicia sling her right eyebrow. "It was a joke."

"Oh, good, I was about to say."

"I guess the only thing I can do is take pictures," Heaven says.

"I need headshots to send to a local production company. I'll pay you to take some, but you have to be good, because I've already had one photographer who wasn't."

"I'm good. I have a portfolio you can look at."

"What are you doing tomorrow?"

"I'll probably look for an apartment, but I really need to find a job first so I can qualify. I would rent another house, but I can't go through that again. I was paying rent every month, but my landlord pocketed the money and now he's being foreclosed on. Can you believe that?"

"Sadly, yes, I can. That happens a lot in LA."

"Well, it won't be happening to me . . . not anymore. My utilities were too high anyway."

"So, if you could live anywhere . . . where would you live?"

"I used to want to live out of state. Never LA. Maybe Atlanta, I guess, because that's all I really hear about as far as being a cool place for blacks to live. I would go to North Carolina, but it's best to deal with my nana long distance. But really, I just want to stay in Detroit. There's one place I have in mind . . . but please don't laugh."

"I won't. Just tell me."

"I've always wanted to live in the Jeffersonian."

"The Jeffersonian? On Jefferson?"

"That's why it's called the Jeffersonian."

"That place is like a hundred and fifty years old."

"It's not that old, more like fifty years old."

"My point is, there are so many newer apartments downtown. Why that place?"

Heaven shrugs. "I've always loved that building and those huge balconies that stretch the whole width of your apartment. My best friend Angelica and her parents used to live there on the thirtieth floor with a view of the Detroit River. I loved going over there. Honey, baby, let me tell you something—if I lived there, couldn't nobody tell me nothing."

Alicia smiles. "I can tell you're excited. It would be hard for me to live downtown, because there're no grocery stores down here, no retail. It's just not convenient. I can't even get a Starbucks. . . . Now, if Starbucks isn't even coming here, you know something's wrong."

"I don't care about all that. Why would I want to spend that much on a cup of coffee anyway? I just want a nice place to call home."

Alicia thinks it's sweet that Heaven can get excited about the old apartment building. Alicia had driven past almost a week ago with Sir when they were on their way to Belle Isle Park, and it didn't even catch her eye enough for her to take a glance. "Well, let's take a tour."

"For what?"

"Because that's where you want to live one day."

"No. I'm not into window-shopping."

"It's not window-shopping—it's more like window-dreaming."

"I'm not into that either."

"We're going. Today. Right now."

"With this rag on my head . . . I don't think so. Not today, maybe tomorrow, and I don't care what you say. Plus, all that window-dreaming isn't good for you."

"**W**e can pretend," Alicia had told Heaven before they left Andiamo the day before. "Pretend you have money. Pretend I'm your manager and you need an apartment . . . a second residence."

In some ways, she didn't understand why they had to go through all that just to get a tour of an apartment, but then she figured Alicia just missed LA . . . missed her acting classes . . . missed pretending.

"Just follow my lead," she tells Heaven as Alicia pulls her stepfather's black Escalade through the attended gatehouse. She pulls up to the front of the building and tosses the keys to a valet as she and Heaven stroll confidently through the front door of the Jeffersonian, which is held open by a doorman. They are greeted by an attractive young man in his early- to mid-thirties, professionally dressed in a navy suit with a striped tie and a crisp white shirt. He walks with them to the leasing office, where Alicia exchanges a few words with him.

"So, Miss Star, you are from Los Angeles?" the leasing agent asks Heaven.

Heaven looks over at Alicia.

"Tempest is a new artist signed with Motown, and she needs a two- or three-bedroom apartment for roughly a year . . . something with a great view on your highest floor—the thirtieth."

"Our thirtieth floor is our mechanical room. So our highest floor with apartments is the twenty-ninth."

"You don't have a penthouse on the thirtieth floor?" interjects Heaven. "Are you sure?"

"I'm positive," he says with a smile. "A lot of people do inquire about penthouses, but we don't have any here. All of our apartments have spectacular, unobstructed panoramic views, though. So you're with Motown?" the leasing agent asks Heaven.

"Please, I'll be handling this, so you can direct all of your questions to me," says Alicia.

"Didn't Motown leave Detroit in the seventies? Is it even still in existence?"

"Of course, it merged with Universal like so many record labels did."

"So, she just wants to move to Detroit because Motown *used* to be here?" the leasing agent asks.

"Okay, listen, Tempest wants to look around. Do you have something to show us on the twenty-ninth floor or not?"

The leasing agent nods, not wanting to put up a fight. "Well, we have a very nice apartment available. It has three bedrooms, three baths, and two thousand eighty-nine square feet. I just need your driver's license and I can show it to you."

"It's exciting to know a major artist signed to Motown is considering living here," the leasing agent says, as he takes Alicia's license and writes her name down on a log. Alicia toggles through her Black-Berry and dials Benita as they head for the elevator. "India wants to fly down next week to work on the album. She and Stevie are doing a song together. After we leave here, I'm going to drive out to the airport and pick up Nelly," she tells Benita, who plays along. She's used to Alicia's window-dreaming.

Benita says, "You didn't get my e-mail. We have a limo service picking up Nelly."

"Oh, a limo service is picking him up. Perfect, because we have to get ready for Aretha's dinner tonight."

"Your cell phone may cut off on the elevator," the leasing agent says as he presses the elevator button.

"I've got to run, but Tempest and I will be back in LA early next week."

Alicia and Heaven walk into the elevator. Alicia turns toward Heaven and says, "After this, I need to swing by Anita Baker's place." Heaven doesn't respond. She looks at Alicia as if she's a weirdo. She's pretended on an occasion or two while she was shoplifting, but now she sees just how strange it is.

"A few things about our property . . . Laundry facilities are on each floor," the leasing agent says as they walk down the long hallway heading to the apartment. "There are a few amenities that Miss Star may find of interest. We have a twenty-four-hour door person, a twenty-four-hour-attended gatehouse, along with twenty-four-hour valet service. Our parking garage is covered and has an enclosed walkway." He sticks the key in the apartment lock. "Each apartment is cable ready with high-speed Internet access. As you can see, the private balconies are quite spacious," he says as he opens the door and allows Heaven and then Alicia to step out ahead of him. "We have a heated Olympic-sized pool and tennis courts," he says as they look over the six-acre property. They step back inside the apartment and head for the kitchen. "Our kitchens come fully equipped with GE appliances."

"How much does this rent for?" asks Heaven.

"Thirteen hundred ninety-six dollars."

"For a three-bedroom with three baths and more than two thousand square feet?" Heaven emphasizes to Alicia.

"And the rent includes your water, heat, and air-conditioning."

Heaven clears her throat. "What did you just say? That includes your water, heat, and air?"

"Yes."

"How much are your one bedrooms?"

"Our one bedrooms are eight hundred square feet and start at five hundred seventy-eight dollars."

"What?" Heaven is elated. She is tired of pretending now. She's ready to sign on the dotted line and be done.

"Well, we will certainly consider this," says Alicia, hanging on to the property's brochure. "But we do have a few other properties to take a look at. I have your card here, and I'll call if we're interested."

On the ride back to Heaven's house, Heaven says, "You're a good actress. You almost had me believing I was an up-and-coming celebrity. It felt good to window-dream."

"It does. . . . I told you it does."

"I Googled that man. That director . . . Marcus Toller. You didn't tell me he made *Tenacity*. I love that movie even more than *The Shawshank Redemption*." Heaven thinks about her last comment. "Well, maybe not more than *Shawshank* but almost as much, and that says a whole lot. So I called him a couple days ago," she says nonchalantly, "but he was busy."

"Heaven . . . He's an Oscar-winning director. . . . You can't just call him on the phone like he's J.R."

"Who is J.R.?"

"Nobody . . . That's my point exactly."

Heaven shrugs. "Well, yes you can, 'cause I did. His number is listed—Envision Entertainment. Full address and phone. Why would he list it if he didn't want anybody to call him?"

"That's his film and television production company. And the contact information wasn't listed on his Web site, was it?"

"No, but all I had to do was Google it."

"So you actually called him, and what happened? Who answered?"

"An answering machine picked up . . . not even a voice mail . . . an answering machine like old people used to use back in your day. But I didn't leave a message."

"My day? I'm only thirty-two."

"I'm just teasing . . . but seriously, I was expecting the man behind *Tenacity* to at least have a personal secretary screening his calls."

"Secretary . . . who says secretary? You mean assistant, don't you? How old are you? Someone would think you were my age."

"Okay, okay, I get your point, but actually I did mean secretary. I used to be one for the board of education. Anyway, I didn't leave a message. I'll just call back."

"No, Heaven, you won't. I plan to return to LA one day. I don't want to be known as the woman who had her little sister call one of the top Hollywood directors and beg for a job."

Heaven smiles. "You called me your little sister. But anyway . . . Ain't nobody gonna beg for it. I'm merely going to state the facts. He'd be a fool to pass you up. You wanted to go to the Jeff and window-dream. Well, what's wrong with me calling up a director and stating the facts? You deserve that role."

"I hope that's not what you were planning to tell him."

"I'm not sure what I plan to tell him."

"Heaven, you won't be telling him anything, because you won't be calling him back." Alicia looks over at Heaven when she stops at a red light. She's not sure if someone as young as Heaven, someone who has lived her entire life in a dying city, can understand the politics of Hollywood. "Please promise me."

Heaven's eyes fall toward the word *Platinum* above the walnut wood trim near the glove compartment. She doesn't understand how Alicia can accept defeat so easily; how she can be so close to her dream and pull back.

"Promise," Alicia stresses.

"I promise."

The next day, in the midafternoon, Heaven is over at Trina's, helping her move into a two-bedroom apartment in a new complex in Farmington Hills, roughly five miles away from Trina's old apartment where Nicolette still lives and away from all memories of Heaven's only sexual experience with a female that she will never admit to having had. Heaven is staring at the phone and wondering why it is so easy for her to be so defiant sometimes. But in this case it's only because she feels so strongly that this is the right thing to do. She can feel bad about stealing her sister's identity and charging up thousands of dollars; she can feel bad about her on-again, off-again relationship with Donovan; but she doesn't feel bad about the call she is getting ready to place.

"Wait," says Trina. "Don't call yet. Maybe we should practice this first."

"I don't need to practice. I know what I want to say."

"Girl, you have to speak a certain way when you're conducting business."

"I know how to talk right when I need to."

She begins dialing the number on her cell phone. She is nervous—more nervous than she's ever been when she was inside a store breaking the law and getting away with thousands of dollars in merchandise.

"Envision Entertainment . . . Marcus Toller's office."

"I was trying to reach Mr. Toller. Is he in?" asks Heaven as she stays focused on Trina, who shakes her head.

"Who shall I say is calling?" asks the woman.

"Heaven."

Trina's head shakes furiously.

"Your last name, please?" asks the woman.

"Oh, I'm sorry . . . Jetter . . . Heaven Jetter."

"From?"

"From?" Heaven shrugs. "From Detroit."

Trina covers her face with both of her hands.

"Please hold," the woman says.

Heaven mutes the phone. "What?" she asks Trina.

"You need to sound more professional. As if you're calling the White House for President Obama. Would you just say Heaven? From Detroit. Did you really say that?"

"I know. . . . I'm nervous. Be quiet. I'll get it together."

"You better."

"Miss Jetter, he can speak to you now."

"He can speak to me . . . okay," she says with a nod. She mouths to Trina, "Oh . . . my . . . God."

"I'll transfer you to Mr. Toller now."

"Okay." Heaven shrugs.

"This is Marcus," the man says quickly.

"Mr. Toller, hi, my name is Heaven Jetter."

"You're with the *Detroit News*, right?"

"With the *Detroit News*?" She hesitates and begins to stutter. "N-no, I'm calling on behalf of my sister."

"Your sister? Who the hell is your sister?"

"No need to get hostile. My sister is Alicia Day. I'm not sure if you remember her, but I'm calling because she would never call you herself, but she didn't put me up to this. It's just that she really wants this part in your movie. I mean she read the book when she was in high school and she knows she would really do the role justice."

"She read the book when she was in high school. That's interesting. This movie isn't based on a book."

"Oh, well, she read books in high school. I guess not that book."

"No, not that book, because there is no book. What's this all about? Make it quick."

"My sister . . . Alicia . . . She just needs a chance. Is there any way you can reconsider your choice and make her an offer?"

The line goes silent for a few seconds, and then he gives a deep sigh. "I really have to hand it to you—this is a first. And, yes, I do remember your sister, but even if I didn't find this call to be highly annoying, which I do, and extremely unprofessional, which I also do, I still couldn't consider Alicia because I'm about to start filming. You just happened to catch me in the office on a day I agreed to do phone interviews with the media, and that's the only reason I'm on this line now. I thought you were with the *Detroit News*. Ironically, I have a one-o'clock phone interview with them, and bingo, this is them on my other line."

"So there's no way you could consider it?"

"Listen, the only way I would is if Aubrey Daniels drops dead before we start filming," he says, and then hangs up.

"What? What's wrong?" asks Trina. "Why are you giving me that look?"

"He said the only way he'd consider Alicia is if Aubrey Daniels dies. Man, they are really heartless out there."

"So, what, you think we should try to kill her or something?"

"Be serious, Trina. We're shoplifters, not murderers." Heaven sighs. Now she feels bad for going against Alicia's wishes. What if her entire plan backfires and Alicia finds out when she goes back to LA that Heaven annoyed a famous director? What if she decides to never speak to her again?

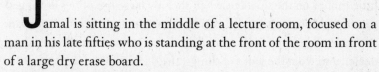

Jamal is sitting in the middle of a lecture room, focused on a man in his late fifties who is standing at the front of the room in front of a large dry erase board.

"All right guys," the man says as he claps his hands together loudly to gain the attention of the other men in the room. "This is the second warrant for the day, and this one is a little different. We will be assisting the FBI. The suspects are all wanted for several armed bank robberies as well as auto theft. But here's the rub—we have absolutely no idea exactly how many are in their crew. They have an informant, but recently he's stopped cooperating. The reason we're getting involved is because several of the identified suspects all have prior records for drug possession with intent to sell. Their drug operation took a substantial hit during a DEA raid about six months ago that netted more than three million in cash. It's believed that the members of the crew who weren't busted turned to bank robbery as a means to get some cash to refuel their drug business. It's been hard to pin down all the various spots they operate from as well as all the players. It's a fairly large operation, well organized, and they move around from various houses often, so we should have a few warrants to serve in the next few days. Right now, we have a person of interest under surveillance." A male's picture flashes on an overhead projector. "His name is Donovan Davis, known on the streets as Scarface. Right now he is just a person of interest."

Heaven had come to Donovan's house to finally break it off. But when a teen boy allowed her to enter through the side door after another man left, she stumbled upon something she hadn't expected to see. Looking back, she was surprised she hadn't realized what was going on before. After all, there were always people coming and going from Donovan's house, he did move quite often, and his cell phone was constantly ringing. She just figured he was cheating on her all this time. That was probably part of it, but it definitely wasn't the whole story.

She had guessed he might be a small-time weed dealer to make a little money on the side, but when she saw large quantities of bagged cocaine and some other drugs laid out on the table before Donovan, she realized he was much more than that. He was a full-fledged drug dealer, and from the looks of things, she'd guess he was a pretty powerful one.

"What you doing here?" asks Donovan, as he sits in a wingback chair in the living room, counting cash with a money counter. "You let her in?"

"This your girl, right?" the teen asks.

"You don't just let people come through the door unannounced, fool. Get on out of here," he says to the teen with a dismissive wave. "What's up?" he asks Heaven. "Since when you start just dropping by?"

She tries to hand him *The Black Male Handbook: A Handbook for Life*. "I bought this for you."

"You can keep it," he says as he continues to use his money counter.

She shakes her head. "So this is who you are? I knew you were doing something, but I didn't know you were into it like this." She sighs and shakes her head. "I'm leaving you."

"Where you goin'?" he asks, rising from his seat and yanking her arm.

"Stop grabbing on me like that," she says, snatching her arm away. "I'm not going to be here when this place gets raided. And it will get raided." She'd finally finished all of her community service hours, and last month was her last month on probation. She doesn't want to risk it all. For a minute, she thought maybe she could help Donovan get his life back on track. But now she realizes that she has to focus on herself.

She turns to head for the door, but Donovan shoves her into the wall. When she turns toward him, she sees the most evil look in his inky eyes. She throws up one hand, gesturing for him to remain calm. *It's over, there's no need to get into it and start a fight*, she tells herself. *Simply move toward the door and leave.* And that's when he does one of the foulest things she can imagine; he churns his mouth and spits a foamy wad of saliva in her face. "That's what I think of you, bitch." She wipes the saliva from her face, trying hard to keep her cool, and heads for the door. If she can just reach it, she promises herself she will never see him again.

He forces her to the floor after he rams his foot into the small of her back, and at that moment a knock-down fight ensues as they bang into cheap furniture, tripping over an end table, and the digital scale he uses to weigh drugs falls from the table to the floor. It breaks, causing his anger to escalate even more. All she can do is pray that neither of his friends, who've been sitting at the kitchen table with the drugs the entire time, come to his aid. Ending this fight—the last fight—is the only thing on her mind.

She manages somehow to make it out the door. It's over. . . . She knows that this time it's over. He will never lay a finger on her again.

At ten in the morning, Heaven and Alicia enter the county clerk's office—room 928.

Heaven is there to file a personal protection order against Donovan. After Heaven had run out of Donovan's house the day before, she didn't go home. She didn't want to in case Donovan did what he would often do, which was come to her house and harass her further; intimidate her; scare her into staying. It was fear, Alicia explained to Heaven when she met her at Sir's loft later that evening, that kept Heaven in the relationship, when it should have made her want to leave.

Heaven ended up spending the night at Alicia's parents' home and waking up at eight in the morning to an annoying cell phone alarm just so they could make it downtown by ten.

The room feels cramped, but after a fairly long wait—long enough to make Heaven reconsider her actions but not enough to change her mind—Heaven is seated with a victim's advocate.

"May I see your driver's license?" asks the advocate.

"Yes," Heaven says as she removes her wallet from her heart-patterned canvas bag and slides her license over to the woman.

The advocate takes Heaven's license and uses it to fill out a portion of the form. She hands Heaven a "complaint for abuse prevention" form. "What I'm going to need for you to do with that form is provide us with the defendant's home and work addresses."

"He doesn't work."

"Okay, then just leave that part blank. We'll need you to list all of his phone numbers, as well as a description and plate number of the abuser's car."

"I have no idea what he's driving now. Lately, he's been changing his cars. Plus he just moved to his new place, and I don't have the exact address. I just know it from sight."

"Does he have a history with drugs or gun ownership?"

"I've never seen him with a gun." That is true, though she doesn't doubt he has one, judging from his line of work.

"What about drugs?"

Heaven shrugs. "Not really." She drops her head, disappointed that she is still trying to protect him because she realizes this will probably screw up his probation.

"If you could briefly write down on the form the most recent incident of violence and try to be very descriptive."

Heaven looks at the form, looks up at Alicia, and points to the word *Plaintiff*.

"That's you," says Alicia.

Heaven writes down her name.

"Do you have any questions for me?" asks the victim's advocate.

"Yes, if he's on probation, will this interfere with that? Will it be a violation of his probation?"

"No. A PPO itself is not a criminal charge, but if he were to violate the order, then it could become criminal and possibly interfere with his probation. What is he on probation for?"

"DUI," says Heaven.

Heaven focuses on filling out the form attached to the clipboard as Alicia stands over her. Several minutes later, after she completes the form, she is taken into the courtroom by the victim's advocate to have her paperwork reviewed by the court. The entire process from the time they arrive until the final determination by the court takes nearly three hours. And when she leaves, she is given a notice of hearing and told the defendant will be served to appear in court.

"How do you feel?" asks Alicia as they walk out of the Coleman A. Young Municipal Center.

"I'm trying not to think about it. I just want him to be served and have this all be over. She spots the hot dog stand. "And I feel like I want a hot dog loaded with onions."

"A hot dog loaded with onions sounds cheap enough for me to treat," says Alicia.

Heaven and Alicia head toward the hot dog stand. Heaven is worried. She knows for certain that Donovan will come after her when he is served. She thinks she should take Trina up on her offer of a LadySmith revolver so she can be prepared.

Loud, angry male voices drift by Heaven's rental house as she stands on her front porch, fumbling with her door key in the darkness. The streetlights on the block are still out—the aftermath of another forceful storm that had swept through southeastern Michigan three days earlier and left thousands without electricity. There are no downed trees on the street, but there are a few on some of the neighboring streets. Though things are bad for her, she remembers the house she saw one street over with a tree jammed through the front window—a reminder that things can always be worse.

She is afraid.

Her fear is not of a tree falling or of the strange men lurking around her unsavory neighborhood. She is afraid of Donovan, who is suddenly standing so close behind her she can smell the vodka on his breath before he even speaks.

He had called her while she was at Rumor Nightclub about being served earlier that day. He was angry and yelling, and telling her that she was really trying to mess up his life. Only he didn't say it that nicely. He cursed her out and hung up the phone. But now, as she eases her front door open and realizes Donovan is behind her, she knows he has much more to say.

Donovan slams her head into the cracked frame and then pushes her inside. Splintered wood sticks out of her temple. Small amounts of blood drip. But she doesn't feel pain; at least not yet—not even after he grabs her long hair extensions, spools her hair around his wrist, and pulls her head back.

"I used to think this was all your real hair. But you're just like ninety percent of the bitches in the D . . . fake and so beneath me," he says, anger raging. "My mom is right. I can do better."

Heaven doesn't say a word. "I bet I can get you to give me a kiss now." Her eyes focus on his thin lips. She tries to pull free, but he throws her to the dusty hardwood floor. He flings a loose track of her hair from his hand and whips her in the face.

She gathers herself quickly, running into the kitchen to retrieve a knife.

He follows closely behind her, grabbing her waist and pulling her away from the kitchen drawer.

She runs out of the kitchen, heading for the front door. He tackles her legs and she falls hard. "You don't even know who I am," he says, standing and pouncing on her fleshy thighs with his white gym shoes. He looks down and notices a red speck on his once-spotless gym shoes. "You got blood on my new Jordans!" He kicks her right shin.

She scoots away from him and rests her back against the wall of her bare living room.

"Look at you," he says, pacing the empty room. "Looking all scared. You scared."

He turns his back toward her for just a few seconds.

She grabs her white hearts purse from the floor by the bamboo handles, drags it over to her, and pulls out the LadySmith revolver Trina had given her just hours after she filed the PPO.

When he turns back around, she says, "I swear to God if you take one step toward me, it will be your last." He steps toward her, taunting her. "Stop, Donovan, and put your hands up. I ain't playing. I will protect myself." She eases herself off the floor and keeps both hands steadied on the revolver.

"So, what, you gonna kill me now?" asks Donovan as he takes yet another step.

She fires the gun, lodging a bullet into the floor less than an inch from the tip of his left sneaker.

He jumps back. "Okay . . . okay, hold up," he stutters. "I'ma need you to calm down—"

"Look at you, looking all scared," she says, mockingly. She digs in her purse, retrieving her cell phone to dial 911 while her eyes remain on Donovan. "I told you I'm serious. I'm not trying to hurt you, but I'm not trying to get hurt either."

"I know you're not calling the police? Don't do this to me."

"Do it to you? What about me? You put your hands on me . . . again."

"Baby, I'm sorry. I don't want to go to prison—"

"Maybe that's where you need to go. You've got problems and I'm tired of it all . . . you, your problems . . . everything. I can do better and I will do better. Much better, you just wait and see."

"I want you to do better with me. I'll do better. We can do better together." His voice softens, and for a moment he looks so sincere.

She shakes her head. "Shut up," she says, confusion creeping inside her mind again.

"Do you want me to go to prison? Because if you call the police, that's what will happen. How will that make you feel? That you were responsible for another black man going to prison?"

"I wouldn't be responsible for that. You would. I'm tired of you talking down to me . . . hitting me. I don't need this," she says more for herself than for him. Heaven is young, but she isn't stupid. She's been through a lot and knows she needs to do so much better. But the excuse of doing her best instead of doing what's best is one she has used too often.

"Go on and call the police. But think about this—you're the one pointing a gun, not me. So where did you get that gun from? Is it registered to you? That's what the police are gonna wanna know."

She lets out a heavy sigh. She knows what he's saying is the truth. Going to jail would be her worst nightmare come true.

"You will never hit me again, I swear to God," grunts Heaven, stopping short of dialing the last one in the 911 emergency number, the gun pointed in his direction. "Take off all of your clothes."

"Take off all my clothes for what?"

"Take them off . . . and hand me your keys and your cell phone . . . now!" shouts Heaven.

He tosses over his car keys and cell phone and takes off his shirt.

"Your pants too, and your gym shoes."

"I'm not giving you my gym shoes."

"Take them off," she demands, steadying the gun in his direction. He takes off his shoes and his blue jeans, which leaves him wearing only his boxers and crew cut socks.

"Now, let's go. Keep your hands up and walk out the door." She walks behind him, leaving quite a bit of distance. "Don't turn and look at me. Just walk out the door." He swings open the front door and the barred security door. She stands on the porch and quickly locks both doors. "All right, now walk as far away from this house as you can."

"What about my car? That's a brand-new LS 10. I'm not going to leave it here," he says, attempting to turn toward her.

"I said don't turn around and I mean it."

"I'm not leaving my car here—that's a Lexus."

"Then fetch," she says, tossing his key far off in the darkness along with his cell phone. By the time he finds his keys and cell phone, if he ever does, and has the opportunity to call any of his friends, she'll be long gone. Sure, she's left her camera and laptop inside, but she still has her life, and those other things aren't rightfully hers anyway. When it's all said and done, the only thing that does belong to her that she is concerned for right now is herself. She hops into her car and speeds off, leaving Donovan several houses down from hers, searching through bushes for his belongings.

"Heaven, what's wrong?" asks Alicia on the other end of the line.

"I couldn't get a hold of my friend Trina, and I don't have anywhere else to go. Can I please come there?"

Alicia doesn't even need to ask any questions. "Yes, come over."

On the morning of the hearing, Heaven is nervous as she steps into the elevator. The heels of her navy two-inch pumps tremble as she stands toward the front of the elevator near the controls. But she isn't alone. Alicia is with her for moral support. Heaven notices the button for the ninth floor is already lit, which gives her the slightest twinge of relief—one less thing she has to do. She feels a sharp pain pierce a nerve in the back of her neck. Her right eyelid twitches. Her armpits are moist and sticky. She takes a deep breath. She stands in the middle of a pack, surrounded by a dozen or more people. Her arms are hugging a manila folder pressed firmly against her chest. The folder holds evidence; photos, notes, and a digital tape recorder are all inside.

A few days earlier, Heaven wrote a list of things she wants the judge to know, such as the fact that she's called 911 previously and officers were dispatched to her home. She leaves out the minor detail that she'd told them to go away once they'd arrived. She'd gone around her old house, taking pictures of the holes in the wall and the bathroom door hanging off the hinges. And the more she wrote down, the more Heaven began to see, with her eyes wide-open, that

314

she truly was in an abusive relationship. Maybe, since she wouldn't always back down, she didn't realize he was abusing her. Just because she'd sometimes push back whenever he shoved her didn't mean she was on equal footing. She should've known when he started using a closed fist to throw punches against her face and body that they were never on equal footing.

She has had many low points with Donovan before this final breaking point. She asks herself what kind of man puts his hand on a woman. He never once sincerely apologized for the ringing he caused in her ears or the stiffness in her back after a beating. Instead, she apologized for making him snap. And then they went upstairs and had sex right after. He moaned out her name and told her how good she felt, which for Heaven was better than any apology he could have possibly given her.

But no more.

Heaven steps off the elevator, donned conservatively in a teal paisley printed silk twill dress. Accented with a tie neck, the dress falls almost an inch below her knees. She purchased the outfit from Sym's especially for the occasion. Alicia follows behind her, and they both move toward Judge Stanford's courtroom twenty minutes before her scheduled hearing time.

When they enter the courtroom, there is another hearing in session, a nondomestic personal protection case involving former business partners. She waits patiently for an appropriate moment to approach the clerk. When it's time, she tells the clerk that she is there for a hearing and she is representing herself. Then she and Alicia each take a seat in the back of the courtroom and wait for her case to be called. There is no sign of Donovan, even though he phoned her the day before and informed her that he would be there and would be bringing a surprise witness.

Heaven Jetter's name is finally called thirty minutes after the scheduled hearing time. If Donovan is not here after thirty minutes, she assumes he's not coming. She prays he doesn't show so she won't have to look at him.

Heaven steps toward the podium while Alicia sits behind it.

"It is my understanding," says the judge, "that you come before the court today as the petitioner in sole representation to ask the court to grant a domestic personal protection order against Donovan David Davis; is this correct?"

"Yes, Your Honor," says Heaven.

"You may start by stating the facts of your case," says the judge.

She begins with a ruffle of a few pages; three sheets of lined paper noting incidents spanning their volatile relationship. "Your Honor," she says, clearing her throat, "the reason I'm here today is to ask the court to grant my request for a personal protection order against Donovan David Davis. He has threatened me on numerous occasions, and I stand before you in fear of my life."

At this point Donovan enters the courtroom, sporting a conventional pair of blue slacks; clean, well-polished, lace-up black leather shoes; a white long-sleeved button-down dress shirt with French cuffs that fits him nicely and conceals his many tattoos, and a simple silk tie. His diamond earrings have been removed from both of his ears. He has on prescription metal frame glasses, and his hair is freshly cut. He is flanked by two women. One is Nubia, a former friend of Heaven's. She and Heaven met at Wayne County Community College during the first and only semester Heaven attended, but the pair fell out shortly after Heaven started dating Donovan and discovered the two secretly exchanging sexually explicit text messages. The other woman with short reddish blond hair is someone Heaven doesn't recognize, at least not by her face.

"Are you the respondent in this case?" the judge asks Donovan.

"Yes, Your Honor," he says as he takes his place at the podium while the two ladies take their seats in the chairs behind him.

"Miss Jetter," says the judge, "you may continue telling the court the nature of your case."

Heaven takes a deep sigh and tries her best not to lose track by glancing in Donovan's direction. Nubia's presence throws her off more than Donovan's.

She gives a trenchant account of their relationship. "He has hit me with a closed fist on numerous occasions, Your Honor," she says, glancing down at her paper, her finger pointing at the words she's sprawled within each line. "The first time he hit me was January 1 of this year. We'd gone to a seventies New Year's Eve party, and he felt I was getting a little too friendly with the bartender, but that was only because I knew him. He grew up in my neighborhood, so of course I was going to speak to him. So, after we left the house, he threw me against the hood of his car and called me the b-word and made several negative references toward me that I can't even repeat in this courtroom."

"Did you report this incident?" asks the judge.

"Um, well . . . no, Your Honor," she says hesitantly, "at the time I didn't."

"At a later time did you?" asks the judge.

"Well, no, Your Honor . . . I didn't at any time, but that's exactly what happened. He's a very violent person."

"Hearsay," says Donovan.

"You'll get an opportunity to speak," says the judge. "Miss Jetter, please continue."

"After that time nothing happened for several weeks, and I dismissed that incident due to the fact that he may have been drunk or just snapped from jealousy, so I just let that go. Things seemed pretty good for a while, but then on February 14, we went to a concert he had obtained some tickets for illegally—"

"I didn't obtain the tickets illegally. We're in court on one matter that you're lying about and now you're trying to lie on me about something else. That would be like me bringing up your DUI."

"Mr. Davis, as I stated, you will have your opportunity."

"I know, Your Honor, but I can't let her stand up here and lie on me about something that's not even relevant. First of all, it wasn't even a concert—it was a local artist doing spoken word at the Music Hall that she said she wanted to go to."

"Words and Rhythms of the D was the name of it, Your Honor."

"The tickets were cheap," says Donovan, "so why would I obtain some illegal tickets to that? Who does?"

"I'm sure someone does. People do just about anything in this world," the judge says before turning back to Heaven. "Miss Jetter, I'd like you to continue, but please stick to the merits of this case. Also, I am very curious as to how you know these dates—do you keep a journal?"

"No, but New Year's Day is a very easy day to remember, and so is February 14—Valentine's Day. There are many more incidents that occurred, but for which I have no idea of the date or time."

"I'm also curious as to why it took you so long to finally come to court."

"I try not to make excuses. I can tell you I've asked myself that same question time and time again. I think it's because I was brought up in an abusive household, so I never really had a good idea in my head of what a healthy relationship is like or what a good man is and how he is supposed to treat a woman. But recently my sister has come into my life, and she's been helping me to see some of the things that I couldn't . . . that I was too blind to see. And I've been exposed to more things and different types of people, and all men aren't like Mr. Davis"—she shrugs—"but I used to think they were either like him or worse."

"Like me or worse. I got three years of college, Your Honor. I come from a good family. My father was a doctor, and my brother's a corporate attorney and my mother is very active in the community. I don't think she did too bad with me."

"That's where you came from, but that's not who *you* are," Heaven says.

"I don't want to hear another outburst," the judge says. "I don't want the two of you speaking directly to each other in my courtroom. Is this your sister behind you?" the judge asks Heaven. She takes his question as a form of disbelief.

"Yes, Your Honor, one of them. I know we don't look alike."

"I wasn't making any reference as to whether or not the two of you favored. Is she here as a witness to some of this?"

"No, Your Honor, she's just here for emotional support. It's been hard, being with him and trying to make something work that never was meant to." Heaven starts to cry, and the bailiff takes a box of tissues to her. "Thank you," she tells the bailiff after removing a few from the box. "When I was little my mother told me that if a man is jealous and hits you from time to time, you know he truly loves you. And she used to say the fun is in the making up."

"Your mother used to tell you that?" the judge asks.

"Yes, Your Honor."

The judge shakes his head. "Well, I hope you have learned that's not true."

"Yes, Your Honor, I have."

Heaven continues with more incidents after the judge instructs her to. Occasionally Donovan interrupts, but the judge gives a final warning. And then she produces her tape. "I'd like permission to play this tape. It includes various voice mail messages of a threatening nature that he left on my cell phone."

"Let me hear them," the judge assents.

She presses the button to the digital recorder, and the tape starts off with a male's voice in laughter that continues with an expletive directed toward Heaven. The message is three minutes long and is filled with words she is just as tired of using as she is of hearing, so when she plays back the recording, she lets her mind bleep out all of the expletives; all the vulgar language and descriptions of his sexual organ; all the things they'd done in bed; all those things he's made up. She only tunes back in on the tail end of the message to the part that matters only because she assumes it's true. She starts to listen at the point that he says, "You think I'm kicking your ass now. You just wait—" And it continues with more threats and more cursing and more vulgarity. "You think some muthafuckin' judge can stop me. . . . Can't nobody stop me. . . . I'm Scarface, bitch—you got that?"

"Oh yeah, she got that—she got that on tape." The judge extends his open hand toward Heaven. "I've heard enough."

"There's a lot more."

"I'm sure there is, but I don't need to hear any more—that was plenty." The judge turns in Donovan's direction. "Okay, Scarface, so what do you have to say for yourself? Was that you on the tape?"

"First, I'd like to call both of my witnesses to the stand."

"Witnesses?" the judge snaps. "I haven't even heard from you yet. Was that you on the tape?" the judge asks again, this time escalating his voice.

"Yes, it was me."

"'Yes, it was me, Your Honor.' Show some respect, and I'll be the one to call up witnesses. So what does Mr. Scarface have to say for himself? Why did you leave such threatening messages? You must think you're above the law or something. Is that what you think?"

"You should hear the messages she's left for me to make me respond that way."

"Do you have any that the court can hear?"

He shakes his head. "No, Your Honor, because I don't save every message. Only a crazy person does that."

"No, only a crazy person does not. A smart person trying to provide the evidence necessary to prove their case does, and she is proving her case. The burden of proof falls back on you to prove you didn't do these things." The judge shakes his head. "That's the game some of you young men try to run on young women nowadays. I see it every day in my courtroom. And it's pathetic."

"She doesn't need to take a PPO out against me, because I have moved on. I don't want anything to do with that girl. This is my girlfriend now," he says, pointing to Nubia. "And she used to be her friend, and she can tell you some things about our relationship, which is why I brought her along as a witness . . . and she can tell you about Heaven too."

"What is she going to tell me, Mr. Davis? You don't know how many cases like this I've seen. So what is the former friend of your ex-girlfriend who is now your girlfriend going to tell me that I'm going to believe?"

"Well, I'm going to let her tell you."

Nubia steps to the podium. She is wearing a short black minidress with a plunging neckline that exposes her large breasts.

"Please state your full name."

"Nubia Lexus Hill . . . My friends call me Nubee."

The judge chuckles and shakes his head. "Your friends? Okay, well, you're in a courtroom, and I'm going to call you Miss Hill. What do you have to offer the court that relates to this case?"

"Just as a witness to say that she's crazy," Nubia says as she points to Heaven, then spins her forefingers in a circle around the side of her face. "All she wants to do is sit around and drink and get high. She was the violent one in the relationship. She would go through his phone and call the numbers to see who was calling him."

"Is that all you have to offer to the court?"

"Yeah, that she's crazy and a liar and that he's not abusive."

"Miss Hill, please sit down. You come in my courtroom dressed inappropriately. You used to be her friend, but now you're her ex-boyfriend's girlfriend, and you expect me to believe one word you have to say? I know the game, and I'm just waiting to see how many months it will be before you're in my courtroom standing in Miss Jetter's same spot and asking me for the same thing. Who is this next witness you've brought in here, Mr. Davis? Your other girlfriend?"

"Your Honor, my next witness is Jiwana Moore, my ex-girlfriend and mother of my son."

"Okay, what do you have to offer?"

The woman steps up to the podium. "Your Honor, I was with Donovan for four years, and we have a three-year-old son together, Donovan Jr. We broke up after he met her, basically. She used to call me and harass me all the time."

"Your Honor, that is a lie," Heaven interjects. "I have never even seen this woman before in my life. I know her by name, but that's it. We've never even spoken before."

The woman shakes her head. "No, I don't have you confused. It was you. I know she is lying about Donovan, because he never laid one finger on me. And, as a matter of fact, this bitch over here—," she says, stopping abruptly when she fails to catch the curse word. She covers her mouth with her hand.

"Is this how you speak in my courtroom? Mr. Davis, you provide the court with two witnesses. One can't dress appropriately; the other can't speak appropriately," the judge says. "Do you have any reliable witnesses?"

Jiwana rolls her eyes. "I meant to say 'Miss Jetter,'" she says.

"Miss Moore, you may sit down too."

"She busted out the windshield to my car. She's the one who's violent," the woman adds.

"Miss Moore, I said you may sit down. The only person in this courtroom today who has proven her case is Miss Jetter. Mr. Davis, you can bring your girlfriend, ex-girlfriend, next girlfriend; I'm not impressed. I am going to issue a personal protection order that will forbid the respondent, and that's you, Mr. Davis, from entering Miss Jetter's home or coming within fifty yards of Miss Jetter or her property. You must not assault, attack, beat, or wound her, much less threaten to kill or physically harm her. Miss Jetter, do you have any children?"

"No, Your Honor," Heaven responds.

"He shall not interfere at your place of employment. He shall not contact you by telephone or mail, and this includes any form of electronic mail, e-mail, text message, all social networking sites such as Twitter, MySpace, Facebook, etcetera. Mr. Davis, you are prohibited from purchasing or possessing a firearm. And in the event that you break any of these mandates imposed against you, you will be punished to the full extent of the law. Do you understand?"

Donovan shrugs.

"'Yes, Your Honor' is what I expect to hear."

"Yes, Your Honor."

"Good." He hits his gavel. "The case is closed."

Later that afternoon, around two, Heaven, Alicia, and Sir meet for lunch at Detroit Breakfast House & Grill on Woodward Avenue just minutes from the municipal center where court was held.

They are sitting in a partial booth, Alicia and Sir on the cushioned seats against the wall and Heaven in a chair directly across from Alicia. Sir had emphasized to Heaven that the meal was his treat and she could order anything off the menu she wanted, regardless of price. Alicia and Heaven order two separate breakfast entrées they plan on sharing while Sir orders the Breakfast House Combo—a T-bone steak, eggs, two pancakes, and hash browns—and jokingly tells the ladies he doesn't need help with eating and therefore won't be sharing.

"How is staying with Trina working out?" Alicia asks.

"It's not the Jeffersonian. But it's working out for now. I've stayed with her before, but I really want my own place soon. By the way, do either of you have experience with caulking? I might need some help repairing some damage that was done to the rental house before I move so I can get my security deposit back."

Alicia says, "Heaven, do you honestly think he'll give you back your security deposit even if you do fix up the place? Wasn't he using your money for his own mortgage?"

"If he doesn't give it back, I'll take him to court, and I don't want to give the judge any reason not to rule in my favor."

"I don't have any experience with caulking, but I'm sure we can figure it out," says Alicia. "Right, Sir, we can figure it out and help her get the place together?"

"Of course, whatever you need. But for now, I think we should make a toast," says Sir as he holds up his water glass and the two ladies hold up their glasses of orange juice. "To independence, a whole new start, and never accepting less than you truly deserve."

Heaven smiles as her glass touches both of theirs. "And to finally getting that fool out of my life. Now, if Hope and Havana could just come back into it, I'd be even better."

PART THREE

You Are Not Alone

Alicia arrives at Hope's home unannounced and for good reason—for Heaven. She ensconces herself behind the wheel of her mother's compact car as she parks on the quaint tree-lined street in front of a small yet charming brick ranch-style home with a three-tier cast-iron water fountain. The seemingly stable working-class neighborhood in Oak Park, Michigan, is sprinkled with FOR SALE signs. As she stands on the front porch of Hope's house with her feet and eyes planted firmly on a welcome mat, she briefly wonders if Hope will actually welcome her. There's only one way to find out, she muses as she aims her finger at the doorbell and lets out an uneasy sigh.

A few seconds later, Havana opens the door.

Hope's voice sounds loudly in the background, chastising her daughter. "Always wait for me before you open the door. You know better."

Havana's eyes bulge. "But, Mom, there's a lady at the door who looks exactly like you."

"Who looks like me?" asks Hope as she steps around her daughter and stares at Alicia through the locked screen door. "May I help you with something?" Hope asks.

"I'm Alicia."

"Your sister," says Havana, remembering from a phone conversation she'd overheard some time ago.

"Havana, go to your room."

"Why, Mom? If she's your sister that also means she's my aunt."

"Because I said so. Now go to your room."

Havana huffs away, turning once to look back at Alicia and waving after Alicia does.

"I don't have to ask how you got my address. Heaven would give my child away if she had the chance."

"That she wouldn't do—she adores Havana."

"So, you've been around her for what, a couple months, and all of a sudden you know her better than I do? I doubt that."

"May I come in?"

"No offense, but I don't know you, and I teach my child not to go with strangers, so I'm not about to let one into our house."

"Technically, I'm family."

"Why, because my father got your mother pregnant when he was too young to know better?"

"You know what, forget it. I don't know what I was thinking. . . . Yes I do. . . . I was thinking about Heaven, who misses you and Havana. . . . I was thinking how much of a shame it is that two sisters who have the same parents and were raised together aren't even close. I don't understand why Heaven loves you so much. But family gets disowned every day . . . so I'm going to have to tell Heaven to move on, because you, for some reason, are heartless. Maybe it's because of your loss that you're the way you are, and I'm sorry to hear about that. I know it must've been awful, but what about the living?"

"My loss?" asks Hope. "The only thing I've lost is money messing around with Heaven. You think I'm heartless, but you just don't know. You think I don't love my sister?" She steps onto the porch, moving toward Alicia. "I love Heaven very much, but I'm tired of being disappointed. If a man doesn't kill her, one of her no-good friends probably will. Nobody she deals with has a real job.

My advice to you, since Heaven says you're an actress, is to act like you never met her."

"She's a good person who just needs some guidance, and I'm glad I met her."

"And while you're guiding her, she's going to be ripping you off. She's stolen from me. Used my credit so she could buy a laptop and camera and lenses. I'm sure she didn't tell you about that."

"Yes, she did."

"I could have prosecuted her if I wanted to, but I didn't. I didn't because I love her, but maybe I should have so she could learn that you have to pay for what you want in this world. You don't go around taking from people. Really, if she will take from her own flesh and blood, where will she draw the line?"

"She's a good person. And I know she has some issues, but so did I when I was her age. Didn't you?"

"When I was her age, I was married with a child. Nobody helped me get my life together. God helps those who help themselves. Heaven is a waste of time."

"What is wrong with you? You really do have a problem, don't you?" asks Alicia, tired of Hope's negativity. "Why are you mad at the world?"

"I'm not mad at the world . . . just at Heaven. You don't know what we've been through."

"She told me a little."

"Heaven was all I had for a while. She was all the family I had. I'm her big sister. Did I do something wrong? Sometimes I lie in bed thinking one day the phone is going to ring and they're going to say Heaven's in jail, or worse, she's dead . . . killed by a man just like our mother was."

Alicia pauses. "Killed by a man just like your mother was? Your mother was killed? She didn't have cancer?"

"Our father killed our mother, and that's why I don't understand Heaven and why she would want to be with any man like our father. I understand the whole thing about the cycle of abuse being hard to break free from, but I don't buy into that theory. She doesn't tell people the truth about our parents. We were both there, and we saw him shoot her. That's not something you want to tell anyone. Trust me. It's not something you want to remember."

Alicia is stunned into a moment of silence. Their father, who is also her father, killed Heaven and Hope's mother. Alicia thinks of her own mother and then of her stepfather. She can't imagine how she'd feel if something like that happened to her. She also couldn't imagine her stepfather doing something like that.

"I am so sorry," says Alicia.

Hope waves her hand dismissively. "Yeah, so am I, but that's life."

"Hope, we don't have to become friends or even get to know each other, but for Heaven's sake—"

"For Heaven's sake? Just leave, okay. What about for Hope's sake? What about for me? I'm happy for the first time . . . truly happy."

"If you're truly happy," Alicia says as she steps off the porch, "then your heart should be big enough to forgive your sister. Don't let money come between blood."

"You don't have to give me advice on how to handle *my* sister."

"Fine, if you ever change your mind, just call me. I'm sure my number is on your caller ID."

"Good-bye," Hope says coldly, then walks inside her house and slams the door.

Alicia walks down the sidewalk toward her mother's car. Detroit isn't even half as bad as she imagined it would be. But Hope is much worse. It's as if the heavy weight of Hollywood, the ball and chain of feeling required, obligated, duty-bound, to succeed in Los Angeles, was removed with her tumor, and her urge to return no longer exists, because there's nothing there to return to. Besides, how can she leave Detroit? How can she leave Heaven?

Minutes later, once she gets in the car, Alicia's phone rings. It's the law office in Beverly Hills, California, that sent her a demand letter weeks ago. Alicia's parents had advised her to call them and try to work things out, but she hadn't been able to get through and had left a message instead.

"Ms. Day, this is Attorney Foxmoore. I was cleaning up my case files and realized I never got back to you in regard to Mr. Ruckus. He is no longer a client of ours."

"So does that mean I'm not getting sued?"

"Well, not by our firm. In fact, just between you and me, I don't think you'll be sued by anyone."

"Can you tell me why? I'm just curious as to what happened."

"I suppose I can. Mr. Ruckus was sued himself for plagiarism and settled the case. He won't be making that movie, and therefore your contract isn't valid."

"Thank you," Alicia says with a twinkle in her eye. She can't believe her luck. Karma is in motion, and it's finally on her side.

With traffic, it took Ezra and Hope just over twenty minutes to cross into Canada at Goyeau Street from the Detroit entrance off East Jefferson. Ezra drove through the highway tunnel underneath the Detroit River. Hope was frightened after realizing it was just one lane in each direction, especially once she'd convinced herself she saw water seeping down the tunnel walls.

Before long, they had reached the point of international crossing marked by a U.S. and then a Canadian flag on the tunnel's wall. Hope was ashamed to admit it, but she finally told Ezra that she had not once been to Canada—not as a child and not as an adult. And he didn't laugh. In fact, he was excited that he had the opportunity to treat her to a fabulous weekend in Windsor, Ontario, while Havana spent the weekend with her father and his family.

Once parked, they took the escalator up to the promenade level and checked in at the hotel's front desk. From there they rode the elevator to the twenty-seventh floor to exit, taking a sharp left at the hallway's corner toward the specialty suite.

"Such a show-off," Hope says as she enters the suite, immediately making herself comfortable in one of the two red swivel chairs near the entrance. She drums her nails against the glass table.

"You want to order room service?" he asks as he props the one piece of rolling luggage they shared for the trip against the wall and picks the menu up from the glass table.

Hope stands and shakes her head. "There you go again, wanting to stay in." She walks around the suite. "This is really nice." She weaves in and out of the living room, sweeping through the bedroom before stopping at one of the large windows.

"If I was really a show-off," he says, placing his arm around her waist as she stands at the window glancing across the Detroit River at their city's skyline, "I would have rented the executive suite."

"It's such a beautiful view." She turns and takes his face in her hands and plants a wet kiss on his lips. "We're going downstairs right now, and we're going to eat at Nero's Steakhouse, and then we're going to go to the casino and try to win some money," says Hope with a snap of her fingers. He checks his watch. It's close to four in the afternoon, still early. "I've always had this dream since I was a kid— Heaven and I, both, have always dreamed of hitting the lotto or a lot of money in the casino."

"Honey, I think a lot of people have that same dream."

"You're making fun of me. At least I'm not like Heaven. Come rain or shine, she's playing the lotto. That means if she has to collect the deposit on cans to get the money to buy the lotto ticket, she will, whatever she has to do. At least I'm not like that."

"Maybe you already won the lottery," he says as he hugs her.

"You can't buy my love, mister. You have to earn it."

"I think I can do that too. And if all else fails"—he shrugs—"I'll just buy it. Everyone has a price," he says with a teasing grin. "I just wonder what yours is."

"Nope. I can't be bought. You have to earn my love through honesty. I need to trust you." They stare into each other's eyes. Hope wonders what the rest of their night may bring. "I'm going to change into a nice dress, and we're going downstairs where the people are."

"Oh, the hell with the people," he says as she rolls her suitcase into the bathroom. But Hope insists they go downstairs.

She slips into a printed, long-sleeved, scoop-neck dress, and the pair heads down to the casino.

Free drinks are carried on trays by the scantily clothed cocktail waitresses circulating the casino floor on the second level. Hope is seated at a Crystal Fortune nickel slot machine with Ezra standing beside her.

"It should come as no surprise to me that I'm not lucky," she says as she feeds a dollar into the coin receptor. Seconds later, $786.13 flashes on the small screen above her slot machine.

"Looks like your luck is changing," Ezra says with a broad smile. "Dare I say it has anything to do with, I don't know . . . me?"

Hope glows with happiness. "Maybe," she says, inching two fingers closely together, "maybe just a little. I'm going to cash out. I don't press my luck." She takes her voucher to the closest redemption machine. "And you wanted to eat first," she reminds him as she cashes in her winnings. "Then I probably wouldn't have won."

"Yes, you would have. You're with me, remember?"

"Nero's Steakhouse is straight ahead," she says, reading the overhead sign that directs them to the Forum tower lobby. They are welcomed into the restaurant by an estatelike entryway with majestic iron gates, stunning leather-wrapped columns, and a stone fireplace at the top of marble steps. Intricate filigree screens encompass the fifty-six-hundred-square-foot venue, creating an intimate, semiprivate seating area for more than a hundred guests.

For starters they order a quarter pound of king crab legs and chilled jumbo shrimp cocktail. Hope orders the bone-in New York strip with steamed asparagus. Ezra asks for the wild king salmon with butternut squash. For dessert they both order chocolate mousse with ganache.

"We'll have to take Havana out to dinner. What weekends do you have Havana?"

"What weekends?" she snaps. "You make it sound like my ex

has joint custody or something. I have full custody and he gets some weekends, but only because I allow it."

"Why are you so angry?"

Hope dabs each corner of her mouth with the white cloth napkin. "I don't know. I guess because I'm black," she says with emphasis. "I know that's what you're thinking."

He starts to chuckle. "I think it's just because you're angry. I know plenty of black people who aren't." He eases the dessert plate away from her. "I think something's in your dish. You took a spoonful and just started going off. The hardest problem I'm going to have with you is your stubbornness."

"Well, bail out now, because that's not going to change."

"And so we have a conundrum, because I'm not leaving you."

"Ditto."

"Ditto? Very sexy. I like that. I say I love you, and you say ditto." He watches her face light up with laughter, and he smiles in response.

"You didn't say you love me."

"But I've said it, and I've never heard you say it back."

"I love you," says Hope. "Is that better?"

"I don't know. . . . Is it even true?" he asks with a smile.

"Of course it's true. I do love you. Aside from Havana, you're the best thing I have going."

Ezra's smile grows. "Well, now that I know that, I know you won't be turned off by my news. I've decided to have my right arm amputated below my elbow."

"Why?"

"It's just sort of hanging here doing nothing . . . all crispy."

"Crispy?" Hope covers her mouth. "I'm not even going to laugh at that."

"It's okay. You can."

"I hope you're not doing that because of me, because you've had that arm for five years."

"It was suggested at one point, but I resisted." Ezra shrugs. "Some men get cars to impress a woman. I'm getting a fake limb."

"You don't need to impress me. I'm already impressed. But if it's something you want to do, then you should."

"The technology they have now will blow you away. The prosthetic I'm getting acts pretty much like a real arm. It'll be better than this one. I'll be able to use my hand. The face, though . . . I can't do anything about my face. Sorry."

When they finish, Ezra leans over and kisses her on the cheek. "As usual, dinner was wonderful. I look forward to taking you and Havana out. The first annual Detroit Restaurant Week will be starting soon."

"We'll have to check a few of those places out. Havana would really like that. She really likes you."

"I know, she's told me."

"Told you . . . What did she tell you?"

"Don't worry about it. We talk . . . and it's not all about Harry Potter and Artemis Fowl either."

"Well, what's it about?"

"Don't worry about it. That's for me and Havana to know and for you to find out about very soon."

Later that evening, just before ten, they return to their room.

"I'm having so much fun," she tells Havana on the phone. She covers the mouthpiece and says to Ezra, "She wants you to know she's almost done with *Lost Colony*, and she can't wait to discuss it with you. And she wants us to have plenty of fun all weekend." She turns to the phone again. "No, I'm not going to tell him that. No, I'm not giving you the phone so you can say it either."

After she hangs up, Hope sighs. She doesn't want to admit it, but she has to. "He's really a good father," she tells Ezra. "She seems to be having a great time."

"Good." Ezra smiles. "So, you trust him now?"

"I'm not going that far. . . . Maybe I should have said he *seems* to be a good father."

Ezra shakes his head and sighs. "You're a tough woman to please.

So, what did Havana want you to tell me?" Hope shakes her head and waves him off with her hand. "Oh, I'm sure she's already told me. And she doesn't have to worry about that."

"She doesn't?"

"No, that will be happening soon."

"Will it?"

"Absolutely."

"So which book series are you going to buy her next? Because I told her I wasn't going to ask you to do that, but she said you wouldn't mind."

Ezra is embarrassed. He was certain Havana had told Hope that she wanted him to ask her mother to marry him and that she wanted her mother to have someone to love the way her father did, because Havana had told him that during one of their book discussions. "No, I don't mind, but I really thought she was talking about something else . . . something pertaining to us."

Hope looks at him curiously but decides not to push the issue. She relaxes on the sofa facing the water.

"I've really been curious about something," Ezra says.

Hope shrugs. "About what?"

"Your sisters."

Hope shrugs. "Heaven?"

"Both of them," he says as he sits on the sofa beside her.

"I only have one sister. If you want to get technical, I'll say one and a half."

"My parents were both married before they had me. So I have three half sisters and two half brothers, and we're all very close. The way I look at it, she is your sister and she probably just wants to get to know you. What's wrong with that? There's no reason to have a Napoleon complex about this kind of thing."

"I don't act tough because I'm little. And I'm not that little," she says, shoving him against his injured arm. He grabs his arm and moans. "I'm sorry, did I hurt you?" Her face displays concern.

"Gotcha," he says, pointing toward her.

"That wasn't funny."

He smiles. "But in all seriousness, what do you have against them?"

"You don't understand."

"I'm trying to. . . . Help me to."

She sighs heavily. "I'm mad at Heaven because I'm scared for her—scared for the way she's living. We both have had problems with trust, and for her to be the one to betray me . . . I can't explain the way that feels, especially when she did it during what I thought was the worst time in my life . . . when I was in mourning. As for Alicia . . . I don't know why I'm not as happy as Heaven to know I have another sister. Maybe because Heaven has always been enough."

"You miss Heaven, don't you?"

Her eyes begin to swell with tears. She nods. "Well then, you'll just need to see her. Promise me you will."

"I promise . . . I will." She notices his look and can tell he isn't quite buying it, nor can she say she blames him. For Hope, it's all about trust. As far as she is concerned with Heaven, she is and will always be her baby sister. But she needs to trust her again before she can let Heaven back into her life.

"You know," says Hope, "the last time we had a conversation about Heaven while we were alone, it ruined what could have been a wonderful evening. I don't want that to happen this time."

"Honestly, I thought you may not have wanted to make love to me because of my burns."

"I told you, your burns don't bother me."

"Yeah, they don't bother you, I get that, but I'm sure they don't turn you on."

"Just like my stretch marks probably won't arouse you . . . or the raised scar I have on my bikini line from my C-section. Yuck . . . They're not a pretty sight."

"A keloid?"

"How do you know?"

"I'm a doctor, remember? Well, I used to be. A keloid doesn't frighten me."

Hope shrugs. "I guess we all have something we want to change." He sits close, and she scoots even closer. She holds his face in her hands and kisses him all over his face, working her way back around to his lips.

"I love you, Hope . . . and I want to make love to you."

She unbuttons his long-sleeved shirt, sweeps her hands over his chest, and lightly touches the burns on his chest that stop just below his collarbone. "And I want to make love to you." She helps him take off his shirt, and they move from the living room into the bedroom.

He immediately turns off one of the lamps on the nightstand nearer the entrance and a lamp that is on the dresser, but as he walks over to the nightstand nearer the ceiling-to-floor windows that overlook the Detroit River and the Detroit skyline, she asks him to keep the light on. "I don't want to be in total darkness."

"Neither do I." He shrugs. "I guess you've seen all of my burns. But I do want to close the curtains. He pulls the sheer curtains closed, leaving open the drapes.

She pulls her dress over her head and nestles herself on top of the bedsheets between a mound of pillows.

"You're beautiful," he tells her as he looks at Hope as she lies on the bed in a shell pink corset bra with matching V-string panties.

"Are you sure?" she asks as she fluffs up her short locks that she recently started growing out. "Because, you don't seem in any rush to come join me."

He removes his pants, leaves on his boxers, and snuggles in the bed beside her. "Are you kidding? I just didn't want to come across as desperate."

"You have a nice body," she says to him, "and your legs aren't skinny at all."

"You have a gorgeous body," he tells her as he snuggles up to her even closer and nibbles on her ear.

"Do you really love me?"

"I wouldn't lie about that. I love you very much. Can't you feel how hard my heart is beating?"

Hope covers her mouth for a second. "When you said 'hard,' I thought Mr. Hansen was about to say something freaky . . . and I wasn't ready for that."

"Oh, Mr. Hansen can get freaky. Just think of the kind of role-playing we can do. I can be Freddy Krueger, and I won't even need a mask."

"Stop talking down about yourself. You don't look anything like Freddy Krueger . . . and now that I've seen all your scars, I guess it's time for you to see mine," she says as she slinks out of her panties and bra. She looks into his eyes and realizes she's finally found love and prays that it will last.

He moistens his lips at the sight of her naked body. It's been five years since he's had sex, since he's even wanted to. His eyes study her movement.

"You're more curvaceous than I thought," he says. "I love it."

"I've gained some weight and I feel much better for it. . . . All I needed was closure."

"Is that all you need?" he asks, his excitement transforming his breathing into soft groans.

"I need more than that now—now, I need you," she says as she lies on her back, her arms pulling him toward her. "I need you," she repeats as he slides out of his boxers and dispels the myth that white men have small penises. His body blankets hers. His lips begin kissing her body all over. He offers compliments; tells her how wonderful she smells, how soft her skin is, how he wants their first night together to last forever. He tells her things she didn't know, about how long he's fantasized about having her sexually. She remains quiet, but he can tell from her movement and her moans that she is aroused by him and his words, by what his tongue is doing to her. Much later, their moans of satisfaction fill the entire suite.

September

"**I** know one person I don't miss," says Alicia. "My period." She picks up an egg slice from the salad bowl and plops it in her mouth. She is in the kitchen of her parents' home, assisting her mother as she fixes dinner by preparing a salad.

"Your period was a person?" her mom asks with a laugh.

"Yes, because that thing had a life of its own." She picks up another egg slice. "I must be starving or something, because this is a really good egg."

"I get my eggs from a Mennonite woman down at the Eastern Market. They are good, aren't they? You remember the Eastern Market, don't you, baby? I go there and get my produce."

Alicia nods. "I used to love going down there on weekends."

"That's funny, you always did, but we could never get your brother into it."

"You know how Max is. That's too much like grocery shopping to him, but it wasn't like that for me."

"You should go on a Saturday." Alicia's mother catches Alicia in deep thought. "What's on your mind? You know you don't have to go back to LA if you don't want to. You can always stay here."

"I'm not moving back in with my parents at thirty-two."

"Lots of people are moving back home. Some older than you . . . with families even. Your aunt was living with your grandparents, and she was in her forties."

"She wasn't really living there. She was living in the Embassy Suites in New York during the week, and it made sense for her not to get a place just for the weekends."

"I'm not saying you have to stay here for the rest of your life."

"Actually, I wasn't really thinking about that. I was thinking about Hope." Alicia picks out a baby carrot from her salad bowl to crunch on. "I don't get her."

Alicia's mom has warmed up to Alicia's having another family, especially after meeting Heaven, who seemed very warm and personable, though also a little troubled. But from what she's heard of Hope, she remains less than impressed. "Just because someone is your blood doesn't mean by default they'll also be your friend . . . or sister. Some siblings really can't stand one another."

"You mean like you and Auntie."

"No, not like me and Auntie. Your auntie and I love each other very much and we *are* friends."

"Aww, that's the same thing she said about you."

"And I think children will definitely do Olena a world of good. She'll be a great mother."

"She will," says Alicia with heavy sighs.

"You can't force yourself on another person, sweetie. That doesn't just apply to men . . . just people in general. Either they want to be your friend, want to get to know you, or they don't. She doesn't, and that's her loss."

Several minutes later, after she's completely finished making the salad and they have moved on to a different conversation, Alicia glances down at her cell phone that has just started to ring.

Alicia's eyes widen. "I can't believe she's calling me," she says. "I hope nothing's wrong with Heaven. "Hello," she says quickly.

"Hi, Alicia, this is Hope. You said if I change my mind I should give you a call. Well, I'd like to try to get to know you. . . . Havana really misses Heaven too . . . and so do I."

"Oh, I'm so glad you called. I think that would be wonderful. If I plan something, you'll show up, right?"

"Yes, I will. Havana and I both will. I know I wasn't nice to you at all when you came to my house, and I'm not going to blame it on PMS. The truth is I have very little patience for nonsense, and the way Heaven has been living really gets to me, but I do miss her. And I would like to get to know you."

Alicia smiles broadly. She can't believe Hope's turnaround. "I'll plan for us to all get together," she says. "A nice outing for this coming weekend, or is that too soon?"

"This weekend will be great. I'm not working as many weekends now that our bank has changed ownership again, so that will work fine."

Alicia pulls in front of Hope's home in her stepfather's SUV with Heaven in the passenger seat. It is the Saturday before Labor Day and the perfect day for them to visit Eastern Market, pick up some fresh fruits and vegetables, a plant for her mother, and grab lunch at one of the restaurants.

"I pray this goes well," she tells Heaven.

"I think I should wait in the car," Heaven says.

"And send me to her door all by myself? It didn't go so well the first time I came over here, so I don't feel completely comfortable doing that."

"I'll go," says Heaven with a shrug. "All she can do is cuss me out."

"She won't cuss you out. She said she missed you."

"She actually said that?"

"Yes, she actually said that. She said that she and Havana both do."

Hope and Havana exit their house while Alicia and Heaven are still sitting in the SUV debating who will go to the front door.

Havana is wearing her latest outfit from Justice Clothing for Girls; a pair of pink cuffed denim pedal pushers along with a long-sleeved crewneck graphic T-shirt and a pair of multicolored lace-up high-tops with sequins and a peace-sign print.

Hope has on a fashionable Nike sweat suit in purple and a pair of gym shoes that match.

"I've never seen her wear a sweat suit," Heaven mumbles to Alicia. "She picked up a little weight and she's letting her hair grow." She gets out of the SUV to greet them.

"I missed you, Auntie," says Havana as she runs up to her and draws her arms around Heaven's waist with a smile. "More than you know . . . more than I can even explain."

"Aww, I missed you too," says Heaven, wiping away tears and kissing her niece's forehead.

Hope observes Heaven for several minutes before awkwardly breaking her silence.

"I think we should get something to eat first," demands Hope. "Havana and I didn't have much for breakfast."

"That's fine," says Alicia, picking up a moody vibration from Hope. "I heard there's a really good pizza place down there."

"Great . . . pizza . . . again," Hope says sarcastically.

"We love pizza," says Havana. They climb into the SUV and they pull off.

Red walls. Metal artwork sculptures. Communal tables. A large brick oven. These are the things Hope notices as she enters Supino Pizzeria, trailing behind Alicia and Havana as they walk up to the counter to place their order.

In the SUV on the ride down, something happened to Hope. She expected to be happy, but she wasn't. She was envious of the relationship between Heaven and Alicia. She felt like an outsider. She heard them laugh about things they'd done together, mostly just the two of them—something that happened downtown at the Jeffersonian; yoga on the riverfront; an overnight stay at the hospital; someone named Gigi Mama, and some man they only referred to as Sir, never by his first name, which Hope initially thought was strange until she figured out that Sir was his first name. By the time Alicia found a parking space, Hope's bad mood had returned. What was she thinking by calling Alicia?

She knew what she was thinking. She was thinking about Ezra and making him happy. He had said it would make him happy if she at least tried to get along with her family—including Alicia. Then she had made a promise . . . and she wanted to make good on her end.

"What's so great about this place?" Hope asks under her breath.

"Mommy," whines Havana. She points to the words on her T-shirt, MAKE PEACE HAPPEN. "If Ezra brought us here, you wouldn't be acting like this."

Hope smiles. "You're too grown up . . . but I guess you're right."

Alicia and Heaven focus on the chalkboard overhead. Hope notices the bond again between them. "I think we should try that Bismarck," says Alicia. "Doesn't that sound interesting?"

Hope reads the ingredients: fresh mozzarella, prosciutto, tomato sauce, and a sunny-side-up egg. "Sunny-side-up egg on a pizza? No, thank you. This sure isn't Buddy's. I'm ordering a pepperoni for Havana and me. It's always best to stick to what you know when you go somewhere new."

"Auntie, I'll eat some of your pizza with you."

Hope wrinkles her brow and shakes her head at her daughter. Why, she wonders, does her daughter feel so comfortable with a stranger whom she insists on calling Auntie?

"Young lady, let's go to the restroom," says Hope to her daughter. Hope takes Havana under the guise that they need to wash their hands, but after they enter the restroom, she pulls her to the side and says, "We don't know her."

"She's your sister. She looks just like you."

"She's a child my father had—a mistake."

"Mom," Havana says shaking her head, "God doesn't make mistakes." At that moment Alicia enters; it's hard to tell if she may have overheard.

"I need to wash my hands too," says Alicia.

Hope gently guides Havana toward the sink so she can wash her hands, and then Hope does the same.

Alicia pulls a paper towel from the wall dispenser and dries her hands. "You're right," she says to Havana. "God doesn't make mistakes."

Heaven enters the bathroom just as Hope, Havana, and Alicia are leaving. "I need to wash my hands too."

The only available table is one near the soda dispenser, which starts off a chain of complaints on Hope's part. She complains that the chairs remind her of ones she sat on in elementary school. Once the pizza arrives, Hope is turned off by the runny egg in the center of Alicia's Bismarck. She wonders whose bright idea it was to get such small, thin napkins. "Don't they know pizza is greasy and napkins are important? I would have been more impressed with a roll of paper towel than this," she says, pulling out another napkin and waving it in the air like a distress signal.

Alicia sighs. She had picked the place at her mother's recommendation and the *Detroit Free Press*'s stellar review, which recently named Supino the best pizzeria in the metro area.

"Look at these beat-up tables. I don't get this. I'm not impressed. Is this place going for a certain look? If so, they should keep looking."

"Actually, these are recycled work tables from a Flint plant," says Alicia, recalling details from the newspaper article as she thumbs the surface.

"I hope you plan on washing your hands again," says Hope. Alicia takes out a small bottle of hand sanitizer and rubs it over her hands. "That stuff doesn't work."

Alicia clears her throat. Since her surgery, she hasn't had one mood swing, so she knows what she's experiencing isn't hormones. What she is experiencing right now, which is causing her heart to beat so fast she can both feel and hear it, is anger. *Yes, I do count. And no, I am not a mistake, but perhaps this meeting was.* Alicia is amazed that someone like Hope can have a daughter like Havana, a well-behaved child with the sweetest disposition. What made Hope even reach out to her in the first place if this is the kind of attitude she's going to maintain?

Alicia takes a bite of her first slice at the same time Havana does. "Mmm, this is soooo good!" says Alicia. Havana nods and smiles in agreement.

"I was skeptical about the egg too," says Heaven, "but I have to admit it is pretty good." They await the verdict from Hope, the ultimate cynic. She takes a bite of her pepperoni, batting her long lashes as she chews.

"Well?" asks Alicia.

"It's okay," says Hope.

"Okay?" asks Havana. "Mom?"

"It's good. I guess. Okay, it is pretty good." Hope notices Heaven glance down at Hope's bare wedding finger. "Yes, I finally took it off."

"I'm surprised," Heaven says, "but glad you're ready to move on."

"Apparently Roger had moved on long before he disappeared. I finally got in contact with Michael Beck, and he told me that Roger wasn't even on the boat when it capsized. He was off with some woman." She'd already explained the sordid details to Havana, so if Heaven is curious to know more, she doesn't mind telling the story in front of her daughter.

"What the f-u-c-k?" Heaven asks, spelling out the word.

"I know how to spell, Auntie."

"I know, but it still sounds better if I spell it out instead of say it. Are you serious?"

Hope nods. "Yep, I am one hundred percent serious. And I'm so glad I finally know the truth, because I'd rather spend the rest of my life alone than spend one day with a liar."

"But you won't have to spend the rest of your life alone," Havana says with a giggle.

Hope smiles down at her daughter. "We'll see."

"So if he's alive, where is he?" asks Heaven.

"I don't know and I don't care. I'm moving on."

"Don't you want to talk to him and find out why he did what he did? Aren't you curious as to where he is right now?" asks Heaven.

"No, I'm not. Not in the least." There is a little part of Hope that wonders about him; wonders if he's still alive—not that she cares. She should have moved on with her life long before now, she tells herself. To mourn for a time was fine, but not two years, and it was certainly not fine to mourn that long for a man she didn't really know. She's not going to waste any more time or any unnecessary energy on making him reappear just for the satisfaction of asking him why . . . especially if he's just going to lie to her again.

The day ends much better than it began. Hope stops with her complaints while they are in the flower section of the largest open-air public market in the country. She and Havana wait near a large flower display stand while one of the growers puts the plants Alicia is buying in beautiful ceramic pots. Alicia had browsed rows of live plants looking for one to take back to her mother before settling on one a grower recommended—an *Oxalis regnellii*, also referred to as a shamrock plant. The grower explained the cheery plant with purple leaves and white flowers is not only easy to care for and nearly impossible to kill, but it is also the perfect gift, symbolizing good luck and fortune. It's then that she decides to buy three; one for Heaven, another for Hope and Havana, and the third for her mother.

"That's really nice of you," says Hope as she takes the plant from Alicia, "but you didn't have to."

"I know. I wanted to. We can all use good luck and fortune."

"We sure can," Heaven agrees.

"Yeah." Hope sighs. "I guess we can."

It's Sunday, the day before Labor Day, and Somerset Mall is swarming with people looking for deals at the one-day-only sales. Heaven and five others are looking for something a lot more substantial—top-of-the-line designer merchandise to abscond with.

Will this be Heaven's last time? The time before was supposed to be. The run at Novi at Twelve Oaks Mall was supposed to be the last. But the plan was carried out so smoothly that she just couldn't stop then—not yet. Maybe after this one, though. The only reason she doesn't go back to the mall in Novi is because she feels funny stealing so close to where Alicia is living. She could easily bump into her at one of the four stores she lifted from that day. Even worse would be running into her mother. And seeing them would throw her off her game for sure. It would also remind her of how she should be living.

Heaven slips into a fitting room with a Nordstrom shopping bag in one hand and six pairs of jeans tucked under her arm. The two salespeople from that department are both being distracted by two women in their early twenties, who are part of Trina's recently assembled shoplifting crew. Trina has big ideas. She fantasizes about the crew appearing on *America's Most Wanted*—one of her favorite shows—as outlined figures that have never been caught by surveillance cameras, and described by John Walsh as America's most notorious shoplifting ring.

"Let's get a real talent," Heaven suggested to her friend several times. "You're good with putting on makeup. You could be a makeup artist. I'm a photographer. Maybe we could open a studio."

"A studio? And do what, take wedding photos? Girl, please. We gonna make this quick money."

"Not that kind of studio, maybe like a self-esteem studio . . . I don't know. Something for women. . . . something to make women feel better about themselves. You'd be surprised what a nice photo can do to change a woman's opinion of herself. You should've seen Patty's face glow when I gave her hers. And she didn't even have any makeup on." But Trina didn't like that idea either. She didn't understand how they could provide a service that they themselves needed. And for some reason, Heaven always went along with Trina's ideas—partly because shoplifting was a way for her to get a little extra cash, and it was harder to say no to Trina when Heaven was now living with her rent free.

Heaven has to act quickly. She lays down six pairs of high-priced jeans from various high-end designers on the bench in her fitting room, then takes out one store shopping bag and two pairs of pliers from her large hearts canvas bag. She removes each security tag by placing a pair of pliers on each side. She bends the pliers down toward the ground and snaps off the tags.

She folds the jeans and places three pairs in one of the shopping bags underneath the merchandise she purchased from another store earlier that day. She places the other three pairs in the empty shopping bag. She tosses inside, along with the jeans, some lingerie she'd purchased earlier. Then her phone erupts. Panic. She touches the red icon on the screen quickly so the noise won't alert anyone. She has three minutes to not only get out of the fitting room, but also out of the store. The plan is for the ladies to occupy the salesperson for seven minutes.

But she notices the missed call is from Hope.

She turns her ringer off. At the same time a text comes through.

I want to try to trust you again...because i miss u and i love u and u seem to have changed...I forgive U. everyone deserves a second chance. We R family.

Heaven stands in disbelief. She faces the floor-length mirror and sees herself for the first time as someone who isn't deserving of anything...not if she doesn't change. What she's doing isn't right, and she feels the text from her sister is her warning. But she promised Trina—Trina, who opened her apartment up to her.

A few minutes later she leaves the fitting room with two shopping bags in her hand. The two young women are gone. The saleswoman picks up the phone and dials two numbers after eyeing Heaven. She is calling security; Heaven is sure of it. Off to the side, she sees the two women being led away to a back room by two men wearing navy-colored suit jackets. So she hightails it toward the escalator. She doesn't wait for the moving staircase to carry her down. She briskly walks down the escalator, practically running as she anxiously heads toward the door. But before she gets close enough to exit, a black woman wearing blue pants and a short-sleeved powder blue blouse approaches her.

"I'm with store security," she says, flashing a badge. "We need for you to come with us, please."

"For what?" Heaven asks.

"I know you have stolen merchandise in those bags. Did you also steal from Nordstrom?"

"I didn't steal from anyone. I don't know what you're even talking about."

"You can either come with us or we're calling the police and they can deal with you."

"If you call the police, I'll sue you."

"Open your bags," the woman says firmly. "If you want to play that game, fine, but I'll show you who's going to win. Open your bags and produce all of your receipts for the merchandise."

Heaven opens the first shopping bag that has two T-shirts inside and the receipt in the bag. She opens the second bag that has a night-gown, bra, and panties along with the receipt. "I bought all of this. The receipts are in there to prove it."

"Open your purse."

"For what?"

"You can either open your purse for me or for the police. Which would you prefer?" Heaven opens her hearts canvas bag. The woman slips on a light blue rubber glove and forages through the inside.

"Is there a reason for these?" the woman asks Heaven as she removes two pairs of pliers.

"Yes," says Heaven. "I'm going over to my sister's house to help her put up a desk she just purchased. Is it a crime for me to have those too?"

"Why were you running down the escalator?" the woman asks.

Heaven shrugs. Why was she running? She didn't even know.

"I don't know if you got a heads-up or what the deal is, but I know you were with the other two women."

"Unless you have a valid reason to detain me, I'm leaving right now." She takes the pliers from the woman's hands and tosses them back in her purse. "My sister is waiting."

Heaven strides out of the upscale department store and into the mall's large parking lot.

She pulls out her phone and dials Trina as she walks toward her car, but hangs up.

Why should she call Trina? She doesn't want to think about what just happened in there.

She sticks her key in her car's ignition. It was Hope's text that caused Heaven to reconsider the way she'd been living, so she phones Hope instead. While she was in the fitting room, she also thought about how appalled Alicia was over bootlegging DVDs, and Heaven realized for the first time that there were people who lived their life right. She wanted that second chance Hope mentioned. She wanted to be someone anyone, especially her sisters, could trust, so she'd left all six pairs of jeans folded neatly inside the fitting room and she left. It was one of the best decisions she ever made in her life.

"Hey, Hope, I got your text. It was really sweet and it made my day."

"Made your day," laughs Hope. "It was just a text."

"No, believe me, it was more than just a text. And I want us to be more than just sisters. . . . I want us to be friends."

The more Heaven thinks about what Hope told her, the angrier she becomes. Trina was wrong when she'd said it was none of her business. What Roger did to her sister is every bit her business. Hope wasted two years of her life mourning a man who wasn't even dead; a man who obviously didn't love her and is now living in Tampa, according to the report she'd obtained from a people search directory for which she'd paid $39.95. The report included everything Hope would ever want to know about Roger Teasdale.

Trina lent Heaven her credit card so she could sign up for the people search service. And she went to Kinko's to run off two hard copies of the report—one for her and one for Hope. But Heaven was going to make the first call.

She'd studied his full report. He had aliases, but to find out about his aliases would cost even more, so she was just going to leave that up to Hope. She was shocked to see a long list of addresses attached to his name, from Deer Park, Washington, to Boston, Massachusetts— and several states in between. But even more startling was Haley Teasdale—the woman listed on the report as his spouse. How was he able to pull that off? she wondered.

"I'm trying to reach Roger Teasdale," Heaven says in her most professional voice.

"Roger? That's my dad's middle name," a young preteen girl says.

"Is his last name Teasdale?"

"Yeah."

"What's his first name?"

"David."

"Okay, may I speak to him?"

"Dad!" the girl screams. "Phone!" Heaven had waited to call until seven o'clock on a Thursday evening—a time when most people were home. She had already called most of the numbers she found on the report and finally it looks like one of them is going to pay off.

"Dad!" the girl screams again, but this time much louder. "Telephone!" A few seconds later the young girl comes back to the phone. "Who is this?"

"Carmen Harlan," says Heaven, taking her acting cues from Alicia and impersonating a Channel 4 newscaster in Detroit. "Is Haley, your mother, in?" she asked, remembering the woman's name listed as spouse on the people-search report.

"No, she's with my sister. But isn't it my dad you want to speak to?"

"Either one is perfectly fine."

"Are you a teacher?"

"No, I'm not. I have good news for them . . . a surprise. Can you give me your mom's cell phone so I can call her after I talk to your dad?"

The young girl rattles off the number and then shouts to her dad again. "Some lady named Carmen Harlan is on the phone for you."

A few seconds later, a man comes to the line sounding out of breath, almost as if he'd run up a flight of steps. "I have the phone, Marissa. You can hang it up." He was a lot older than he'd led her sister Hope to believe—ten years older according to the report. "Hello," he says.

"Hello, is this Roger Teasdale?"

He hesitates. "Who is this?"

"I know this is you, Roger or David or whatever your name is. "This is Carmen Harlan from Channel Four news in Detroit. I'd like to get you on our program for an interview."

"Interview me? Interview me about what?"

"About polygamy and the death you faked."

"What are you talking about? Who are you? I never faked my death. How did you get my number?"

"I'm a reporter. We have our ways. How do you feel about your double life? Does Haley know? How would your kids feel if they knew you'd gotten married to someone other than their mother?"

"Who is this?" Roger says, bringing his voice down to a whisper. "I know you're not Carmen Harlan."

"Don't you think the people in your life would like to know how you've been deceiving women? How you faked your death?"

"Is this . . . Heaven? It is, isn't it? Heaven, I never faked my death."

"Oh, you didn't? So I'm talking to a dead man right now?"

He sighs heavily. "Look, I don't know what to tell you."

"You don't have to tell me anything. Tell my sister why you did what you did."

"I can't talk to her."

"She's your wife."

"Look, the boating accident just made it convenient for me to stop the lies and come back to my real family and be the husband and father I should have been. I was separated from my wife at the time I met your sister. . . . I never meant to hurt Hope. . . . Things happen, you know."

"No, I'm sorry, I don't know," Heaven says, giving up the Carmen Harlan ruse. "Maybe your wife will, though. I'm calling her next on her cell phone." Heaven hangs up as Roger starts pleading with her.

Heaven decides to leave the conversation with Roger's wife for

Hope. She rushes over to Hope's house with a copy of the report on her ex-husband folded neatly and tucked inside her red canvas purse. She doesn't even think to call first. She's too excited and just wants to get her all of the information as soon as possible, tell her about the phone conversation she had with Roger, and tell her how easy it was to find him.

Heaven receives a call from Alicia as she's driving. "Are you ready for your big chop tomorrow?" she asks.

"I'm not even thinking about that right now. I called Hope's husband. I actually talked to him. I'll have to tell you later what I found out, because I want to tell Hope first. She's going to be so excited. I even have his wife's cell phone number for Hope to call."

"So he already remarried?"

"No, it turns out he was married to this other woman—Haley—before he married Hope," she says as she parks in Hope's driveway. "I cannot wait to get her this information. This is definitely going to give her closure."

"I think she already found that. Are you sure you want to tell Hope anything about this guy? You two just made up. I think you should just work on your relationship and not bring up anything that's a sore spot for her."

"No offense, Alicia, but I know Hope way better than you do. She's going to want to know this."

"Okay, well, you're right, you do know her better than I do, because I barely know her at all. I was just putting myself in her shoes. And I'm just worried that she might get mad that you did that."

"Well, don't. It'll be fine. I'll call you later."

Heaven springs from her car and hurries to Hope's front door, ringing the bell three times before she answers.

"Hey, can I come in?" asks Heaven after Hope comes to the door.

"Yeah," says Hope as she moves away from the threshold to allow Heaven to enter.

"What are you and Havana up to?"

"Havana just finished her homework, so she's getting ready for bed, and I just finished talking to Ezra."

"Well, guess whom I found and called today?" She digs in her purse, takes out the folded report, and hands it to Hope. "Roger was married before he married you. His real name is David. Roger is his middle name. That report has everything in it . . . and I wrote his wife's cell phone number at the top of the report in case you want to tell her everything."

"His wife's cell phone number?" Hope asks, confused.

"You should call her right now," says Heaven as she snatches Hope's cordless phone from the base. "Tell her what her husband did to both of you. Now you can really get closure."

"No, Heaven, now I feel as though I'm back to square one." She grabs the phone from Heaven's hand. "Why did you do that? Why, Heaven? What's wrong with you? You had no right to take it upon yourself to contact that man. And now you expect me to call his wife and say what? Tell her that her husband is a psycho? I don't want to have anything to do with that man."

"You don't even want to know what he told me? I talked to him."

"Why?" Hope asks in a voice drowning in disappointment. Her head begins to shake. "People would ask me . . . why I wasn't closer with you. And all I could say was it was hard to explain . . . that they had to know you. It's because of things like this that I can't be close to you. You had no right to contact that man. Just like you had no right to steal my identity and open up credit cards in my name. I tried to forgive you. Tried to give you a second chance. But I've had it this time." Hope walks to the door and opens it. "It's time for you to leave."

"Why? You're mad at me again? Just because I was looking out for you? You hate me for that?"

"I don't hate you, Heaven, but you've got to start getting your life together and thinking about the consequences of your actions. What do you think a man like Roger, or whatever his name is, someone who is so skilled at deception, is capable of? You ever think of that? I don't want to be fearful of my life or my daughter's. No, I'm not going to call his wife. What for? Just to anger that fool and have him, I don't know, put a hit out on me?"

"Put a hit out on you?" asks Heaven, spitting out laughter.

"This is my life you're laughing about. Good-bye, Heaven," Hope says firmly. Heaven walks out of her sister's front door in silence with her head hanging low. As the door closes, Heaven's eyes begin to water. Yes, it is easy for Heaven to cry, just as Trina always says, because she has so much to cry over.

Back at Trina's apartment, Heaven walks past Trina into the kitchen and removes a pair of black-handled scissors from the nine-piece knife set. She walks into the bathroom, locks the door, and flips on the light switch. She stands in front of the vanity mirror. A few seconds later—snip, and her hair falls into the basin. Fake hair at first. Then her real hair. An hour later, she unlocks the door and stomps out.

Trina is in the living room, blasting music and smoking weed. She glances over at Heaven. "You're bald!" she says, and breaks out in laughter.

Alicia and Heaven had planned a full day of events before Heaven decided to investigate Hope's no-good husband. First, they were going to take pictures—outdoor shots downtown at Campus Martius Park, the two-and-a-half-acre public square and home to year-round entertainment. Then, they were going to stick around for WDET's *Essential Music Tuesdays*. After that, they were supposed to meet at Sir's loft so Alicia could cut all of the relaxer from Heaven's hair. Heaven has been excited about this day for the entire preceding week, but now their plans have changed.

She thought about wearing a wig before Alicia came to pick her up from Trina's, because she isn't yet used to having just an inch of hair—a TWA, or teeny-weeny Afro. But then, at the last minute, she snatches off her wig and decides not to cover up who she is . . . how she really looks now. She needs to go through the process, no matter how long it may take to change her hair—and herself.

"Do you have a dollar I can borrow?" asks Heaven after spotting a customer walking from the gas station holding a string of lotto tickets. Heaven remembers that the Mega Millions jackpot is huge—$229 million—and the drawing is tonight.

"All you need is a dollar?" asks Alicia as she pumps gas.

"Just a dollar. It only takes one ticket to win."

Alicia smiles at her as she hands her a twenty-dollar bill. "Play the whole twenty—I like to better our chances if we can. And you don't have to pay me back, but if you win I want half."

"A third. I'll have to give Hope a third too."

Alicia laughs. "That's fine."

Alicia watches her sister prance into the gas station. She wonders what happened to make her cut her own hair and oversleep for their photo shoot that morning. Heaven didn't want to talk about it, but Alicia already knows. If she had to guess, Hope didn't appreciate what Heaven told her about Roger Teasdale.

Inside the gas station, Heaven stands in line. The man in front of her has several lottery slips. He purchases one hundred dollars' worth of tickets—one hundred dollars' worth. She should go back outside and ask for at least another twenty dollars to purchase more tickets herself. But what she has will have to do. It's nineteen dollars more than she even asked for—more than she claimed she needed.

"Let me get twenty easy picks," she tells the man behind the counter.

"Twenty?" the young man asks. But it was the way he asked that made her contemplate her answer. Why should she do all easy picks?

"I'll be back." She steps out of line. She decides to pick the numbers for just one ticket. She uses a combination of all the sisters' ages, along with Hope's birthday. She chooses twenty-nine for the Mega Ball number in honor of Angelica's apartment. *Or should I pick thirty?* she ponders. She really thought they'd lived on the thirtieth floor in the penthouse the Jeffersonian never had. Maybe that's what her nana meant when she'd said that Heaven had made up the whole thing— her best friend, her parents, the penthouse, everything. Could that be possible? That the family she'd spent so much time with wasn't even real? Her pencil heads for the number thirty but at the last minute she circles in the number twenty-nine. She hates picking the Mega Ball number. It's the difference maker; the number that can change a person's winnings from something they can live off for a little while to something they can live off for the rest of their life.

She walks out of the gas station waving the tickets as she comes toward Alicia. "Who wants to be a millionaire?" she asks her.

"You could live in the penthouse at the Jeffersonian if we win," jokes Alicia.

Heaven smiles. "The twenty-ninth floor. That's the number I used for the Mega Ball, honey child. I'd have so much money I could buy the Jeffersonian."

"Smile with your eyes," Heaven tells Alicia as Alicia poses in Sir's living room. "Think about all that money you're going to have in less than an hour. Think about what you're going to do with your portion. . . . Perfect," says Heaven once Alicia's eyes light up. She walks over to Alicia with her camera to show her some of the shots from the display screen on the back of the digital camera. "Just use this button to toggle through."

While Alicia is looking through the large array of pictures Heaven took of her, Heaven helps herself to some of the Happy's Pizza leftovers. All of the pizza is gone, but there are still a few rib tips and a couple of spoonfuls of Greek salad. While she eats salad and rib tips, she sends a quick "I miss you" text to Jamal.

He answers right away.

Miss u 2. When r u going to take me out to dinner to experience ur culture

Soon.

She texts back with a smile.

"These are really nice pictures, Heaven. You do a great job."

Heaven smiles. "It's going to be hard for me to decide which to choose."

Sir is there, but he is staying out of the ladies' way. He's in his bedroom watching television. By this time, Alicia is at the kitchen sink with Heaven, washing Heaven's hair because Heaven has been complaining nonstop all day about how badly her scalp is itching.

Suddenly Sir yells from the bedroom, "Turn on the TV—they're about to draw the numbers!"

"Oh my God," Heaven says, springing from the chair with water and conditioner dripping down her face and into her eyes. "Give me a towel so I can see," she shouts as the balls start spinning.

Alicia runs back into the kitchen to retrieve a bath towel and hands it to Heaven, who is still searching through her wallet for the ticket. "I can't even find the ticket. I hid it from myself," she says before finally pulling the stack from the inside zipper pocket of her bag.

"Do we have any numbers so far?" asks Alicia. She turns to look at Heaven once she doesn't hear a response. "Heaven, what's wrong?"

"Shh, I'm trying to go through all these numbers."

"Once again, the Mega Millions numbers for this evening are twenty-one, twenty-seven, thirty-two, ten, twenty-six."

"Oh my God . . . Oh my God, we got five. . . . We got five!" Heaven shouts.

"And the Mega Ball number is . . . thirty."

"Did she just say thirty?" Heaven asks in disbelief. "Please tell me she didn't just say thirty."

"Yes, she said thirty. Did you have thirty?" asks Alicia with excitement.

"No, but I started to play thirty." Her fist pounds Sir's coffee table.

"Whoa, what's up?" asks Sir as he walks out of his bedroom and joins them.

"I started to play thirty, but I played twenty-nine instead, because . . . well, it doesn't even matter why now. I can't believe it. I didn't play thirty. It made more sense to play thirty."

"Well, how many numbers did you get?" Sir asks.

"Five."

"Five?" he asks. "That's still going to be a lot of money. You got five numbers out of six."

"But we didn't get the Mega Ball, so what's it going to be? About ten thousand?"

"No, I think it's about two hundred and fifty thousand."

"Two hundred and fifty thousand?" asks Alicia, and she looks over at Heaven.

"Two hundred and fifty thousand dollars is nothing compared to two hundred and twenty nine million. God." She buries her face in her hands. "God, I should have listened to my first thought."

"Don't beat yourself up over it. You still won," says Sir.

It all boiled down to that one number—the Mega Ball—the difference between paying off bills and paying in installments. Between never worrying about money again and a temporary fix.

Theirs is a temporary fix.

She takes a deep breath and starts to snap out of her disappointment. "That's right—we did. And something is better than nothing at all."

She immediately picks up the phone to dial Hope, who, of course, doesn't answer. She starts to leave a message until Alicia says, "Let's just go to her job tomorrow and surprise her with the good news."

"While we're on our way to the lottery office, right? Because I want to go there tomorrow. I don't want to be walking around with a winning ticket for too long."

God has answered Heaven's prayers.

Now she can take part of the lotto money and buy a house—nothing real fancy, as Jamal had recommended. He is pretty confident she can get a decent home in the city for around forty or fifty thousand—a home that in a few years will appraise for three times that. She just needs to take her time and look. She could even get something cheaper. Spend five to ten thousand fixing it up, then a couple thousand on furniture. But Heaven can't get over the idea of living at the Jeffersonian.

Heaven and her sisters have won big. They haven't won multimillions, but enough—more than enough to get each of them started. And this is her way of paying back Hope for the camera, and then some.

Alicia and Heaven stand inside near the doors for nearly ten minutes, waiting patiently for Hope to finish with her customer.

Hope sits at her desk across from Ezra, wondering why they are there at all and wondering why Heaven, who even as a little girl has always been so obsessed with having long hair, is now practically bald.

She takes her time with Ezra. She isn't going to rush on their account. Especially when they didn't even have the decency to call her first. She takes her work very seriously. She isn't into nonsense—and anything personal is just that. Who does that—simply pop up unannounced to a person's place of employment? she wonders. But what does either one of them know about professionalism? One is unemployed, and, well, the other one is worse—an actress.

Everything happens so quickly. Out of nowhere, Hope notices four men enter shortly after Ezra walks out. Two with high-powered machine guns burst through the bank. One immediately grabs Heaven.

"Everybody hit the ground!" says the man who grabbed Heaven.

Hope gets down and tries to remain calm. Are there four men or five? Suddenly, she can't remember. All she can see is the ground. And all she can think about is Havana. She doesn't want to leave her in this world alone . . . without her mother to raise her.

Heaven is standing in the middle of the bank beside Alicia, who is facedown on the floor. The robbers don't say another word. They let their actions speak for them. Their actions say if anyone moves, Heaven is going to die. If they have problems getting money from the teller stations, Heaven is going to die. If they have problems getting money from the vault, Heaven is going to die. If the police come before they get out of the bank, Heaven is going to die. Hope suddenly begins to panic, and she realizes she would be devastated if something happens to Heaven. She begins to pray.

Later, the police will say the bank robbery occurred in less than five minutes. But to Hope it feels like an eternity. There is one man going around to the handful of customers on the ground, taking any jewelry that seems of value. When they get to the woman lying facedown on the floor beside Hope, they immediately snatch a ring from her finger so hard it removes a small piece of her skin and causes her ring finger to bleed. She moans loudly from the pain. The bank robber shoves the assault rifle at the back of her head and says, "Shut up or get your head blown off." Hope keeps her head down, trembling and crying out in fear of what will happen next. When she hears movement, Hope raises her head just a little.

Heaven screams as they drag her from the bank toward the car. Hope doesn't know what to think at that moment. She sees the fear in Heaven's eyes and she wonders if this will be the last moment she will see Heaven; the moment she feared would one day come.

"God, don't let them hurt her," says Hope.

Police sirens sound in the near distance. The robbers leave, pushing Heaven to the ground before they speed off. Heaven is left kissing the ground and hanging on to what remains of a cheap cloth purse. Two bamboo handles are all she has left.

And for a brief moment, before Hope rushes outside, the thought crosses Hope's mind—is it possible that Heaven was behind this bank robbery in any way? She stands still and watches as Alicia runs to her sister's aid. And what about Alicia? What does Hope even know about this half sister?

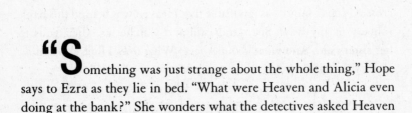

"**S**omething was just strange about the whole thing," Hope says to Ezra as they lie in bed. "What were Heaven and Alicia even doing at the bank?" She wonders what the detectives asked Heaven when they interviewed her at the bank.

"I'm sure you were scared to death, but, baby, don't try to overanalyze." He strokes her hair and releases sighs of worry. "I'm just glad you didn't get hurt. I could not believe that all of that happened right after I walked out. When I heard it on the radio, I immediately made a U-turn and headed back. That's when I really knew. I mean . . . if anything had happened to you . . . I couldn't take losing someone else I love."

She turns and places her hand over his mouth. "I couldn't take losing you," she says, still shaken from the events that occurred earlier in the day. She'd asked Havana's father to pick Havana up from school, and he offered to watch her for the next few days in addition to the coming weekend. And she agreed, because if something had happened to her, she realized for the first time that he would be the person to raise her child. She needs the relationship to be a good one—a healthy one.

She laments over the day and says, "I'm sorry, but I do not want to die at work, of all places."

"If it were left up to me, I wouldn't want you ever going back. And I want you to know you do have that option. You don't have to go back if you don't want to."

Hope plants a kiss on Ezra's lips. "Where do you come from? How can you be so perfect?"

"I'm not perfect. Can't you see I'm not perfect?"

"You're perfect for me. You're what women dream of. I want to be loved and desired, and I want to feel secure. Of course, I could never accept such an offer since I'm way too independent, but it's nice to know you would take care of me . . . that you care about me enough."

"Well, if you won't let me take care of you, will you at least do me another favor?" he asks, slipping around the open ring case that he'd been hiding out of sight. "Will you marry me?"

Her eyes glance down at the large emerald-cut diamond ring. "Marry you?" she asks as she turns to face him. "Are you sure?" She's certain of what her answer will be, but she needs to know that he is ready to truly move on. She doesn't want a third marriage to fail.

"I'm one hundred percent sure. I absolutely want to marry you. I want you to become my wife. I want to take care of you and Havana, and I want you to take care of me, and I want to make you and Havana happy, and yes, eventually, when you're ready, I want you to quit your job and concentrate on having some babies."

"You want to have babies?"

"Try for three. You want more?"

"I do want more. I've always wanted more," she says, glowing with happiness.

"Okay, well, I asked you if you'll marry me, and I'm still waiting for your answer."

"Of course I'll marry you." Hope throws her arms around Ezra.

"The proposal was going to be much more romantic than this," he says as he pulls away and slips the engagement ring on her finger.

"I had reservations at Coach Insignia for next weekend, and Havana was going to be there, but after what happened today, I couldn't wait."

"Are you real?" asks Hope.

Ezra nods. "Are you?"

Hope returns the nod. "As real as the diamond in this ring."

"Well, that's unfortunate, because that's a cubic zirconia."

"You know what?"

"You're going to have to get used to my sense of humor, baby. . . . If you give me an opening, I'm going to take it. . . . You should know that by now."

She lets out a deep sigh and shakes her head with a smile. Her life feels almost complete, except for one major thing—Heaven and Alicia. It's nice to have family . . . nice to have friends. If she and Heaven had been speaking, she would have immediately phoned her to tell her the good news, to check to see how she was doing, but Hope's stubbornness prevents her from picking up the phone.

At seven at night, Jamal picks Heaven up from Trina's suburban apartment in a black Charger. The temperature is in the low fifties—cool enough, she convinces herself, to wear a turtleneck to cover up her tattoo. The fade cream is working, but not fast enough. Now, instead of saying *Donovan*, it says *Dono* with a black smudge at the end. She was going to use some of her lotto winnings to get the tattoo removed by laser. But no use in going over what she was going to do. The ticket is gone now, and the fade cream is all she can afford to use.

She twirls her finger around her long silky straight Beverly Johnson wig with brow-skimming bangs. She's wearing a wig, not because she's afraid to spring her new natural look on Jamal, but because of the bank robbers. They were all wearing masks, and although she wouldn't be able to identify any of them on the street, they could identify her, so her wig is her mask, at least for tonight.

"I'm surprised I get to see you so soon," says Heaven to Jamal as he drives the Lodge Freeway southbound. "You're always so busy."

"I'm never too busy to eat," he says. "If you want to see me more, all you have to do is cook. I like home-cooked meals."

"Me? Cook? If I were to start cooking, you would get too busy to eat for real, trust me. You'd avoid my kitchen like the plague."

"Another contemporary woman with nothing to offer but a bangin' body and a beautiful smile," he says jokingly.

Heaven smiles. "Thank you."

"And she takes it as a compliment," he says as he smiles and looks over at her. "What do you think about you and me?"

"Me and you?" she asks.

"You and me? Me and You? Us?"

"You seem cool."

"I am cool . . . very cool."

"But, there are things about you that I don't know."

"I'm sure there are things about your ex-man that you didn't know," he says, tugging at her turtleneck. "I appreciate the cover-up."

"Oh, yeah, there were a lot of things about him that I didn't know."

"Did you all ever live together?"

"No. He stayed over at my place a lot."

"Why did he stay over at your place if he had his own place? He did have his own place, right?" asks Jamal, digging for information.

"Why so many questions? I don't think about him. He's in the past, thank God. I haven't heard from him since we went to court. Except one time I got a call from an unknown caller. I picked up and nobody said anything. I know it was him. But I don't ever want to hear from him again, so I just hung up. Anyway . . . let's change the subject . . . or listen to music." She turns up the volume to his Jay-Z CD and starts shoulder dancing in her seat.

Twenty-five minutes after he picks Heaven up from Trina's, they stroll into the restaurant after he parks in the adjoining lot. "I mean if you want me to learn how to prepare Mezze and farr . . . farr—"

"Farrouge Moussahab . . . Aww see, you're learning," Jamal says as he opens the door for her.

"I can do that, but right now I'm trying to expose you to my culture."

"By taking me to Steve's Soul Food?"

"Exactly, where else you want to go? 'Cause this right here is our culture."

"I've been going to Steve's for a while now," Jamal admits. "I've never been to this location, but I've been to the one on Grand River. I was expecting you to take me to maybe, I don't know, the Blue Nile."

"The Blue Nile? What's that?" asks Heaven as she moves down the line.

"It's an Ethiopian restaurant."

Heaven smiles wide. "Oh my God . . . Ethiopian, really?" She fans her hands in her face. "Do I really look Ethiopian to you?"

"Your features and your complexion. Your ancestors may have come from there."

"You do know this ain't my real hair, right?" Heaven says.

He shrugs. "I'm just keeping it real. I'm looking at your face and your rich complexion, not your hair."

"Rich." She nods. "Yeah, I like the way that sounds. A man has never told me I have a rich complexion." She whispers in his ear, "You must be trying to get yourself some tonight, but I'm not that type of girl."

"I'm not trying to get any."

"Oh no, why not?"

"Maybe I'm not that kind of guy."

She pushes her tray and moves farther down the line, then stops to inspect the menu board. "Let me have barbecued pig's feet. Nah, better yet, let me get the catfish."

"Two sides?" the lady asks.

"Corn bread dressing, of course . . . You know what, let me have the fried chicken instead."

"Is it really that difficult?" asks Jamal.

"Shut up," Heaven says playfully. "Give him the barbecued pig's feet."

"What?" asks Jamal.

"You ordered for me when I went to your restaurant. I'm exposing you to my culture, remember? Give him the pig's feet with candied yams and black-eyed peas, and with my chicken give me the corn bread dressing and candied yams."

"We need a green vegetable," Jamal says as he leans into her.

Heaven sighs. "And two orders of green beans."

"Any dessert?"

"Ooh yes, definitely. Umm, sweet potato pie for me and give him the peach cobbler."

"You're funny," says Jamal as they sit in a booth and enjoy their meal. "So, how is your sister from LA doing?"

"We could all be doing better." She considers telling him about her lotto ticket. But, she admits, she's paranoid. Detroit can seem small at times. Everyone knows someone who knows someone else who knows them. They stole her purse, but hopefully they'll never find the ticket. Why should someone else benefit from her lottery winnings? It's still very hard for her to believe that all that money is gone, just like that. But after having the barrel of a gun pressed so firmly against her temple, she's just glad to be alive.

The rest of the night at the restaurant, Heaven tries to probe into his true profession, asking him questions about the gas station where he supposedly works with his father or grandfather. But he says he doesn't want to talk about work, so they talk about everything but work. She talks about the bank robbery, but he doesn't want to talk about that much either. So then they don't talk—they eat. And when they finish eating, Heaven walks briskly back to his car, practically running. She should have worn a coat. Her hands are so cold she wishes she had gloves. The temperature has dropped even lower; it feels like it's in the forties. He unlocks the door with his key fob and she hops inside while he is just making it to the parking lot.

She blows into her hands. She's freezing. She wonders if he has some gloves as she pulls open his glove compartment. Right away, she spots a small plastic bag. She is slow in removing the bag, but after opening it and peering at its contents, she's quick to shove it back inside and slam the compartment door shut. Inside the plastic bag was a black ski mask. Beneath the bag was a Smith & Wesson gun.

Her heart is racing. The ski mask looked exactly like the kind that the robbers were wearing. And now that she thinks about it, he was silent every time she brought up the robbery. Was Jamal the one who had the gun pressed against her head. *Jamal?*

"What are you doing?" asks Jamal once he gets behind the wheel.

"I was cold, and I was hoping you had some driving gloves or something I could put on to warm my hands."

"Oh no, I don't," he says, locking the glove compartment.

"Did you rob my sister's bank?" she blurts out without thinking. But why shouldn't she just ask him? She wants to know, and she also wants her purse back.

"What are you talking about?" asks Jamal.

"Are you about to kill me?"

"What? You're joking right now, right?" he asks as he starts up the engine and pulls out of the parking lot.

"No, I'm not joking," she says, raising her voice. "I'm scared right now. Maybe I didn't have a right to go into your glove compartment before asking, but I'm glad I did. You were supposed to be different."

"I am different."

"Yeah, you are. I never dated a bank robber before. Can I at least have my purse back?"

"I'm not a bank robber," he says.

"Then why would you need a ski mask and a gun?" She sees Jamal's back stiffen. Then he casually shrugs.

"I just thought you were some small-time drug dealer and that was bad enough, but I never thought you were a bank robber."

"Heaven, listen—you really just have to believe me. I'm not a bank robber or a drug dealer."

"Then why didn't you want to talk about the robbery at dinner?"

"Because I wanted to talk about something else."

"I don't believe you. You helped rob that bank. Didn't you?"

"I'm not a bank robber," he says, his voice low.

"Then explain the mask. Are you a terrorist, just like my nana said? I didn't want to believe her. You're a terrorist. You're not really Catholic are you? Do you have explosives in your trunk?"

"What?"

"You do, don't you? Stop the car and open your trunk."

"I'm not going to open my trunk. You're sounding real racist right now."

"I don't care how I sound. You had a gun to my head. I liked you . . . a lot. And you had a gun to my head." She starts to hit him wildly with her fists.

"What are you doing? Do you want me to crash the car?" he asks.

"You're not going to strap a bomb to me and blow me up," she yells.

He rubs his head after she peppers him with blows. "Do you have to be so stereotypical? I'm not a terrorist, I'm not a drug dealer, and I'm not a bank robber."

"There are a ski mask and gun in your glove compartment, and God knows what else could be hidden in this car. Who needs a ski mask in the summer? Who needs a ski mask anytime?"

"A skier, maybe?" he says.

"Yeah, right, a skier. Let me out of this damn car, Jamal. You're no better than Donovan."

"Oh, I'm a lot better than he is."

"Let me out of this car right now," she screams.

"I'll let you out, but only after I take you home. It's not safe for a woman to be walking the street at night."

Heaven bursts out laughing. "No, it's much safer for me to be riding in the car with a bank robber slash drug dealer who has a gun in his glove compartment."

"Don't forget terrorist too."

"Let me out! I'll take my chances on the street."

"No, you won't."

She rides in silence while he travels northbound on the Lodge Freeway. He keeps telling her that he wishes he could explain, but some things are better left unsaid. She wonders if he'll even take her home. She ponders all the way while she sits in silence, right until he pulls in front of Trina's apartment building.

"I didn't rob the bank," he tells Heaven as she steps out of his car.

She doesn't respond. She doesn't look back at him. She doesn't want to believe that a man with so much pride would stoop so low. But she also knows, after everything she and her sister have been through, that anything is possible.

Atlas Global Bistro in the historic Addison Building is their first stop on inaugural day of Detroit Restaurant Week. Ezra's plan for the two of them is to dine at four of the seventeen award-winning restaurants participating in Restaurant Week over the next two weekends. The event, the first of its kind in the city, runs for ten days, starting on September 18, and offers a three-course meal for twenty-seven dollars. He had already made reservations for six in the evening on opening day at the restaurant *Metro Times* readers voted best restaurant under fifty dollars. He had the entire evening planned a couple weeks in advance. Of course, he had no way of knowing, just two days earlier, the bank where Hope worked was going to get robbed. But he didn't want to cancel, because he felt that Hope needed to step out and stop focusing so much on the robbery. He wanted her to put the terrible event behind her so they could move on.

Inside, the restaurant is beautifully designed with soaring ceilings, exposed brick walls, and vintage wood floors. They sit beside a large window with a view of Woodward Avenue and the Detroit skyline.

"Do you want to ride the new dining car?" asks Ezra as he dips his spoon into the crunch caramel coating of the dark chocolate spiced custard. Although they had hoped to each order a different dessert and share, neither was interested in the raspberry sorbet, so instead they both ordered the Mexican chocolate brûlée.

"Why, do they serve food in there or something?"

"No," he chuckles. "They've painted one of the cars of the People Mover with restaurant logos."

"Pugh," she spits, "I don't need to see that. I guess that's good for people who are visiting from out of town." She thinks of Alicia. She wonders if she and Heaven are still bonding, then tosses out the image of the two of them coming into the bank and the subsequent robbery. She shakes her head.

"What's wrong?"

"I'm just thinking about my sister," she says, shaking her head again. "Is it crazy for me to wonder if she and Alicia had something to do with the bank getting robbed?"

"Hope, I don't think your sisters had anything to do with that."

"My sister and half sister," she snaps a correction. "Besides, you don't know Heaven."

He reaches his hand over to touch hers. "Why would your sister rob a bank, baby?"

"Maybe that thought is a little bit paranoid. It's one thing to rob me—I'm just family—but robbing a bank is a federal offense," she says, "and I don't suppose she'd do that."

"What is your issue with your sister?"

"We've been through this."

"Money? Are you telling me this is all over money?"

"If you can't see my point of view, why should I continue talking about this? All I'm saying is if a person can kick you while you're already down, that's someone who doesn't care anything about you and someone you definitely can't trust. She kicked me when I was down, and I would have never done her like that. I always protected her when we were growing up. Always."

Ezra notices Hope's eyes tear up. "Don't cry, baby. I understand."

She dabs the corner of her eyes with the cloth napkin. "I want to forgive. I swear I do. But she keeps messing up."

The next morning Heaven Jetter receives a call from an FBI agent, informing her that they'd recovered her purse after the Feds, along with the Detroit Police, raided the home of a suspected bank robber.

She closes her eyes. "Is his name Jamal Bashi?" she asks the officer.

"Whose name?"

"The suspect in the bank robbery."

"No, ma'am. But your purse was at the scene, and you can come down to our field office to pick it up at any time."

She gives a sigh of relief. She thinks she may have jumped to conclusions. But then her mind turns to her purse, and she wonders whether the ticket will still be inside.

She doesn't let a full hour pass before heading down to the station. The lotto ticket would sure come in handy.

"My name is Heaven Jetter, and I'm here to see Detective Murphy," she says as she approaches a woman sitting at the front desk.

The female officer picks up the phone to call Detective Murphy's office. "You can go on back through the door and turn left."

Heaven walks toward the door in the back of the station and waits for someone to allow her access. What if her wallet is inside her purse and the ticket is still there? That would make almost everything right again.

Once inside, she notices a tall white-haired man standing outside an office door directing her to come his way.

"You have my purse?" she asks as she enters his office. And immediately she spots her former probation officer, Debra Thomas.

"I do," he says, pulling her purse from the bottom of his drawer with an evidence sticker attached. "Please sit down."

"I can't stay. I just came to pick up my purse."

"I understand, but we received a lead during our investigation and your name came up."

She immediately thinks of her shoplifting. "What kind of investigation?"

"Bank robbery and narcotics investigation. We have reason to believe that you have information on a Donovan David Davis aka Scarface."

She nods. "I've heard him refer to himself as that before."

"So you do know the suspect?"

"Yes, he's my ex-boyfriend."

"What can you tell us about him?"

"I have a PPO out against him and he's crazy . . . but that's all I know."

"But do you think he had something to do with the bank robbery? Your sister works at that bank. . . . Isn't that correct?"

"Yes."

"Did you have anything to do with the robbery?"

"No, I didn't. Is that why you're here?" Heaven asks her probation officer.

"No, Heaven, but they need you to cooperate."

"Heaven, we're going to need your help."

"My help?" she asks, curious as to how she could possibly help them.

Half an hour later Heaven walks out of the office with Mrs. Thomas by her side. "Detective Murphy is a good man. Just work with him, Heaven."

"So how come you came down here? I'm not on probation anymore. So if I don't work with him, am I going to get in trouble?"

"He wanted me to talk to you. We know all about the code of silence. But Heaven, I can't stress enough how serious this is. This guy you were with isn't a part of something small time. He's hooked up to a pretty elaborate network."

"I haven't talked to him, Mrs. Thomas. I told him all I know."

"Well, if anything else comes up, you have my card and you have his."

Heaven focuses on Mrs. Thomas' feet. "Christian Louboutins,

Mrs. Thomas? Keep it up and I'm gonna think you're a part of that same network."

"You know better than to think that."

"I know you got those shoes at Saks," Heaven says as she moves toward her car, "and I also know they weren't on sale."

"Every now and then you got to splurge."

"Yeah," Heaven says as she swings open her car door, "but you have a whole lot of nows and a whole lot of thens." With so much on her mind, she almost forgets to look inside her purse for the wallet before driving away. The detective had explained to her that a suspect had been picked up on a drug warrant and had implicated Donovan, and in the midst of questioning, Heaven's name was mentioned. The detective told her not to discuss the case with anyone and not to tell anyone she'd even come to their office. But she'd already told Alicia she was going to pick up her purse.

The suspect, the detective said, referring to Donovan, was armed and dangerous. He had a previous drug conviction and had spent eighteen months in the state penitentiary for a possessions charge. He has a warrant for his arrest on an attempted murder charge for an altercation occurring at a nightclub on the east side a couple of weeks earlier, and he was on the FBI's most wanted list.

At the first red light, she says a silent prayer and pulls her wallet from her purse. She searches the hidden compartment for the ticket. She sees a tiny piece of folded paper buried deep inside. She pulls it out with a trembling hand and gasps. It's the lotto ticket. Unbelievable. In her excitement, she blows her horn right before the person behind her blows theirs.

"I won." Her eyes cloud with tears of joy as she proceeds down the street.

"Go to TMZ right now," says Benita through Alicia's cell phone.

"I'm not even home. I'm driving on my way home."

"You should be home so you can read about this."

"What happened?"

"Oh my freaking God . . . Aubrey got fired off the set of *Innocence*."

"What?" shouts Alicia. She slams on the brakes at a green light nearly ready to turn yellow. The woman in the car behind her swerves to the opposite lane, giving Alicia the finger and blowing her horn as she passes through the light. "How do you know it's true?" she asks as she stays put for the red light.

"It's true. It's all over the Internet. Something big had to go down. This has to be good for you, huh? Surely he'll remember you. It's not like you have to worry about J.R. anymore."

"That's true." But then Alicia thinks about it. "I'm sure he's not thinking about me now. You know how they are in Hollywood. Out of sight, out of mind."

"Still, this could be an opportunity for you."

"I wonder what happened. Did they say?"

"It just says, 'Story developing.'"

"I hope she's okay."

The phone goes dead silent. "She was trying to ruin you, and you hope she's okay? Who cares how she is? I don't. I told you about karma. And I also told you about her. You'll start listening to me now."

Several hours later, after Heaven has driven all the way to Lansing and back to claim the prize, she phones Alicia. The thought to keep the full amount never crosses her mind.

"Guess what?" asks Heaven after Alicia answers her cell phone.

"I have something to tell you too, but you go first."

"They found my purse . . . and guess what?"

"What?"

"I found our lotto ticket. Can you believe it?" she shouts. "We're two hundred and fifty thousand dollars richer."

"You can keep my cut."

"What? Why? Why would I do that?"

"That can be your agent fee."

"My agent fee? What do you mean by that?"

"First, I received a call from my roommate, Benita, telling me they'd fired Aubrey off the set of the movie that was supposed to be mine. Aubrey was being real difficult on the set, and they found drugs in her trailer. Then, about an hour or so later, Marcus Toller called."

"So did you get the part?"

"He said he was glad you called him. Under different circumstances I'd be pissed, but he said that even though he found it to be crazy, he also believes everything happens for a reason . . . and your call reminded him of that."

"So what are you saying? Do you have the part?"

"Yes, I have the part, and I'm about to have a whole lot of money, so you can keep my portion."

"Oh my God . . . Oh . . . my . . . God. We have to celebrate."

"Yeah, we should."

"Somewhere really, really nice."

Alicia laughs. "So you're tired of the two-dollar tacos? I'm sure Sir will know of another good place."

In as short a time as fifteen minutes and for as little as fifty cents each, the three of them—Hope, Havana, and Ezra—ride the entire loop of the People Mover, an automated light rail system that operates on an elevated single-track loop. They make their way to the Marriott Hotel and end where they started—the GM Global Renaissance Center. They conclude their day at Coach Insignia, the eclectic chophouse located on the seventy-first and seventy-second floors, making the restaurant the second highest in the United States.

Havana looks down at the five-story Winter Garden Atrium as the glass elevator whisks them up seventy-two flights over sweeping and breathtaking views of Detroit and the Windsor skyline.

After taking their seats in the circular dining room at a square table accented with a smooth white tablecloth, Hope begins to marvel at the view through the ceiling-to-floor windows.

"Do you see the Ambassador Bridge, Havana?"

Havana nods; then her eyes immediately light up. "Mom, look!"

"I think I see Hope," says Heaven to Alicia as they head to their table.

"Hope?" asks Alicia as both Alicia and Sir crane their necks to look around the restaurant. "Are you sure?"

"Yes ... I know my sister. That's Hope and Havana and Ezra. I'm going over there."

"Wait a minute, Heaven. Are you sure?" Alicia asks. "You never know what kind of mood she's in."

"I don't care what kind of mood she's in. I want to tell them the good news."

Hope's plate of braised beef short ribs has just arrived when she spots Heaven heading in her direction. Havana is almost jumping out of her seat.

"Havana, don't shout. We're in a public place."

Ezra leans in toward Hope's ear. "Take your own advice."

"Why would I shout?"

"Just be nice."

"Auntie," says Havana, leaping out of her seat and wrapping her arms around Heaven.

"Hello, Miss Fierce." Heaven walks her fingers down the center part in her niece's hair.

"Hello, Heaven. How are you? Have the police found your purse yet?" Hope asks politely.

"As a matter of fact," Heaven says, turning to Hope, "I have something for you."

"Something for me? Like what?"

"Like some money—a lot of money. I won the Mega Millions lottery."

"I guess I'm supposed to laugh now, right?" asks Hope.

"No, the police recovered my purse, and inside was a lotto ticket— a winning lotto ticket. I only matched five numbers, so we're not mil- lionaires, but I have enough to pay you back five times what I took.

That's why Alicia and I were at the bank on the day of the robbery. We played the lotto and won. I told you I'd pay you back, plus interest, and I meant it. I love you, Hope. And I'm trying; I just want you to see that."

Hope slumps back in her chair and says, "God, you actually won the lotto?"

"I actually did."

"Why don't you, Alicia, and your . . . friend join us?"

"Seriously?" Heaven asks with a wide smile, and Hope nods. "Let me go get them."

After Heaven walks away, Hope turns to face Ezra, raising her right eyebrow.

"That's why a person needs eyebrows. If I had any, I'd be able to give you the same look."

The three take a seat at the table beside Hope's. And as the appetizers are carried to their table, the conversation begins to flow. Hope smiles as she looks over at her sister Heaven and then over at Alicia. Alicia tells a Hollywood story about how she'd once tripped down a flight of stairs at an after party, right after Denzel Washington and his wife Pauletta walked in. "I'd never seen him in person before," she explains, "and I really wanted to take his picture with my cell phone and send it to my aunt. I guess that's what I get for trying to be sneaky." They laugh the night away and have a wonderful time, and they promise to meet up again soon.

"Maybe you all can go out on a triple date," says Havana. "Do you have a boyfriend, Auntie?"

Heaven thinks of Jamal and what might have been. "No, I'm single . . . and loving it," she proclaims.

Jamal stands in front of a large dry erase board that has the outline of two homes drawn. He begins briefing the Special Response Team, the Detroit Police Department's version of SWAT.

"We will be conducting two simultaneous raids this morning. Initially, we had our target house as one single-family home, highly fortified. We've done two raids on this home in the past. The first time we made a buy bust, and we had no problem securing the entrance to the home. The next time they'd put down between fifteen to twenty cement bags at the front and rear doors of the home. We've obtained some new leads on the house two doors down, which is also operating as a drug house. I made a buy at this home early this morning. It is a one-story, single-family home of white cinder block brick with red trim. Our seller is believed to be Donovan David Davis, a black male, twenty-four years of age, five-foot-nine, one hundred eighty pounds, medium complexion and medium build with short black hair. He has been known to carry a gun. He has served time in prison for a possessions charge and he has an outstanding warrant for attempted murder. We've had surveillance on the first home for three days and the second home for one day, and both homes are still active. So let's get ready to move."

Jamal pulls a department-issued police mask over his face, similar to the black one Heaven had seen in the glove compartment of his car when she assumed it was a ski mask. The black mask covers every feature of his face, exposing only his eyes. He then places a black bucket hat on his head with the word POLICE in white letters across the front. He is wearing black nylon gloves and a bulletproof vest. He is an undercover narcotics officer, and he can't risk blowing his cover, but he is coming to the scene for one major reason: He's familiar with one of the two homes being raided, and this bust is personal.

He climbs in the backseat of a black GMC Savana filled with other narcotics officers. SRT is in the black van ahead of theirs, and a thirteen-ton armored personnel carrier is ahead of them. Another armored unit known as a GIMP is traveling along to breach the back door of the second house, and two undercover narcotics cars are behind the van.

"UC was able to make a buy at our first target," says a man over the radio. "However, our second target would only sell through a slot, so it is unknown whether or not our suspect is inside. We will proceed as planned."

Two blocks away from the suspected drug houses SRT lowers the APC handle, known as the boom, preparing to breach the front door.

"We have to get in there with one hit," Jamal says. "Can't give them time to flush."

Within minutes they are at the scene. The narcotics van stays back and allows SRT to breach both locations. Once SRT has cleared out the location and taken down the suspects, narcotics will go in and sweep for drugs.

Several narcotics officers are standing in the street between both residences. Most are covered from head to toe in police gear and masks to conceal their identity. They are an intimidating force, with at least thirty officers covering the perimeter of both houses and the street out front.

The APC drives onto the front lawn of the second home and rams the boom at the front door, tearing down the door and pushing it inside the residence. Officers quickly descend on the property.

Within seconds, Jamal hears an officer yell over the radio, "We are clearing out both houses now. The suspect, Donovan David Davis aka Scarface, is not here. Repeat. The suspect is not here."

Heaven's next-door neighbor's dog, Cody, a solid black rottweiler–pit bull mix, is barking furiously. Heaven stumbles out of her front door into Donovan's hardened chest. The menacing look in his eyes serves as Heaven's warning, but the mere fact that he is standing in front of her despite a PPO order from the court has her the most concerned.

"You know you aren't supposed to be here," says Heaven. If she could call the police she would, but her cell phone is inside her purse, which is inside her car. She had just finished stuffing her trunk with two garbage bags filled with clothes, and she had headed back inside for more of her things.

"Moving?" he asks as he notices a garbage bag. "Or just taking out the trash?"

She hadn't been back to the house to spend a night since the night she and Donovan got into the big fight . . . since the night she pulled the gun on him. She was just there waiting on Alicia and Sir to come help her repair some of the damage both she and Donovan caused over the course of the tumultuous year they were together. She left her purse inside the locked car while she ran inside to get a bag of shoes, many of which belonged to Trina, before she left to pick up some takeout from China Wok for them. Heaven had been inside the house only a matter of minutes when Donovan appeared from out of nowhere.

He doesn't say another word, as if he decided he doesn't need to because, as he quickly makes it known to Heaven while shoving her back inside the house, he is carrying a gun. She drops the bag of shoes on the porch, and shoes topple out as she falls inside the rental house.

————

Narcotics had found a large amount of money at the scene. Some of the bills were those they'd used for the buy. Jamal did a quick walk-through, along with a couple other undercover narcotics officers who all remained hidden behind their masks and dark clothing.

During the raid they recovered two digital scales (one broken), thirty grams of heroin, a hundred grams of crack cocaine, two hundred sixty grams of PCP, twenty grams of ecstasy, forty grams of marijuana, a tube full of loose cocaine, a 9mm pistol, and a twelve-gauge shotgun, but not their primary suspect, Donovan.

The narcotics sergeant tells the suspect they've apprehended, "You know you're taking the hit for all this, right?"

"Me?" asks the teen who is lying facedown on the living room floor, hands secured behind his back in heavy-duty white plastic ties—temporary cuffs. Two narcotics officers pick him up by his arms. "Why I got to take the hit? I was just in the wrong place at the wrong time, man."

"You can say that again," says the sergeant. "Right now it's got to suck to be you."

The officers walk him out of the house, and Jamal follows.

"Nah, see y'all got the wrong dude. The dude that owns this house—that's all his. You can find him over at his girl's house."

"Oh, yeah, what's his girl's name? Where does she live?"

"Man, you know what?" He shakes his head. "Forget this. I ain't sayin' no more."

Jamal takes out his cell phone and dials Heaven's number. The phone rings a few times, but no one answers. He then texts her and asks her to please return his call or send him a text. They hadn't spoken since that night they went out to dinner and she found his mask and gun.

Jamal walks over to his narcotics sergeant and says, "He may be over at his ex-girlfriend's house. That's what I'm thinking. She's already been working with police." Then, without waiting for a return call, he requests that units be sent over to Heaven's home.

"God," says Alicia, pressing her cell phone to her ear, "she's probably cursing us out right now. We were supposed to have been over there an hour ago. I hope she got my messages. Maybe she's on the other line and doesn't want to click over or something."

"She knows we're coming," says Sir. "She knows we wouldn't stand her up."

Once at Heaven's house, Alicia notices something strange. Shoes are falling out of a large black garbage bag all over her porch, with several pairs on the steps. She can see Heaven's purse as she walks by her car. She phones Heaven again and can hear her cell phone ringing from inside the car. She tries the doors, but they're locked. She notices the dog next door pacing and barking furiously. Then she thinks she sees one of the blinds open and close quickly.

"I'm calling the police," says Alicia to Sir as she rushes back to his car. "Something's wrong. The dog is acting real funny. And all of her shoes are just lying all over the place. I tried to call her, but her phone is in her car. And I really think I saw someone, a man, peek through the blinds," she says as her fingers dial 911. "She has a crazy ex-boyfriend, remember? I'm calling the police, and then I'm calling Hope."

"When did the 911 call come through?" asks Jamal. "Okay, several units are on their way now, and we're on our way as well." He hangs up the phone and sits quietly in the passenger seat of a tinted, unmarked police car.

"So the suspect is at his ex-girlfriend's."

"We believe so," says Jamal. "Her sister called the police. Says she was supposed to meet her more than an hour ago, and when she came to the house, she found that her sister's purse, along with her cell phone, was inside the car, and shoes were all over the front porch. She also believes she saw a male peek through the blinds. At this point we believe our suspect has barricaded himself inside his ex-girlfriend's home." Jamal is concerned. He's seen situations like this end very badly. Donovan has been in prison before, and he has an outstanding warrant on a felony count. Most of the time ex-cons are fully aware of the amount of time they can expect for each charge. The kidnapping charge will be a federal crime, and the sentence must be served in its entirety. Adding the possessions and weapons charges, and a few other charges they can throw into the mix, including unlawful entry, Donovan probably knows he'll be a very old man if he's lucky to see the outside world again.

When Jamal arrives at the scene, SRT officers are already posted at the entry and perimeter of the home that sits in the middle of the block. Neighbors are in clusters in a few areas on the street, keeping a watchful eye on the house and all of the police presence.

One of the SRT negotiators is speaking to Alicia, trying to get information from her on both Heaven and Donovan.

"I know he's violent. I know he's beaten her on several occasions and she has a PPO against him," says Alicia to one of the officers.

"What can you tell us about the layout of the house?"

"I've never been inside her house," says Alicia. "But our other sister should be here any minute. I called her too, and she doesn't live too far away."

Several minutes later, in the midst of Alicia's conversation with the negotiator, Ezra pulls up with Hope in the passenger seat. She jumps out of her parked car and runs toward Alicia.

"Oh my God, what is happening?" asks Hope frantically.

"Ma'am, we have a hostage situation, and we need you to calm down and tell us about the house. Is there a landline inside?"

"No, she has only a cell phone," says Hope.

"Do you know his cell phone number?"

"Whose?" asks Hope.

"Her ex-boyfriend, Donovan"

"I don't even know who he is."

"Okay, we'll need the layout of the house because we're going to drop a phone inside." The hostage situation complicates things. An hour has passed; normally they would have deployed tear gas with a gas gun by now, but they are trying not to put Heaven in any more immediate danger than she already is.

"I don't know the layout. I've never been inside. I'm sorry. I should have been a better sister. . . . I'm sorry, but I can't help you," she says, falling into Ezra's arms.

"That's fine. To get the layout we can speak with one of the neighbors who may have a similar house."

"But are you going to save her? Can you promise me that you'll save her? I really need you to promise me you will."

"That's what we're all here to do."

The police negotiator retreats back inside one of two mobile command posts set up on the street. Two men approach the rear of the house using the side of the APC and a shield as cover. They break the window and drop a cell phone inside.

The negotiator, who is sitting at a desk inside the mobile command post, says through a loudspeaker, "We want to hear your side of the story. Come outside with your hands up. We do not want to harm you. In the back bedroom there is a phone. Pick up the phone so we can hear your side of the story. Otherwise, things are going to change, and they're going to change quickly."

The negotiator calls the number to the phone that was dropped inside the house. After five rings, Donovan answers. "Hello."

"Hey, Donovan?"

"Yeah."

"This is Ron from the Detroit Police Department. We need you to come out or at least release Heaven. Is she okay?"

"Yes."

"Can we talk to her?"

The phone is silent for a few seconds, and then a woman says frantically, "Hello."

"Are you okay?"

"No."

"Has he hurt you?"

"Not yet."

"Hello," says Donovan after taking the phone away. "I'm going to come out. Just give me about five minutes and then call me back."

"Why are we calling you back?" asks the negotiator. "Why can't you just come out?"

"I'm going to come out. Just call me back in five minutes."

"Can you send Heaven out, and then we'll wait the five minutes and call you?"

"We're both going to come out in five minutes."

"Okay, I'm going to call you back in five minutes." The police negotiator hangs up the phone and looks up at his partner. "I don't like that 'Give me five minutes.' He's playing us, but we're in a bad situation. He has the upper hand." He releases a deep breath and waits out the time. In exactly five minutes, the negotiator calls Donovan back and he answers.

"Hello," says Donovan.

"Yeah, Donovan, this is Ron again. So you're coming out now?"

"Yeah, getting ready to. I just need a few more minutes, so can you call back?"

"I just called back. . . . What's going on, man? I need you to work with me."

"I know . . . and I am working with you, but can you call back again . . . in about fifteen minutes?" asks Donovan.

"Why do I have to call back in fifteen minutes? We need to end this now and end it safely. We want to hear your side, but I can't keep calling back."

"Okay, well then don't call back," he says, and hangs up.

The next-door neighbor's dog is standing at attention before he begins to pace inside his large cage, keeping an eye on Heaven's house.

"This is the Detroit Police Department," says the negotiator over the loudspeaker. "We have the house completely surrounded. We want you to come outside, surrender, and talk to us. Release the young lady unharmed. We're not going to go anywhere until you and the young lady come out. We know you care about your children—your baby daughter and son. So let's go ahead and end this so everyone can go on with their lives. We're not going anywhere until you and the young lady come out."

After another hour passes, they move to the next level. Back at the second command post, Donovan's mother has taped a message to her son that is delivered to the negotiator who then plays the message over the loudspeaker.

"Donovan, please come out of the house, son," says his mother in a weary voice. "I want to see you. I miss you and I love you. Your children miss you and love you. We can work this out. Please, Donovan . . . Please come out."

The negotiator tries to call the house again and after several rings, Donovan finally answers. "Hello."

"Donovan. . . . It's Ron. Are you ready now to come out so we can work this out?"

"Yes, sir, I am."

"Good. That's good. I just need you to leave any weapons you have inside—"

"This is what I'm going to do. I'm going to say a prayer, and then we're going to come out. So I need about ten minutes to do that."

"Okay, well, you can say your prayer with me on the phone," says the negotiator.

"No, sir, I can't do it that way. I need to say a prayer alone. This is between me and God. I need ten minutes."

"Okay, well, I can't give you any more time. If you want to release Heaven, then I can see about giving you some more time, but with Heaven inside, we can't keep this going on any longer."

"All right, well, then, in that case . . . we're going to come out. Are there any ambulances outside?"

"An ambulance?" asks the negotiator. "No. Is someone hurt?"

"Okay, well, can you get an ambulance? I'm going to need two stretchers, and I'm going to say my prayer and come out. But you need to have that ambulance ready."

"Why would we need an ambulance?" asks the negotiator. Seconds later he hears a dial tone. The negotiator removes his headset and looks up at his partner. "I don't like this. What do you think he's thinking?"

"It sounds like he's setting this up for a murder-suicide. Saying a prayer, requesting an ambulance. Sounds like he's not planning on coming out of that house alive."

Seconds later, Donovan calls back the negotiator on his line.

"I'm not really a violent person. I mean, I really try hard not to be," he says with a lifeless voice, "But if my life is over, so is hers. Y'all try to come in this house to get me, I'm blasting her head off. You don't believe me, try me."

"Well, we definitely don't want that to happen, Donovan," says the negotiator in a firmer tone. "How can we prevent that?"

"How can you prevent it?" repeats Donovan. "Get me a helicopter and let me fly up out of here. And I'm going to need some money . . . a million dollars."

"That's not going to happen. . . . That's the movies; you know that."

"That's the movies? But this ain't no movie in here. And it ain't gonna be the movies when you need two body bags either. I don't want you coming near the house. If you come near the house, she's going to die. I promise you," Donovan says, and then ends the call.

The negotiator tosses his headset on the ground and begins wringing his hands. "If we go in and he kills her . . . We can't go in. We can't endanger her life any further."

"Tell the guys this could end up being a long night. . . . He has a hostage, and there's no way we're going to be able to go in."

Night begins to fall.

Inside the house, the blinds are drawn. Donovan is sitting in the bare living room on the wood floor, occasionally tapping the back of his head against the wall. Heaven is sitting in the center of the same room, trying to decide if she should attempt to make a run for it, but Donovan locked the security bar on the front door after forcing entrance, so that thought is no longer a viable option. She can tell he's scared, but she isn't sure if that is a good or bad sign for her. He'd spent the last several hours berating her, calling her stupid, telling her the entire ordeal was her fault. But she remained calm. She apologized. Even she is in shock that he has gone to this level. He has never pulled a gun on her. He never seemed capable of what he is telling them he's going to do to her—not murder. At least she never thought so.

He walks into the kitchen and notices a pile of mail on the counter and a letter addressed to Heaven from a man with the same last name from a prison. Donovan tosses it in her lap, and she sets it to her side.

"You don't want to read the letter your dad sent you before you die?"

"It's his fault I'm dying."

"It's not his fault," screams Donovan. "It's yours." He snatches the envelope off the floor, rips open the letter, and throws it in her face. "Read it."

It is nine eastern time, six central, and Alicia's "Superstar" ringtone sounds. She answers out of habit.

"Alicia, thank God," says Heidi, the agent. "I've been trying to reach you all day. I have great news for you."

"I'm in the middle of an emergency," says Alicia, suddenly breaking down in tears.

"When can you call me back? This is very important. You have a movie deal. Remember—"

"Look, I don't have time for this," interrupts Alicia. "What you have to say isn't as important as this. Hollywood will be there; my sister may not."

"When can you call me back?"

"Never. This isn't business; this is personal." Alicia hangs up the phone.

Sir draws her into his chest and strokes her curly locks gently. "It's going to be okay, baby," he says as he kisses her forehead.

"They don't see any movement inside," says Hope. "I heard one of the officers say they don't see any movement." Hope reaches for Alicia's hand after Sir releases Alicia from his embrace. The two sisters stand hand in hand near the command post.

"You still have the opportunity to come outside with the young lady and no one is going to hurt you. If you aren't ready to surrender yourself, please release the young lady unharmed, and then we can talk about this. Remember you have a newborn daughter, Mona, and a four-year-old son, Donovan Jr. They love their father, and they want you to be around to raise them."

A gunshot is heard coming from the house, and Hope collapses in Ezra's arms. A few minutes later, the front door opens and Heaven stands behind the barred door in tears, wrestling with the key to put it inside the lock. She flings open the barred door and bolts across the street into the arms of her sisters.

"Did he shoot himself?" asks one of the officers.

She shakes her head. "He's getting ready to come out," Heaven tells the officer. "Dad's letter saved my life," she says as she hands the letter to Hope. "He saved my life."

Several minutes later, Donovan walks out of the home with his hands up, immediately dropping to his knees, placing his hands behind his back as officers rush toward him.

Jamal stands in Heaven's presence, a few steps away, completely concealed, but as she finishes giving her statement to the police, her eyes remain focused in his direction. She steps toward him, away from the direction of her family, and that is his cue to walk away in the opposite direction, toward his unit. When she gets within mere inches, two narcotics officers stop her.

"I'm sorry, young lady, but this area is restricted right now. All our UCs are back here."

"What is a UC?"

"Undercovers."

"And they wear those ski masks," she says, the realization dawning on her features, "to conceal their faces."

"Yes, but you can't come in this area, I'm sorry. We do need to speak with you, so can you come with me, please?"

Heaven nods and walks alongside the officer, turning her head several times in the direction of the UCs.

Hope opens the letter from Glenn and starts to read it silently.

Dearest Heaven,

I am in receipt of your letter, and while your words have cut to my deepest core, I understand your anger. I had no right to kill your mother, an act that in turn has left our innocent children without either one of their parents and with the burden of carrying around their father's guilt. I am thankful to your nana for doing what I didn't have the courage to do—raise you. I have now come to accept complete responsibility for my actions. After thirteen years in this hell, I finally realize I was wrong; that I allowed my anger and ego to cloud my better judgment. Why did I do it? That was your question—why did I kill your mother? I don't know why. Honestly, I don't. I was high. I know that sounds like a cop-out, but I was a ticking time bomb who refused to live right. We were arguing. I wasn't bringing home any money. Nothing was going right for me, and then she said she was leaving. She had someone else. There's no excuse for what I did. Young men come in here every day—many for murder. When they first come, I can tell they haven't allowed their minds to settle on the fact that this will be their permanent home and that they have ruined their whole life with a split-second decision. Many of them are younger than you, and sometimes it takes them a few weeks before the truth settles in. Sometimes it takes months; for many it takes years, but when it does, you can see the change that starts in their eyes. Almost like zombies, they carry an empty stare. Nothing out there in the world is worth sacrificing your freedom. I had a choice and I made the wrong one. I was always a thief; never a murderer. But I've come to realize there really isn't a difference. In both cases, I stole. If I could do anything to repair the hurt I have caused so many, I would. I pray every day, all day, that somehow you and your sister will smile again. Maybe one day you will forgive me for what I stole from you. Maybe one day you will trust and that trust will be worth the risk. God granted me the gifts of three girls. I pray you and your sister Hope will one day meet your older sister Alicia and the three of you will become inseparable. Keep God in your heart and allow faith to rule the world.

Love always,
your father

October

Visiting hours for prisoners whose last names begin with the letters A through J are on Saturday afternoon from one o'clock to four thirty for a maximum-allowed time of two hours.

They start out from downtown Detroit at seven in the morning. Sir is driving. Havana wanted to come along and Hope was going to let her, until they learned that a prisoner is allowed only three guests per visit. So Havana stays behind with Ezra. At the end of the month, Hope and Ezra will wed. They don't need to wait. They don't need to waste a year on planning one day; they want to get on with the rest of their lives together.

Hope muses over the upcoming visit. She prays it will be positive; it is the first time she or Heaven has seen their father in more than thirteen years. And for Alicia, it's been even longer. Regardless of the circumstances, he is still their father, even though he did a terrible job being one. She can only pray she can truly forgive him—forgive both of her parents for a childhood she wishes to forget. She has grown to realize it's not her place to judge either of them for their parenting skills and that the forgiveness he is seeking must come from God. Finally, though, she has forgiven him for killing their mother. Anything could have happened in that house the way their parents were attempting to coexist while under the influence. She and Heaven witnessed their mother's death. She witnessed a lot of things in that house that they never should have been exposed to as children. Perhaps she can forgive, but she certainly can never forget.

As they are traveling northbound on Interstate 75, Sir says to Alicia, "I'm a friend. I'm someone who's going to be with you whether you're up or down. I'm going to expand your brand. I'll have you doing Revlon and Maybelline commercials at the same time—they're just going to have to work it out. I'm going to have you rapping and singing gospel. You're going to have a clothing line, a perfume line, a food line, a shoe line. . . . When I get finished working my magic, you'll have a factory line. . . . You're from the Motor City. . . . You think I can't make that happen? You're going to be making movies and cars."

"Hair product line," Heaven chimes in.

"I like the way you think," Sir says, nodding as he flashes a smile at Heaven through the rearview.

After several hours on the road and one bathroom stop and a food run, Heaven asks, "Can we have some music?"

"I don't know how many stations we can get out here," Sir says. "You might be able to listen to some country."

"Nobody has an iPod? Sir, you don't even have Sirius radio in here?"

"No, I don't even have Sirius. I'm sorry. I bought the cheapest Three Hundred on the lot."

"No iPod. No Sirius. Just turn on the radio then. At this point, I'll listen to anything. I'm a country girl at heart."

Even Hope, who has remained relatively quiet in the backseat beside Heaven most of the drive, has to laugh at that.

"What's so funny? I am a country girl at heart." And to prove that she is, she sings along to "When I Get Where I'm Going," the Brad Paisley song that begins playing on the first station they can get reception to.

When Dolly Parton begins to sing along on the chorus, Heaven bolts out, "'Yeah, when I get where I'm goin' there'll be only happy tears. I will shed these sins and struggles I have carried all these years.'"

"We might have the next American Idol," says Sir. "A black country singer . . . with soul. You can sing girl, you can surely sing. What you say now?"

Heaven smiles. "Country's not bad—I love the lyrics." Heaven hums along with the rest of the song. "You know what, that song is asking a very good question. When are we going to get where we're going? Where are we going? Is the prison out of state or something?"

"Might as well be. It's four hundred and twelve miles, and it took us seven hours to get here," says Sir. "Welcome to Munising."

Hope's stomach is churning, especially once they turn right at West Industrial Park Drive and she sees the correctional facility on the right. They had each applied for visitation at the latter part of last month and were approved within a week. All three of their names have been on their father's visitation list for as long as he's been in prison, though he told Hope on the phone that he never thought he'd see them—especially not Alicia, and definitely not all three together.

The three sisters report to the second floor of the prison for a non-contact visit, while Sir waits in the car outside in the visitors' lot.

They are seated when their father walks out wearing an orange jumpsuit. Some signs of aging are visible. His shiny black hair is now highlighted with gray. He has cut off his signature long braid and wears a low cut. But his complexion is clear, better than it has ever looked. This is probably because he's drug free and in good shape. All things considered, he looks better than he did before he went in.

He takes his seat and presses the palm of his hand to the window that separates the sisters from him, and then he picks up the phone.

"God is so good," he says through the phone. "Even to someone like me. This is how I know he can forgive. All three of my daughters . . . He brought all three of them to me."

Heaven is the first to speak. "The letter you sent . . . It saved my life, and in a strange way it let me know that you didn't completely abandon us. For the first time, I realize that I'm responsible for the choices I make. When you know better, you do better, and I know better now."

He closes his eyes for a moment and replays her words. "I wish I had known better," he says after opening his eyes. "I have to live with what I did . . . and it's not easy. But God . . . God is good. He takes away the sins of the world. And he has mercy . . . even on someone like me."

Heaven nods, wipes away tears, and hands the phone to Hope.

"Hi, Glenn," says Hope.

"I would really love it if you called me Dad. I know I don't deserve that, but I want to prove I can be a father in some way even from inside here."

Hope hesitates. "Dad," she says, her heart softening, "you look good."

"So do you . . . all of you. I wish I could have seen my grandbaby."

She releases a deep sigh. "Maybe I'll bring her up to visit with my fiance next time."

"You're getting married?" he asks.

She nods. "Yes, at the end of this month. So I guess he'll be my husband the next time I see you."

"To a good man this time?"

Hope nods again. "Yes, he is a good man . . . a very good man." She struggles to find the words. "You know, just because you're in here doesn't mean you can't do the world some good. You can still have a purpose."

He nods. "I believe that," says their father. "And I want to do something to right my wrong."

"That's good, Dad. I hope you do. I'm going to let you talk to Alicia, our movie star." Hope hands the phone to Alicia.

"You mean I have a daughter who's a star? I mean, all of my daughters are stars in their own right, but you're a Hollywood star?"

"Not yet."

"But you're going to be—you have to believe that. So how are you?"

A smile slowly surfaces. "I'm good. I'm enjoying being with my sisters."

"That's good. That's how I always wanted it to be." He shakes his head. "I wasted my life. I want you girls to make great use of yours. So are you ready to start filming the movie?"

She takes a deep sigh. "I will be. I actually play a female inmate who was sentenced to life without parole. I'm having a hard time finding my objective with the role. I did a good reading, but I need to become her."

"That's ironic," he says. "Well, you know I know a lot about that, so if you want, I can call you from time to time to help you get in the right frame of mind.

"When you play someone like that, you need to take yourself through the five stages of dying, because when you are sentenced to a life in prison, essentially you are sentenced to death. And you must first learn to accept that you will feel dead inside well before your spirit leaves your body. My life is gone. This is what I see," he says, moving his hand over the room; the guards, and other prisoners. "Imagine being the kind of woman who never thought she would end up behind bars, but then suddenly she is and it doesn't feel real to her." He shrugs. "I guess the way I'd been living, I should have known. But if you can take a person like that who did this horrible thing and get them to accept what they did, and if you can get your audience to not only understand but also feel compassion for someone who doesn't deserve any, then you will give the performance of a lifetime."

"I didn't even tell you what the movie was about, but I feel like you've already read the script."

He chuckled softly. "I live the script."

Their two-hour visit ends with each of them touching their father's hand through the glass.

They walk out of the prison, hand in hand and amazed at how a visit to a prison could lift their spirits and bring them even closer together.

"I've never seen you look so happy," says Heaven as she lowers her camera. "You're so beautiful." Both of Hope's sisters assigned themselves a task. Heaven, of course, is photographing the wedding, and Alicia will perform a monologue for the small number of guests prior to the start of the ceremony.

I'm so happy," Hope says. "I really know the man I'm marrying as much as I can know someone other than myself. I trust him completely. Every Wednesday at the bank we would talk. For more than a year, we would just pour our hearts out—grieving. I just connected with him instantly. We bonded. We helped each other." Hope's eyes begin to water. "I love him so much."

"Don't cry," Alicia says, rushing over with a tissue to pat the corners of Hope's eyes. "You can't ruin your makeup."

"You don't understand. He thinks he's this marred man, but when I look at him, all I see is his beauty. It's incredible. I've never in my life experienced it," she says, crying her eyes out. "Every time I look at him he looks better and better."

Alicia smiles and says, "You are making me want to marry Sir. I wonder if he'll ask me."

"You're going to have to ask him," says Heaven as she slips into a rouge stretch-satin sheath dress. Havana, the flower girl, doesn't want to see her mother before the wedding—even though that superstition only applies to the groom—so she is waiting with her father, stepmother, and stepsisters.

The three sisters traveled by ferry to Mackinac Island, a small island on the eastern end of the straits of Mackinac within Lake Huron, Michigan, a few days before the groom and guests arrived. They wanted some bonding time. And fall is such a beautiful time of the year. It is a little cool in Michigan in October, but still, they are at the perfect place for a romantic wedding.

Hope and Ezra had decided upon the historic Grand Hotel as the location for their intimate wedding and reception that will take place at two o'clock that afternoon. The hotel's wedding coordinator handled all of the details, from the salon services for the bride and her sisters, to the lilac floral arrangements, to the west front porch venue with a view of the straits and Mackinac Bridge, to the nonalcoholic dinner reception complete with a classical band, a fifty-dollar-a-plate meal, and the couple's three-tiered wedding cake.

"Well, ladies," Alicia says, "we have a wedding to go to. Ready?" she asks Hope.

Hope nods and stands.

"You look beautiful," says Heaven.

Alicia nods in agreement. "You do, Hope. . . . You are just beaming."

"Let's go," Hope says as she hurries toward the door. "I don't want to be late for my own wedding."

Alicia steps up to the microphone. "Respected guests, we welcome you on this glorious day for the union of our beloved Hope Jetter and Ezra Hansen. Please, all rise." Havana walks from a side entrance of the hotel onto the west porch just a little ahead of her mother, tossing lilacs in her path. Hope, resplendent in an ivory embroidered sequined sheath dress with a matching jewel-neck jacket, smiles through her eyes as she walks, holding a lilac bouquet, from the Grand Hotel onto the porch.

Alicia and Heaven break down at the first sight of their sister—love beaming from the tip of her head throughout her entire body. It is hard for Alicia to imagine this to be the same woman who could always find something to complain about. She takes one glance at Ezra and Hope as they join before the minister and she thinks of the cliché, like two hearts beating as one. That is what they are. She knows this beautiful union will truly last until death, an uncommon certainty these days. She glances at Sir, seated in the second row of five, and smiles after reading his lips. "We're next," he mouths with a wink. Maybe, she muses, blushing back at him.

At the reception, inside the Grand Hotel, Heaven is buzzing around with her camera and photographing anything she finds that will evoke loving memories to treasure once the moment itself has passed. She has been photographing her sister for three days in order to have enough pictures to create a coffee-table wedding book as a gift to the couple.

Everyone's happy. Her niece has two complete families now, and Heaven is certain Hope will have another child before long, or a few more, because Hope always wanted a large family. Alicia will be filming her movie soon. She already has another film scheduled in preproduction that will be filming in Detroit, so it's not the end of the sisters' being together after all. As for her, she has put love on hold. She hasn't seen her friend Jamal, but she is almost certain she knows why he had that mask in his car. She is almost sure he was that undercover narcotics officer. She can feel it. But she doesn't want to dwell on it. Maybe one day she'll run into him on the streets of Detroit. She doesn't want to leave him in the past, though she knows some things are meant to be left behind, things such as her Donovan tattoo, which she has finally managed to remove.

She has concrete plans now for her nonprofit organization that will mentor young girls. She is happy to be alive, to experience life and the lives of those she loves—her family, her friends—in person and through her camera lens.

She captures the perfect shot of Heaven and Alicia standing together in laughter. And they hug. But she realizes what is missing is a picture of all three of them.

"Sir," she says, rushing over to him with her camera. "Take a picture of us?"

She hands him the camera. "Do you know how to use it?"

"I think so. They're all built on the same general principle."

"Where's Havana?" Heaven asks.

"She's zipping around with her sisters," Hope says.

Heaven gathers her sisters and the three of them pose.

"Okay, Sir, just snap us real quick, and then we'll take one with Havana."

"Everybody give a big smile and say, 'When I Get Where I'm Going.'"

The sisters smile and say, "Cheese," laughing as he snaps their picture.

Sixteen Months Later

There she is—seated inside the Kodak Theatre—adorning a sparkling body-hugging gown from the Armani Privé collection. Her flawless skin is illuminated. Her curly hair is swept into a meticulously sculpted up-do. She feels the need to be pinched again to ensure this isn't another one of her recurring dreams, so Sir takes a nip at the skin on her arm for the tenth time.

This time it really is real. She saw Jeremy Piven—not Ari Gold. He didn't walk up to her as he had in her dream, but several members of the media who were on the red carpet did. One of them suggested to Sir that he move to the side, but she held Sir's hand even tighter—she didn't want him to leave her side, not even for one moment.

She knows that her family is plastered in front of the television in one of their adjoining suites at the Hollywood Roosevelt Hotel, waiting to crack open a bottle of Moët & Chandon to celebrate in the hotel's restaurant for the private celebration among family and close friends—her parents, her brother, her aunt Olena and uncle Jason, her grandparents, two uncles along with their wives, and Benita. And of course, Hope and Heaven.

Hope is sharing custody of her daughter with her first husband

and expecting her second child with her new husband, Ezra, who is also back at the hotel celebrating. And Heaven, well, Heaven's still working on herself and doing a good job turning her life around. She has so many things she wants to do; now the only thing left is to figure out which one she wants to start first.

And Alicia can't wait to join them all.

But she is very nervous. To go from one day being an unknown to overnight becoming a sensation, lauded by the media as a "breakout star," feels better than a dream. This is nothing she could have ever imagined. She's practiced her Oscar speech in the mirror millions of times, but even with her speech written on a paper folded in four and tucked inside her jeweled clutch, waiting to be read, she knows she'll still be at a loss for words. She's had plenty of practice with acceptance speeches after being nominated for twenty-five awards, many of which she has already won—not least of all the Golden Globe and SAG awards. But none are as important to her as winning an Academy Award—the most prominent and oldest award. Four other women are in her category. Three are legends, but the fourth, Aubrey Daniels, is the one she'd really like to beat.

Barr Edmunds strolls onstage to present the best actress category.

"It is my distinguished honor to present the nominees for outstanding performance by an actress in a leading role . . . and the nominees are . . . Aubrey Daniels in *One Fatal Dawn* . . . Alicia Day in *Without Innocence* . . . Jessica Hill in *Extreme Madness* . . . Mary Piper in *The Ends* . . . Molly Smith in *Forever Goes Love* . . . And the Oscar goes to . . ."

Barr looks down as he opens the envelope slowly. He closes his eyes, shakes his head once, and smiles wide. . . . "Alicia Day in *Without Innocence*."

Alicia spends a second with her face buried in the palms of her hands. She hugs and kisses Sir. Then she stands and rushes to the podium to accept her award.

She releases a laborious sigh and raises her Oscar toward the ceiling. She has a long list of people to thank, but her written speech is inside her clutch that she gave to Sir before she left her seat. But this will come from the heart. "To think, I had almost given up." She wipes away tears. "God is good. I really didn't want to cry. I know my makeup probably looks horrible right now, but I don't care. This Oscar isn't for me. . . . This is for all of those people out there who have been clinging to a dream . . . their dream . . . so long that sometimes they confuse it for a nightmare. Don't you give up. If you only knew the road I traveled to get here . . . When I say it can happen, you better believe me. Auntie, this is for you, thank you for being the first to truly believe, and to keep believing. Of course, I want to thank the entire cast and crew and Marcus Toller—what an amazing director you are. To my new agent, Mitzy—you put Ari Gold to shame. To my mother and both of my fathers—I love you all very much. My brother, Max . . . Oh God, I can't believe this. I'm shaking. I can't believe this. I walked away from Hollywood almost two years ago—I needed to take some time out to smell the roses. And I found two of them in Detroit; my sisters, Heaven and Hope. I love you both very much. I know I'm forgetting a lot of people. I'm sorry, it's not every day you win an Oscar, so please forgive me if I didn't mention your name." She turns to walk away from the podium and then turns back. "Oh, I almost forgot. Sir . . . will you marry me?"

Sir stands up and shouts from the crowd, "Yes, I will!"

"Heaven," Hope says, holding up Heaven's clutch, "your phone is vibrating."

Heaven walks over to Hope, retrieves her phone, and reads the text message that just came through from Jamal.

I'm watching the oscars. I'm happy for your sister—winning for her first role.

She never worried that Jamal might text her on Oscar night. She told all of her other friends not to until the next day, because the Academy Awards broadcasts live in the other time zones and they would see the show three and a half hours before those on the West Coast. Heaven didn't want to know the results ahead of time. But, oh well, she knew now and she was ecstatic, but she couldn't let on for several more hours or else she'd spoil it for the rest of her family.

She texts back.

Thank you. And I'm sorry I didn't believe you weren't a bank robber or terrorist. I hope we can remain friends.

Of course, I'll be here when you get back and we can just rewind.

I'd really like that.

"Oh my God," says Heaven as she stands in front of a large-screen television in the spacious party room filled with Alicia's family and friends. "He yelled out 'Yes, I will!'" She shakes her head. "That's going to be all on YouTube tomorrow. You know it will. And I can't wait, because I want to upload it to my Facebook."

Heaven's smile lights the room.

"Who was that?" Hope asks.

"A really good friend."

She walks over to the DJ and steps up on his elevated booth. "Do you have the song 'When I Get Where I'm Going'?"

"We can get anything. I can download it and mix it in. Just give me a second."

She steps out of his booth but notices him motioning to her, so she returns.

"The only song I see with that title is a country song. I know you're not talking about that . . . are you?"

"Yeah, that's the one. Can you do it?"

"Oh, I can make it work. This is about to turn into the hippest country song you've ever heard. Just give me another minute."

"Actually, can you wait until Alicia Day walks in and mix it in then?"

"Yeah, I can do that."

About an hour later, when Alicia walks through the doors with Sir, the DJ mixes the song in and it begins to play. And Heaven, Hope, and Alicia immediately start smiling. It is the perfect song to top off what is truly just the beginning.

When I Get Where I'm Going

cheryl robinson

A CONVERSATION WITH CHERYL ROBINSON

Q. *How long did it take you to write* When I Get Where I'm Going, *and what was the process?*

A. It took about ten months. I started writing the book in March 2009, but I had a two-month lapse in between. I finished the final draft with edits in February 2010. As for the process, it started with an idea, and not as much time as I truly wanted to try to execute my idea. Or so I thought. I was working a full-time job five to six days a week, but deep down I really wanted to write full-time. I was patient. I'd always told myself, "One day I'm going to write full-time."

A couple months later, I had to have surgery and I was off for seven weeks from my full-time job. While I was nervous about being put under anesthesia for the surgery, in the back of my mind I was so happy I'd have seven weeks off to write. My surgery went well and while I was recovering, I started writing as much as I could. Time flew by, and just like that my seven weeks were up. I can remember so vividly the day I returned to work. My drive to the office was seventy-seven miles one way, and during the entire drive I was thinking, "What if today is my last day at work?" I just had a feeling it could be. Ironically, not even two hours after I arrived, it was announced that our entire department was being laid off that day. They took each of us into an office, one by one, with an HR representative and a manager to give us our layoff packages and go over all the details. Before they started the process, they asked for volunteers to go first, and I immediately raised my hand. I felt like everything was happening for a reason. And the sooner I could pick up my papers, the sooner I could head back home and finish the chapter with Alicia, Aubrey, and Benita having brunch at the seaside restaurant.

It took a couple of weeks for the reality of my situation to hit, and during that period I really couldn't write that much. I was laid off, no one was hiring, I had plenty of time on my hands; yet I couldn't do what I'd been asking God for years to allow me to do full-time—write. I experienced firsthand the saying, "Be careful what you wish for." I was scared of this next phase of my life— scared to fail. I had had a good job with what was once a great company that offered plenty of opportunity and great bonuses. Now that company is slowly going out of business, phasing out departments until eventually, in the next year or two, the entire company will be closed.

Eventually, I snapped out of what may have been a depression. I counted my blessings, opened my journal, and started writing. I reminded myself of what I truly wanted from life, and I started going after my dream. I haven't stopped writing since. Writing this book was one of the best experiences of my life.

Q. *Detroit is your hometown. Is that the reason most of your novels are set there?*

A. I know Detroit very well. My sister and one of my nephews and a few friends still live in the city and surrounding suburbs. I lived there until I was in my early thirties. And I love the city. Nearly every place I mentioned in the novel, with the exception of Karen's House and Mercury Bank, are actual places. Detroit is also a city that most people are familiar with, even if they don't live in Michigan, because it's the headquarters of Ford, GM, and Chrysler, and still houses Hitsville USA, which is now the site of the Motown Historical Museum. Many people have or had relatives who moved to the city years ago for factory jobs. Detroit has a lot of history and was once booming, so it saddens me to hear my hometown referred to as a dying city. I can't sugarcoat what plagues Detroit, because the city is definitely having its share of problems—not just the city but the entire state that depended upon the automobile industry for years. So I did want to show the plight in the book, but not make it a primary focus. I wanted the city to reflect the sisters—like them, it needs work, but has lots of potential.

Q. *Tell us what you see* When I Get Where I'm Going *being about?*

A. *When I Get Where I'm Going* is a story about family and togetherness. It's about three women who happen to be sisters who are each trying to find their way through life. In the process of searching for themselves, they find one another. Each of them is going through a lot of drama and heartache, and they eventually turn to one another to overcome life's obstacles.

Q. *What made you decide to write a book about family that centers around three sisters?*

A. I knew after writing my last book, *In Love with a Younger Man,* that Alicia Day, who was a minor character, would be one of the main characters in my next book, so after I went probing into her life, I discovered her two sisters and began to ask questions about who they both were. Before long, one theme led to another, which ended up being a book about sisters and family and life in general. Not everyone has a sister, but everyone has family, even if it's not one they want. And everyone is dealing with the ups and downs of life.

Q. *Do you have a favorite character in* When I Get Where I'm Going? *Is there one sister you can relate to more than the others? One sister you feel will be the most misunderstood?*

A. I like each of the sisters. All three of them are different. At times Heaven is my favorite, even though she is the most confused of the sisters. In my opinion, her story line carries the most drama, and yet I understand how she can allow herself to get caught up in so many of the things that she does. Deep down, she really wants to change. She's very young. I really just want her to get her life together.

I can relate to Alicia most of all. Being in the arts, I understand her dream and relate to how long she's pursued it without giving up. But I think of all three sisters, Hope may be the one who is the most misunderstood and will possibly be disliked by some readers. I'll just have to wait to hear what they say.

Q. *Speaking of Hope, does she really dislike her own race?*

A. I don't believe it is ever implied that Hope doesn't want to be black. But certain facts are stated. Though her first husband is black, he left the marriage, and the next man she married was white. Her new husband, Ezra, is white. If you consider the way she feels toward Rico Johnson, the young man who works at the bank, one could make a case that she dislikes black *men* specifically. In the scene when Heaven is at the Coleman A. Young Municipal Center, she wishes Hope were there to see that "fine black men with decent jobs really do exist." I think Hope's feelings come from her relationship with her own father and the hurt she experienced from her first husband.

Q. *In the book, Heaven is in an abusive relationship, yet she continues to stay in it much longer than she should. Why did you write her character that way?*

A. I believe it takes Heaven a long time to realize she is actually being abused. Heaven is a tough girl and she fights back most of the time, so in her mind, in some ways, she feels they are on equal footing and they are both possessive. I could have written an exit for Heaven much earlier, but ultimately, I had her leave when she was ready . . . when she'd had enough.

Q. *Putting the sisters aside, who is your favorite character?*

A. Ezra. He is the person some of us try desperately not to look at and others of us stare at a little too long. He is someone who could really be any one of us, and I think he handles his situation the best he can. I enjoyed the scenes I wrote that involved him.

Q. *Tell us about Jamal in general, and the love connection that was hinted at with Heaven.*

A. Jamal is a character inspired by someone I had spoken to by phone a few times. I was considering writing a book about an undercover narcotics officer, but I didn't know much about that profession, and I had lots of questions I couldn't find answers to. I have a friend who is a police officer, and he introduced me to his friend who, at the time, was an undercover narcotics officer. I loosely based Jamal on him.

As for the love connection, it was obvious she was attracted to him, and I hope it was indicated that he also was attracted to her. I wouldn't say they were complete opposites, but they were very different and those differences seemed to work for the most part. I did have her display a degree of prejudice toward him also. When she found the ski mask, she thought he was a terrorist because he was Middle Eastern. So, even though she was open to dating a man of a different race, she still held on to negative views when something happened that she didn't understand. People often give a person within their own race the benefit of the doubt, but when a person of another race does the same thing, people aren't always as kind.

Q. *In fiction, writers are given a lot of leeway. How much do you take and how much do you research?*

A. Even though my stories are fictionally based, I like the story to seem as real as possible. Some people may think that doesn't provide the reader with a good enough escape, but I feel that it still does. It allows them to enter someone else's world. So, I definitely do research. In my last novel, *In Love with a Younger Man*, I researched plastic surgeons in the Atlanta area, because my character was considering going to one. I found a female plastic surgeon by the name of Dr. Nedra Dodds, who has her own practice in the Atlanta area. One day, months after the book was released, I received an e-mail from a Dr. Nedra Dodds. I kept looking at the name, wondering why it looked so familiar, and then as I read her e-mail I realized why. I was blown away that she'd contacted me. She'd ordered my book online and she thanked me for the mention. I was very happy about that. And I was also touched when one of the cousins of the late Darrent Williams, who was a Denver Bronco and was slain on New Year's in 2007, also e-mailed me. The subject line of the e-mail read: *Showing Love from the Family of Darrent Williams*. She told me how his aunt and mother had read my book *Sweet Georgia Brown*, and how it was very emotional for them when they read the part in the book where one of my characters learns his favorite football player was murdered. I was very touched by her e-mail and how very appreciative she said their family was. It reinforced to me another reason that I write—and not only a reason, but also how you can never know who's reading what you write or how your words may affect them. I used to wonder why I'd become so attached to media stories. I would go back for several days to weeks trying to find updates on stories I grew attached to; Darrent's story was one of those. But I quickly noticed that the media will tell you the breaking story and drop it after a few days or weeks without a conclusion. Writing is the perfect way to continue the story or, in Darrent's case, just to remember him.

Q. *Tell us about the Michael Beck subplot. How did that come about?*

A. When I began to write Hope's character, the only thing I knew was that she was a young widow. Initially, I really thought he was going to be dead, until the bookstore scene. I learned when Hope did that he wasn't dead, so then I had to figure out how this could happen. The question I tried to raise was how well do you really know someone? I had read about a man who married two women who both lived in the same apartment complex and I thought, if he could pull that off, anything is possible. The fact that he was leading a dual life was the only explanation for why he wouldn't simply return home to Hope, even if he wasn't on the boat.

What I didn't show as much, but implied, was just how obsessed Hope was with finding out the truth. She'd pretty much put her life on hold for a couple of years. But in that time, she never admitted to herself that she really didn't know Roger that well. It's one of those things that you'd never believe unless it happened to you. As someone who is pretty obsessed with the national news, I can say stranger things happen every day.

Q. *What did you leave on the chopping room floor?*

A. A lot—too much to remember without referring back to the extra scenes I have saved. Even the tone of the story changed. This always happens. I write a draft and I think this is the story, and then I let it rest for several days and refer back and wonder what I was thinking. Usually it isn't the story at all, just a start to the story. I used to get really frustrated about that. I'd think about all the work I did. But I really love the revision process now. The first draft is the framework for something bigger developing. I usually rewrite the story two more times. That's why you may hear writers talking about how lonely the process is. You can't do all of this while you're talking to someone or watching television. It's just you and your laptop or typewriter or paper and pen—however you write your novel.

QUESTIONS AND TOPICS
FOR DISCUSSION

1. What are some of the underlying themes of the book? In your opinion, what are the primary motivations and/or goals of each of the sisters?

2. What is the first thing to come to mind when you think of Heaven? Hope? Alicia? Use one word to describe each sister.

3. What was your first impression of each sister and did it ever change? If so, in what way and why?

4. How would you react if you discovered you had a sister or brother you never knew existed? Do you think you would welcome him/her into your life? Do you understand Hope's reluctance?

5. Which sister did you like the most and why? Which one did you like the least and why?

6. For each of the sisters, an argument could be made that they hold on too long to something—a dream, a loss, an abusive relationship. What are your feelings about each of the sisters and their resistance to change?

7. With regard to Alicia and her experiences with Hollywood, do you consider most of her struggles due to her race, her lack of experience, Aubrey, her agent, or a combination of all of these factors? Do you think black actresses, and minorities as a whole, still

struggle today with securing the kind of roles that garner an Oscar nomination?

8. What does Hope and Heaven's past reveal about who they are? In what way do you feel their past shaped their lives? How do you think the murder of their mother by their father affected their relationship with men?

9. Heaven states that one of her biggest fears is going to jail. Yet her actions, from driving under the influence to shoplifting, are completely reckless. How do you explain this?

10. Think of each sister and begin by pointing out their strengths and weaknesses. What, if any, similarities do they share? What is the catalyst for the shifts in their relationships? Is there more than one such catalyst?

11. Aside from the sisters, who are some of your favorite characters and why?

12. What is the most memorable scene for you and why?